BEST DETECTIVE STORIES
OF THE YEAR–1972
26th Annual Collection

BEST
DETECTIVE STORIES
OF THE YEAR
1972

26th Annual Collection

Edited by
ALLEN J. HUBIN

E. P. DUTTON & CO., INC. / NEW YORK / 1972

Published simultaneously in Canada
by Clarke, Irwin & Company Limited, Toronto and Vancouver

SBN: 0–525–06431–1

Library of Congress Catalog Card Number: 46–5872

Contents

6

Introduction

A friend of mine, after reading one of the recent anthologies in this series which I'd edited, remarked that he liked the stories—but that he had a quarrel with the title. *Detective* stories?

To those of you who, like my friend, remember fondly the days when detective stories were (in the traditional sense) stories of detection, a few comments may be in order, which may also serve to set the present anthology in perspective.

The period between the world wars is generally thought of as the Golden Age of Detection. It was during this period that a host of notables arose—Ellery Queen, John Dickson Carr, Agatha Christie, Dorothy Sayers, Anthony Berkeley, Freeman Wills Crofts, S. S. Van Dine, and many others—and what they wrote was classical detective fiction. During these decades the puzzle was king, fair play to the reader was his throne, on his right hand stood S. S. Van Dine and on his left Ronald Knox encoding the principles of his reign, and kneeling before him were the members of London's Detection Club, chanting their unswerving allegiance.

This was the time when wits were matched in a game devised by the author, a game wherein reader and detective together saw each and every clue and red herring, and the reader was challenged to interpret the data correctly and identify the culprit before the detective did so.

There are still aficionados extant for whom this *is* the detective story; everything else is something very other.

But the mournful fact, at least for those thus inclined, is that the quantity of short fiction so narrowly defined as "detective" has steadily declined since 1940, to the point where it is now practically a vanished species.

To some, like myself, this is not *entirely* a calamity. While we might wish for the continued leavening of some pure detection, we think it would be a shame to close off or ignore the intriguing new avenues down which detective fiction more broadly defined has developed since World War II.

Detective stories? Well, perhaps that's not the most descriptive term, but you will find detection herein, however modernized. I might prefer the generic expression "crime stories," but after more than a quarter-century the title *Best Detective Stories of the Year* is rather too well and favorably established to cast aside. In any event, there is a prior claimant, at least in England, to the title "Best Crime Stories."

Thus, be they detective, mystery, or crime stories, here follows a selection of the best published in the United States for the first time during 1971.

ALLEN J. HUBIN

January 16, 1972

Detective fiction and science fiction are kindred genres, as may be suggested by the considerable overlap not only in readership but also in authorship. For proof, note the bylines appearing in this anthology, among them Michael Crichton, a medical student who became a highly successful author while still in his twenties. He is most widely known in fiction for his best-selling novel The Andromeda Strain, *a chilling projection of a possible space-program mishap. Not so well known is the fact that as Jeffery Hudson he wrote* A Case of Need, *awarded an Edgar by the Mystery Writers of America as the best mystery novel of 1968; nor the fact that as John Lange he authored a series of suspense novels. And the tidy tale which follows nicely confirms this duality of creative enterprise.*

MICHAEL CRICHTON

The Most Powerful Tailor
in the World

John Hansen, a Presidential science adviser, was reviewing some CIA reports on Russian ICBM launch-pad locations when the telephone rang. The President said, "John, I'd like you to come into my office," and hung up.

Hansen could tell nothing from the tone, but then, he never could. He locked the CIA reports in the lower drawer of his desk, along with some data on civilian fusion reactors, and went down the hall to the West Wing of the White House. This was usually a nice little ego trip; as a young, handsome physicist with influence at the top, he was a great favorite among the secretaries. But today he was ignored—the secretaries and the lower staffmen were all whispering among themselves.

Ethel, the President's secretary, said, "You can go right in, Dr. Hansen," and pressed the button by her desk to unlock the door. He noticed that some refurbishing was taking place in the anteroom. Workmen in coveralls were repositioning portraits on the walls, and it seemed to him that they were a little tense, on edge.

Hansen said, "What is it, Ethel?"

Ethel rolled her eyes upward. "You won't believe it," she said.

Hansen went into the Oval Room office, where, to his astonishment, he found almost half the Cabinet—including the Secretaries of Defense, State, Housing and Urban Development—and the President's foreign-policy adviser. They were all standing, looking very uncomfortable. Even the President was standing.

One man was sitting, and Hansen looked at him curiously. He was a little man, neatly dressed in a gray suit, chubby and white-haired. He must have been sixty at least, but he was snappishly alert, and his eyes were compelling.

The little man swung his eyes over to Hansen. "Who are you?" he demanded. The authority in his voice disturbed Hansen. Most people were awed to be received by the President. This man acted as if he were surrounded by servants.

The President cleared his throat. "This is Dr. Hansen, my science adviser," he said. "Dr. Hansen, Mr. Borak."

Borak laughed. "So you called in a scientist," he said. "You think that'll help?" He crossed his legs, folded his hands in his lap, and looked at Hansen contemptuously.

"I want another opinion," the President said mildly. And Hansen realized with a shock: *He's afraid of this man.* He looked around at the others. He now sensed that they were all afraid.

The President said, "Mr. Borak came to our attention two hours ago. He first visited John Harper—you know him, don't you?—the Undersecretary of Housing and Urban Development—"

"The *late* Undersecretary," Borak said, and laughed.

"And eventually was brought here. He is making a rather interesting set of demands, which I'd like you to hear." The President's voice remained mild and controlled. But Hansen could see the faint line of sweat on his upper lip.

"What happened to Harper?" Hansen asked. He had had lunch with him only a week before.

"Incinerated," Borak said, and he chuckled with a sort of childish glee.

The room was very quiet. "I don't understand," Hansen said. He heard his own voice becoming as mild and controlled as the President's.

"Mr. Borak is a tailor from Cincinnati, and—"

"Not *originally* from Cincinnati," Borak said, interrupting again. "Originally from Dayton, but the past ten years, Cincinnati. I have a place on Front Street, part of a dry cleaner's. I do reweaving and mending. I'm a widower; my wife died five years ago. No children. Last year, I made six thousand, three hundred dollars, and I paid all my taxes on it. I've been a registered Democrat all my life. Does that help you?"

"Not much," Hansen said.

Borak laughed with genuine pleasure. He sat back in his chair and looked up at all the men standing around him. "None of it helps you," he said. "Admit it. Like my wife says, there isn't a damn thing you can do."

There was silence in the room for a moment. Finally, the President said, "Mr. Borak has demanded the sum of five hundred million dollars from us for—"

"Call it half a billion. It sounds better, half a billion."

"For 'protection.'"

"Protection?" Hansen said.

"You may not think so," Borak said, "but I have had a very unusual life. Very unusual. When I was young, I heard voices and they told me what to do. I often had the feeling of doing something I had done before, in another incarnation. Several times, I traveled out of my body to India, Japan, and Kansas."

This guy is a screaming nut, Hansen thought. He listened, nodding politely.

"Then, after my wife died, I was very lonely. A man with no children is lonely. So I tried to contact her, and finally succeeded two years ago. I have psychic powers, you see. It was my wife who suggested that I try to move things. It was—"

"Move things?"

"You know, ashtrays and books at first, moving them around the house. Opening and closing doors, with my mind."

"I see." Hansen worked to suppress a smile. The psychic little tailor from Cincinnati.

"It was an exercise," Borak continued. "Just getting in shape. Nothing much happened until I discovered I could make things catch fire. In fact, I have a special talent for this, a gift, you might call it. I practiced, strengthening my powers of concentration. Finally, a month ago, after consulting with my wife, I set a factory on fire." He rummaged in the pockets of his suit. "I have the clippings here. . . ."

"That's all right," Hansen said. He had already made up his mind. They were dealing with a psychotic of some kind. Probably he'd sneaked out and set a few fires like any other pyromaniac, then constructed an elaborate rationalization to explain it and to handle his guilt.

"It was a four-million-dollar fire," Borak said proudly. "It got a lot of attention," he said, and giggled.

"Speaking of fires, you might want to look at these," the President said, giving Hansen some Polaroids. They showed a Government office in several views. "They were taken half an hour ago."

Hansen studied them. He could see evidence of fire damage in each, but one shot in particular caught his attention. It showed a desk and a blackened lump in the chair behind the desk.

"The Undersecretary of Housing and Urban Development," the President said, nodding.

"Sorry about that," Borak said. "But it was his own fault. He made me lose my temper. The things he said about me! He called me a screaming nut, for instance."

"Who observed this sequence of events?" Hansen asked, still staring at the Polaroids.

"An administrative assistant and a speechwriter," the President said. "They have been heavily sedated now, but they were in the room at the time, and their stories match Mr. Borak's account of what happened. Mr. Borak, according to all accounts, closed his eyes, mumbled something, and Mr. Harper burst into flames. They were separated by a distance of several yards at the time."

"Distance has nothing to do with it," Borak said. "Distance makes no difference."

"Mr. Borak claims," the President said, "to be able to do the same thing to the city of New York if we do not give him the money he demands."

"Terrific," Hansen said. "But I think we should pay only *if* he promises to burn New York to a crisp." He said it as a joke, and he laughed, but he kept his eyes on Borak's face. He was testing. A joke like that would drive a psychotic up the wall. Borak was not amused—but neither was he livid with fury.

He said, "I see that you are still skeptical. Very well. Please remove your tie." Feeling odd, Hansen took off his tie and held it out in his hand. "That's fine," Borak said. He bent over, closed his eyes, and whispered something quickly under his breath.

The tie burst into flames. Hansen gasped, dropped it, and stamped out the fire with his shoes. When he looked up, the little man was smiling blandly. "Have I convinced you?"

Hansen did not speak. He was staring at the charred pieces of cloth, trying to remember where he had bought the tie, who might have gotten to it, treated it with chemicals, prepared it for this little trick. After a moment he shook his head. It could not be a trick.

His mind spun crazily. As a physicist, he was accustomed to thinking of alternative explanations, contrasting mathematical models to describe physical events. But this was flatly impossible in any system. It couldn't be done.

"Now, then," Borak said, turning to the President. "Unless there are further questions, I would like to turn to the matter of payment."

The President, looking pale, nodded.

"In return for maintaining secrecy and withholding my powers, I will receive from you half a billion dollars, tax-free, to be paid through the Defense Department. Furthermore—"

Hansen stopped listening. His mind was turning inward, considering all the possibilities and ramifications. He tried to think of what he had seen as a true manifestation of psychic power, psychokinesis. If so, what followed? How could it be dealt with logically? "Just a moment," he said. "I have some questions."

The tailor Borak looked at him with obvious hostility. "Yes?"

Hansen knew that he would have to proceed cautiously. The picture of the charred lump remained in his mind. "Mr. President," he said, "it seems to me that we may be able to use Mr. Borak's skills to our own advantage. In fact, I think he may be worth a great deal more than he is asking. Someone who could invisibly and immediately incinerate Peking, Havana, Moscow—that's a talent to have on our side."

The President stared at him as if he had gone mad.

But Borak was nodding slowly, thinking about it seriously. "Yes," he said, "possibly. . . ."

"We also ought to determine," Hansen said, "what other powers Mr. Borak has that might be useful. For instance, can you see the future, Mr. Borak?"

Borak shook his head. "I've tried," he said, "but I can't. Even in communication with my wife I can't. But I'm very good at dealing with the present."

"You certainly are," Hansen said. He concealed a sense of triumph. He knew now what he had to do. "I want to thank you, Mr. Borak," he said, "for a most stimulating morning." He went to the door. "Mr. President, it's my recommendation that you do as Mr. Borak asks, with the condition that you have a legal option on his services in the future."

The President nodded curtly, though he looked angry and frustrated. "That's your final conclusion?" He'd obviously been half-hoping that Hansen could produce some scientific miracle that would prove Borak a fraud.

"Yes," Hansen said. "Absolutely." And then he walked out of the room.

In the anteroom, he smiled at Ethel, who was nervously smoking a cigarette. "How is it in there?" she asked.

"No problem," he said, still smiling. He went over to the workmen and whispered to them for a moment.

Fifteen minutes later, when Mr. Borak, the psychic tailor from Cincinnati, emerged from the office of the President of the United States, Hansen was there to greet him.

"I want to thank you," Borak said. "I didn't expect a scientist to understand."

"Scientists are logical people," Hansen said, "and I'm only doing my job."

And then he swung one of the workmen's hammers down on Borak's head, killing him instantly. Ethel screamed. After a moment, the President and his advisers came out of the inner office and looked down at the body. Then they looked at the bloody hammer. Finally, they looked at Hansen.

"He couldn't see the future," Hansen said.

There was a brief silence. Then the President said "Ummm" in a distracted way and went back into his office. His advisers followed him. The door closed. Hansen went back down the hall to his office. And there the matter ended.

The cipher has been a legitimate feature of the detective story since E. A. Poe penned "The Gold Bug" in 1843. What better literary ancestor could the tale which follows have than this? Added to this, Mr. Young contributes a fine sense of history and a striking revelation of character.

ALAN K. YOUNG

Ponsonby and the Classic Cipher

Professor Ponsonby smiled at his old friend across the study hearth. "Well, Rene," he asked, "is it time?"

Rene LeBreau withdrew, startled, from whatever distant fantasy he had been pursuing in the depths of his brandy glass. He was a small man, with small nervous hands and a lined red face that was dwarfed by his unruly halo of white hair. At sixty-eight he was ten years younger than his host, Briarwood College's professor of English emeritus, but he could have passed for the same age.

"Time, Amos?" he asked. "Time for what?"

"Time to tell me what has kept you so distracted this evening. When I broached the subject earlier, you suggested it wait till after dinner. How was it Browning's Bishop Brougham put it? 'I promised, if you'd watch a dinner out, we'd see truth dawn together—truth that peeps over the glasses' edge when dinner's done.'" Ponsonby raised his own snifter. "More brandy?"

"No, thank you." LeBreau's accent was primarily Oxonian, with only the barest hint of his native French. "And I hadn't forgotten, Amos. But I've been sitting here asking myself if it *was* time—if it would ever be time, in fact. What started my wool-gathering was your telling me before dinner how you'd helped your local police solve one or two little puzzles recently. That set me to thinking about an unsolved puzzle of my own which I've carried about with me now for twenty-six years. Actually, it's a letter—in cipher—from a friend. I don't believe I've even had it out of my wallet in a decade, yet scarcely a day goes by that I don't give it at least a passing thought."

"And in twenty-six years you've never succeeded in deciphering it?" Ponsonby chuckled. "I'm sure I'd have given up long ago and simply asked my friend what he meant by it."

"I last met this man on the street in Gramonte just two days before he sent it. That was June 2, 1944. I never saw him again."

"Ah," said Ponsonby. "Lost in the war?"

"Yes—lost in the war."

"And in all these years you've never asked an expert to decipher it for you? Do you suspect it of being too personal?"

"No—at least, I don't think so. And I doubt if it's really that difficult, if I could just put my mind to it long enough. But the night I first received it I had only a few hours to work on it before the Gestapo came for me. Then after the war, when I got home from the concentration camp and got it out from where I'd hidden it, I found I simply couldn't concentrate on it long enough. I tried telling myself it was just because it wasn't important any-more, but in my heart I knew—" The little Frenchman lifted haunted eyes. "Quite frankly, Amos, I've always been afraid to discover what it says!"

Ponsonby regarded his friend sympathetically. "Would it help to tell me the whole story?"

LeBreau stared into the fire for several moments. At last he said, "Perhaps it *is* time, after all. Do you remember, Amos, the weekend you visited me in Normandy before the war? You'd spent the summer at Oxford and came over to France in early September."

"The autumn of thirty-six—how could I forget? Your Château Montclair was the most beautiful estate I'd ever seen, and your Denise the most beautiful hostess."

"Ah, yes, my two great loves. And how I enjoyed showing them off! I still do the château, of course, although it's not the same since Denise died. But do you recall having met a friend of mine named Victor Mornier that weekend?"

"A short, rather dark chap with an infectious laugh?"

"Yes, that was Victor. My oldest and dearest friend, even though, God help me, I was forced to cut him dead the last dozen times we met."

"Tell me," said Ponsonby softly.

The Frenchman hefted his brandy glass as though hoping to find in its weight some suggestion of where best to begin his story. "Have you ever had the kind of friendship, Amos," he asked at last, "that is at once both a close friendship and a keen rivalry? Because that's the way it was with Victor Mornier and me, almost from the cradle. We played together as children, went camping together on holidays, attended the local academy together, where we vied for the same scholastic prizes, played on the same teams, even courted the same girls. But the honors were remarkably even, so our rivalry served as a spur to our friendship rather than a handicap.

"Then in 1921 as we both went off to university in England— Victor to Cambridge and I to Oxford. Unfortunately, Victor had to drop out after a year; his father had died, and far from being the wealthy man we had all supposed, the settlement of his estate showed him to have been quite deeply in debt. But I was able to help out, and Victor managed to save part of his father's land, and by the time I was graduated and had returned to Normandy, he had a flourishing business going.

"It wasn't long before our rivalry was going again, as keen as ever." LeBreau smiled, remembering. "There was scarcely any skill in which we didn't feel compelled to compete—tennis, golf, bridge, chess. But most of all we liked to challenge each other with—what shall I call them?—puzzles, riddles, conundrums of all kinds. Evening after evening we would sit over our cognac just as you and I are doing tonight, testing each other with little-known facts, or playing 'Who Said That?' with obscure quotations from French or English or American literature. Victor's knowledge of your language and literature was equal to mine—his library of English books was just as extensive.

"There was only one area where I really outshone him in those days, and I'm afraid it does me no credit. I was far more of a dilettante; I played harder, I dabbled more, I squandered my time and money, while Victor had to work hard to pay off his father's debts. In fact, he was just beginning to get his head above water in that dreadful autumn of thirty-nine when the world changed so abruptly for all of us."

Again LeBreau fell silent, staring into the fire. Finally he resumed his story. "But as terrible as the war was, Amos, the most terrible thing for us in France was the suddenness with which it ended—officially ended, at any rate. That was the blackest day of our lives, and only one thing sustained us: we knew, as surely as we knew the sun would rise the next day, that our country would one day be free again. And we knew that until that day, if we were to salvage anything of our national honor, those of us in occupied France would have to keep right on fighting the Nazis in every way we could.

"Half a dozen of us gathered at Montclair one evening in June 1940 to organize the Resistance in our arrondissement. The plan we finally settled on was to organize *two* underground networks, one of which would concern itself exclusively with espionage—gathering information about German troop movements and defenses to be passed on to the Free French and the British—while the other would be responsible for sabotage—derailing trains, blowing up bridges, smuggling out escaped prisoners. And because the two networks would be independent of each other except at the very top, only a few key people would know the makeup of both groups. Thus the betrayal or infiltration of one would not necessarily jeopardize the members of the other. Or so we thought then."

LeBreau paused to take a sip of his brandy. "Victor and I were chosen to head the two networks. Victor was mayor of Gramonte at the time, and we knew that the Nazis preferred to work with local officials, provided they showed signs of cooperating; accordingly, Victor was chosen to organize a group which would appear to collaborate with the Germans and would thus be relatively free to come and go, to mingle socially, to watch and listen and find a hundred opportunities to ferret out the information the Allies would need. And it fell to me to organize the other network—the dynamiters, the saboteurs, even the assassins." LeBreau shuddered, remembering.

Without asking, Ponsonby picked up the decanter and refilled his friend's glass. The firelight glinted warmly on the dark liquid as the Frenchman continued his tale.

"Because my network was to be responsible for all the hostile activities, it was decided that I should maintain contact with London by setting up a shortwave radio station in the wine cellar at Montclair. But this presented a problem: if Victor's group was to gather the information the Allies would need, and I was to provide the link with the free world, we would need some means of frequent contact between us.

"It was Denise who had—what is it your American advertising people call it?—the brainstorm. She would provide the liaison by the simple expedient of having an 'affair' with Victor. The stolid, unimaginative Germans would never suspect the proud seigneur of Château Montclair of knowingly countenancing midnight trysts between his wife and the notorious puppet mayor of Gramonte, so if Denise were to seize every opportunity to sneak off for an hour or so with Victor, the Nazis would be amused rather than suspicious.

"So, as far as the enemy was concerned, I became a cuckold,

Denise an adulteress, and Victor a collaborator. And it worked, Amos; we had one of the most successful underground operations in occupied France, until"—LeBreau stared at his host as though he still did not quite believe the import of his next words—"we were all betrayed."

Ponsonby could not bear to look into his friend's memory-haunted eyes; he swirled his brandy snifter, creating a miniature whirlpool in its depths. "Do you know by whom?" he asked.

"No. We never found out. At the time of the Gestapo raids there were just nine of us who knew enough to accomplish so sweeping a betrayal. Of the nine, three died that night, either slain trying to escape capture or executed on the spot by the Gestapo, and the rest of us were arrested and sent to concentration camps in Germany. Of those six, two are known to have died in the camps, while two others vanished, swallowed up in the confusion of Germany's defeat. I alone survived to return to France after the war. I've always assumed that the traitor must have been one of the two who disappeared in Germany, but I've never been certain."

Ponsonby frowned. "You said, Rene, that three died the night of the betrayal, two died in concentration camps, two disappeared and only you survived the war. But that adds up to only eight. What of the ninth?"

"Eh?" LeBreau appeared to drag his mind back from some lonely distance. "Oh, I should have said that of those who survived the night of the raid, all but one of us were arrested. The Nazis never bothered Denise. I've often thought that the traitor, whoever he was, must have been in love with her—God knows there were enough of us who were—and so kept silent about her role in the Resistance."

Ponsonby carefully set down his brandy glass. "Tell me about the night of the betrayal."

"It was June 4, 1944, just two days before D-day. We didn't know that then, of course, but we did know that an Allied landing was imminent. It was just after midnight when one of my lieutenants arrived at the château with word of the betrayal. My people were being arrested all over the arrondissement; it was obvious that my entire network had been smashed and that it was only a matter of time before the Gestapo would come for me.

"But I still didn't know that the betrayal had included Victor's group as well, so I sent Denise off to warn him. It wasn't the first time she'd slipped away to see him after I was supposedly asleep, so I knew the Gestapo wouldn't be suspicious of her absence, and I wanted to get her away from Montclair before they arrived —I was hoping her cover might still be intact. She didn't want to leave me, of course, but I was able to make her see it was the wisest course.

"It wasn't until eleven months later, when I returned from the concentration camp, that I learned what had happened to her that night: how she'd arrived in sight of Victor's house just as a carload of Gestapo agents had pulled up in front and gone storming inside; how she'd hidden in a nearby barn until after dawn and then returned to Montclair, to find the château deserted; how she'd lived for months in an agony of doubt, expecting the Gestapo to come for her at any moment.

"And of course all that time she didn't know what had become of me, either; she assumed I'd been arrested and taken to Germany, but she couldn't be certain. And of course she knew nothing about Victor's letter."

"Tell me about the letter," said Ponsonby.

"Victor's messenger arrived at Montclair with it about half an hour after Denise had left to warn him. And those next two hours, Amos, were the longest and most agonizing of my life. I knew—I *knew!*—that I should go at once to the shortwave radio in the cellar and send the message on to London, where it could be deciphered by experts. But instead I sat there—tired, terrified, sick with worry over what might be happening to Denise, what would soon be happening to me, cursing Victor for having chosen such a time to challenge me with one last puzzle, yet unable to let go of it.

"I was in the grip of that damned rivalry, don't you see? Because I knew that Victor, pressed for time and under the most harrowing circumstances, had still managed to devise that cipher, and I simply refused to admit that I couldn't solve it under equally trying conditions. I knew I was behaving like a fool—but I couldn't stop. God help me, Amos, I was like a man possessed! It didn't even occur to me to send it on to London and *then* try my hand at deciphering it. I had to try it then and there.

"Then suddenly the Gestapo were pounding on my door. I managed to hide the letter where it would be safe till after the war, but by then, of course, it was too late. Denise saw that. She saw what it was doing to me and begged me to destroy it. I realize now, of course, that she was terrified that I would discover—"

A log shifted in the fireplace with a sputter. LeBreau's unfinished sentence slid into the momentary diversion like a snake disappearing into tall grass.

"Tell me about the letter," Ponsonby repeated hastily. "What sort of cipher did Victor use?"

"Two ciphers—rather, one cipher and one code. There's a solid block of symbols, and the letter itself, although only Denise and I would have realized that the letter was some kind of code. At least, the second and third paragraphs are, because otherwise they don't make sense.

"May I see the letter?" asked Ponsonby.

LeBreau hesitated only a moment. Then, removing his wallet from his inside breast pocket, he extracted a small square of paper, which he unfolded and handed to Ponsonby.

The latter's eyebrows registered his surprise. "But it's in English! Wasn't that unusual?"

"No. Victor and I agreed when we organized our underground networks that if written communication between us became absolutely unavoidable, we'd use English. That was less to deceive the Germans than to keep some young courier—and we were using virtual children in those days, God help us!—from being tempted to read something he'd be better off not knowing."

Ponsonby turned to the letter. It was written in longhand on a single sheet of paper, badly soiled with age and handling. "Dear Rene," it began; "The cover of both our networks has been broken and our entire organization betrayed. The Gestapo will doubtless be coming for all of us before morning. As soon as I've finished this note I plan to go into hiding until the Allies arrive. Perhaps I've been a fool to have spent a whole hour devising this message, but I'm certain you will understand why I felt impelled to do so. You will not consider it good news, but it's something I wanted you to know."

Ponsonby paused, glancing at the Frenchman over the top of the letter. "And you say that these second and third paragraphs must be a code of some sort?"

LeBreau nodded and Ponsonby resumed his reading.

"And so for now, Rene, good-bye. When this war is over and these troubled days are behind us, what do you say we round up the old gang and go on a glorious holiday to that little inn near Cremona that we enjoyed so much? How was it called? *L'Insetto d'Oro*, wasn't it? You may remember that Jean, Kirk, Quentin, and several others weren't with us there before, but this time perhaps they'll all come. At least we can send each one a letter and let him answer for himself! Then we can all sit on the terrace of an evening, sipping our wine and watching the barges drift lazily down the river into the sunset. Remember?

"Yes, Rene, let's do it! We'll leave the world behind, and anyone who would give us away can be dealt with as the need arises by you or I (although my role will have to be a small one, as I will also be busy with other matters). There is a certain fat couple whom I think we should leave at home this time—I am sure you know the ones I mean and so will not dirty my page with their names. I have stuck behind them through thick and thin, yet I know they would betray us if they could. In their place I suggest we invite one who is known to us all, a familiar substitute, a good Christian gentleman whose son will also be of the party. Again I will not say his name, lest this fall into the wrong hands, but I am confident that you will take my meaning.

"But listen to me!—running on like an old fishwife when the Gestapo may be arriving at any moment! Does it all sound a crazy dream, Rene? Perhaps it is, but a dream worth dreaming, isn't it? Think about it, please!"

It was signed simply "Victor," with the signature followed immediately by a solid block of letters, numbers, and symbols:

:2X¶3 (*u20ıxz96iz]X (4 († (‡‡:¶09*2†z23040ıXz*u6 (xzXix0]
¶ (4*u6i‡2zk6¶xzı3 (0930z44ı6u*i0?X¶3 (*u (9i¶] (9xz4u20ı4)
6 ı‡] i‡ı]¶Xu;i43zko20ı69z*¶† (‡‡:uXi (6? (9z‡kz2*¶93Xu9z3‡z4
36i9¶ (4) z‡‡6 (8z‡20ı (9†uz‡Xz4 (9z‡‡i‡4¶20ı636 (ı*k) z93?6
(u9] 8 (x 306

After several minutes of careful study Ponsonby lowered the letter to his lap. "Fascinating. Most intriguing," he said.

LeBreau had been watching him intently. "The block looks familiar to you, of course?"

"It does. To anyone with an interest in the detective story and a knowledge of its landmarks, the similarity is inescapable. Even if Victor hadn't put such an obvious clue in his letter."

"Ah, so you spotted that, too? That's what I meant by the thing's not making sense; a group of us *had* gone to Italy on holiday before the war, but we'd stayed in a little village on the Ligurian coast near Genoa, and at the Hotel Emmanuel. In any event, we were nowhere near Cremona."

"I assume that the source to which Victor was referring would have been available among the English books in his library?"

"Undoubtedly. In a French translation, too, most likely; we French regard it as a classic of your American literature."

Ponsonby was again studying the letter. "And the other statements in these second and third paragraphs are also meaningless to you?"

LeBreau nodded. "Those names Victor mentions, for instance. We did have many mutual friends, but Jean and Kirk and Quentin I couldn't place at all. And then there's all that mumbo-jumbo about whom we would or would not invite. Victor pretends to pass it off as a bit of gossip, but neither Denise nor I had the vaguest idea whom he was talking about."

"So that those two paragraphs are almost certainly the key to the cipher which follows." Ponsonby gazed thoughtfully at his old friend, then nodded brusquely, as though confirming a sudden decision. "Tell me, Rene," he said, "why *have* you been so reluctant to decipher Victor's message?"

The Frenchman gestured impatiently. "But I thought that would be obvious, Amos. Remember, Victor sent that letter just two days before D-day, which we all knew to be imminent. So what more likely than that somehow he'd discovered vital information about the German defenses that might have saved thousands of Allied lives if he could have gotten word of it to London? What else would have made him take so much time over that message when he should have been running for his life?"

"But that still wouldn't explain the necessity for a cipher, Rene. If the Germans had intercepted a letter containing information about their own defenses, it would scarcely have been news to them."

"Ah, but it might have been a tremendous surprise to them to learn that the Resistance had that information too! And if it was vital information, Victor wouldn't have stopped at just one attempt to get word out; he'd have kept on trying to get his message to London from wherever he was, so that even if the Germans *had* intercepted his letter to me, it would still have been essential that they not be able to read it, at least not until after the invasion."

The little Frenchman leaned forward earnestly. "Don't you see, Amos, that *has* to be the explanation of those rambling nostalgic paragraphs? Victor must have been hoping that if the Germans intercepted his letter they'd take the paragraphs at face value, and so concentrate their efforts on the cipher block. Because he knew that if his letter reached me, I would immediately recognize those paragraphs as being the key to his cipher and pass that information on to London. So whatever his message was, Victor didn't care if the Germans found it out eventually, just so long as they didn't find it out at once. Which makes it all the more likely that it had something to do with the Allied invasion."

"I suppose that does make sense," admitted Ponsonby.

"You *know* it does, Amos. And *I* know that's what Denise thought, too. She was afraid if I deciphered Victor's message I'd realize that my vanity and stupidity had very likely caused the deaths of hundreds of Allied soldiers. That I was not only a fool, but a murderer as well!" LeBreau buried his face in his hands. "And how in the name of God could I live with knowledge like that?"

Ponsonby stared in sympathy at his friend's bowed head. "I'm sorry, Rene. I never should have pried—"

"No!" LeBreau sat up briskly. "I've been a coward long enough! I should have asked someone less involved than I am to decipher Victor's message for me years ago. I'm afraid I can't delay my departure for the Coast tomorrow, but I'll leave the letter with you and stop by again on my return next week. At which time, Amos"—terror and hope fought in the Frenchman's voice—"I will expect you to give me Victor's message!"

The grandfather clock in the corner of the study was striking noon the following day when Ponsonby laid down his pen and leaned back in his chair. Victor Mornier's deciphered message lay on the desk before him.

He had set to work on it immediately following LeBreau's departure that morning. His first step had been to select, from the section of his library devoted to nineteenth-century American literature, a handsome calf-bound volume which he knew to contain the two passages he must consult in order to solve the mystery. The first of these was a solid block of symbols strikingly familiar to the one in Victor's letter:

53‡‡†305)) 6*;4826) 4‡.) 4‡) ;806*;48†8¶60)) 85; ;]8*;:‡*8†
83 (88) 5*†;46 (;88*96*?;8) *‡ (;485) ;5*†2:*‡ (;4956*2 (5*__
4) 8¶8*;4069285) ;) 6†8) 4‡‡;1 (‡9;48081;8:8‡1;48†85;4) 485†
528806*8ı (‡9;48; (88;4 (‡?34;48) 4‡ı6ı;:188;‡?;

The second, a few pages on, was the deciphered version:

"A good glass in the Bishop's hostel in the Devil's seat—twenty-one degrees and thirteen minutes—northeast and by north—main branch seventh limb east side—shoot from the left eye of the death's-head—a beeline from the tree through the shot fifty feet out."

For ten minutes Ponsonby had diligently matched alphabet letter to symbol. Then he had sat in silence for almost an hour, frowning over Victor's letter. The first six sentences in the second paragraph had given him no trouble, nor had the entire third paragraph—it had been easy enough to see what Victor was getting at there, especially with the help he had received from William Legrand. But the long sentence near the close of the second paragraph—Victor's nostalgic reminiscence about sitting on the terrace of an imaginary Italian inn at sunset—had stumped him.

Stumped him until he had muttered, "Confound it, the thing's impossible!"—and slapped his desk with such vehemence that he had started the globe on one corner to gently spinning. In that instant he had known the solution to Victor Mornier's final challenge. "Because it *is* impossible," he had murmured, reaching out to stop the spinning earth.

Now another hour had passed, and Victor's message lay unmasked before him. Ponsonby sighed as he thought of the awful moment when he must show it to LeBreau. How right, he thought, how prophetically right, Thomas Gray had been: "Where ignorance is bliss, 'tis folly to be wise."

"Tell me, Amos, how did you go about deciphering Victor's message?" It was a week later, and Rene LeBreau once again faced Ponsonby across the study hearth. The Frenchman sat stiffly erect, obviously braced for the worst.

Ponsonby seized the reprieve which LeBreau's question had offered. "I began," he said, "by accepting your interpretation of Victor's basic plan—that he intended to devise a secret message and then give you an advantage over the Germans by hiding certain clues to its solution in a chatty, seemingly innocent letter. But even if that were so, I reasoned, his first concern must have been the cipher itself.

"It's no mean trick to devise any kind of code or cipher on the spur of the moment, and this one presented definite problems. If he made it too simple and the Germans did intercept his letter, they'd very likely break it in a matter of hours, even without the help of his clues. Too hard, and composing a letter of clues would become impossibly difficult in the short time he could spare.

"I pictured him sitting at his desk racking his brain for a solution to his problem, when suddenly it occurred to him that there was a *ready-made* cipher available in his library, which, thanks to your extensive collection of American literature, was almost certainly available in your library as well. He was thinking, of course of Captain Kidd's cipher in Edgar Allan Poe's story, 'The Gold-Bug.'

"Thus Victor adopted that famous cipher as the basis for his own, and in case you failed to recognize it, he gave you a hint in the first of his covering-letter clues by 'recalling' an imaginary visit to Cremona—a city on Italy's *Po* River—and an equally imaginary sojourn at an inn called *L'Insetto d'Oro,* which, of course, is the Italian for—"

" 'The Gold-Bug,' " interrupted LeBreau. "That much I had worked out for myself."

"You may have deduced some of the rest,' said Ponsonby. "Now, Poe's story does not list Captain Kidd's cryptographic alphabet in full, but it would have taken Victor only a few minutes to work it out. He would then have discovered, however, that since Kidd's deciphered message makes no use of the letters *j, k, q, x,* and *z,* there are no symbols for those letters in 'The Gold-Bug' cipher.

"That, of course, was no great stumbling block, but Victor probably decided that Poe's cipher would be easier to modify, as he felt it advisable to do, if he had a complete alphabet to work with. Accordingly, he hit on the simple expedient of having each of the missing letters represent itself. That's what he means in his next clue: the phrase 'Jean, Kirk, Quentin, and several others' refers to the missing letters—*j*, *k*, *q*, *x*, and *z*—and the operative words in the next sentence are 'each one a letter' and 'answer for himself.' "

Ponsonby frowned thoughtfully as he continued his explanation. "I was assuming that the idea of using the Captain Kidd cipher had appealed to Victor because Poe's works are not as well known in Germany as they are in France, so that even a German intelligence officer would be less likely to recognize the source than you would. But it must then have occurred to him that that was by no means a certainty, and that it would be wise for him to make some basic change in Poe's alphabet so as to foil the rapid solution which must otherwise follow recognition of his source.

"I was convinced that his next sentence contained a clue to such a change, but I was at a loss to grasp it until I finally had sense enough to refer to my globe and realized—something I should have recalled at once—that the Po River flows into the Adriatic Sea. That is to say, it flows toward the *east*, so that it would have been impossible to have watched barges '*drift* . . . into the sunset.' In short, Victor reversed the direction of the river to indicate to you that he had reversed the alphabet in 'The Gold-Bug.' "

"So that the symbols for *a, b, c,* and so on in Poe's cipher—?" began Lebreau.

"Became the symbols for *z, y, x,* and so on in Victor's. Precisely. But even with that change, as Victor himself must have then realized, he still had a cipher that was no great challenge. Consequently, I pictured him next as thrashing about in his mind for some way to make it just a bit more difficult. And since he had recalled Poe's story for his basic cipher, it seemed logical that he should also recall William Legrand's method of decipherment. You'll remember that Legrand used the prevalence of the letter *e* and the frequency with which it is doubled in English.

"Accordingly, I assumed that the phrase 'anyone who would give us away,' near the beginning of Victor's third paragraph, referred to the letter *e,* and that the balance of that clause—'can be dealt with . . . by you or I'—indicated something he planned to do to it. Now, no man with a command of English such as you attributed to Victor Mornier was likely to use 'I' as the object of a preposition. Accordingly, I suspected the error to have been deliberate, and my suspicion immediately pointed to the meaning of his clue: orally, you see, *you* and *I* are letters as well as words, and Victor was here indicating his intention of using those letters as additional symbols for *e,* thus giving him three possible *e*'s and frustrating any attempt to break his code on the basis of simple letter frequency.

"In the parenthetical phrase which follows"—Ponsonby stressed the key words as he read aloud from Victor's letter—" 'although my role will have to be a *small one,* as *I* will also be *busy with other matters,*' he acknowledges the fact that capital *I* is used elsewhere in Poe's cipher, so that it will have to be a small, or lower-case, *i* which serves as one of his stand-ins for *e.*"

Ponsonby paused to marshal his thoughts. "Now, I should point out that throughout these deductions I had been ignoring the step which Poe correctly observes to be primary in solving any cipher: that of determining the language of the original message. Because I wasn't working with the cipher itself, you see, but merely with Victor's clues, and I was confident that once I had worked out his alphabet, words in one language or another would begin to emerge from his cipher. Even Victor's concern with the letter *e* was no indication, since that letter is even more prevalent in French than it is in English.

"His next clue, however, made it clear that his deciphered message must be in English, for, again following Legrand's lead, he next turned his attention to the combination *th,* which occurs with great frequency in English but relatively seldom in French. Victor identifies it as 'a certain fat couple . . . I have stuck behind them through *thick* and *thin*'—as of course *i* does."

Ponsonby stopped abruptly, startled by the awkward sound of the phrase. Then he smiled wryly at his own ingrained purism and resumed his explanation. "To replace *th,* Victor tells us, he is going to use 'a familiar substitute,' and of course the most familiar substitute for the unknown in the realm of symbols is the capital X. An illiterate man will substitute it for his signature, or an advertiser will substitute the term 'Brand X' when he wishes to refer to a rival product. And Victor then goes on to describe X as 'a good Christian gentleman' because X has stood for centuries as a symbol for the name of Christ. Finally he adds, 'whose son will also be of the party,' by way of acknowledging the fact that a small *x* is in use elsewhere in his cryptographic alphabet and should not be confused with the capital X which will serve as his substitute for *th*.

"So to sum up, Victor took the incomplete alphabet invented by Poe for his story 'The Gold-Bug,' filled in the gaps, reversed it, added additional symbols to disguise the most obvious weak spots in any English cipher—that is, the letter *e* and the combination *th*—and arrived at the following." Leaning forward, Ponsonby handed LeBreau a sheet of paper on which he had written out these symbols:

a = z	j = q	's = 4
b = :	k = .	t = 3
c = x	l = ‡	u = I
d =]	m = *	v = 8
e = ¶, u or i	n = 9	w = †
f = ?	o = 0	x = __
g = ;	p = k	y = 2
h =)	q = j	z = 5
i = (	r = 6	th = X

LeBreau studied the paper for several seconds. Then he took a deep breath, like a man about to plunge into an icy river, and asked, "And Victor's message?"

Ponsonby picked up a second sheet of paper from the table. "I'm afraid it explains a great deal, Rene. We both should have realized all along that Victor would not have been so foolish as to think that any spur-of-the-moment cipher could baffle German experts for more than a few hours. But of course it wasn't the Germans he was trying to deceive."

"Please," said LeBreau, holding out his hand.

Ponsonby sighed, and handed the deciphered message to his friend. He himself knew it by heart, so often had he read it over:

"By the time you can read this I will be on my way to South America. The code is merely a precaution to assure me of the time I need in case you should elude the Gestapo. Your name will be their final payment. Then at last, Rene, I shall rival you in wealth as in all else. Your triumphant friend, Victor."

LeBreau finished, then slowly crumpled the paper in his hand. He lifted his haunted eyes to Ponsonby. "How could I have been so blind, Amos? So completely mistaken?"

"War can do strange things to a man, Rene. I'm sure the Victor Mornier who sent you that message was not the same man you had known in happier days."

"But all these years I've thought—"

"That he was dead? But even if he wasn't, Rene, even if he's still alive somewhere in South America, do you think his conscience has ever given him a moment's rest? A man who betrayed his friends, his country—"

"No, Amos"—LeBreau gestured feebly—"you don't understand. I've known all along that Victor was dead. A neighbor found him a few days after the betrayal. The Gestapo had taken him down to his cellar and made him kneel before a crude swastika scratched on the wall and then shot him in the head. I realize now they were simplying ridding themselves of a French traitor who had outlived his usefulness, but in Gramonte we assumed he'd been executed for his role in the Resistance. And of course I always believed he'd sacrificed a chance to escape just to encipher a message that, thanks to me, never even reached the Allies."

With a groan LeBreau hurled the crumpled paper into the fireplace. "Don't you see, Amos? For twenty-six years I've been haunted by the guilt that, no matter what was in Victor's message, *I* had betrayed *him*."

Jack Ritchie—a most reliable contributor to these pages in recent years—has recently launched a beguiling series of short stories. Picture, pray, a high-principled homicide cop who bestows a traffic ticket upon the drunken son of the mayor, and for his sins is banished to the Records Division, there to sit in dusty solitude over crimes ancient and unsolved, ancient but not unsolvable....

JACK RITCHIE

Take Another Look

It had been my misfortune to arrest the mayor's son for drunken driving.

Captain Milliken saw me alone in his office. He smiled tightly. "Henry, why don't you resign?"

"No," I said firmly.

"Why don't I fire you?"

"Because we both know that firings are reviewed by the Police Board, and it is composed of civilians who might create a stink."

He winced at the word "civilians." "Why did you do it?" he demanded again. "You were off duty. Besides, you're in Homicide."

"A policeman is *never* off duty."

"Didn't he *tell* you he was the mayor's son?"

"Yes, but anybody could claim that."

"Didn't you *look* at his driver's license?"

"Of course. However, Johnson is such a common name . . ."

It had been my day off and I had been returning from the main library downtown when I noticed the car in front of me weaving considerably from side to side. I had blown my horn and pulled cautiously alongside, waving my wallet and its badge. The driver had been still sufficiently in possession of his senses to pull to the curb.

Upon further investigation, I quickly determined that he was in no condition to walk. As a matter of fact, he fell asleep when I pocketed his car keys and went to the nearest public phone to summon a patrol wagon.

Milliken got to his feet. "Come with me, Henry."

I followed him out into the corridor. We walked side by side for some time and then stopped before a door marked "Records Division." We entered.

Some twenty civilian clerks were busy at work in the large room.

"Are you transferring me?" I asked.

Milliken continued walking.

We passed through the room to a blank door at the farther end of the department. Milliken unlocked it, and we went in.

"What is this?" I asked.

"Your new assignment," Milliken said. He grandly indicated the wooden filing cabinets. "Here we have the case records of murder, robbery, rape, arson, breaking and entering, litterbugging, and whatever—none of which have ever been solved." He smiled, revealing remarkably sharp teeth. "Henry, it is now your job to review these cases to see if something can finally be done for the triumph of justice."

The word "finally" caught my attention. "The filing cabinets look awfully dusty."

Milliken revealed his teeth again. "And they should be. Every case in this room is at least twenty-five years old. Some of them even go back to the founding of the police department. I believe that was in 1842."

I blinked. "You mean I'm supposed to review cases that are more than twenty-five years dead?"

"Not dead, Henry. Just resting. And I expect you to wake them up." His smiled increased. "No hurry, Henry. You've got *all* the time in the world." He dropped the key into my palm. "Don't forget to turn off the lights and lock up when you leave. And *do* have fun."

He disappeared the way we had come.

I sighed and proceeded to examine the room. It was windowless. I wandered through the aisles of filing cabinets and found a small island of space which contained a battered flat-top desk and a swivel chair.

Ah, evidently someone had once lived here.

I turned on the drop light above the desk, and the area warmed up a bit. I returned to the filing cabinets and began examining labels. Yes, Milliken had been right. Almost every crime conceivable—and unsolved—resided here, and all of them were at least twenty-five years old.

I found the section devoted to homicides and opened one of the filing cabinet drawers at random. I pulled out a thick cardboard container, went back to the desk, and began reading the contents.

The murder had taken place at six-forty on the first Friday of a rather warm day in November 1941.

It was at that time—give or take a minute—that the immediate neighbors of Mrs. Irene Brannon had heard her scream. They had rushed to their windows, and one of them, a Mrs. Wilson, claimed to have seen a dark figure rush out of the back of the Brannon house. She had been unable to describe it further, the night being almost moonless and the sun having set officially at 4:46 P.M.

Mrs. Wilson had immediately phoned the police.

When they arrived, they found Mrs. Brannon dead on the floor of her kitchen. She had been stabbed three times, and the murder weapon was missing.

On the floor beside her body, the police found a diamond

bracelet which the department experts estimated to be worth approximately ten thousand dollars.

The police had taken the necessary photographs and measurements and removed the body to the morgue for the mandatory autopsy.

Two detectives—one of them a Sergeant Dunlap—remained at the Brannon home until approximately eleven o'clock, at which time Mrs. Brannon's husband, Dennis, returned home.

They informed him of what had happened, and he seemed to be properly shaken by the news. Upon questioning, Dennis Brannon denied having any part in the murder. He claimed he had spent the entire evening—from six to approximately ten-thirty—at the home of his twin brother, Albert.

Brannon had been taken to the station for further questioning, but he continued to deny any knowledge concerning his wife's death.

His brother, Albert, also brought to the station, backed up Brannon's statements completely.

The police had released Dennis Brannon at five-thirty in the morning and had assigned someone to follow him when he left.

Brannon had gone directly to the six-o'clock Mass at St. John's Cathedral. It appeared that he attended Mass every morning, come rain, shine, or murder.

I read on.

The cardboard container held everything—the official forms, some of them now obsolete, the records of the interviews, the questionings. There were the descriptions, the statements, the biographies. It was all here—everything the police could unearth—but still the crime remained unsolved.

When I finished my reading, I glanced at my watch. More than two hours had passed by. I turned back to the papers spread out on the desk. Yes, I could almost see and hear Dunlap interviewing the suspects, the witnesses.

I leaned back thoughtfully and promptly fell over. Now I realized why this particular swivel chair had been consigned to the scrap heap. I got off the floor, put the chair back together, and gingerly sat down again.

Where was I? Oh, yes. Seeing Sergeant Dunlap interrogating people; Mrs. Wilson, for instance.

Mrs. Wilson was sharp-eyed and eager. "I really don't know *too* much about the Brannons. They moved into the neighborhood only six months ago."

"Tell us what you can."

"Well, I'll say one good thing for her. She always did her wash on Mondays. Not like *some* people in this neighborhood. You know, Tuesdays, or Wednesdays, or whenever. And her clothesline was always orderly."

"Orderly?"

"Yes. All the pillow cases hung together. Socks with socks, and all the shirts on one line. Some people in this neighborhood put up their laundry just helter-skelter. All mixed up, you know."

"Yes. Well, you heard Mrs. Brannon scream at six-forty, and you went immediately to the window?"

"That's right. There wasn't much light, but I could just make out this figure running across the back lawn and into the alley."

"Mr. Brannon?"

"I really couldn't *swear* to that. Just a figure. It could have been anybody."

"The Brannons were quiet neighbors? No loud arguments, for instance?"

"Very quiet neighbors. Almost ideal, you'd think. Except for the vodka bottles."

"Vodka bottles?"

"Yes. Every other day or so, Mrs. Brannon used to *sneak* out of the back door of her house with an empty bottle, and she'd push it *under* the other trash in the ash box. I just *happened* to be outside when the trash men came—they collect only once in two weeks now, you know. Garbage once a week, but trash only every second week—and I *noticed* that all of the bottles were vodka bottles. Eight or nine bottles every two weeks."

"The Brannons drank?"

"Well . . . I don't think that he drank at all. I can usually *tell* just by looking at a person." She held a small, tight smile. "Don't people drink vodka because it has no *smell?* I mean, she could drink and hide those bottles, and he'd never *know,* would he?"

"Did the Brannons have many friends? Visitors?"

"Not many visitors. But I do think that *she* had a *special* friend."

"Someone who visited her frequently?"

"Not exactly visited. It was sort of halfway."

"Halfway?"

The light in her eyes became brighter. "Well . . . my sister lives just four blocks away from here—around the corner and straight on—and I do go there fairly often. Four or five times a week, I'd say. This one afternoon about eight weeks ago, Maggie and I were having tea at the living-room window when I noticed Mrs. Brannon walking up the street. She stopped at the corner, and I thought she might be waiting for the bus. But several of them passed by, and she still stood there."

"Yes?"

"Well, I said to myself, that's odd. So we just watched, Maggie and me, and after about five minutes more, this great big car with a *man* driving pulled up, and Mrs. Brannon got into it." Mrs. Wilson paused for a moment. "That was on a Wednesday, and on *Friday,* Maggie and I happened to be sitting there again when the same thing went on—Mrs. Brannon waiting there and getting into the same big car. And so we . . . *Maggie* . . . decided to keep a weather eye out at two o'clock in the afternoons, and what do you know, Mrs. Brannon would get picked up by that car at least two or three times a week."

"Could you describe the car?"

"I really don't know that much about automobiles, except that it looked expensive. And I couldn't describe the man either. He never got out of the car. *However* . . ."

"Yes?"

Slight color came to Mrs. Wilson's cheekbones. "My *sister* did happen to copy the license number of the car. I mean, it was all a little *suspicious*, you know, and I . . . *she* . . . thought that it wouldn't do any *harm* to take it down, just in case *something* might come up . . ."

Yes, she had given Sergeant Dunlap the license numbers of the car, and the State Motor Vehicle Department had come up with the name of Charles Colling, 2481 N. Simmon Avenue.

Colling proved to be in his late forties and the senior vice-president of our largest department store. Also he was married and had two children in college.

Colling had been wary. "What can I do for you, Sergeant?"

"Do you know a Mrs. Irene Brannon?"

Colling frowned thoughtfully. "Brannon? Brannon? No, I'm afraid I don't know anybody by that name."

"Would this photograph help you to refresh your memory?"

He had glanced at it and paled slightly.

"When was the last time you saw her?"

"I said I don't know anybody named Brannon."

"You were seen with her on a number of occasions—by reliable witnesses who took the trouble to jot down your license-plate number."

Colling licked his lips. "What is this all about?"

"Mrs. Brannon was murdered last night."

Colling lost more color. "And you think that I had something to do with the killing?"

"Where were you at approximately six-forty last night?"

"Is that the time she was murdered?"

"Please answer the question."

Colling thought for a moment and then almost smiled. "At six-forty last night I was at the State Businessmen's Association banquet in Park Falls. That's over thirty miles from here."

"Do you have anyone who could verify that?"

"Of course. Nearly a hundred people. As a matter of fact, I was the principal speaker at the banquet. I arrived early, at six, for the predinner drinks. The dinner itself was served at seven, and I gave my speech at seven-thirty."

"What was your relationship with Mrs. Brannon?"

Colling cleared his throat. "We were just friends."

"Friends enough so that you found it necessary to meet secretly? Friends enough to buy her a ten-thousand-dollar bracelet? We are in the process of tracing it now, Mr. Colling. It shouldn't be too difficult, but could you save us time?"

Colling looked away. "All right. I bought it for her."

"How did you happen to get acquainted with Mrs. Brannon?"

"Just one of those things. Met her at a bar, and one thing led to another." He smiled faintly. "Her husband didn't understand her."

"Did you ever make her any promises?"

"Promises?"

"A man doesn't casually give a woman a ten-thousand-dollar bracelet, does he? Did you ever make her feel that the affair was more than just an affair? That perhaps it would lead to marriage?"

"No," Colling said firmly. "Absolutely not." Then he hedged. "Possibly she might have *misunderstood*, but never, *never* did I promise her anything like that." He took a breath. "Sergeant, is there any need to drag my name into this? I mean, I'm a married man with two children. It would cause nothing but harm if my *friendship* with Mrs. Brannon came to light. After all, I had nothing to do with her murder."

"You could have provided the motive."

Colling paled again.

Again I found myself on the floor. I got up, put the chair together, and turned back to another group of papers.

Dennis and Albert were twins; not identical twins, but just your ordinary run-of-the-mill twins. Their immediate friends had little or no difficulty in telling them apart.

Their parents had, at the very beginning, determined that each of the twins would be allowed to develop a personality of his own. While they advanced in schooling at the same rate—receiving similar, though not identical grades—they were seldom ever assigned to the same classroom. They were never dressed alike, each having his own wardrobe.

Probably as a consequence of this, as adults they diverged to some degree, though still maintaining a warm personal relationship. Dennis turned to Catholicism, his father's faith, and Albert became a Quaker, his mother's persuasion. In the field of vocation, Dennis turned to accountancy and Albert became a librarian.

Librarian? Somehow one always thinks of librarians as women, at least in branch libraries.

My mind went back to my own boyhood branch library and Miss Lucinda Swenson. She had always worn a severe center part and an authoritarian frown. I had been perhaps eight and determined upon my own reading program, but Miss Swenson had kept trying for months to shoo me back into the juvenile section.

Finally I bit her. After that she let me alone.

I turned to the sheaves of papers covering the questioning of Dennis Brannon. There was quite a bit of material—he had been interrogated a number of times—but I consolidated.

Dennis Brannon was a rather small, light-haired man, in his middle twenties.

"You say you spent the evening at your brother's house?"

"Yes. I arrived there at about six o'clock."

"How long did you stay?"

"Until ten-thirty. Then I went home and found the police waiting for me."

"You had dinner at your brother's place?"

"Yes. I stayed there for dinner."

"What did you have to eat?"

Dennis frowned for a moment. "Roast beef with fried potatoes. Sliced tomatoes. Canned peaches. Coffee."

"Your brother is single?"

"Yes."

"Who made the meal?"

"His landlady. Albert rents a small upper flat. Mrs. Porter—she lives below—cooks his evening meal four or five times a week and brings it up."

"She served it to both of you?"

"No. She had made it earlier and brought it up. Albert kept it in the oven until I arrived, and we ate alone."

"Did Mrs. Porter see you at all? Arriving, perhaps?"

"I really don't know."

"What did you do after you ate?"

"Albert and I played chess."

"All evening?"

"Yes. I'm afraid I won every game. Albert isn't really a good player. I suppose that's because he's not exactly fascinated by the game."

"He's not interested in chess, and yet he played it for more than three hours?"

"Yes. Albert is very accommodating, and I was his guest."

"Have you any idea who might have wanted to kill your wife?"

"None at all. It must have been a prowler or someone of that sort."

"Did you and your wife quarrel?"

"Occasionally. I suppose all married people do."

"What did you quarrel about?"

"Nothing really serious. The usual small things."

"Do you know anybody named Colling? Charles Colling?"

Dennis Brannon shook his head. "The name means nothing to me."

"You saw the bracelet we found next to your wife's body?"

"Yes."

"Do you know anything about it?"

"No. Nothing at all. I never saw it before in my life."

I riffled through another set of papers. Mrs. Porter had been questioned. She had not seen or heard Dennis arrive at his brother's upper flat, but she thought she had heard him leave at about ten-thirty.

I paged through the questioning of Albert Brannon.

"Do you have your brother over for dinner often?"

"Not really. But last night happened to be one of those times. Dennis came over at six. We had dinner and spent the evening playing chess."

"How many games?"

"I can't say exactly. Perhaps half a dozen."

"You won about half of them?"

"No. Dennis won them all. He's quite good at the game."

"You had the radio turned on?"

"No."

"I believe you had lamb chops for dinner?"

"No. Roast beef. Potatoes. Tomatoes. Canned sliced peaches."

"Mashed potatoes?"

"No. Fried."

"How many drinks did Dennis have?"

"He doesn't drink. We had coffee. With cream and sugar."

"Why didn't you invite your brother's wife over too?"

"I used to. However, I'm afraid that I really bore her. So now she prefers to stay home. With a headache, of course."

I heard footsteps, and Captain Milliken appeared. "Well, well, still here? The work must be interesting. Your sister phoned me and said you didn't show up for supper. I had to come all the way back to headquarters, because I'm the only one who knows where you are or how to reach you."

I glanced at my watch. It was past eight in the evening. I got to my feet and began gathering together the Brannon papers.

Milliken sat down in the swivel chair I'd just vacated. I watched hopefully as he leaned back, but nothing happened.

I sighed and returned the Brannon records to their place in the filing cabinet.

We made our way back to the records room, where I said good night to Milliken. I lingered behind to ask one of the night crew for a copy of the city directory.

I found no Dennis Brannon listed, but I did find an Albert

Brannon. I was a bit surprised to discover that he still lived at the same address he had in 1941.

I phoned my sister to tell her that I was still alive and well, and then drove to the Albert Brannon address.

It proved to be in a quiet tree-lined residential district. I parked my car and walked up to the porch. I pressed the buzzer connecting the upper flat.

After a few moments the hall leading to the second floor lighted up and a voice called down to inform me that the door was unlocked.

I was met on the top landing by a small man in his middle fifties, with graying hair, but a generally youthful appearance.

"Albert Brannon?"

He nodded.

I hesitated a moment and then pulled out my wallet and showed the badge. "My name is Sergeant Henry H. Buckle."

He looked past my shoulder. "I thought you detectives worked in pairs?"

I looked back myself. "At the moment I'm on special assignment and haven't got a partner. Could you tell me where I could find your brother?"

He smiled faintly. "You don't know where he is?"

"No."

He invited me in.

I found a pleasant small kitchen, and beyond I caught a glimpse of a book-lined room. The rooms melded the odor of books, pipe tobacco, and possibly roast beef.

He filled his pipe at a canister. "Why would you want to know where Dennis is? After all these years?"

"Could you tell me?"

He nodded. "Dennis died in 1944."

"In 1944?"

Albert explained further. "The last of the good wars, you know. He was killed during the invasion of Kwajalein Atoll in the Marshall Islands. What did you want him for now?"

I felt a bit uncomfortable. "It was about the murder of his wife."

Albert raised an eyebrow. "Don't tell me you've finally solved it?"

"Well . . . yes."

"You *know* who killed her?"

"Yes. Your brother, Dennis, did."

He waited with interest.

"The way I reconstruct the crime is that your brother discovered his wife had been having an affair with Charles Colling. I imagine he accidentally discovered the bracelet and demanded to know how she got it. He happened to catch her at a moment when she'd had a bit too much vodka, because she not only admitted the affair, but got defiant about it. So Dennis grabbed the nearest kitchen knife and killed her. Then he fled to this place—probably dropping the knife into a convenient sewer on the way —and the two of you cooked up the alibi."

"Really? And what makes you think the alibi wasn't genuine?"

I smiled triumphantly. "There has been considerable liberalization in the practices of the Catholic church since 1941, but at that time no good practicing Catholic—as was Dennis Brannon— would have eaten *meat* on a *Friday,* and such was the day of the murder." Now I smiled tolerantly. "Why didn't you simply tell the police that the two of you ate fish on that evening?"

He joined my smile. "Mrs. Porter had prepared beef roast and brought it up before Dennis showed up so unexpectedly. She was also questioned by the police, you know. If we'd told them that we'd eaten anything but roast beef, they would have realized immediately that something was fishy, if I may use the word," Albert explained.

"Ah," I said. "You *admit* the fabrication?"

He shrugged. "I suppose so."

I studied him severely. "There's just one thing about this case that I still can't fit into the picture. The *twins* business."

He looked puzzled. "What twins business?"

"Whenever there are twins involved in a murder case, you sort of *expect* some kind of hanky-panky. Like a *switch.*"

Albert Brannon blinked. "Why should we switch identities? I don't see any point in that. Besides, most people could tell us apart quite readily. If you don't believe I'm Albert, you could check my fingerprints against my birth records."

"I believe you're Albert," I said. "It's just that it seems almost *mandatory* that . . ." I felt a bit warm. "I mean, it's almost *traditional* that whenever twins are involved . . ."

He regarded me with what I uneasily felt was a clinical interest. "Sergeant Buckle, if, thirty years ago, Dennis had been confronted with the fact that he supposedly consumed meat on a Friday, do you *actually* expect that he would have leaped forward with a full confession?"

"Well, no, but . . ."

"Do you think that a *jury* would have condemned a good Catholic to life in prison simply because he *forgot* the day of the week?"

"But I don't think that he forgot the . . ."

"Perhaps not. But that is what we would have claimed if that slight discrepancy in his alibi had been brought to the attention of the police." Albert smiled in a kindly fashion. "Did you know that Dennis was a war hero?"

"No, but I don't see how that has any . . ."

"Enlisted the day after Pearl Harbor. *Two* Silver Stars, three Purple Hearts, four battle stars. Even a Good Conduct Medal. Would you now, *thirty* years later, sully the reputation of a dead war hero?"

"It isn't a question of sullying . . ."

"And what do you expect to do now? Arrest me for being an *accessory* to murder? Isn't there a statute of limitations?"

"Not for murder."

"How about *accessory* to murder?"

"I don't know. I'd have to look that . . ."

"And do you think that *today* a jury would convict me of being an accessory to murder simply because my dead-brother war hero forgot to eat fish on a Friday thirty years ago?"

"But you just admitted . . ."

"All of which I would deny to anyone else. It is your word against mine."

I experienced the strong impulse to bite another librarian.

Albert patted my shoulder and spoke quietly. "Sergeant Henry H. Buckle, don't you think it would be wiser to let sleeping dogs lie?"

After several long moments of thoughts, I sighed.

I also went home and had *three* shots of brandy before I went to bed.

I took a thick and dusty cardboard container from the Homicide files and brought it back to the desk.

The year 1862?

Hm, I thought, that could be interesting.

I sat down, leaned back, and . . .

Damn. . . .

Read through the various histories of the mystery/detective story and you will find the con man—or, from antiquity, the rogue— looming large on the literary horizon. Curious how our sympathies are enlisted by someone who robs the robber, who with finesse seems to prove what in our most rational moments we may profoundly doubt—that the end justifies the means, that frustrated justice sometimes whips off her blindfold and achieves her ends through cunning. . . .

ROBERT EDWARD ECKELS
Vicious Circle

All in all, it was a pretty good night for the middle of the week. I was behind the bar as usual, busy and making money, but not really rushed. Best of all, there was enough of a crowd in the barroom to cover the number of cars in the parking lot, so that any cop who stuck his nose in wouldn't have any reason to suspect that a high-stakes poker game was going on upstairs. From which the house—me—got its cut, of course.

The Mind was at his usual corner table, and by now a fair-sized group had gathered around to try to stump him. And not having any luck, because the Mind had a memory that never let go of anything it ever got hold of—who played second base for the Senators in 1934, big-band theme songs, old movies, anything, you name it. He could even recite word for word the pledge from the old "Mr. District Attorney" radio show—which, considering who and what the Mind was, was really something.

The smart money didn't try to stump the Mind. Instead, they'd bet among themselves and use the Mind to settle it, paying the Mind off with a free drink. But, of course, there was always a sucker around who had to try it. Just as there was always a sucker in the game upstairs who was sure his luck was bound to change if he could just hang in there one more round.

And that was the reason the Mind hung around my place. Not for the suckers with the questions they were sure he couldn't answer, but for the suckers upstairs in the poker game. The memory thing was just a sideline with him. His real business was loan-sharking for the Organization. And when the sucker upstairs was ripe, the Mind was right there on hand to slip him a couple of hundred or thousand at five percent a month. Of course, there's no such thing as luck, and almost before the sucker realized it, he was well on his way to being owned body and soul by the Organization.

A lot of bartenders I know don't like having Organization types like the Mind around. But the way I figured it, he was good for business. Besides, the world's divided into those who take and those who are taken. I like to be on the side of the takers.

This particular evening there was only one guy in the place I didn't know by name or by sight—a tall rangy man with fair hair and the kind of open fleshy face that seems to go with work in the outdoors. He was sitting down toward one end of the bar and listening to the group around the Mind without really being a part of it. He didn't look like a cop, but it never paid to take chances. So the first opportunity I got, I moved down the bar to where he was sitting and stuck out my hand.

"Hi," I said, giving him the hearty-host treatment. "I'm the Johnny they call this place 'Johnny's' after. I don't think I've seen you around before."

The guy jumped as if startled, then smiled sheepishly and

grasped my hand across the bar. "Earl Sanders," he said. "And you're right. This is my first time here."

"Well," I said, smiling more naturally now, because he didn't sound like a cop, "don't let it be your last. I can use all the business I can get."

Just then one of my regulars—a jerk named Evans—sitting about two stools down, decided to butt in. He put one elbow on the bar and leaned toward us. "That's a laugh," he said. The liquor hadn't hit his tongue yet, but his eyes glittered and his face was shiny from one drink too many. "Ever since they opened that government office building across the way, this place has been a gold mine. And Johnny's got a fat five-figure bank balance to prove it." He grinned foolishly and let his elbow slide closer to us. "I ought to know. I'm his banker."

I gave him a cold look. "Keep talking like that," I said quietly, "and you won't be much longer."

That sobered him up in a hurry, because Evans was just a teller in the neighborhood bank, and it wouldn't do him any good at all if I dropped the word to his bosses that he was spending his evenings drinking and blabbing bank business.

Sanders seemed to have missed the byplay between me and Evans, though. Or the last part of it, anyway. He was staring morosely at his glass. "That's the way it goes," he said in the half-wistful, half-bitter voice of a born loser. "Some guys get the breaks and make out, and others don't. It's the same in my business."

"What kind of a business is that, Mr. Sanders?" I said, more to change the subject than from any real curiosity.

"Construction work," Sanders said.

Instinctively my eyes dropped to his hands. They were smooth and soft. Sanders followed my gaze and gave me that same sheepish grin.

"I don't mean I do it myself," he said. "I'd probably be better off if I did, the kind of wages I have to pay." He rolled his glass between his hands, and his grin became rueful. "I have my own

company. Sanders Construction. Page 397 in your Yellow Pages."
He said it with such defensive pride that I was sure the listing
was a single line or at best an eighth-of-a-page ad. In any case, I
figured I had nothing to worry about from Sanders. So I stood
him a drink on the house and let him go back to listening to the
Mind.

Sanders got to be a pretty steady customer after that, dropping
in maybe three or four times a week. Occasionally he'd drop by in
the evening, but more often he'd come in early, before the five-
o'clock after-work crowd hit, and have a couple of beers and shoot
the breeze with me. I figured that if this was the way he ran his
business, it was no wonder he wasn't making any money. But
that was his problem, not mine.

Anyway, about a month or so later, Sanders dropped in at his
usual time and ordered his usual beer. But this time, instead of
chatting, he sat quietly at the end of the bar, flipping through
the pages of a magazine he'd brought with him. If he didn't
want to talk, I wasn't going to push him, so I kept myself busy
polishing glasses.

Finally Sanders sighed and pushed the magazine to one side.
"You know, Johnny," he said, "I sometimes wonder why I
bother to subscribe to this thing. All I do is torture myself with
it."

I put down my towel now that he was showing an inclination
to talk, and moved closer to him. "How's that, Mr. Sanders?"
I said.

Sanders turned the magazine around so I could see it. "It's a trade
magazine for engineers and contractors," he said. "It lists invita-
tions to bid on construction jobs. Not little piddling jobs, either,"
he added, "but the kind you always dream about. The kind that'll
put you up there with the big-money boys."

He turned the magazine halfway around to where we both
could read it, and began to leaf through it rapidly. Once he
almost knocked over his beer, but he caught the glass in time and
moved it out of the way.

"See that?" he said, finding what he wanted in the magazine and pointing with his finger. "That's an invitation to subcontract on a job putting in a city subway system out West." His voice grew in enthusiasm as he went on. "Now, that's a job that's right up my alley! I could cut it real close on the bid to be sure of coming in low and still make a tidy profit."

I looked down at the page without really trying to read it. "Why don't you bid on it, then?" I said.

Sanders laughed shortly. "Because they freeze the little man out," he said. "To get a bid even considered, you've got to prove you have the right equipment to do the job." His voice took on that loser's quality again. "And, of course, I don't have the right equipment. Or the money to buy it with. It just goes to show— like they say, you've got to have money to make money."

I watched him impassively, thinking how he sounded just like the suckers in the poker game. This was a different game, but the players were divided the same way—winners and losers, takers and taken. And if anybody was ripe to be taken, it was Sanders, I thought. Somebody could pick up a nice small construction company dirt cheap. It was kind of a pity that it would be the Organization and not me. Still, there would be a nice commission for me for making the referral, and the Organization took care of its friends in other ways, too. So I wouldn't lose by it in the long run.

"That's a shame," I said. "Maybe you could get a loan, though, to cover the down payment on new equipment."

Sanders snorted derisively. "A loan!" he said. "A lot you know about banks, then. They won't give me a loan on a job like this unless I've already got the contract. And I can't get the contract. And I can't get the contract unless they give me a loan. It's a vicious circle."

"I wasn't thinking about a bank," I said. "I was thinking about the Mind. He's got money to lend. It's Organization money, and it don't come cheap. But it would get you your equipment."

Sanders bit on his knuckle, "I see," he said. He brooded on it a while, then said slowly, "I'd need at least fifty thousand dollars. Would the Mind be able to swing that much?"

It sounded a bit steep, but let the Mind worry about whether Sanders was worth it or not. "He could get it," I said. When Sanders still looked undecided, I added, "I know you don't cotton to the idea of dealing with a loan shark. But look at it this way—you'll only need the money until you get your contract. Then you can get a regular loan from the bank, pay the Mind off, and be on your way."

"That's right," Sanders said, catching fire. "And I could pay the bank off out of my profits from the job." He slapped the bar with his hand and said with sudden decisiveness, "Where can I find the Mind?"

I shrugged. "I don't know where he lives," I said. "But he'll be in here later tonight. All you have to do is stop by his table and tell him you want to talk business. He'll do the rest. And—uh —don't forget to mention that I sent you over."

"I sure won't," Sanders said, standing up and tossing a five-dollar bill down on the bar. "I don't think you realize how big a favor you've done me, Johnny," he said. "But thanks to you, I'll end up a millionaire yet."

And you, I thought as I watched his departing back, don't realize how big a favor you're doing me. Neither did I at the time.

The Mind came in around nine-thirty that evening as usual and stopped by the bar to pick up his first drink. Generally it was the only one he paid for himself.

"Slow evening," he said, looking around while I mixed the drink for him. He was a poker-faced little guy with a nose too large for his face and thick glasses too large for the nose. He kept his voice mild and as empty of expression as his face. Only his eyes behind the big glasses seemed alive. They moved restlessly, and you were always glad when they passed away from you.

"It'll pick up now that you're here, Mind," I said, grinning and handing him his glass. It was on the tip of my tongue to tell him about Sanders, but I decided not to in case Sanders had had second thoughts about getting mixed up with the Organization.

"Hope so," the Mind said. He slid a bill across at me, waved away the change, and strolled over to his corner table.

And just as I'd predicted, things did start to pick up. He'd no sooner gotten settled when two guys went over to ask him to decide a bar bet. I didn't hear his answer, but a minute later one of the guys was heading for the bar to order the payoff round plus one for the Mind.

It looked like it was going to be a good evening, after all.

It looked even better a half-hour or forty-five minutes later when Sanders came in and beelined to the bar.

"Is the Mind here yet, Johnny?" he said in a hushed, anxious voice as I came up to him.

"Right over there," I said, nodding.

Sanders looked around in the direction of my nod. As anxious as he sounded, I figured he'd head straight over. But instead he ordered a Scotch and water and took his time drinking it. Getting up his nerve, I decided, because every time I had a free minute he'd call me over to talk about nothing in particular.

Finally, though, he tossed off the last of his Scotch and stood up. "Wish me luck," he said.

I gave him the "O" sign with my thumb and forefinger and watched him walk over to the Mind's table and speak to him. A moment later he pulled a chair around and sat down.

I got kind of busy after that and lost track of them until Sanders came back to the bar. The way he looked, I was afraid the loan hadn't gone through and I'd lost my commission. So first chance I got, I went over to him.

"How'd it go?" I said, casual and friendly-like.

A funny little smile twisted Sanders' mouth. "All right, I guess," he said. "I got the loan, but it's costing me more than I expected. Five-percent-a-month interest."

"Well," I said, relieved, "you knew it wouldn't be cheap."

Sanders nodded. "You're right," he said. "So I guess I can't complain." He put his hand in his pocket. "Oh," he said, "by the way, the Mind said to give you this. He pulled out a roll of bills and handed it to me.

I thumbed through it rapidly before sticking it in my own pocket. Fifty bucks. That was five times what the Mind usually paid for a referral. But then I'd never referred this big a loan to him before. And in any case, who was I to argue with fifty dollars?

I caught the Mind's eye, patted my pocket, and nodded my appreciation. The Mind made a slight gesture with his hand to say it was nothing. That was the kind of a guy he was—as long as you were on the right side of him, that is.

I didn't see Sanders around for about five or six weeks after that. It was nothing to me, of course, and when I thought about it at all, I figured he was out West arranging the details of his contract bid.

Then one afternoon he walked in out of the blue. It was early again, and the place was empty. Only this time Sanders looked like this wasn't the first place he'd hit. His tie was loose at the collar, and his face was flushed.

"Whiskey, Johnny," he said, sliding onto one of the bar stools. "And keep it coming until I tell you to stop. Only I won't tell you to stop." He didn't look or sound like he was celebrating. On the other hand, there's no law that says you can only serve happy people.

I poured him a shot. "What happened, Mr. Sanders?" I said. "Your contract fall through?" It was the only thing I could think of that would set him off like this. And, of course, it was what I'd expected to happen all along, anyway.

Sanders laughed bitterly. "You know, Johnny," he said, "I almost think I'd feel better if it had." He picked up his glass, drained it, and put it back down so hard that it rang against the bar. "No," he said, "everything worked out just as I planned it. I was low bidder, and the job's mine. But those damn lawyers won't sign until all the other subcontracts are buttoned up. And that won't be for another two months."

"So what's your problem?" I said. "You just wait out the two months, and then you're in clover."

Sanders shook his head. "That's the problem, Johnny," he said. "I can't wait out the two months. I've got a payment coming due to the Mind tomorrow, and my credit is stretched so tight I can't raise a dime."

"That is tough," I said. "The Mind doesn't like people missing payments."

Sanders laughed even more bitterly than before. "You think so?" he said. "There's nothing the Mind would like *more* than for me to miss a payment. Then he and the Organization can take over my company and a job that practically guarantees a profit of a million bucks. And if I try to stop him, I'll end up dead in an alley somewhere."

I caught my upper lip between my teeth and chewed on it softly. "A million bucks," I murmured.

"At least," Sanders said. "And it would be mine except for a measly five-thousand-dollar payment I can't make and can't raise."

I looked at Sanders for a long minute and made my decision. It was dangerous crossing the Mind, but he didn't have to know. And the profit made the risk worth it. "I've got five thousand dollars," I said.

Sanders looked up suddenly, and relief flooded his face. "Look, Johnny," he said, his hands making little shaking motions, "you lend me that money and I'll guarantee you'll have it back in two months at the latest with a profit of ten—no, twenty percent." He smiled tentatively. "So, how about it? Is it a deal?"

I smiled tightly and shook my head. "I wasn't thinking of a loan," I said. "What I had in mind was an investment. Like, say, a half interest in your million-dollar profit."

Sanders looked at me aghast. "You can't be serious," he said.

"Why not?" I said. "The way I look at it, I'm doing you an even bigger favor than before. Because without my five thousand you've got nothing except a load of trouble. With it you get to keep your company and make half a million bucks for yourself."

I had him over a barrel, of course, but I didn't want to be

unreasonable. Because a happy sucker is better than an unhappy one any day, and it wouldn't be long before I'd squeezed him out altogether anyway. So in the end we settled on a one-fourth interest for ten thousand dollars.

I hung a "Closed" sign on the door and took Sanders over to the bank to get the money out before he could change his mind.

"You're a good businessman, Johnny," Sanders said as we counted the last of the money into his attaché case.

"I try to be," I said. I patted the pocket holding the partnership agreement, all legal and binding, that I'd written out and made him sign. "No hard feelings, I hope?"

"No," Sanders said, "of course not. Business is business, and that's all there is to it." He closed the case and tucked it under his arm. "Well," he said, "I guess we both have things to do and people to see." He crossed to the door. "I'll be in touch. And if you see the Mind before I do, be sure to tell him I'll meet him at his usual table tomorrow to make the payment."

"Sure," I said, thinking about what I was going to do with all that money.

That evening the Mind stopped in as usual, and when I handed him his glass, I said casually, as if I'd just remembered it, "By the way, I saw Sanders today. He said to tell you he'd meet you at your usual table tomorrow with the money."

"Sanders?" the Mind said. "Who's Sanders?"

"That big blond guy," I said. "He borrowed fifty thousand dollars from you as a down payment to buy new equipment for a construction job out West."

The Mind shook his head. "Not from me he didn't," he said.

"About five or six weeks ago," I said, the bottom of my stomach falling out. "He went over to your table to make the loan, and afterwards you sent him back with fifty dollars for me for making the referral."

The Mind let his eyes rest on me. Then he said, "Yeah, I remember the guy. But he didn't make any loan. He said he had a bet with you over who was the first to break the four-minute mile. I said it was Roger Bannister, and he said in that case he owed you fifty dollars. That's all. Why he'd want to tell you he'd made a loan, I sure don't know."

I had a pretty good idea, but just to make sure, the next morning I looked up the Sanders Construction Company in the Yellow Pages. It was there on page 397, all right, but when I phoned at nine on the dot and asked to speak to Mr. Earl Sanders, the girl who answered told me that there hadn't been a Mr. Sanders in the company since the present owner's father-in-law died in 1953.

So, really, what can you believe in anymore? Especially these days. . . .

It's a pleasure to welcome the first appearance in this series of Richard Matheson—another author of unusual skill who too infrequently crosses over into our genre from his usual haunts in fantasy. His story is one which rises to piercing tension—because, I suspect, it reflects, in subtle yet identifiable terms, the deadly contest between everyman and implacable, inexplicable, murderous doom: the stuff of modern daymare.

RICHARD MATHESON

Duel

At 11:32 A.M., Mann passed the truck.

He was heading west, en route to San Francisco. It was Thursday, and unseasonably hot for April. He had his suit coat off, his tie removed and shirt collar opened, his sleeve cuffs folded back. There was sunlight on his left arm and on part of his lap. He could feel the heat of it through his dark trousers as he drove along the two-lane highway. For the past twenty minutes, he had not seen another vehicle going in either direction.

Then he saw the truck ahead, moving up a curving grade between two high green hills. He heard the grinding strain of its motor and saw a double shadow on the road. The truck was pulling a trailer.

He paid no attention to the details of the truck. As he drew behind it on the grade, he edged his car toward the opposite lane.

The road ahead had blind curves, and he didn't try to pass until the truck has crossed the ridge. He waited until it started around a left curve on the downgrade, then, seeing that the way was clear, pressed down on the accelerator pedal and steered his car into the eastbound lane. He waited until he could see the truck front in his rearview mirror before he turned back into the proper lane.

Mann looked across the countryside ahead. There were ranges of mountains as far as he could see and, all around him, rolling green hills. He whistled softly as the car sped down the winding grade, its tires making crisp sounds on the pavement.

At the bottom of the hill, he crossed a concrete bridge and, glancing to the right, saw a dry stream bed strewn with rocks and gravel. As the car moved off the bridge, he saw a trailer park set back from the highway to his right. How can anyone live out here? he thought. His shifting gaze caught sight of a pet cemetery ahead, and he smiled. Maybe those people in the trailers wanted to be close to the graves of their dogs and cats.

The highway ahead was straight now. Mann drifted into a reverie, the sunlight on his arm and lap. He wondered what Ruth was doing. The kids, of course, were in school and would be for hours yet. Maybe Ruth was shopping; Thursday was the day she usually went. Mann visualized her in the supermarket, putting various items into the basket cart. He wished he were with her instead of starting on another sales trip. Hours of driving yet before he'd reach San Francisco. Three days of hotel sleeping and restaurant eating, hoped-for contacts and likely disappointments. He sighed; then, reaching out impulsively, he switched on the radio. He revolved the tuning knob until he found a station playing soft, innocuous music. He hummed along with it, eyes almost out of focus on the road ahead.

He started as the truck roared past him on the left, causing his car to shudder slightly. He watched the truck and trailer cut in abruptly for the westbound lane and frowned as he had to brake to maintain a safe distance behind it. What's with you? he thought.

He eyed the truck with cursory disapproval. It was a huge gasoline tanker pulling a tank trailer, each of them having six pairs of wheels. He could see that it was not a new rig but was dented and in need of renovation, its tanks painted a cheap-looking silvery color. Mann wondered if the driver had done the painting himself. His gaze shifted from the word FLAMMABLE printed across the back of the trailer tank, red letters on a white background, to the parallel reflector lines painted in red across the bottom of the tank to the massive rubber flaps swaying behind the rear tires, then back up again. The reflector lines looked as though they'd been clumsily applied with a stencil. The driver must be an independent trucker, he decided, and not too affluent a one, from the looks of his outfit. He glanced at the trailer's license plate. It was a California issue.

Mann checked his speedometer. He was holding steady at fifty-five miles an hour, as he invariably did when he drove without thinking on the open highway. The truck driver must have done a good seventy to pass him so quickly. This seemed a little odd. Weren't truck drivers supposed to be a cautious lot?

He grimaced at the smell of the truck's exhaust and looked at the vertical pipe to the left of the cab. It was spewing smoke, which clouded darkly back across the trailer. Christ, he thought. With all the furor about air pollution, why do they keep allowing that sort of thing on the highways?

He scowled at the constant fumes. They'd make him nauseated in a little while, he knew. He couldn't lag back here like this. Either he slowed down or he passed the truck again. He didn't have the time to slow down. He'd gotten a late start. Keeping it at fifty-five all the way, he'd just about make his afternoon appointment. No, he'd have to pass.

Depressing the gas pedal, he eased his car toward the opposite lane. No sign of anything ahead. Traffic on this route seemed almost nonexistent today. He pushed down harder on the accelerator and steered all the way into the eastbound lane.

As he passed the truck, he glanced at it. The cab was too high for him to see into. All he caught sight of was the back of the truck driver's left hand on the steering wheel. It was darkly

tanned and square-looking, with large veins knotted on its surface.

When Mann could see the truck reflected in the rearview mirror, he pulled back over to the proper lane and looked ahead
again.

He glanced at the rearview mirror in surprise as the truck
driver gave him an extended horn blast. What was that? he
wondered; a greeting or a curse? He grunted with amusement,
glancing at the mirror as he drove. The front fenders of the
truck were a dingy purple color, the paint faded and chipped;
another amateurish job. All he could see was the lower portion
of the truck; the rest was cut off by the top of his rear window.

To Mann's right, now, was a slope of shalelike earth with
patches of scrub grass growing on it. His gaze jumped to the clap-
board house on top of the slope. The television aerial on its roof
was sagging at an angle of less than forty degrees. Must give great
reception, he thought.

He looked at the front again, glancing aside abruptly at a sign
painted in jagged block letters on a piece of plywood: NIGHT
CRAWLERS—BAIT. What the hell is a night crawler? he wondered.
It sounded like some monster in a low-grade Hollywood thriller.

The unexpected roar of the truck motor made his gaze jump
to the rearview mirror. Instantly, his startled look jumped to the
side mirror. By God, the guy was passing him *again*. Mann
turned his head to scowl at the leviathan form as it drifted by.
He tried to see into the cab but couldn't because of its height.
What's with him, anyway? he wondered. What the hell are we
having here, a contest? See which vehicle can stay ahead the
longer?

He thought of speeding up to stay ahead but changed his mind.
When the truck and trailer started back into the westbound
lane, he let up on the pedal, voicing a newly incredulous sound
as he saw that if he hadn't slowed down, he would have been
prematurely cut off again. Jesus Christ, he thought. What's *with*
this guy?

His scowl deepened as the odor of the truck's exhaust reached his nostrils again. Irritably, he cranked up the window on his left. Damn it, was he going to have to breathe that crap all the way to San Francisco? He couldn't afford to slow down. He had to meet Forbes at a quarter after three, and that was that.

He looked ahead. At least there was no traffic complicating matters. Mann pressed down on the accelerator pedal, drawing close behind the truck. When the highway curved enough to the left to give him a completely open view of the route ahead, he jarred down on the pedal, steering out into the opposite lane.

The truck edged over, blocking his way.

For several moments, all Mann could do was stare at it in blank confusion. Then, with a startled noise, he braked, returning to the proper lane. The truck moved back in front of him.

Mann could not allow himself to accept what apparently had taken place. It had to be a coincidence. The truck driver couldn't have blocked his way on purpose. He waited for more than a minute, then flicked down the turn-indicator lever to make his intentions perfectly clear and, depressing the accelerator pedal, steered again into the eastbound lane.

Immediately, the truck shifted, barring his way.

"Jesus Christ!" Mann was astounded. This was unbelievable. He'd never seen such a thing in twenty-six years of driving. He returned to the westbound lane, shaking his head as the truck swung back in front of him.

He eased up on the gas pedal, falling back to avoid the truck's exhaust. Now what? he wondered. He still had to make San Francisco on schedule. Why in God's name hadn't he gone a little out of his way in the beginning so he could have traveled by freeway? This damned highway was two-lane all the way.

Impulsively, he sped into the eastbound lane again. To his surprise, the truck driver did not pull over. Instead, the driver stuck his left arm out and waved him on. Mann started pushing down on the accelerator. Suddenly, he let up on the pedal with a gasp and jerked the steering wheel around, raking back behind the truck so quickly that his car began to fishtail. He was fighting to control its zigzag whipping when a blue convertible shot by him in the opposite lane. Mann caught a momentary vision of the man inside it glaring at him.

The car came under his control again. Mann was sucking breath in through his mouth. His heart was pounding almost painfully. My God! he thought. *He wanted me to hit that car head-on.* The realization stunned him. True, he should have seen to it himself that the road ahead was clear; that was his failure. But to wave him on. . . . Mann felt appalled and sickened. Boy, oh, boy, oh, boy, he thought. This was really one for the books. That son of a bitch had meant for not only him to be killed but a totally uninvolved passerby as well. The idea seemed beyond his comprehension. On a California highway on a Thursday morning? *Why?*

Mann tried to calm himself and rationalize the incident. Maybe it's the heat, he thought. Maybe the truck driver had a tension headache or an upset stomach; maybe both. Maybe he'd had a fight with his wife. Maybe she'd failed to put out last night. Mann tried in vain to smile. There could be any number of reasons. Reaching out, he twisted off the radio. The cheerful music irritated him.

He drove behind the truck for several minutes, his face a mask of animosity. As the exhaust fumes started putting his stomach on edge, he suddenly forced down the heel of his right hand on the horn bar and held it there. Seeing that the route ahead was clear, he pushed in the accelerator pedal all the way and steered into the opposite lane.

The movement of his car was paralleled immediately by the truck. Mann stayed in place, right hand jammed down on the horn bar. Get out of the way, you son of a bitch! he thought. He felt the muscles of his jaw hardening until they ached. There was a twisting in his stomach.

"*Damn!*" He pulled back quickly to the proper lane, shuddering with fury. "You miserable son of a bitch," he muttered, glaring at the truck at it was shifted back in front of him. What the hell is wrong with you? I pass your goddamn rig a couple of times and you go flying off the deep end? Are you nuts or something?

Mann nodded tensely. Yes, he thought; he *is*. No other explanation.

He wondered what Ruth would think of all this, how she'd react. Probably, she'd start to honk the horn and would keep on honking it, assuming that, eventually, it would attract the attention of a policeman. He looked around with a scowl. Just where in hell *were* the policemen out here, anyway? He made a scoffing noise. What policemen? Here in the boondocks? They probably had a sheriff on horseback, for Christ's sake.

He wondered suddenly if he could fool the truck driver by passing on the right. Edging his car toward the shoulder, he peered ahead. No chance. There wasn't room enough. The truck driver could shove him through that wire fence if he wanted to. Mann shivered. And he'd want to, sure as hell, he thought.

Driving where he was, he grew conscious of the debris lying beside the highway; beer cans, candy wrappers, ice-cream containers, newspaper sections browned and rotted by the weather, a FOR SALE sign torn in half. Keep America beautiful, he thought sardonically. He passed a boulder with the name WILL JASPER painted on it in white. Who the hell is Will Jasper? he wondered. What would he think of this situation?

Unexpectedly, the car began to bounce. For several anxious moments, Mann thought that one of his tires had gone flat. Then he noticed that the paving along this section of highway consisted of pitted slabs with gaps between them. He saw the truck and trailer jolting up and down and thought: I hope it shakes your brains loose. As the truck veered into a sharp left curve, he caught a fleeting glimpse of the driver's face in the cab's side mirror. There was not enough time to establish his appearance.

"Ah," he said. A long, steep hill was looming up ahead. The truck would have to climb it slowly. There would doubtless be an opportunity to pass somewhere on the grade. Mann pressed down on the accelerator pedal, drawing as close behind the truck as safety would allow.

Halfway up the slope, Mann saw a turnout for the eastbound lane with no oncoming traffic anywhere in sight. Flooring the accelerator pedal, he shot into the opposite lane. The slow-moving truck began to angle out in front of him. Face stiffening, Mann steered his speeding car across the highway edge and curved it sharply on the turnout. Clouds of dust went billowing up behind his car, making him lose sight of the truck. His tires buzzed and crackled on the dirt, then, suddenly, were humming on the pavement once again.

He glanced at the rearview mirror, and a barking laugh erupted from his throat. He'd only meant to pass. The dust had been an unexpected bonus. Let the bastard get a sniff of something rotten-smelling in *his* nose for a change! he thought. He honked the horn elatedly, a mocking rhythm of bleats. Screw you, Jack!

He swept across the summit of the hill. A striking vista lay ahead: sunlit hills and flatland, a corridor of dark trees, quadrangles of cleared-off acreage and bright-green vegetable patches; far off, in the distance, a mammoth water tower. Mann felt stirred by the panoramic sight. Lovely, he thought. Reaching out, he turned the radio back on and started humming cheerfully with the music.

Seven minutes later, he passed a billboard advertising CHUCK'S CAFÉ. No thanks, Chuck, he thought. He glanced at a gray house nestled in a hollow. Was that a cemetery in its front yard or a group of plaster statuary for sale?

Hearing the noise behind him, Mann looked at the rearview mirror and felt himself go cold with fear. The truck was hurtling down the hill, pursuing him.

His mouth fell open and he threw a glance at the speedometer. He was doing more than sixty! On a curving downgrade, that was not at all a safe speed to be driving. Yet the truck must be exceeding that by a considerable margin, it was closing the distance between them so rapidly. Mann swallowed, leaning to the right as he steered his car around a sharp curve. Is the man *insane?* he thought.

His gaze jumped forward searchingly. He saw a turnoff half a mile ahead and decided that he'd use it. In the rearview mirror, the huge square radiator grille was all he could see now. He

stamped down on the gas pedal and his tires screeched unnerv-
ingly as he wheeled around another curve, thinking that, surely,
the truck would have to slow down here.

He groaned as it rounded the curve with ease, only the sway of
its tanks revealing the outward pressure of the turn. Mann bit
trembling lips together as he whipped his car around another
curve. A straight descent now. He depressed the pedal farther,
glanced at the speedometer. Almost seventy miles an hour! He
wasn't used to driving this fast!

In agony, he saw the turnoff shoot by on his right. He couldn't
have left the highway at this speed, anyway; he'd have overturned.
Goddamn it, what was wrong with that son of a bitch? Mann
honked his horn in frightened rage. Cranking down the window
suddenly, he shoved his left arm out to wave the truck back.
"Back!" he yelled. He honked the horn again. "Get back, you
crazy bastard!"

The truck was almost on him now. He's going to kill me! Mann
thought, horrified. He honked the horn repeatedly, then had to
use both hands to grip the steering wheel as he swept around
another curve. He flashed a look at the rearview mirror. He could
see only the bottom portion of the truck's radiator grille. He was
going to lose control! He felt the rear wheels start to drift, and
let up on the pedal quickly. The tire treads bit in, the car leaped
on, regaining its momentum.

Mann saw the bottom of the grade ahead, and in the distance
there was a building with a sign that read CHUCK'S CAFÉ. The truck
was gaining ground again. This is insane! he thought, enraged and
terrified at once. The highway straightened out. He floored the
pedal: seventy-four now—seventy-five. Mann braced himself, trying to ease the car as far to the right as possible.

Abruptly, he began to brake, then swerved to the right, raking
his car into the open area in front of the café. He cried out as the
car began to fishtail, then careeened into a skid. *Steer with it!*
screamed a voice in his mind. The rear of the car was lashing from
side to side, tires spewing dirt and raising clouds of dust. Mann

pressed harder on the brake pedal, turning further into the skid. The car began to straighten out, and he braked harder yet, conscious, on the sides of his vision, of the truck and trailer roaring by on the highway. He nearly sideswiped one of the cars parked in front of the café, bounced and skidded by it, going almost straight now. He jammed in the brake pedal as hard as he could. The rear end broke to the right and the car spun half around, sheering sideways to a neck-wrenching halt thirty yards beyond the café.

Mann sat in pulsing silence, eyes closed. His heartbeats felt like club blows in his chest. He couldn't seem to catch his breath. If he were ever going to have a heart attack, it would be now. After a while, he opened his eyes and pressed his right palm against his chest. His heart was still throbbing laboredly. No wonder, he thought. It isn't every day I'm almost murdered by a truck.

He raised the handle and pushed out the door, then started forward, grunting in surprise as the safety belt held him in place. Reaching down with shaking fingers, he depressed the release button and pulled the ends of the belt apart. He glanced at the café. What had its patrons thought of his breakneck appearance? he wondered.

He stumbled as he walked to the front door of the café. TRUCKERS WELCOME, read a sign in the window. It gave Mann a queasy feeling to see it. Shivering, he pulled open the door and went inside, avoiding the sight of its customers. He felt certain they were watching him, but he didn't have the strength to face their looks. Keeping his gaze fixed straight ahead, he moved to the rear of the café and opened the door marked GENTS.

Moving to the sink, he twisted the right-hand faucet and leaned over to cup cold water in his palms and splash it on his face. There was a fluttering of his stomach muscles he could not control.

Straightening up, he tugged down several towels from their dispenser and patted them against his face, grimacing at the smell of the paper. Dropping the soggy towels into a wastebasket beside the sink, he regarded himself in the wall mirror. Still with us, Mann, he thought. He nodded, swallowing. Drawing out his metal comb, he neatened his hair. You never know, he thought. You just never know. You drift along, year after year, presuming certain values to be fixed; like being able to drive on a public thoroughfare without somebody trying to murder you. You come to depend on that sort of thing. Then something occurs and all bets are off. One shocking incident and all the years of logic and acceptance are displaced and, suddenly, the jungle is in front of you again. *Man, part animal, part angel.* Where had he come across the phrase? He shivered.

It was entirely an animal in that truck out there.

His breath was almost back to normal now. Mann forced a smile at his reflection. All right, boy, he told himself. It's over now. It was a goddamned nightmare, but it's over. You are on your way to San Francisco. You'll get yourself a nice hotel room, order a bottle of expensive Scotch, soak your body in a hot bath, and forget. Damn right, he thought. He turned and walked out of the washroom.

He jolted to a halt, his breath cut off. Standing rooted, heart-beat hammering at his chest, he gaped through the front window of the café.

The truck and trailer were parked outside.

Mann stared at them in unbelieving shock. It wasn't possible. He'd seen them roaring by at top speed. The driver had won; he'd *won!* He'd had the whole damn highway to himself! *Why had he turned back?*

Mann looked around with sudden dread. There were five men eating, three along the counter, two in booths. He cursed himself for having failed to look at faces when he'd entered. Now there was no way of knowing who it was. Mann felt his legs begin to shake.

Abruptly, he walked to the nearest booth and slid in clumsily behind the table. Now wait, he told himself; just wait. Surely, he could tell which one it was. Masking his face with the menu, he glanced across its top. Was it that one in the khaki work shirt? Mann tried to see the man's hands but couldn't. His gaze flicked nervously across the room. Not that one in the suit, of course. Three remaining. That one in the front booth, square-faced, black-haired? If only he could see the man's hands, it might help. One of the two others at the counter? Mann studied them uneasily. Why hadn't he looked at faces when he'd come in?

Now *wait,* he thought. Goddamn it, *wait!* All right, the truck driver was in here. That didn't automatically signify that he meant to continue the insane duel. Chuck's Café might be the only place to eat for miles around. It *was* lunchtime, wasn't it? The truck driver had probably intended to eat here all the time. He'd just been moving too fast to pull into the parking lot before. So he'd slowed down, turned around and driven back, that was all. Mann forced himself to read the menu. Right, he thought. No point in getting so rattled. Perhaps a beer would help relax him.

The woman behind the counter came over, and Mann ordered a ham sandwich on rye toast and a bottle of Coors. As the woman turned away, he wondered, with a sudden twinge of self-reproach, why he hadn't simply left the café, jumped into his car, and sped away. He would have known immediately, then, if the truck driver was still out to get him. As it was, he'd have to suffer through an entire meal to find out. He almost groaned at his stupidity.

Still, what if the truck driver *had* followed him out and started after him again? He'd have been right back where he'd started. Even if he'd managed to get a good lead, the truck driver would have overtaken him eventually. It just wasn't in him to drive at eighty and ninety miles an hour in order to stay ahead. True, he might have been intercepted by a California Highway Patrol car. What if he weren't, though?

Mann repressed the plaguing thoughts. He tried to calm himself. He looked deliberately at the four men. Either of two seemed a likely possibility as the driver of the truck: the square-faced one in the front booth and the chunky one in the jump suit sitting at the counter. Mann had an impulse to walk over to them and ask which one it was, tell the man he was sorry he'd irritated him, tell him anything to calm him, since, obviously, he wasn't rational, was a manic-depressive, probably. Maybe buy the man a beer and sit with him awhile to try to settle things.

He couldn't move. What if the truck driver were letting the whole thing drop? Mightn't his approach rile the man all over again? Mann felt drained by indecision. He nodded weakly as the waitress set the sandwich and the bottle in front of him. He took a swallow of the beer, which made him cough. Was the truck driver amused by the sound? Mann felt a stirring of resentment deep inside himself. What right did that bastard have to impose this torment on another human being? It was a free country, wasn't it? Damn it, he had every right to pass the son of a bitch on a highway if he wanted to!

"Oh, hell," he mumbled. He tried to feel amused. He was making entirely too much of this. Wasn't he? He glanced at the pay telephone on the front wall. What was to prevent him from calling the local police and telling them the situation? But, then, he'd have to stay here, lose time, make Forbes angry, probably lose the sale. And what if the truck driver stayed to face them? Naturally, he'd deny the whole thing. What if the police believed him and didn't do anything about it? After they'd gone, the truck driver would undoubtedly take it out on him again, only worse. *God!* Mann thought in agony.

The sandwich tasted flat, the beer unpleasantly sour. Mann stared at the table as he ate. For God's sake, why was he just *sitting* here like this? He was a grown man, wasn't he? Why didn't he settle the damn thing once and for all?

His left hand twitched so unexpectedly, he spilled beer on his trousers. The man in the jump suit had risen from the counter and was strolling toward the front of the café. Mann felt his heartbeat thumping as the man gave money to the waitress, took his change and a toothpick from the dispenser and went outside. Mann watched in anxious silence.

The man did not get into the cab of the tanker truck.

It had to be the one in the front booth, then. His face took form in Mann's remembrance: square, with dark eyes, dark hair; the man who'd tried to kill him.

Mann stood abruptly, letting impulse conquer fear. Eyes fixed ahead, he started toward the entrance. Anything was preferable to sitting in that booth. He stopped by the cash register, conscious of the hitching of his chest as he gulped in air. Was the man observing him? he wondered. He swallowed, pulling out the clip of dollar bills in his right-hand trouser pocket. He glanced toward the waitress. Come *on*, he thought. He looked at his check and, seeing the amount, reached shakily into his trouser pocket for change. He heard a coin fall onto the floor and roll away. Ignoring it, he dropped a dollar and a quarter onto the counter and thrust the clip of bills into his trouser pocket.

As he did, he heard the man in the front booth get up. An icy shudder spasmed up his back. Turning quickly to the door, he shoved it open, seeing, on the edges of his vision, the square-faced man approach the cash register. Lurching from the café, he started toward his car with long strides. His mouth was dry again. The pounding of his heart was painful in his chest.

Suddenly, he started running. He heard the café door bang shut and fought away the urge to look across his shoulder. Was that a sound of other running footsteps now? Reaching his car, Mann yanked open the door and jarred in awkwardly behind the steering wheel. He reached into his trouser pocket for the keys and snatched them out, almost dropping them. His hand was shaking so badly he couldn't get the ignition key into its slot. He whined with mounting dread. Come on! he thought.

The key slid in, he twisted it convulsively. The motor started and he raced it momentarily before jerking the transmission shift to drive. Depressing the accelerator pedal quickly, he raked the car around and steered it toward the highway. From the corners of his eyes, he saw the truck and trailer being backed away from the café.

Reaction burst inside him. "No!" he raged and slammed his foot down on the brake pedal. This was idiotic! Why the hell should he run away? His car slid sideways to a rocking halt and, shouldering out the door, he lurched to his feet and started toward the truck with angry strides. *All right, Jack,* he thought. He glared at the man inside the truck. You want to punch my nose, O.K., but no more goddamn tournament on the highway.

The truck began to pick up speed. Mann raised his right arm. "Hey!" he yelled. He knew the driver saw him. *"Hey!"* He started running as the truck kept moving, engine grinding loudly. It was on the highway now. He sprinted toward it with a sense of martyred outrage. The driver shifted gears, the truck moved faster. "Stop!" Mann shouted. "Damn it, *stop!*"

He thudded to a panting halt, staring at the truck as it receded down the highway, moved around a hill, and disappeared. "You son of a bitch," he muttered. "You goddamn, miserable son of a bitch."

He trudged back slowly to his car, trying to believe that the truck driver had fled the hazard of a fistfight. It was possible, of course, but, somehow, he could not believe it.

He got into his car and was about to drive onto the highway when he changed his mind and switched the motor off. That crazy bastard might just be tooling along at fifteen miles an hour, waiting for him to catch up. Nuts to that, he thought. So he blew his schedule; screw it. Forbes would have to wait, that was all. And if Forbes didn't care to wait, that was all right, too. He'd sit here for a while and let the nut get out of range, let him think he'd won the day. He grinned. You're the bloody Red Baron, Jack; you've shot me down. Now go to hell with my sincerest compliments. He shook his head. Beyond belief, he thought.

He really should have done this earlier, pulled over, waited. Then the truck driver would have had to let it pass. *Or picked on someone else,* the startling thought occurred to him. Jesus, maybe that was how the crazy bastard whiled away his work hours! Jesus Christ Almighty! was it possible?

He looked at the dashboard clock. It was just past twelve-thirty.

Wow, he thought. All that in less than an hour. He shifted on the seat and stretched his legs out. Leaning back against the door, he closed his eyes and mentally perused the things he had to do tomorrow and the following day. Today was shot to hell, as far as he could see.

When he opened his eyes, afraid of drifting into sleep and losing too much time, almost eleven minutes had passed. The nut must be an ample distance off by now, he thought; at least eleven miles, and likely more, the way he drove. Good enough. He wasn't going to try to make San Francisco on schedule now, anyway. He'd take it real easy.

Mann adjusted his safety belt, switched on the motor, tapped the transmission pointer into drive position, and pulled onto the highway, glancing back across his shoulder. Not a car in sight. Great day for driving. Everybody was staying at home. That nut must have a reputation around here. When Crazy Jack is on the highway, lock your car in the garage. Mann chuckled at the notion as his car began to turn the curve ahead.

Mindless reflex drove his right foot down against the brake pedal. Suddenly, his car had skidded to a halt, and he was staring down the highway. The truck and trailer were parked on the shoulder less than ninety yards away.

Mann couldn't seem to function. He knew his car was blocking the westbound lane, knew that he should either make a U-turn or pull off the highway, but all he could do was gape at the truck.

He cried out, legs retracting, as a horn blast sounded behind him. Snapping up his head, he looked at the rearview mirrow, gasping as he saw a yellow station wagon bearing down on him at high speed. Suddenly, it veered off toward the eastbound lane, disappearing from the mirror. Mann jerked around and saw it hurtling past his car, its rear end snapping back and forth, its back tires screeching. He saw the twisted features of the man inside, saw his lips move rapidly with cursing.

Then the station wagon had swerved back into the westbound lane and was speeding off. It gave Mann an odd sensation to see it pass the truck. The man in that station wagon could drive on, unthreatened. Only he'd been singled out. What happened was demented. Yet it was happening.

He drove his car onto the highway shoulder and braked. Putting the transmission into neutral, he leaned back, staring at the truck. His head was aching again. There was a pulsing at his temples like the ticking of a muffled clock.

What was he to do? He knew very well that if he left his car to walk to the truck, the driver would pull away and repark farther down the highway. He may as well face the fact that he was dealing with a madman. He felt the tremor in his stomach muscles starting up again. His heartbeat thudded slowly, striking at his chest wall. Now what?

With a sudden, angry impulse, Mann snapped the transmission into gear and stepped down hard on the accelerator pedal. The tires of the car spun sizzlingly before they gripped; the car shot out onto the highway. Instantly, the truck began to move. He even had the motor on! Mann thought in raging fear. He floored the pedal, then, abruptly, realized he couldn't make it, that the truck would block his way and he'd collide with its trailer. A vision flashed across his mind, a fiery explosion and a sheet of flame incinerating him. He started braking fast, trying to decelerate evenly, so he wouldn't lose control.

When he'd slowed down enough to feel that it was safe, he steered the car onto the shoulder and stopped it again, throwing the transmission into neutral.

Approximately eighty yards ahead, the truck pulled off the highway and stopped.

Mann tapped his fingers on the steering wheel. *Now* what? he thought. Turn around and head east until he reached a cutoff that would take him to San Francisco by another route? How did he know the truck driver wouldn't follow him even then? His cheeks twitched as he bit his lips together angrily. No! He wasn't going to turn around!

His expression hardened suddenly. Well, he wasn't going to *sit* here all day, that was certain. Reaching out, he tapped the gearshift into drive and steered his car onto the highway once again.

He saw the massive truck and trailer start to move but made no effort to speed up. He tapped at the brakes, taking a position about thirty yards behind the trailer. He glanced at his speedometer. Forty miles an hour. The truck driver had his left arm out the cab window and was waving him on. What did that mean? Had he changed his mind? Decided, finally, that this thing had gone too far? Mann couldn't let himself believe it.

He looked ahead. Despite the mountain ranges all around, the highway was flat as far as he could see. He tapped a fingernail against the horn bar, trying to make up his mind. Presumably, he could continue all the way to San Francisco at this speed, hanging back just far enough to avoid the worst of the exhaust fumes. It didn't seem likely that the truck driver would stop directly on the highway to block his way. And if the truck driver pulled onto the shoulder to let him pass, he could pull off the highway, too. It would be a draining afternoon but a safe one.

On the other hand, outracing the truck might be worth just one more try. This was obviously what that son of a bitch wanted. Yet, surely, a vehicle of such size couldn't be driven with the same daring as, potentially, his own. The laws of mechanics were against it, if nothing else. Whatever advantage the truck had in mass, it had to lose in stability, particularly that of its trailer. If Mann were to drive at, say, eighty miles an hour and there were a few steep grades—as he felt sure there were—the truck would have to fall behind.

The question was, of course, whether he had the nerve to maintain such a speed over a long distance. He'd never done it before. Still, the more he thought about it, the more it appealed to him; far more than the alternative did.

Abruptly, he decided. *Right,* he thought. He checked ahead, then pressed down hard on the accelerator pedal and pulled into the eastbound lane. As he neared the truck, he tensed, anticipating that the driver might block his way. But the truck did not shift from the westbound lane. Mann's car moved along its mammoth side. He glanced at the cab and saw the name KELLER printed on its door. For a shocking instant, he thought it read

KILLER and started to slow down. Then, glancing at the name again, he saw what it really was and depressed the pedal sharply. When he saw the truck reflected in the rearview mirror, he steered his car into the westbound lane.

He shuddered, dread and satisfaction mixed together, as he saw that the truck driver was speeding up. It was strangely comforting to know the man's intentions definitely again. That plus the knowledge of his face and name seemed, somehow, to reduce his stature. Before, he had been faceless, nameless, an embodiment of unknown terror. Now, at least, he was an individual. All right, Keller, said his mind, let's see you beat me with that purple-silver relic now. He pressed down harder on the pedal. *Here we go,* he thought.

He looked at the speedometer, scowling as he saw that he was doing only seventy-four miles an hour. Deliberately, he pressed down on the pedal, alternating his gaze between the highway ahead and the speedometer until the needle turned past eighty. He felt a flickering of satisfaction with himself. All right, Keller, you son of a bitch, top that, he thought.

After several moments, he glanced into the rearview mirror again. Was the truck getting closer? Stunned, he checked the speedometer. Damn it! He was down to seventy-six! He forced in the accelerator pedal angrily. *He mustn't go less than eighty!* Mann's chest shuddered with convulsive breath.

He glanced aside as he hurtled past a beige sedan parked on the shoulder underneath a tree. A young couple sat inside it, talking. Already they were far behind, their world removed from his. Had they even glanced aside when he'd passed? He doubted it.

He started as the shadow of an overhead bridge whipped across the hood and windshield. Inhaling raggedly, he glanced at the speedometer again. He was holding at eighty-one. He checked the rearview mirror. Was it his imagination that the truck was gaining ground? He looked forward with anxious eyes. There had to be some kind of town ahead. To hell with time; he'd stop at the police station and tell them what had happened. They'd have to believe him. Why would he stop to tell them such a story if it weren't true? For all he knew, Keller had a police record in these parts. *Oh, sure, we're on to him,* he heard a faceless officer remark. *That crazy bastard's asked for it before, and now he's going to get it.*

Mann shook himself and looked at the mirror. The truck *was* getting closer. Wincing, he glanced at the speedometer. Goddamn it, pay attention! raged his mind. He was down to seventy-four again! Whining with frustration, he depressed the pedal. Eighty!—Eighty! he demanded of himself. There was a murderer behind him!

His car began to pass a field of flowers; lilacs, Mann saw, white and purple, stretching out in endless rows. There was a small shack near the highway, the words FIELD FRESH FLOWERS painted on it. A brown-cardboard square was propped against the shack, the word FUNERALS printed crudely on it. Mann saw himself, abruptly, lying in a casket, painted like some grotesque mannequin. The overpowering smell of flowers seemed to fill his nostrils. Ruth and the children sitting in the first row, heads bowed. All his relatives—

Suddenly, the pavement roughened and the car began to bounce and shudder, driving bolts of pain into his head. He felt the steering wheel resisting him and clamped his hands around it tightly, harsh vibrations running up his arms. He didn't dare look at the mirror now. He had to force himself to keep the speed unchanged. Keller wasn't going to slow down; he was sure of that. *What if he got a flat tire, though?* All control would vanish in an instant. He visualized the somersaulting of his car, its grinding, shrieking tumble, the explosion of its gas tank, his body crushed and burned and—

The broken span of pavement ended and his gaze jumped quickly to the rearview mirror. The truck was no closer, but it hadn't lost ground, either. Mann's eyes shifted. Up ahead were hills and mountains. He tried to reassure himself that upgrades were on his side, that he could climb them at the same speed he was going now. Yet all he could imagine were the downgrades, the immense truck close behind him, slamming violently into his car and knocking it across some cliff edge. He had a horrifying vision of dozens of broken, rusted cars lying unseen in the canyons ahead, corpses in every one of them, all flung to shattering deaths by Keller.

Mann's car went rocketing into a corridor of trees. On each side of the highway was a eucalyptus windbreak, each trunk three feet from the next. It was like speeding through a high-walled canyon. Mann gasped, twitching, as a large twig bearing dusty leaves dropped down across the windshield, then slid out of sight. Dear God! he thought. He was getting near the edge himself. If he should lose his nerve at this speed, it was over. Jesus! That would be ideal for Keller! he realized suddenly. He visualized the square-faced driver laughing as he passed the burning wreckage, knowing that he'd killed his prey without so much as touching him.

Mann started as his car shot out into the open. The route ahead was not straight now but winding up into the foothills. Mann willed himself to press down on the pedal even more. Eighty-three now, almost eighty-four.

To his left was a broad terrain of green hills blending into mountains. He saw a black car on a dirt road, moving toward the highway. *Was its side painted white?* Mann's heartbeat lurched. Impulsively, he jammed the heel of his right hand down against the horn bar and held it there. The blast of the horn was shrill and racking to his ears. His heart began to pound. Was it a police car? *Was* it?

He let the horn bar up abruptly, *No,* it *wasn't.* Damn! his mind raged. Keller must have been amused by his pathetic efforts. Doubtless, he was chuckling to himself right now. He heard the truck driver's voice in his mind, coarse and sly. *You think you gonna get a cop to save you, boy? Shee-it. You gonna die.* Mann's heart contorted with savage hatred. *You son of a bitch!* he thought. Jerking his right hand into a fist, he drove it down against the seat. Goddamn you, Keller! I'm going to kill you, if it's the last thing I do!

The hills were closer now. There would be slopes directly, long steep grades. Mann felt a burst of hope within himself. He was sure to gain a lot of distance on the truck. No matter how he tried, that bastard Keller couldn't manage eighty miles an hour on a hill. But *I* can! cried his mind with fierce elation. He worked up saliva in his mouth and swallowed it. The back of his shirt was drenched. He could feel sweat trickling down his sides. A bath and a drink, first order of the day on reaching San Francisco. A long, hot bath, a long, cold drink. Cutty Sark. He'd splurge, by Christ. He rated it.

The car swept up a shallow rise. Not steep enough, goddamn it! The truck's momentum would prevent its losing speed. Mann felt mindless hatred for the landscape. Already, he had topped the rise and tilted over to a shallow downgrade. He looked at the rearview mirror. *Square,* he thought, everything about the truck was square: the radiator grille, the fender shapes, the bumper ends, the outline of the cab, even the shape of Keller's hands and face. He visualized the truck as some great entity pursuing him, insentient, brutish, chasing him with instinct only.

Mann cried out, horror-stricken, as he saw the ROAD REPAIRS sign up ahead. His frantic gaze leaped down the highway. Both lanes blocked, a huge black arrow pointing toward the alternate route! He groaned in anguish, seeing it was dirt. His foot jumped automatically to the brake pedal and started pumping it. He threw a dazed look at the rearview mirror. The truck was moving as fast as ever! It *couldn't,* though! Mann's expression froze in terror as he started turning to the right.

He stiffened as the front wheels hit the dirt road. For an instant, he was certain that the back part of the car was going to spin; he felt it breaking to the left. "No, don't!" he cried. Abruptly, he was jarring down the dirt road, elbows braced against his sides, trying to keep from losing control. His tires battered at the ruts, almost tearing the wheel from his grip. The windows rattled noisily. His neck snapped back and forth with painful jerks. His jolting body surged against the binding of the

safety belt and slammed down violently on the seat. He felt the
bouncing of the car drive up his spine. His clenching teeth
slipped and he cried out hoarsely as his upper teeth gouged deep
into his lip.

He gasped as the rear end of the car began surging to the right.
He started to jerk the steering wheel to the left, then, hissing,
wrenched it in the opposite direction, crying out as the right rear
fender cracked into a fence pole, knocking it down. He started
pumping at the brakes, struggling to regain control. The car rear
yawed sharply to the left, tires shooting out a spray of dirt. Mann
felt a scream tear upward in his throat. He twisted wildly at the
steering wheel. The car began careening to the right. He hitched
the wheel around until the car was on course again. His head was
pounding like his heart now, with gigantic, throbbing spasms.
He started coughing as he gagged on dripping blood.

The dirt road ended suddenly, the car regained momentum
on the pavement, and he dared to look at the rearview mirror.
The truck was slowed down but was still behind him, rocking
like a freighter on a storm-tossed sea, its huge tires scouring up a
pall of dust. Mann shoved in the accelerator pedal and his car
surged forward. A good, steep grade lay just ahead; he'd gain that
distance now. He swallowed blood, grimacing at the taste, then
fumbled in his trouser pocket and tugged out his handkerchief.
He pressed it to his bleeding lip, eyes fixed on the slope ahead.
Another fifty yards or so. He writhed his back. His undershirt
was soaking wet, adhering to his skin. He glanced at the rearview
mirror. The truck had just regained the highway. *Tough!* he
thought with venom. Didn't get me, did you, Keller?

His car was on the first yards of the upgrade when steam began
to issue from beneath its hood. Mann stiffened suddenly, eyes
widening with shock. The steam increased, became a smoking
mist. Mann's gaze jumped down. The red light hadn't flashed on
yet but had to in a moment. How could this be happening? Just
as he was set to get away! The slope ahead was long and gradual,
with many curves. He knew he couldn't stop. Could he U-turn
unexpectedly and go back down? the sudden thought occurred.

He looked ahead. The highway was too narrow, bound by hills on both sides. There wasn't room enough to make an uninterrupted turn, and there wasn't time enough to ease around. If he tried that, Keller would shift direction and hit him head-on. "Oh, my God!" Mann murmured suddenly.

He was going to die.

He stared ahead with stricken eyes, his view increasingly obscured by steam. Abruptly, he recalled the afternoon he'd had the engine steam-cleaned at the local car wash. The man who'd done it had suggested he replace the water hoses, because steam-cleaning had a tendency to make them crack. He'd nodded, thinking that he'd do it when he had more time. *More time!* The phrase was like a dagger in his mind. He'd failed to change the hoses and, for that failure, he was now about to die.

He sobbed in terror as the dashboard light flashed on. He glanced at it involuntarily and read the word HOT, black on red. With a breathless gasp, he jerked the transmission into low. Why hadn't he done that right away! He looked ahead. The slope seemed endless. Already, he could hear a boiling throb inside the radiator. How much coolant was there left? Steam was clouding faster, hazing up the windshield. Reaching out, he twisted at a dashboard knob. The wipers started flicking back and forth in fan-shaped sweeps. There had to be enough coolant in the radiator to get him to the top. *Then* what? cried his mind. He couldn't drive without coolant, even downhill. He glanced at the rearview mirror. The truck was falling behind. Mann snarled with maddened fury. *If it weren't for that goddamned hose, he'd be escaping now!*

The sudden lurching of the car snatched him back to terror. If he braked now, he could jump out, run, and scrabble up that slope. Later, he might not have the time. He couldn't make himself stop the car, though. As long as it kept on running, he felt bound to it, less vulnerable. God knows what would happen if he left it.

Mann stared up the slope with haunted eyes, trying not to see the red light on the edges of his vision. Yard by yard, his car was slowing down. Make it, make it, pleaded his mind, even though he thought that it was futile. The car was running more and more unevenly. The thumping percolation of its radiator filled his ears. Any moment now, the motor would be choked off and the car would shudder to a stop, leaving him a sitting target. *No,* he thought. He tried to blank his mind.

He was almost to the top, but in the mirror he could see the truck drawing up on him. He jammed down on the pedal and the motor made a grinding noise. He groaned. It had to make the top! Please, God, help me! screamed his mind. The ridge was just ahead. Closer. Closer. Make it. "Make it." The car was shuddering and clanking, slowing down—oil, smoke, and steam gushing from beneath the hood. The windshield wipers swept from side to side. Mann's head throbbed. Both his hands felt numb. His heartbeat pounded as he stared ahead. Make it, please, God, make it. Make it. *Make* it!

Over! Mann's lips opened in a cry of triumph as the car began descending. Hand shaking uncontrollably, he shoved the transmission into neurtal and let the car go into a glide. The triumph strangled in his throat as he saw that there was nothing in sight but hills and more hills. Never mind! He was on a downgrade now, a long one. He passed a sign that read, TRUCKS USE LOW GEARS NEXT 12 MILES. Twelve miles! Something would come up. It had to.

The car began to pick up speed. Mann glanced at the speedometer. Forty-seven miles an hour. The red light still burned. He'd save the motor for a long time, too, though; let it cool for twelve miles, if the truck was far enough behind.

His speed increased. Fifty . . . fifty-one. Mann watched the needle turning slowly toward the right. He glanced at the rearview mirror. The truck had not appeared yet. With a little luck, he might still get a good lead. Not as good as he might have if the motor hadn't overheated, but enough to work with. There had to be someplace along the way to stop. The needle edged past fifty-five and started toward the sixty mark.

Again, he looked at the rearview mirror, jolting as he saw that the truck had topped the ridge and was on its way down. He felt his lips begin to shake and crimped them together. His gaze jumped fitfully between the steam-obscured highway and the mirror. The truck was accelerating rapidly. Keller doubtless had the gas pedal floored. It wouldn't be long before the truck caught up to him. Mann's right hand twitched unconsciously toward the gearshift. Noticing, he jerked it back, grimacing, glanced at the speedometer. The car's velocity had just passed sixty. Not enough! He had to use the motor now! He reached out desperately.

His right hand froze in mid-air as the motor stalled; then, shooting out the hand, he twisted the ignition key. The motor made a grinding noise but wouldn't start. Mann glanced up, saw that he was almost on the shoulder, jerked the steering wheel around. Again, he turned the key, but there was no response. He looked up at the rearview mirror. The truck was gaining on him swiftly. He glanced at the speedometer. The car's speed was fixed at sixty-two. Mann felt himself crushed in a vise of panic. He stared ahead with haunted eyes.

Then he saw it, several hundred yards ahead: an escape route for trucks with burned-out brakes. There was no alternative now. Either he took the turnout or his car would be rammed from behind. The truck was frighteningly close. He heard the high-pitched wailing of its motor. Unconsciously, he started easing to the right, then jerked the wheel back suddenly. He mustn't give the move away! He had to wait until the last possible moment. Otherwise, Keller would follow him in.

Just before he reached the escape route, Mann wrenched the steering wheel around. The car rear started breaking to the left, tires shrieking on the pavement. Mann steered with the skid, braking just enough to keep from losing all control. The rear tires grabbed and, at sixty miles an hour, the car shot up the dirt trail, tires slinging up a cloud of dust. Mann began to hit the brakes. The rear wheels sideslipped, and the car slammed hard against the dirt bank to the right. Mann gasped as the car bounced off and started to fishtail with violent whipping motions, angling toward the trail edge. He drove his foot down on the brake pedal with all his might. The car rear skidded to the right and slammed against the bank again. Mann heard a grinding rend of metal and felt himself heaved downward suddenly, his neck snapped, as the car plowed to a violent halt.

As in a dream, Mann turned to see the truck and trailer swerving off the highway. Paralyzed, he watched the massive vehicle hurtle toward him, staring at it with a blank detachment, knowing he was going to die but so stupefied by the sight of the looming truck that he couldn't react. The gargantuan shape roared closer, blotting out the sky. Mann felt a strange sensation in his throat, unaware that he was screaming.

Suddenly, the truck began to tilt. Mann stared at it in choked-off silence as it started tipping over like some ponderous beast toppling in slow motion. Before it reached his car, it vanished from his rear window.

Hands palsied, Mann undid the safety belt and opened the door. Struggling from the car, he stumbled to the trail edge, staring downward. He was just in time to see the truck capsize like a foundering ship. The tanker followed, huge wheels spinning as it overturned.

The storage tank on the truck exploded first, the violence of its detonation causing Mann to stagger back and sit down clumsily on the dirt. A second explosion roared below, its shock wave buffeting across him hotly, making his ears hurt. His glazed eyes saw a fiery column shoot up toward the sky in front of him, then another.

Mann crawled slowly to the trail edge and peered down at the canyon. Enormous gouts of flame were towering upward, topped by thick, black, oily smoke. He couldn't see the truck or trailer, only flames. He gaped at them in shock, all feeling drained from him.

Then, unexpectedly, emotion came. Not dread, at first, and not regret; not the nausea that followed soon. It was a primeval tumult in his mind: the cry of some ancestral beast above the body of its vanquished foe.

This author's name is far better known, I venture, in the field of science fiction, but here he displays a charm and imagination in the crime story worthy of an Avram Davidson. A gaggle of curious, bright, devious, unruffled, inexhaustible kids—Mr. Lafferty clearly knows them well—and the first thing they want to know from Mossback McCarty, the old cop resting his feet in the vacant lot housing their clubhouse, is how to get blood off a knife yet. . . . You can fool a kid some of the time, but beyond question you cannot fool all the kids all of the time.

R. A. LAFFERTY
"Enfants Terribles"

"Mr. McCarty, do you know a good way to get blood off a knife?" asked Carnadine.

"That's an odd question from a nine-year-old girl," said Mossback McCarty, the old cop.

"Going on ten," said Carnadine.

"I would first have to see the knife."

"It was a hypopetical question, you know, that kind. Besides, Eustace has the knife, not me."

"Get Eustace and the knife here at once."

"I don't know where he is."

"Send one of your minions to find Eustace, and the knife."

"I don't know what a minion is."

"Fatty Frost there is a minion of yours."

So they sent Fatty on the mission.

This was almost the only place on his beat where Mossback could sit down and rest, this vacant lot with the little ravine behind it. And on the lot was the clubhouse of the Bengal Tigers with the bench out in front. Mossback was too broad and too tall to enter the clubhouse itself, but he sat every day on the bench and rested.

"You do give us a bad name, though," Carnadine Thompson told him. "All the other clubs despise us because a cop visits here. You know, we're cop killers by our constitution."

"I didn't know the Bengal Tigers had a constitution, Carnadine. Is it a real written one?"

"Well, not exactly a written one. But it's a real one with nineteen bylaws I think they call them. It has been transmitted orally from father to son and from mother to daughter since the club was founded."

"And how long ago was the club founded?"

"Two weeks tomorrow."

Fatty Frost brought Eustace, but without the knife.

"I understand you have a knife with blood on it, Eustace," said Mossback.

"It belongs to me. I won't tell you where it is. Cops steal things from people. They call it impounding the evidence."

"Papa says all cops are crooked," contributed Carnadine. "I said, 'All but Mossback.' He said, 'That's right. He's not crooked, he's just dumb.' "

"Your father is not himself an unqualified genius, Carnadine. Now, then, Eustace, small boys should not have bloody knives. Where is it and where did you get it?"

"I got it out of a man."

"You should say, 'I got it from a man.' Did he give it to you?"

"Not exactly. But he didn't say I couldn't have it."

"Did he say you could have it?"

"No. He didn't say anything. I asked him, but he wouldn't answer. I couldn't get him to wake up."

Mossback began to feel funny.

"Eustace, you will show me the knife, and you will show me where you got it, or I will paddle your pog. I will not be flim-flammed by an eight-year-old boy."

"Going on nine," said Eustace. "I'm going to put the knife back where I got it. And then I'm going to wash my hands of it. With the reputation I got, I can't afford to get involved with the law."

Then he ran off.

Mossback followed the children heavily. He saw Eustace go up and down a tree like a cat. He had had the knife hidden in a crotch of the tree. Then the boy ran down into the ravine with the knife in his hand. But when Mossback came up to the scene, he froze with horror and his hair bristled.

For a shabby dead man lay there, and a knife was prominent in the middle of his chest. And little Eustace had just risen from the dead man.

"Eustace, what have you done?" Mossback whispered.

"Oh, I put it back where I found it, like I said I would."

"And where are you going, what are you going to do now?"

"Why, I'm going to wash my hands of it, just like I said."

Mossback noticed for the first time that it was caked black blood and not dirt on Eustace's hands. And he realized, not for the first time, that the words of children should always be taken literally.

"You may be the stupidest patrolman on the force, Mossback," said Captain Keil. "It's incredible that you should allow a man to be stabbed on your beat, and then allow a small boy to pull a knife from the body, run away with it, hide it in a tree, and finally return and plunge it back into the body again. Do you know who the dead man is?"

"No."

"Do you know who lives in all five of the houses that back onto the ravine?"

"Yes, I know that."

"Who?"

"In the first house, a man whom I have never seen except distantly—he only bought the house a week ago and moved in yesterday—a Silas Schermerhorn who is an ex-magistrate of some sort, and retired. In the second house is Tyburn Thompson, the father of Eustace and Carnadine here, and a terrible-tempered man in his own right. In the third is Carlos Rey, who runs a tobacco store downtown and is a Cuban. In the fourth is Fred Frost, the father of Fatty here—"

"The boy has a given name, I'm sure."

"Finnbar."

"Very well, the father of Fatty here—"

"—who is a competent machinist and an incompetent inventor. What he makes at the one trade, he loses at the other. And in the fifth house is Hatchel Horn, an engraver."

"Get them all here right now, men, wives, children, and domestics; and let nobody else near. We will talk to them right here. It is a shady nook here by the dollhouse."

"It is no more a dollhouse than you are," said Carnadine with some resentment. "It is the clubhouse of the Bengal Tigers, a fraternal organization, and that other word where they have girls, too."

"What, child?"

"Sororical, I think."

"Oh."

They began to arrive.

"I am Silas Schermerhorn," said a gray and polished man, "former judge, though not of this state. I understand there has been an accident."

"And this lady is your wife?"

"Hellpepper no, that's Mama," howled Eustace.

"I could do worse," said the lady. "In fact, I probably have. He seems quite a nice gentleman and should add tone to the neighborhood. But I'm Giddy Thompson."

"Giddy doesn't seem like a proper name."

"It's apt, though it may not be proper. My name is Geraldine Isabella Dorothy Doria Yseult, I being named after five aunts. You can see how this would be shortened to Giddy."

"Yes, I can see how."

"Mrs. Schermerhorn has been dead for many years," said the gray, polished man.

"This is Rose Rey coming in the bathrobe," said Giddy.

"Hi, honey," said Rose. "It seems like a lot of fuss to make just because I ran into a parked car. Why do you have to gather all the neighbors to tell them about it? How did you find out it was me?"

"I don't think it's about that, Rose," said Giddy. "This, Captain, is Annalee Frost, and this is her husband, Fred. My, you look frowsy in the morning, Fred. This is Tootsy Horn. Her real name isn't Tootsy. I was the one who started to call her that—I think it's cute, don't you? And all these children belong to some one or the other of us. Is it necessary to sort them out?"

"Perhaps not at present. Aren't there three men to be accounted for, Mossback? Where are they?"

"At work. They'll be here soon."

"And the domestics? Where are the domestics?"

"You kidding, honey?" asked Rose.

"All of you children go into the dollhouse, and stay there for the present," said Captain Keil. "I don't want you running around."

"I explained once that it was a clubhouse," said Carnadine, her jaw grim, "and besides, Peewee Horn can't come in."

"And why can't he?"

"He isn't an active member of the Bengal Tigers. He is delinquent in his dues."

"This is a direct order from the Police Department," said Captain Keil.

"Oh, all right, then." But they let Peewee in with very bad grace.

Captain Keil took the Frosts aside a few steps.

"Do either of you know anything about this?" he asked.

"I don't even know what it's about," said Fred Frost.

"Did either of you hear any sort of disturbance last night?"

"I was disturbed by our telephone a number of times," said Fred.

"Who was phoning?"

"The neighbors. They complained about the noise of my power tools. I explained to them that the invention I've been working on for the last few weeks is a general-purpose noise eliminator. Still, it is very hard to fabricate a sheet-metal model quietly. And some tempers were lost on all sides."

"And what time did this particular disturbance cease?"

"Oh, they got tired and stopped phoning at two or three in the morning."

"I mean, when did you abate the noise of your power tools?"

"Five o'clock, maybe. Then I went to bed. It seems I had just got to sleep when you had me roused, but I must have slept a couple of hours."

"Did you hear any sort of noise in the ravine last night?"

"I did not. And I'm willing to bet nobody else did. The noise I was making would have effectively drowned out any other sound in the neighborhood."

"Did you go out of the house at all last night?"

"Probably. I get absentminded when I'm working on an invention. I believe I put my lathe on automatic once or twice and went out for a beer."

"Did you walk in the ravine last night?"

"I don't remember it, but I may have. I often do. I never notice where I'm walking when I'm concentrating."

"Did you talk to anyone last night?"

"I am just not sure of that, officer."

"Ask him why he doesn't put the baffled the other way in his noise machine," said Carnadine. "That way he could stop the up-and-down noises as well as the sideways noises."

"Little girl, I told you to stay in that dollhouse."

"It is as much as my life is worth to go back in that clubhouse. I have just been expelled from the Bengal Tigers. It's quite a comedown for me. I was First Stripe, you know."

"No, I didn't know."

"That's the leader. And now I go in fear of my life. As you know, we cannot allow any living ex-members. Our secrets are too horrible. What if the world should learn of them?"

"I shudder," said Captain Keil.

"So now I can only wait the hand of the assassin," said Carnadine. "Fortunately, it will not be long."

"In a way, I hope not," said Captain Keil. "But I believe we can offer you police protection against the worst assassins that the Bengal Tigers can muster."

"A lot of good your police protection did that dead man in the ravine," said Carnadine.

"What? What's this?" asked Fred Frost.

"You will learn in a minute," said the Captain. "Now, you, little girl, go back in that dollhouse and tell the rest of the Bengal Tigers to be quieter."

"All right. But if they kill me, I'll hold you personally responsible."

A surly man came up to the Captain.

"Why don't you quit picking on kids and send for a hacker to pick up that body in the draw?" he asked. "There's one on E Street, the only one left in the county. He makes dog meat out of carcasses. It's going to be offensive as soon as the sun gets to it."

"And just who are you?" asked the Captain.

"I'm Tyburn Thompson. This is my land you're standing on. That is my little girl you were hollering at. Try hollering at me like that, and I'll peel you like a banana. Okay, folks, break it up, all of you beat it. Take that dead hobo with you, Mossback, and old gobblemouth here, too. Why'd you phone me to come home anyhow?"

"I am giving the orders here," said Captain Keil angrily.

"Not to me you're not," said Tyburn.

Two other men came up. "What's the trouble, Ty?" asked one of them, Hatchel Horn.

"Oh, there's a dead bum down in the draw, and the cops think they have to make a noise about it. Give me a cigar, Carlos, you get them wholesale."

"Are you the other two neighbors?" asked Keil.

"We are neighbors," said Carlos Rey.

"Then we all may as well go and view the body, as long as our mouthy friend has already let the corpse out of the shroud."

They went down the incline and gathered around the dead man. Annalee Frost gave a gasp and a slight shriek, then paled and swayed.

"I shall faint," she said.

"You always say that, but you never do," said Tootsy Horn.

"Have any of you ever seen this man before?" asked the Captain.

"I've a dim impression that I saw him yesterday afternoon," said Fred Frost. "Can't say just where or when. Maybe I'm wrong though."

"Did you speak to him?"

"Believe I said, 'It's sure hot.' Seems like I said that to someone yesterday. Does seem I saw that face somewhere."

"Could he have been hanging around the ravine?"

"Could have been. Not sure. I'm absentminded, you know."

"Yes. You mentioned that before."

"I don't believe I ever saw him," said Tyburn Thompson. "I haven't noticed any hoboes around the draw for the last several days. I usually keep an eye open for them and size them up pretty well. On account of the children, you know. None of them ever met a stranger, and some of their best friends are hoboes. The 'boes sleep in the draw sometimes, as it's near the railroad. But I haven't seen this one before."

"I haven't seen him," said Hatchel Horn.

"And I believe I have not," said Carlos Rey. "I would recognize anyone who has ever been in my store. I believe that he has not. I see few people other places. I work long hours."

"Have you ever seen him, Judge?"

"Possibly. My memory, like that of Mr. Rey, is a specialized one. I generally remember the men who have appeared before me in court. I have a definite impression that this man has. Still, a man does not look the same dead; and many of the things by which we recognize—voice, manner—are gone."

"But you think he may have appeared before you?"

"He may have. He has, I would say, a criminal-type face. His suit is of the kind issued to a man leaving prison."

"Yes, I know that. If he has not had it off, and he probably hasn't, then he may have worn it for about five days. And the knife could very well be a prison kitchen knife, but they are not standard. It could be from anywhere. It is quite a cheap instrument. Have any of you ladies ever seen this man before?"

"Good heavens, no!" said Annalee Frost.

"He looks like the President of Paraguay," said Rose Rey. "You think that possible?"

"No," said Captain Keil. "And you, Tootsy—pardon me, Mrs. Horn—have you ever seen this man?"

"It is very unlikely," said Mrs. Horn.

So that was all of it for a while. A few more officers came out. And the neighbors were all cautioned not to move out of the neighborhood suddenly. Then the officials took the dead man away and adjourned downtown.

"It's clear enough, almost too clear," said Captain Gold. "Whoever killed didn't bother to remove his identity."

They were going through the dead man's effects. His billfold was from a prison workshop; they are sold in several states and are recognizable. His prison papers were in order. He had three dollars. Had he been killed by another hobo, he would hardly have been left with the three dollars unless the killing was for a

deeper reason. And his name was Charles Coke. He had been
released from prison exactly a week before. They were waiting
now for his dossier.

"A confidence man," said Captain Gold, "a forger and blackmailer. And he did five years. We are having it checked further."

"Five full years?" asked Captain Keil. "No time off?"

"No. He had a record of altercations inside. He was capable of
violence. Of his previous blackmail victims, none of them live
nearby, and besides, they pretty well revealed themselves in obtaining his conviction. There could have been a victim held in
abeyance while he was in prison; or there could be a new victim
that he had marked out from information obtained in prison. It
almost has to be the blackmail side of his talents. Neither confidence dodges nor forgeries commonly lead to murder."

"Was he killed *in situ?*" asked Keil.

"I don't know," said Gold. "There's no reason to doubt it,
outside of my plain doubtishness. He may not have been killed
in situ, or even in suit—that is, not in the clothes he was wearing."

"Why do you say that?"

"The fit of them was far from perfect."

"Well, it was not a bad enough fit to be grotesque. And prison
fittings are not usually perfect."

"There was one other thing. The absentminded machinist-
inventor, Frost, has come in with a little more information. He is
sure now that he did see the man the day before, but that he saw
him dressed differently, and that it was somewhere in the street,
not in the ravine."

"But is the memory of an admittedly absentminded man
worth anything?"

"Yes. Something. Yet a confidence man will usually acquire
several appearances as quickly as he can. Coke may quite well have
gotten hold of some decent clothes, and yet also kept the prison
issue. He may also have set himself up in two different sets of
rooms, though so far we have not been able to find a trace of any
residence."

"If he had been out only a week, he may not have had any more money than we found on him, and may not have been able to obtain rooms at all."

"Not Coke. From his history he would never have been without operating money. He would not have come out of prison empty-handed."

"Did you tell Frost to be quiet about what he had seen, or thought that he had seen?"

"No, I did not," said Gold foxily. "If even that little news is out, it may worry someone. We haven't much to go on, but the more people we can worry, the more chance we have of smoking something out. And now that we have given it a chance to smolder, I have sent for the five neighbor families to appear again—this time, singly."

But they didn't get much out of them this time either. There is a trick of taking a picture of a site, then a later picture of the same site; then a little business of infrared will reveal any change. Captain Gold had this trick of analyzing evidence. But the variations of the stories told by the neighbors the first and second times were small, and appeared insignificant, and could have been accidental.

Fred Frost could bring no more out of his tricky memory than he had already fished out. Tyburn Thompson had found new words of invective against officialdom, but no new information on the case at hand. Carlos Rey now thought that he might have sold a cigar to that man some years before. But he would not swear to this, nor could he recall for certain the brand of the cigar; besides, it might have been a different man.

Hatchel Horn hadn't known anything about it before, didn't know anything about it now, and didn't expect to know anything about it in the future. And when the sergeant said that Judge Schermerhorn was outside, the captains were still without a lead.

"Good afternoon, Judge. We were wondering if there was anything more you could tell us about the unfortunate affair that happened in your neighborhood."

"Should I have something more to tell you? Has any of the other neighbors been of help?"

"Yes, Fred Frost has been of immeasurable help. He stated that he had seen the dead man on the day before in other and better clothes, in other circumstances, and in a slightly different location."

"I see. I was afraid that he might remember. I should not have been so cowardly from the first. But you would have found out soon in any case. Of course, you have minutely gone over the transcript of his sentencing of five years ago?"

"What? Oh, of course, of course, minutely."

"And naturally the first thing that struck your eye was that I was the sentencing judge."

"What? Oh, naturally, naturally. And then, ah, then we did recall that you had said that just possibly this man had appeared before you, but that you could not be sure: a man does not, as you pointed out, look the same in death. And as a judge has thousands of men appear before him, you could very well not have been sure."

"Quite so. But since you have gone over the transcript, since you read with what violence that man spoke out—for even the typed copy must have carried some echo of the violence in that man—when you had read that he had sworn in court to get me when his time was over, then you realized that I must have re-membered him."

"What? Oh, yes, then we realized it all, didn't we, Keil?"

"Ah, well, why, yes, that was when we realized it."

"So, gentlemen, to save you the time, I have typed a complete summary of my actions in this unhappy affair. Here it is. Please forgive whatever misspellings you find in it. I am a broken man and have been in a highly nervous state for the last several days. You have already guessed the tenor of the contents."

"Ah, yes, we have. Haven't we, Keil? But tell us briefly."

"I had lately retired. I had moved to this town as quietly and unobtrusively as possible, one thousand miles from where he had

seen me last. I learned the day he would get out and I knew that
he intended to kill me. But I had some hope that he would not
be able to follow me here. I was wrong.

"I was not yet settled in my house, I was not entirely moved in,
you understand, when he came up the front steps, nattily dressed.
I thought it was one of my new neighbors calling to welcome me.
I barely recognized him in time. Then I quickly locked the door.
But for the fact that Mr. Frost passed by at that time, I believe
Coke would have broken in the door and had me then. They exchanged some commonplaces, Coke and Frost, and I realized to
my dismay that Frost, who is absentminded, believed Coke to be
me, the man who was just moving in.

"Coke left then. But he called to me that he would be back
after dark, and that there was nothing I could do to prevent his
evening up our score. I spent the next few hours in an agony of
worry. I had no gun in the house, and was afraid to venture out.
Totally unacquainted in town, and with my telephone not yet
connected, I had no idea what to do. And the banshee wails that
rose from the workshop of Mr. Frost after dark added to my
unease. Coke could shoot me a dozen times, and not a soul would
hear."

"And then?"

"Coke came to the front door about midnight and called to me.
There was a hypnotic quality in his voice. I had heard of it, had
felt it before. He said that his was the stronger will, and that he
would force me to open the door, to my own destruction.

"However, as quietly as possible, I slipped through the house,
out the back door, and down to that dark ravine. I thought I
could hide there while he broke into my house, or that I could
get to one of the neighbors for help. I was looking for someone,
anyone, to save me. And I was relieved when I came on a shabby-
looking man there.

" 'My life is in danger,' I said. 'Help me. Help me to get to the
police or to some safe shelter.' I came quite close to him. And
then—"

"Yes?"

"Nightmare of nightmares! I thought I had lost my mind. That shabby man was also Coke! He had tricked me, read my mind. He must have left the front door even before I slipped through the back. I had imagined him nattily dressed, as he had appeared that afternoon. But he had come dressed like a hobo, and he paralyzed me with fright."

"Go on."

"He took out a knife, and we grappled. It was as though he intended to play with me. But he slipped there in the dampness of the ravine. We fell together. And I do not know what fortune it was, good or bad, that ruled; but it was he and not I who died of the knife when we fell."

"Go on."

"There is no more to go on to. I was a coward. I was unsettled in my mind. I went back to my house and did nothing from that time to this. But I swear to God I did not kill him. No, in all truth, I do not believe I would have killed a man, even to save my own life. I am incapable of it. It was sheer accident."

"Naturally. But I would not worry. It is in the five-year-old transcript, as you say, that he swore to kill you. And he came a thousand miles after you immediately on his release; you didn't go after him. I believe that there was never a more clear-cut case of self-defense."

"Well, that rather wraps it up," said Captain Gold. "We should get a commendation for this."

"Tell me, John," asked Captain Keil, "had you read the transcript of the sentencing?"

"Of course not, no more than you did."

"Then you didn't know that Schermerhorn was actually the presiding judge of the case, or that Coke had threatened his life?"

"Naturally not. Let that be our little secret. It is fortunate that Judge Schermerhorn gave us credit for more diligence and more intelligence than we possess."

"Will he get off?"

"Of course he'll get off. Clear-cut a case as I ever saw."

It was early morning. The birds were singing, except that one black one who just pecked and grumbled and hadn't a trace of song in his soul.

Mossback McCarty was resting on the bench in front of the clubhouse of the Bengal Tigers Unaffiliated.

"Mr. McCarty," said Carnadine Thompson. "I have a question to ask."

"This is where I came in. I do not know how to get blood off a knife, nor gore off a bludgeon. I do not even know how to remove telltale marks from a revolver."

"What on earth are you talking about? I wanted to ask you whether you were satisfied with the disposition of our famous criminal case?"

"Why, I suppose so. Shouldn't I be?"

"The Bengal Tigers are not satisfied with it. Or perhaps I should say that I, as First Stripe, am not satisfied with it. Let me ask you: did you ever see a distinguished and dignified-looking judge?"

"Yes, of course. You have only to think of Mr. Schermerhorn."

"All right. Think of some more."

"Why, all of them. All judges are distinguished-looking gentlemen."

"No. Think real hard. Was there ever one?"

"Well, since you insist, no, I never did see a distinguished-looking judge. All of them have something a little furtive about them—fox-faced, sly, rather disreputable."

"Something like the image of a low confidence man?"

"Why, yes, Carnadine, something like that."

"And now tell me: did you ever see a confidence man who looked furtive, fox-faced, sly, disreputable?"

"Why, all of them, Carnadine. We have only to think of Coke when we saw him dead."

"Think of some more. It is possible that you have known more confidence men than I have."

"That's possible. Why, all of them are fox-faced and disreputable-looking."

"Think real hard. Was there ever one?"

"Come to think of it, no. As a matter of fact, all of them have an inspiring presence. They are the most imposing, distinguished, dignified men on the face of the earth. In fact, they look rather like—"

"Like judges? Like judges are supposed to look? Mr. McCarty, you go right downtown and tell them that they may have their men mixed up. Warn them of the dangers of taking things for granted. And tell them that if they take the most elementary fingertip test, which they should have done anyhow, then they can tell for sure. And tell them downtown that you are too good a man to be pounding a beat out here. For the reputation of the Bengal Tigers, we have to get rid of you. And this is the only way I know how to do it."

McCarty went about it rather lamely.

"I have new information from one of the neighbors," he said, "that leads me to believe we are not sure of the identity of the two men."

"From one of the neighbors we questioned?" asked Captain Gold.

"No. From one of the neighbors you neglected to question."

Coke had spoken the truth in one thing. Coke had said that Coke was a man of violence. And so he was for a few moments, until subdued by three burly policemen. Then his violence proved to be short, and he talked easily.

"Oh, well, I guess I've come to the end of my rope in several ways. Details? Oh, the judge was easy enough to find. I'd kept track of him all the way. I even collected a commission when he bought his new house, and that was before I was released. And it didn't take me a week to come the thousand miles; it took me only three hours. I was in town before he was.

"I knew how much money he had transferred here. I knew that I could write his name as well as he could. And I made sure that he had transmitted everything by mail, and was not likely to be known by sight to a single person in this town.

"I observed his moving-in and the fact that he tried to avoid being seen, as he was deadly afraid of me. I figured that his clothing, but not his face, might be familiar to his neighbors from their brief glimpses. And we are nearly the same size. It is true that bumbler, Frost, exchanged civilities with him, and I would have to find a place for that in my story.

"My idea, of course, was to kill the judge and then to become the judge, with access to eighty thousand dollars under the name that I could write as well as he. And that's just what I did.

"I came to his door at night, introduced myself as an insurance salesman with an insurance salesman's voice, and I had one foot in the door before he recognized me. I forced him at gunpoint to strip, and we changed clothes from the skin out. Then I marched him to the ravine and killed him there.

"I had two choices: to do nothing and see if there was any chance of being suspected; or to give up with a maudlin confession in my identity as the judge. If it fell out the one way, I was set up for life here. If it fell out the other way, then I would go through the formality of a short trial, be cleared, and still be settled and respected for life—or at least have a rich base to start from should I become bored and want to return to my regular business again.

"But who is the smart aleck who wanted more positive identification after the case was already wrapped up to everyone's satisfaction? What fresh mind saw the sure-to-be-missed obvious which I was sure would never be seen? Tell me, who outsmarted me?"

"Ah, one of our promising new talents," said Captain Keil. "Our Number Nine, in fact."

"Going on Ten," said Mossback McCarty.

Robert Bloch's laurels are many, his special domain the realm of horror. For some decades he has tellingly explored this fearsome countryside; few of us will forget Psycho. *Hark now to yonder stage: Mr. Bloch gives us not the greatest Hamlet—but "the most memorable performance in* Hamlet"—*as you shall see.*

ROBERT BLOCH
The Play's the Thing

You ask the impossible, gentlemen. I cannot name the greatest Hamlet.

In fifty years as a drama critic, I've seen them all—Barrymore, Gielgud, Howard, Redgrave, Olivier, Burton, and a dozen more. I've seen the play in cut and uncut versions, in modern dress, in military uniform. There's been a black Hamlet, a female Hamlet, and I shouldn't be surprised to learn of a hippie Hamlet today, but I wouldn't presume to select the greatest portrayal of the role, or the greatest version of the play.

On the other hand, if you want to know about the most memorable performance *in* Hamlet, that's another story. . . .

The Roaring Twenties are only a murmuring echo in our ears now, but once I heard them loud and clear. As a young man I was in the very center of their pandemonium—Chicago; the Chicago of Hecht and MacArthur, of Bodenheim, Vincent Starrett, and all the rest. Not that I traveled in such exalted company; I was only the second-string theatrical critic for a second-string paper, but I saw the plays and the players, and in the pre-Depression era there was much to see. Shakespeare was a standby with the stars who travelled with their own repertory companies—Walter Hampden, Fritz Leiber, Richard Barrett. It was Barrett, of course, who played Hamlet.

If the name doesn't ring a bell today, it's not surprising. For some years it had evoked only the faintest tinkle in the hinterlands, where second-rate tragedians played their one-night stands "on the road," but then, for the first time, Richard Barrett brought his production to the big time, and in Chicago he really rang the bell.

He didn't have Hampden's voice, or Leiber's theatrical presence, and he didn't need such qualities; Barrett had other attributes. He was tall, slender, with a handsome profile, and although he was over thirty he looked leanly youthful in tights. In those days, actors like Barrett were called matinee idols, and the women adored them. In Chicago, they loved Richard Barrett.

I discovered that for myself during my first meeting with him.

Frankly, I hadn't been much taken with his performance when I saw it. To me, Barrett was, as they said of John Wilkes Booth, more acrobat than actor. Physically, his Hamlet was superb, and his appearance lent visual conviction to a role usually played by puffy, potbellied, middle-aged men. But his reading was all emotion and no intellect; he ranted when he should have reflected, wailed when he should have whispered. In my review I didn't go so far as to say he was a ham, but I admit I suggested he might be more at home in the stockyards than the theater.

Naturally, the ladies weren't pleased with my remarks. They wrote indignant letters to the editor, demanding my scalp or other portions of my anatomy by return mail, but instead of firing me, my boss urged I interview Richard Barrett in person. He was hoping, of course, for a follow-up story to help build the paper's circulation.

I wasn't hoping for much of anything except that Barrett wouldn't punch me in the jaw.

We met by appointment for luncheon at Henrici's; if I was to have my jaw punched, I might at least get a good meal on the expense account before losing the ability to swallow. As it turned out, I needn't have worried. Richard Barrett was most amiable when we met, and highly articulate.

As the luncheon progressed, each course was seasoned by his conversation. Over the appetizer he discussed Hamlet's father's ghost. With the salad he spoke of poor Ophelia. Along with the entrée he served up a generous portion of opinion regarding Claudius and Gertrude, plus a side-order of Polonius. Dessert was topped with a helping of Horatio, and coffee and cigars were accompanied by a dissertation on Rosencrantz and Guildenstern.

Then, settling back in his chair, the tall Shakespearean actor began to examine the psychology of Hamlet himself. What did I think of the old dispute, he demanded. Was it true that the Prince of Denmark, the melancholy Dane, was mad?

It was a question I was not prepared to answer. All I knew, at this point, was that Richard Barrett himself was mad—quite mad.

All that he said made sense, but he said too much. His intensity of interest, his total preoccupation, indicated a fanatic fixation.

Madness, I suppose, is an occupational hazard with all actors. "Realizing" the character, "losing oneself" in a role, can be dangerous, and of all the theatrical roles in history, Hamlet is the most complex and demanding. Actors have quit in the midst of successful runs rather than run the risk of a serious breakdown by continuing. Some performers have actually been dragged off-stage in the middle of a scene because of their condition, and others have committed suicide. *To be or not to be* is more than a rhetorical question.

Richard Barrett was obsessed by matters extending far beyond the role itself. "I know your opinion of my work," he said, "but you're wrong. Completely wrong. If only I could make you understand . . ." He stared at me, and beyond me, his vision fixed on something far away—far away and long ago.

"Fifteen years," he murmured. "Fifteen years I've played the part. Played it? I've lived it, ever since I was a raw youngster in my teens. And why not? Hamlet was only a youngster himself— we see him grow to maturity before our very eyes as the play goes on. That's the secret of the character."

Barrett leaned forward. "Fifteen years." His eyes narrowed. "Fifteen years of split-weeks in tank towns; vermin in the dressing rooms, and vermin in the audiences too. What did they know of the terrors and the triumphs that shake men's souls? Hamlet is a locked room containing all the mysteries of the human spirit. For fifteen years I've sought the key. If Hamlet is mad, then all men are mad, because all of us search for a key that reveals the truth behind the mysteries. Shakespeare knew it when he wrote the part. I know it now when I play it. There's only one way to play Hamlet—not as a role, but as reality."

I nodded. There was a distorted logic behind what he said; even a madman knows enough to tell a hawk from a handsaw, though both the hawk's beak and the saw's teeth are equally sharp.

"That's why I'm ready now," Barrett said. "After fifteen years of preparation, I'm ready to give the world the definitive Hamlet. Next month I open on Broadway."

Broadway? This prancing, posturing nonentity playing Shakespeare on Broadway in the wake of Irving, Mansfield, Mantell, and Forbes-Robertson?

"Don't smile," Barrett murmured. "I know you're wondering how it would be possible to mount a production, but that's all been arranged. There are others who believe in the Bard as I do; perhaps you've heard of Mrs. Myron McCullough?"

It was an idle question; everyone in Chicago knew the name of the wealthy widow whose late husband's industrial fortune had made her a leading patron of the arts.

"She has been kind enough to take an interest in the project," Barrett told me. "With her backing—"

He broke off, glancing up at the figure approaching our table; a

curved, voluptuously slender figure that bore no resemblance
to that of the elderly Mrs. Myron McCullough.

"What a pleasant surprise—" he began.

"I'll bet," said the woman. "After you stood me up on our
lunch date."

She was young, and obviously attractive; perhaps a bit too obviously, because of her heavy makeup and the extreme brevity of
her short-skirted orange dress.

Barrett met her frown with a smile as he performed the introductions. "Miss Goldie Connors," he said. "My protégée."

The name had a familiar ring, and then, as she grinned at me
in greeting, I saw the glint of her left-upper incisor—a gold
tooth.

I'd heard about that gold tooth from fellow reporters. It was
well known to gentlemen of the press, and gentlemen of the
police force, and gentlemen of Capone's underworld, and to many
others, not necessarily gentlemen, who had enjoyed the pleasure
of Goldie Connors' company. Gold-tooth Goldie had a certain
reputation in the sporting world of Chicago, and it wasn't as a
protégée.

"Pleased to meetcha," she told me. "Hope I'm not butting in."

"Do sit down," Barrett pulled out a chair for her. "I'm sorry
about the mix-up. I meant to call."

"I'll bet." Goldie gave him what in those days was described as
a dirty look. "You said you were gonna rehearse me—"

Barrett's smile froze as he turned to me. "Miss Connors is thinking of a theatrical career. I think she has certain possibilities."

"Possibilities?" Goldie turned to him quickly. "You promised!
You said you'd give me a part, a good part. Like what's-her-name
—Ophelia?"

"Of course," Barrett took her hand. "But this is neither the
time nor the place—"

"Then you better make the time and find a place! I'm sick and
tired of getting the runaround, understand?"

I didn't know about Barrett, but I understood one thing. I rose and nodded. "Please excuse me. I'm due back at the office. Thank you for the interview."

"Sorry you have to leave." Barrett wasn't sorry at all; he was greatly relieved. "Will there be a story, do you think?"

"I'm writing one," I said. "The rest is up to my editor. Read the paper."

I did write the story, stressing in particular the emphasis Barrett placed on realism. BARRETT PROMISES REAL HAMLET FOR BROADWAY was my heading, but not my editor's.

"Old lady McCullough," he said. "That's your story!" And he rewrote it, with a new heading: MRS. MYRON MCCULLOUGH TO FINANCE BARRETT'S BROADWAY BOW.

That's how it was printed, and that's how Richard Barrett read it. He wasn't the only one; the story created quite a stir. Mrs. McCullough was news in Chicago.

"Told you so," said my editor. "That's the angle. Now I hear Barrett's closing tomorrow night. He's doing a week in Milwaukee and then he heads straight for New York.

"Go out and catch him at his boardinghouse now. Here's the address. I want a follow-up on his plans for the Broadway opening. See if you can find out how he managed to get his hooks into the old gal so that she'd back the show. I understand he's quite a ladies' man. So get me all the gory details."

The dinginess of Barrett's quarters somewhat surprised me. It was a theatrical boardinghouse on the near North Side, the sort of place that catered to second-rate vaudeville performers and itinerant carny workers. But then Barrett was probably pinched for funds when he'd come here; not until he met Mrs. McCullough did his prospects improve. The meeting with his wealthy patroness was what I'd come to find out about—all the gory details.

I didn't get them. In fact, I got no details at all, for I went no farther than the hallway outside his door. That's where I heard the voices; in that shabby hallway, musty with the smell of failure, the stale odor of blighted hopes.

Goldie Connors' voice: "What are you trying to pull? I read the papers, all about those big plans of yours in New York. And here you been stalling me along, telling me there was no job because you couldn't get bookings—"

"Please!" Richard Barrett's voice, with an edge to it. "I intended to surprise you."

"Sure you did! By walking out on me. That's the surprise you figured on. Leaving me flat while you went off with that rich old bag you been romancing on the side."

"You keep her name out of this!"

Goldie's answering laugh was shrill, and I could imagine the glint of the gold tooth accompanying it. "That's what you tried to do—keep her name out of this, so I'd never know, or so she'd never know about me. That would queer your little deal in a hurry, wouldn't it? Well, let me tell you something, Mr. Richard Hamlet Barrett! You promised me a part in the show, and now it's put up or shut up."

Barrett's voice was an anguished pleading. "Goldie, you don't understand! This is Broadway, the big chance I've waited for all these years. I can't risk using an inexperienced actress—"

"Then you'll risk something else. You'll risk having me go straight to your great lady and tell her just what's been going on between you and me!"

"Goldie—"

"When you leave town tomorrow night, I'm going with you—with a signed contract for my part on Broadway. And that's final, understand?"

"All right. You win. You'll have your part."

"And not just one of those walk-on bits, either. It's got to be a decent part, a real one."

"A real part. I give you my word."

That's all I heard, and that's all I knew, until five days after Richard Barrett had left Chicago behind.

Sometime during the afternoon of that day, the landlady of the run-down boardinghouse scented an addition to the odors mingling in the musty hallway. She followed her nose to the locked door of what had been Barrett's room. Opening the door, she caught a glimpse of Barrett's battered old theatrical trunk, apparently abandoned upon his departure the day before. He'd shoved it almost out of sight under the bed, but she hauled it out and pried it open.

What confronted her then sent her screaming for the police.

What confronted the police became known in the city newsrooms, and what I learned there sent me racing to the boardinghouse.

There I confronted the contents of the trunk myself—the decapitated body of a woman. The head was missing. All I could think of, staring down at it, was my editor's earlier demand. "The gory details," I murmured.

The homicide sergeant glanced at me. His name was Emmett, Gordon Emmett. We'd met before.

"What's going on?" he demanded.

I told him.

By the time I finished my story, we were halfway to the Northwestern Depot, and by the time he finished questioning me, we had boarded the eight-o'clock train for Milwaukee.

"Crazy," Emmett muttered. "A guy'd have to be crazy to do it."

"He's mad," I said. "No doubt about it. But there's more than madness involved. There's method, too. Don't forget, this was to be his big chance, the opportunity he'd worked and waited for all these years. He couldn't afford to fail. So that knowledge combined with a moment of insane impulse—"

"Maybe so," Emmett muttered. "But how can you prove it?"

That was the question hanging over us as we reached Milwaukee at ten o'clock of a wintry night, and no cab in sight. I whistled one up on the corner.

"Davidson Theater," I said. "And hurry!"

It must have been ten-fifteen when we pulled up in the icy alley alongside the stage door, and twenty after ten by the time we'd gotten past the doorkeeper and elbowed our way backstage to the wings.

The performance had started promptly at eight-fifteen, and

now a full house was centering its attention upon the opening scene of Act Five.

Here was the churchyard—the yawning grave, the two Clowns, Horatio, and Hamlet himself; a bright-eyed, burning Hamlet with feverish color in his cheeks and passionate power in his voice. For a moment I didn't even recognize Richard Barrett in his realization of the role. Somehow he'd managed to make the part come alive at last; this was the Prince of Denmark, and he was truly mad.

The First Clown tossed him a skull from the open grave, and Hamlet lifted it to the light.

"Alas, poor Yorick," he said. "I knew him, Horatio—"

The skull turned slowly in his hand, and the footlights glittered over its grinning jaws in which a gold tooth gleamed. . . .

Then we closed in.

Emmett had his murderer, and his proof.

And I? I had seen my most memorable performance in Hamlet: Goldie's. . . .

*Edward D. Hoch made his first of six consecutive appearances in
this series in 1960 with a story about Captain Leopold of Homicide. The Captain encores here, and like much of Mr. Hoch's
voluminous short-story output, a puzzle is foremost: how may
the inexplicable be explained, the facts (and are they truly facts?)
reshuffled to give a coherent pattern? You may not be able to
solve the case ahead of Leopold by analyzing clues you and he see
simultaneously; this should not, unless you are an unrepentant
classicist, reduce your enjoyment of . . .*

EDWARD D. HOCH
End of the Day

Sergeant Fletcher poked his head around the corner of Leopold's
office doorway. "Captain, I have Mrs. Fleming here, if you can see
her now."

"Send her in," Captain Leopold said. He turned to stare out the
window at the warm June rain so that he would not have to see
her face as she entered. There were moments when he hated his
job, and this was one of them.

"Captain Leopold—"

He swiveled in his chair, seeing a blond young woman of moder-
ate good looks. He'd known Iris Fleming slightly, meeting her at

Copyright © 1970 by Edward D. Hoch; first published in *Ellery Queen's
Mystery Magazine*.

department parties and civic functions. This morning she looked tired, and her finely chiseled face showed the lines of age that usually were hidden. "Yes, Mrs. Fleming, sit right down! Sorry to see you under such tragic circumstances."

"Is it true, what they say?"

"I'm afraid it is, Mrs. Fleming. Your husband shot and killed a man over on the Cross County Expressway."

"Can I see him?"

Leopold shuffled the papers on his desk. "Certainly. But I wish you'd give me a few minutes first. Roger is a detective sergeant under my command. He has killed a person, apparently without any justification. That's bad for my department, bad for the entire police force."

"I'm sure Roger had a good reason for what he did."

"If he did, he hasn't told us yet. The dead man's car was parked off the road for some reason we haven't yet established. Your husband, who was off duty at the time, pulled off the road behind him. He walked over to the driver's side of the victim's car and fired two shots from his service revolver, apparently without even speaking to the other man. Several passing motorists saw the whole thing, and turned off the expressway to call the police. A patrol car reached the scene within five minutes and found your husband's car just pulling away. He offered no resistance, but he refused to talk about the killing."

"Are you so sure he did it?"

"In this case his silence is almost proof enough. His gun had been fired twice, and they're checking it in ballistics now. Several passing motorists identified him, and his car."

"Who's the man he's supposed to have killed?"

Leopold glanced at the report before him. "We don't have an identification yet. The car had Ohio license plates. Do you know anyone from Ohio?"

She shook her head. "No one. Perhaps Roger had seen this man committing a crime, and had chased him. Isn't that possible?"

"I'd like to think so, although it would hardly excuse his killing the man in cold blood. But there's been no report of a crime, and the dead man had no weapon on him."

"And Roger has said *nothing* about it?"

"Nothing, Mrs. Fleming. I'm hoping he'll talk to you. I'll go in with you, and then I'll leave you two alone."

He escorted her down the back hall to the little Interrogation Room, where Detective Sergeant Roger Fleming, smoking a cigarette, sat at the scarred wooden table. Leopold, Fletcher, and Fleming had conducted a hundred or more interrogations in this room over the past few years, and now for the first time, facing Fleming across the table, Leopold realized the utter loneliness of the place. The walls were bare except for a framed photograph of the President which concealed a tiny microphone. The table and four chairs were the room's only furnishings.

"Hello, Roger," Leopold said. It was the first time he'd seen the man since his arrest.

"Hello, Captain. Sorry about all this." He turned to his wife then, hugging her in silence and sighing softly as he finally released her.

"Do you want to make a statement, Roger?"

"No, sir."

"Why did you do it? Why in hell did you do it?"

"I have nothing to say, Captain. I'm sorry."

"Was there some trouble on the highway? Something that angered you?"

Fleming merely stared at him in silence. "All right," Leopold sighed at last. "I'll leave you two alone. Mrs. Fleming, try and talk some sense into your husband."

"Thank you, Captain."

As Leopold reached the door Roger Fleming motioned toward the picture on the wall. "Is the bug on?" he asked.

"No," Leopold answered. "I owe you that much."

Sergeant Fletcher was down in the police garage, going over the victim's car. He glanced up as Leopold approached, turning off the small portable vacuum cleaner he'd been using on the seats.

"Find anything?" Leopold asked, frowning at the car as if somehow it was the cause of the day's woes.

"It's hot, Captain. It was stolen last night from a salesman staying at the Charles Motel."

"Damn!" Leopold kicked a tire in anger. "So why in hell didn't he just say he shot a car thief?"

"Beats me, Captain."

"You know him better than I do, Fletcher. What makes him tick? What's behind that bland face of his?"

"I don't really know him. I'd have a beer with him once or twice a month, but lately we haven't even done that."

"Did he get along with his wife?"

"As far as I know. They've got a couple of kids, in grammar school."

"What about the dead man? Any make on him yet?"

"His wallet was gone, but we found a tailor's tag inside his sleeve. Name is Norman Rossiter, a C.P.A. Got an office in the Grant Building."

"A C.P.A., and he stole a car?"

Fletcher shrugged. "They're human, like anyone else. Why not?"

"The usual motives for car theft are joy riding or simple financial gain. Rossiter wouldn't seem to fit either one."

"But at least he's a local guy, so maybe Roger knew him after all."

"Let's go up and ask his wife," Leopold suggested.

"I'll be along in a few minutes—soon as I finish vacuuming. The lab boys are short-handed today."

Leopold found Iris Fleming sitting in his office, nervously smoking a cigarette. "Did he tell you anything, Mrs. Fleming?"

"No, and frankly I've never seen him quite like this. He just kept telling me not to worry, reassuring me that everything would be all right. I asked him who the man from Ohio was, and he just wouldn't answer."

"The man wasn't from Ohio," Leopold told her. "The car

was stolen. As near as we can tell, the dead man was a local accountant named Norman Rossiter."

That was when Iris Fleming fainted.

Sergeant Fletcher looked depressed, but not half so depressed as Leopold felt. By noon the temperature outside had climbed back into the eighties, where it had been all week, and the humid warmth of the city seemed to hang like a mist over Leopold's office.

"A simple triangle," Fletcher snorted. "She was having an affair with Rossiter, and Roger found out. We have 'em every week of the year, and this one is no different."

"That seems to be it," Leopold agreed. "She admitted as much. The Ohio plates threw her off, so she never gave a thought to Roger having possibly killed Rossiter. She didn't even realize that Roger knew about it—their affair, I mean."

"He knew it, all right."

Leopold patted the moisture on his brow. "When are they supposed to air-condition this place?"

Fletcher shrugged. "It got cut out of the budget again this year." He started to take out a cigarette, then changed his mind. "But why didn't Roger just tell us the whole story?"

"Who knows?" The Captain looked at the list of duty assignments. "He would have been on duty till midnight, and we know he killed Rossiter just before two this morning. That gave him two hours, almost, to track the man down. Where was Roger just before he went off duty?"

Fletcher checked through the morning reports. "Investigating a knifing on Alamanda Street. Family trouble."

"He had family trouble himself."

"He sure did, Captain."

The phone on Leopold's desk buzzed and he answered. "Leopold here."

"Captain, this is Doc Hayes over at the medical examiner's office. We've finished with the man killed over on the expressway."

"Rossiter. Yes?"

"That his name? Well, anyway, I wish you'd drop over. A couple of things of interest."

Doc Hayes was the acting medical examiner while the regular man was on a well-earned vacation. He was a grim little doctor who did his job well and never joked. Leopold admired his efficiency even while thinking he might have been better off teaching at some medical school.

He rose from his desk, all business, as Leopold entered. "Do you want to see the deceased, Captain?"

"Is it necessary?"

"No. I can summarize my findings." He cleared his throat. "The deceased was shot twice by Sergeant Fleming's revolver—ballistics has verified this. One of the bullets entered the left temple, lodging in the brain, while the other shattered the jawbone and passed through the body, lodging in the padded window frame on the right side of the car. I understand that slug was mashed up a bit, but they managed an identification."

"What about your findings, Doc?" Leopold asked, growing impatient. He could read the ballistics report later.

"Well, it's funny the people on the scene didn't notice, but of course it was a warm night."

"Notice what?"

Doc Hayes sighed and glanced around the little office—as if he were looking for a blackboard to continue his lecture. "When a person dies, the force of gravity causes the blood to seep to the body's lowest points. The wounds in Rossiter's head and jaw bled hardly at all, because there was very little blood left in the upper portion of his body by that time. As I say, if it hadn't been such a warm night, rigor mortis would have set in faster and the condition would have been more obvious from the outset."

"Look, Doc, are you trying to tell me that—"

"That the man was already dead for at least two hours when Sergeant Fleming shot him. He'd been killed by a wound from a thin-bladed knife that went between his ribs and straight into the heart."

Leopold went back to his office and told Sergeant Fletcher what he'd learned. Fletcher simply stared at him with widened eyes. "You mean the guy was murdered *twice?*"

"In a manner of speaking," Leopold said. "I don't know if I should feel elated or depressed. It gets Fleming off the hook, but it gives us an unsolved case."

"What now?"

"Get Fleming up here. Maybe he'll be willing to talk now."

A few minutes later Roger Fleming sat in the chair opposite Leopold's desk. "Could I have a cigarette?" he asked.

"Bad for your health," Leopold said, tossing over a pack. "You ready to talk yet?"

"No."

"Suppose I told you Rossiter was already dead when you pumped two bullets into his head."

There was a flicker of something—fear?—across Fleming's otherwise impassive face. He drew slowly on the cigarette and said finally, "I appreciate your seeing me here in your office rather than in the Interrogation Room, Captain."

"That's all you've got to say?"

"That's all."

"Look, Roger, you may be off the hook on the murder charge, but you're finished with the police force unless you change your attitude pretty damn quick. The dead man was having an affair with Iris—that much we already know. If you didn't kill him, who did? Who beat you to it, Roger?"

"What time was he killed?"

"A little before midnight, according to Doc Hayes."

"I was still on duty then, investigating a knifing."

"We know that, Roger. But we want you to tell us what you did after midnight."

Roger Fleming sighed and looked at his hands. "I drove out along the expressway until I saw his car parked. Then I went over and shot him twice through the open window."

"How'd you know he was there? How'd you know which car? The car was stolen."

"God, Captain!" Fleming buried his face in his hands. That was his only answer.

"All right," Leopold sighed. "We'll see how long we can hold you for questioning before your lawyer springs you. When you decide to cooperate and tell a straight story, you know how to reach me."

After Fleming had been taken back to his cell, Leopold buzzed for Fletcher. "I want you to check out Rossiter's movements for all of last night. Then I want you to do the same on Iris Fleming."

"You think she killed him, and Roger's shielding her?"

"At this point I don't know what to think."

Fletcher watched him slip into his rumpled suit coat. "Where can I reach you if I need to, Captain?"

"I'll be down on Alamanda Street, investigating Roger Fleming's last case."

"His last case?"

"Just before midnight he was working on a stabbing. And just before midnight Norman Rossiter was stabbed to death. Funny coincidence—if you believe in coincidences."

Alamanda Street wandered across the backside of the downtown area. It was a section of floppy gray houses and tiny yards crisscrossed by well-worn paths. Now, in the early afternoon of a late-June day, an assortment of noisy children were playing in the yard of the house that Leopold sought.

The woman who answered the door was a big-boned Puerto Rican with a light skin. He showed her his badge. "Leopold of Homicide. I'm here about last night's trouble."

"Wasn't no homicide here," the woman protested. "Just a little knifing, that's all."

"You're the landlady here?"

"That's me. Mrs. Sánchez. But there was no homicide."

"Who got knifed?"

She gestured upstairs. "Mrs. Croft stuck a knife in her husband. Hurt him bad, but didn't kill him."

"The detective came and investigated?"

"Sure."

"Do you remember his name?"

She thought for a moment. "Like that mystery writer—Fleming, that was it. Sergeant Fleming. Good-looking, fairly young."

"How long was he here?"

"Oh, gosh, a couple of hours. He turned Mrs. Croft over to the patrol car, and then he went around questioning all the neighbors. It was after midnight when I saw him get in his car and drive away."

Leopold nodded. Fleming was always a conscientious worker, willing to put in overtime without grumbling. He sighed and wished he had a cigarette with him. There was nothing to connect the knifing of Mr. Croft with the knifing of Norman Rossiter. "Thank you, Mrs. Sánchez," he said, and went out to his car.

He drove around in the afternoon sunshine, trying to get his bearings. It was only a few blocks to the Charles Motel, and the expressway was only a few blocks farther on. He drove to the motel and looked over the parking area, but there was nothing to see. Anyone could have stolen the Ohio salesman's car. Rossiter himself could have stolen it.

But why? It was a nagging point.

He drove out to the little ranch house where the Flemings lived, and found Iris Fleming playing with the children in the back yard. When she saw Leopold, her face clouded over, and she sent the children off to their swings and climbing poles.

"Sorry to bother you again," he said.

"Not at all. Roger just called. He says he expects to be released by tonight. Is that true?"

"Quite possibly. The medical report says that Rossiter was already dead when your husband shot him."

"Oh. Then Roger is innocent!"

"Innocent of murder. But still guilty of enough to get him kicked off the force. Tell me, did Rossiter have any enemies you know of?"

"You're asking me?" Her eyes were all innocence.

"Come off it, Mrs. Fleming," he said with deliberate roughness. "You and Rossiter were having an affair. You admitted that much to us after you fainted this morning."

"But I knew nothing of Norman's business affairs. Perhaps he was an accountant for a gambling syndicate, or for some tax evader who had to silence him."

"Perhaps. Fletcher is checking those angles now."

"Then why are you here?" she asked with a sweet smile that didn't quite make it.

"If Roger didn't kill Rossiter, you become suspect number two."

"So it's like that."

He nodded. "Like that. Where were you just before midnight?"

"Home with the children."

"They were awake?"

"At midnight? Of course not."

"Then you could have left them for a while."

"I wouldn't have done that."

"But you could have. At this stage I'm only interested in the possibilities, Mrs. Fleming."

She got to her feet and started for the house. "When you have a warrant, you can come back and question me some more, Captain. Until that time I'll be indisposed."

He sighed and went back to the car. There was no sense arguing with her. He could take her downtown for questioning, but there was not a shred of evidence against her. He drove back downtown, avoiding the front entrance to headquarters, where reporters would be waiting.

The whole case was beginning to pull apart—like a flimsy kite in a windstorm—and he had the distinct feeling that soon he would be left with only the ruins of his department.

Sergeant Fletcher came back just before dinnertime. He was hot and unhappy, and he wanted to go home. "There's nothing in Rossiter's business or personal life," he assured Leopold. "He was clean—except for Mrs. Fleming."

"That the best you could do after an afternoon's digging? What about his clients?"

"The United Fund, the Red Cross, the Music Association—stuff like that. Not a shady character in the lot."

"All right," Leopold said. "What about the weapon? Anyone find the knife?"

Fletcher shook his head. "I had men out searching where the car was parked, and of course we went over the car itself."

"I suppose he wasn't killed on the expressway. The killer drove him there and pushed him behind the wheel and left him. The knife could be anywhere."

"That could be it, Captain." He started to leave, and then remembered something. "I've got David Thorn outside. Want to see him?"

"Who?"

"Thorn. The salesman whose car was stolen."

Leopold nodded. "Send him in." There was always an angle to be checked. Thorn and Rossiter might have met in a bar, got into a violent quarrel, and Thorn might have stabbed him and then lied about the car having been stolen. There had been a case like that a few years earlier.

"Sit down, Mr. Thorn. This won't take long."

David Thorn was tall and almost handsome. But he was just about over the hill—hair thin to the point of baldness, pouch beginning to show up front. The easy life at middle age.

"Just who are you a salesman for, Mr. Thorn?"

"Ritto Products. School supplies, teaching machines. We're coming out with a low-priced copying machine in the fall."

"Isn't this the wrong time of year for it?"

"On the contrary, this is when they buy for the fall semester."

"Ever call on accountants?"

"No."

Leopold grunted. It had been a passing idea, no more. "What

about your car that was stolen, Mr. Thorn? When did you notice it missing?"

"I didn't. Not until the police phoned and woke me up this morning to ask about it. They'd traced the license number through Ohio and found out from my wife where I was staying here."

"It was taken from the motel parking lot?"

"That's right. Last night I drove around town and went to an early movie. I was back in my motel room by ten-thirty."

"So it was taken sometime after that."

The salesman nodded his balding head. He seemed eager enough to cooperate, and Fletcher said, "Show the Captain your mileage record, Mr. Thorn."

"Oh, yes! I almost forgot. I keep this for tax purposes." He pulled out a little notebook and flipped through the ruled pages. "The odometer reading was 11,362 when I parked it last night."

Sergeant Fletcher flipped open his own book. "And when it was found on the expressway the odometer read 11,369. The car was driven seven miles after it was stolen."

Leopold nodded. "I see what you mean. The distance from the motel to the expressway is only a little over one mile. So the car was driven somewhere else first."

Fletcher nodded. "Now, if only we knew where."

"How about Rossiter's apartment?"

"I'll check it."

Leopold rose and shook hands with Thorn. "Thank you for your cooperation, sir. We'll need your car just a little longer to complete some tests, and then it will be released to you."

He saw the man to the door and went back to his desk. After a while Fletcher returned. "The newspapers want a statement, Captain. They want to know if it's true we're releasing Fleming."

"Sergeant Fleming will be released from custody this evening, but he still faces departmental charges."

"If we announce that, we have to tell the papers that Rossiter was already dead."

"Go ahead. The real killer knows it anyway."

Fletcher nodded. Then, after a moment, he asked, "Captain, why do you think the killer left the car on the expressway? It's a wonder somebody didn't pull up and find the body right away. Whoever left the car had to run through the grass and hop a five-foot fence to get away."

"Unless there was another car."

"Two people?"

"It's happened before."

Fletcher thought about that. "Maybe Rossiter didn't realize how badly he was hurt. Maybe he drove that far alone, on his own, and then suddenly pulled over on the shoulder and died. You said the wound was a narrow one."

"Narrow, but straight into the heart. He didn't drive anywhere after that."

Fletcher looked unhappy, reflecting Leopold's mood. It was a black eye for the department, no matter how you looked at it, and with each hour they seemed to be drawing further away from a solution. "I never saw a case like it," Leopold grumbled. "At the start it was solved, and now it's unsolved, and we're nowhere."

"Do you want to see Fleming again before he's released?"

Leopold considered for a few moments. "Yes. And get his wife back here. I want some answers from both of them."

"Right, Captain. Oh, by the way, I checked a city map. Rossiter's apartment is just under three miles from the Charles Motel."

"Good. Get over there and search the place. Look for signs of a struggle, a bloody knife, anything."

"Why would somebody kill him there and then cart him off to the expressway?"

"I don't know. But I want to find out if that's what really happened."

Leopold had been alone for another ten minutes when a uniformed patrolman poked his head into the office. "Ah, Captain?"

"Yes?"

"I'm Officer Abbot. I patrol the expressway nights—the expressway and that end of the city."

Leopold came alert. "Yes?" The man obviously had something to say, but still he hesitated. "What's it about—the Rossiter murder?"

"Well, it might be, Captain."

"Get to the point."

"We had a call about one o'clock—somebody reported a body on the expressway."

"At one this morning?"

"Yes, sir."

"Man or woman?"

"The officer who took the call couldn't be sure. Husky voice. Anyway, they dispatched my car to have a look. I only went to the city line, of course, and I didn't see any body. So I reported that it must have been a crank call and forgot about it. Gosh, Captain, we get crank calls all the time! One night they told me there was a flying saucer landed out there, with men from outer space!"

Leopold leaned across the desk. "Are you telling me that the car with Rossiter's body wasn't there at one o'clock?"

Officer Abbot seemed to shrivel. "No, Captain. It was there, all right, because I remember seeing it. But I was looking for a body *on* the road—I thought that's what the caller had meant! I saw the car, and the guy sitting behind the steering wheel, and I remembered thinking that I'd go back and check him out if I didn't find anything. It wasn't too unusual, though, because that time of night drivers are always pulling over to doze for a few minutes. He was off the road, not harming anybody. Anyway, I got another call and didn't go back."

"You're sure it was the murder car?"

"I remember the Ohio plates." He quickly added, "It hadn't been reported stolen then."

"All right," Leopold said. "Thanks for telling me now, anyway."

"Does it help any, Captain?"

"Maybe."

Alone once more, Leopold stared out at the city and thought about the case. Here and there, lights were beginning to come on in office buildings, although darkness was still two hours away. He picked up Fleming's personnel file and stared hard at the photo of the man he'd worked with for so many years.

Roger Fleming, detective sergeant.

Then, after a time, he knew what he had to do.

The lights were on in his office when Roger Fleming appeared at the door. He cleared his throat and waited until Leopold looked up, then said, "They're letting me go, but I understood you wanted to see me first."

"Yes, Roger. Sit down, will you?" Leopold motioned to a chair. "Iris is on her way here too. I just wanted to ask a few final questions."

"Iris?" He frowned nervously. "Why drag her into it again?"

"She's into it already, Roger. We know about her relationship with the murdered man."

Sergeant Fletcher came in then, looking tired. It had been a long day for them all. He dropped into the other chair with a sigh. "Still hot out there. Isn't cooling off a bit."

"Did you examine the apartment?"

Fletcher nodded. "Nothing there. No sign of a weapon."

The phone buzzed, announcing Iris Fleming, and Leopold ordered her sent in. She too looked tired, and hadn't bothered to renew her eye makeup. It was the end of the day for all of them.

"Are you ready to go home?" she asked her husband.

"I'm ready."

Leopold cleared his throat, hating what he had to do. "One moment, please. As you know, Roger, you still face departmental charges. You attempted murder, and the fact that your victim was already dead does not greatly alter the situation from the department's point of view. I think I can safely say that you're finished as a detective."

"I suppose so," Fleming mumbled.

"And there's more, because we still have a case to close. There's still the real murderer of Norman Rossiter to be brought to justice."

"Have you found him?" Roger Fleming asked.

"I think so." Leopold leaned back in his chair, trying to keep his eyes off Iris Fleming. "You wouldn't tell us how you knew the car was parked there on the expressway, but of course there's only one way you could have known—only one way, Roger, you could know just where to find Rossiter at two in the morning. And that's if the real murderer told you. But if the murderer told you that Rossiter was in the car on the expressway, not going anywhere, you must also have known he was dead—or at least dying. It doesn't make sense any other way."

"What are you driving at?" Iris asked.

"Only that Roger must have known Rossiter was dead or dying when he fired those shots. Which means he didn't fire them to *kill* Rossiter. He fired them to protect the real murderer. What person would have told him about the killing, told him where to find the car? Who was he trying to protect by taking the blame on himself? No one but his wife. You, Iris. You killed your lover."

"No!" Her hand had flown to her mouth.

Leopold turned back to Roger. "The deception is over, Roger. You can't shield her any longer."

Roger Fleming, his face white as chalk, slowly nodded. "You're right, of course. I thought I could take the blame on myself. You're right. Yes, she killed him."

It was then that Iris moved, springing like a tigress. She screamed and leaped at her husband, clawing at his face.

Fletcher was closest. He grabbed her around the waist and hung on.

Leopold gazed out over the city, seeing only the night lights now. It had been a long, hard day, and his vision tended to blur a bit when he was overtired.

"We've got her calmed down at last," Fletcher said from the door. "God, she was like a madwoman!"

Leopold nodded. "She had reason to be."

Roger Fleming was still in his chair. He hadn't moved since her outburst. Now he started to rise. "I'd better be getting home. The children—"

Leopold said nothing. He opened a drawer in his desk and took out one of the familiar manila envelopes they all used to store evidence. He unclasped it and tipped it upside down. There was a clatter as a narrow-bladed kitchen knife fell out and hit the desk.

Roger Fleming turned his eyes on it, as if seeing it for the first time. "What's that?" he asked.

"The weapon that killed Norman Rossiter. Also the weapon that Mrs. Croft used to stab her husband. I thought you'd have the decency to confess when I accused Iris, but you played it to the bitter end, didn't you?"

"You're accusing me again?"

"Roger, Roger, why in hell did you do it? A smart cop like you, and you let yourself get into a mess like this! Was it worth it, just to kill your wife's lover?"

"I was on duty when Rossiter was killed," he said, but his voice was beginning to crack. "I've got an alibi!"

"Your alibi isn't worth beans, Roger. The lab tests will show two different blood types on this knife blade, and when we start pinning down your exact movements before midnight, we'll find some pretty big gaps. You were called to the investigation of the Croft stabbing, and you found yourself suddenly in a perfect situation for yourself. You had a murder weapon which had already been used for one stabbing, and an hour's time or more for establishing an alibi. After all, what better place to hide a murder weapon than with the evidence of a totally different crime?"

Roger Fleming stirred and glanced at Fletcher, whose face was impassive. They'd both gone through these final moments with Leopold so many times that now it seemed unreal with Fleming as the accused. Finding him at the car with a gun was one thing, but revealing him as a carefully calculating killer was something much more sinister.

"Supposedly you spent nearly two hours questioning neighbors of the Crofts," Leopold continued, "which was a long time for a simple family-trouble call. That made me suspicious from the start, and then I discovered that the Charles Motel was within walking distance of the Croft place. You talked to a few neighbors, then left your car parked where it was and walked to the motel. You stole the salesman's car, drove to Rossiter's apartment, killed him with the same knife that Mrs. Croft had used, and then drove the dead body to the expressway. You left it there, hopped the fence, and walked back to the Croft place—a distance of only a mile. The neighbors thought you'd been there all the time, questioning people."

"Why did he leave the body on the expressway?" Fletcher asked. "I don't understand that part. And why did he go back to it two hours later?"

"That was the key to the whole case. The body was left on the expressway simply so that it would be quickly found—soon enough to make Roger's alibi still valid. As a detective himself, he was well aware of autopsy results, and of the fact that the longer a body goes undiscovered the harder it is to fix the precise time of death.

"He figured someone would stop and find the body right away, but nobody did. Cars kept passing, and nobody stopped. You must have sweated out that hour, Roger, back at headquarters waiting for the report that never came in. You had to establish Rossiter's death as before midnight, in order to be in the clear. You couldn't hang around headquarters all night being seen by people."

"Why didn't he report the body himself?" Fletcher asked.

"He finally did, around one this morning. I just learned that a short time ago. A call came in about a body on the expressway, but no car was mentioned and the investigating officer didn't find Rossiter. By two o'clock you must have been really desperate,

Roger. There was nobody around to alibi you at that time of the morning, and even the bars were closing. You had no place to go for an alibi. In fact, there was a good chance now that the body wouldn't be discovered till morning, and your original alibi would be useless.

"You couldn't pretend to stumble on it yourself, since you were the chief suspect. So you decided on a bizarre and bold plan. You drove out to the stolen car on the expressway, waited till some cars were passing, and fired two shots into Rossiter's dead body. From your police experience you knew it could be shown later that Rossiter was already dead. Rather than place yourself in danger, you actually made sure that the real time of death could be established to clear you."

"Couldn't he just break the guy's wristwatch?" Fletcher asked.

"Would something like that have convinced you? Or the medical examiner?"

"No," Fletcher admitted, "but this way he ruined his whole police career."

"At two o'clock this morning the choice was between his career and his life. It wasn't a difficult choice to make, was it, Roger? It wasn't even difficult to shift the blame onto Iris. After all, she'd betrayed you with Rossiter."

Fleming's lips were dry. "How'd you get onto it?"

"You knew where the car was. Rossiter didn't tell you—he was already dead for two hours. If Iris told you, you'd have tried to hide the body, not take the blame on yourself. And if she didn't tell you, the only way you could have known was if *you* drove it there, if *you* killed him."

"You'll have a tough time proving it," Fleming said.

"Not with this bloody knife."

"Maybe Rossiter and Mr. Croft both had the same blood type."

Leopold smiled. "Feel like gambling your life on it, Roger?"

He didn't feel like gambling. On the way back to his cell he grabbed a gun from the holster of a friendly guard and shot himself in the head.

*This story perhaps ranges farthest of any in this anthology from
the sacred precincts of classic detection, but clearly it deals with
crime, one greater perhaps than the murder of the body—the
stifling of freedom and the annihilation of hope.*

JOAN RICHTER

The Prisoner of Zemu Island

A needle of light pierced the white blaze of African sun and
flickered high in the cloudless sky over Zemu Island. Ras Lazaar
stood at the edge of the airfield, in the shade of a jacaranda tree,
watching the gleaming splinter of steel sprout wings. A fusion
of excitement and sadness held him, as he studied the plane's
gradual descent. He had traveled to the mainland by boat many
times, but he had never flown. He never would now. The new
African government did not allow Indians to leave the island.

He pushed away the wave of self-pity. Unchecked, it would
engulf him in a deep sense of hopelessness.

Thirty passengers were on board the plane today—twenty-nine
Germans on a tour of Africa, coming to spend the afternoon on
Zemu Island, and one American woman traveling alone. Since
Ras was the director of tourism, they were all his responsibility,
especially the American. The decision to grant her entry had not
been reached without argument and threat. Except for newspaper-

Copyright © 1971 by Joan Richter; first published in *Ellery Queen's
Mystery Magazine.*

men whose requests the new government automatically denied, it was a year since an American had sought to come to Zemu Island.

"If she is not what she says she is—if she brings trouble to the New Republic of Zemu Island—you *Indian,* will pay for it!" Prime Minister Masaka's finger had pointed like a gun at Ras's head, firing the abbreviated Swahili with the slur of ethnic superiority. Only Ras's hatred of Masaka exceeded his fear.

When the plane touched the ground and streaked across the far runway, Ras stepped out of the shade of the tree. His stride showed only a bare trace of stiffness from the now year-old wound. He was taller than the average Indian, with the traditional olive skin and gleaming black hair. His frame was held together by pliant muscles developed by years of tennis and swimming. Since the political coup he had done neither, but at twenty-three his body did not show the year's absence from exercise. His mind, too, had survived the trauma of the two-day revolution in which the Indian population of Zemu Island had been decimated.

He had stopped asking why he had lived when so many had died, what instinct had sent him to the ground at the unfamiliar sound of gunfire, by what lucky accident a bullet had struck his leg and not his heart. The Africans had not killed him afterward, when they found him wounded and unconscious; instead they had put him in the care of the Cuban doctors who had come with the revolutionary force. Later, when he was given the position of director of tourism, he began to understand. The Africans needed him—he could read and write both Swahili and English.

It seemed without reason that Masaka should see a threat in the visit of the young American schoolteacher. Yet the attitude was in keeping with the Prime Minister's frequent rages and bursts of irrationality. The pressures of ruling a country were heavy on a man, even when he had the support of his people. Masaka had had that support for only a short time. Suspicion had quickly eaten at the edges of black unity when word spread that the revolution had been the organized effort of a foreign power which had chosen Masaka as its island leader, and not the spontaneous rebellion of Africans against a repressive Indian government.

Sober Africans began to ask questions. Some had begun to demand answers. Yukano was one of them.

Differences between Masaka and Yukano were evident even physically. Masaka was six feet tall, with a round head and enormous hands that were forever washing one another. Yukano was slight, with a thin face and narrow shoulders, and he spoke softly.

At a meeting where Masaka had announced his opposition to the American teacher's visit, Yukano had risen and talked convincingly of Zemu Island's need to reinstate tourism as a source of revenue and prestige. Many were stirred by this argument, but others were unconvinced until Yukano spoke again. "The American, June Hastings, asks to come not just as a tourist but as a scientist interested in Zemu Island's marine life. Do you recall the prestige that came to Tanganyika when Dr. Louis Leakey made his excavations at Oldavai Gorge and found evidence of prehistoric man? How do we know what there is to be found in the waters of Zemu Island?"

Masaka had acceded to the majority, but Ras knew it was a defeat the Prime Minister was not likely to forget. Ras worried about the kind of action Masaka would take to soothe his wounded pride.

The plane came to a stop, and the airfield sprouted life. Africans in ragged shorts and bare feet appeared to unload baggage. Airport officials of the same skin color, wearing starched uniforms and hats decorated with gold braid, stood at attention to some unseen authority. The sun streamed down, and the concrete airfield glistened with the running of dry rivers and shimmering pools.

The first person to disembark was the German tour leader, with whom Ras shook hands. "Lunch is waiting for your group at the Manga Hotel," Ras said. "Afterwards the drivers will take you on a tour of the island." The balding pink-cheeked man mopped his forehead and managed a smile, then went off to tend his flock.

Ras's attention steadied on the young woman who appeared in the plane's doorway. A border of embroidery fluttered at the hem of her dress, the saffron-pink color of a ripe pomalo. A graceful sweep of bronze hair fell across her cheek. He was struck by the expression of expectancy in her eyes as she scanned the horizon of palm trees, then started down the steps.

"June Hastings?" he asked when she reached him.

She hesitated. "Yes."

"I am Rashid Lazaar. We have corresponded. I am with the ministry of tourism."

"I'm glad to meet you, Mr. Lazaar." She offered her hand. "Thank you for arranging for my entry permit."

"My pleasure," he said, a phrase he realized he had not used with any real meaning in a long time. "I think if we go directly to immigration we will save time."

She fell in step beside him. "What about my luggage? Your customs people will want to check that."

"That will be delivered to another place—we must go there after we have finished here."

Though her eyes were veiled by sunglasses, he could see that they were a pale brown, almost golden. There was a question in them. Her bronze head tossed. "Does someone from your office always meet a new arrival?"

"It is the policy of the new government."

"But I must be someone special to be entitled to the director of tourism himself."

The mischief in her voice was clear. It surprised him and reminded him of his sisters, and their playful jibes.

"You *are* special, Miss Hastings. You have not only chosen to visit Zemu Island, you have come for an unusual purpose. Zemu women and children have gathered shells for years and made necklaces of them, but no one has ever thought them of scientific interest."

"Maybe it's time someone did."

"Some in the government are doubtful, others are puzzled. Others still have suggested that you will give Zemu Island prominence by discovering something as important as what Dr. Leakey found at Oldavai Gorge."

She stopped and stared at him. "They don't really think that?"

"It is what has been said."

"By whom?"

Ras shrugged. "A man named Yukano." The name would mean nothing to her—Yukano had become prominent in island politics only a short time ago. But Ras thought he saw a flicker of recognition move across her face. "Have you heard of him?"

"The name sounds familiar, but maybe it's my Western ear. Even now many African names still sound alike to me."

He nodded, assuming she was referring to the last two years she had been teaching school in Kenya. "It is a funny thing. I have the same difficulties with British names—like your own. But Indian names are hard for Westerners, I think."

"Ignorance contributes to the confusion. People of one culture imagine those of another are all alike. Masaka and Yukano, for example. To a person unfamiliar with Africa, they simply are both Africans. No thought is given to the possibility of great differences between them, that they are of different tribes and different persuasions—totally different personalities."

Her voice lowered as they approached the Immigration Building and fell silent when they reached the steps. Ras did not speak either, but his mind was churning. She was well informed, typical of the emancipated American women he had read about. He must be careful not to be guilty of the very thing she had just described. She was more than simply an American. She was an individual who had chosen to come to visit Zemu Island for a special reason. What that reason was, he suspected he had yet to find out.

The immigration check was routine, even to the insolence of the African clerk who looked at Ras and yawned widely. In the past year Ras had learned to ignore such petty insults, but with the young woman at his side he found it difficult to hold back a rebuke. He was glad when they were outside again and he could lead her to the car he had left parked near the jacaranda tree. "Your luggage is being delivered to a building at the other end of the airport—it is just a minute's drive."

As he helped her into the front seat he thought of warning her that this would be no ordinary customs check. Two of the Prime Minister's own men would be in the banda, and their instructions were to go through her belongings with exactness. If they found something they did not like, she would be put on the next plane leaving Zemu Island.

Ras decided to say nothing. A warning would serve no purpose but to alarm her. He hoped her luggage cleared. He wanted her to stay. There was very little he had wanted so much in a long time.

Perhaps he would even take her to Pwani Pwani—he had not been back since the day the guns had fired. He had thought he could never return, to walk over those sands where his mother and his sisters and the girl he had loved had played ball and gathered shells. How pretty they had looked, strolling along the beach, their brilliantly colored saris catching the breeze, like butterflies in flight. Sunday after Sunday they had gone to picnic at Pwani Pwani. One Sunday all of them had died. . . .

"Tell me about the Manga Hotel," he heard June Hastings say. "Is it as nice as it used to be?"

He glanced at her quickly, torn from his reverie. "You know it?"

"I heard of it from someone who had been there years ago when the Norberts owned it. They aren't still here, are they?"

Ras smiled. Anyone who had stayed at the Manga would remember the Norberts. "They're still here. They run the hotel for the government now." He was certain she was aware that the new regime had confiscated all private lands and possessions. "They have kept things up. It is a handsome building, white stone and coral, built around a courtyard that is always in bloom."

Purposely he did not mention the door. For some reason he wanted her to see it for herself, unprompted. He was tempted to

add that a building, no matter how beautiful, did not make a
hotel—only guests could give it life. There had been no guests for
a year. The few boarders were foreign technicians who had come
in the wake of the revolution, from Cuba and Russia and China.
They had come to work, not to play. The lanterns that had always
hung in the flame trees, lighting the terrace on Saturday nights,
had not been lit in a year.

They had reached the end of the concrete runway, where a
wall of tropical forest faced them. Ras found the narrow dirt
track that led to the banda and parked beside a car already
there. It was Masaka's car. His heartbeat quickened, but in a moment resumed its even beat. How else would the two men assigned to check her luggage get to the airport, if not by car? But
it was not like Masaka to let anyone use his.

The shade of the trees was deep and blinding after the brightness of the sun. Inside the banda it seemed darker still. Two
Africans in army uniforms stood behind a table on which her
luggage lay—a blue suitcase and one small metal trunk. Their
black faces shone in the glow from a pressure lamp whose eerie
light did not reach into the far corner to make distinguishable
the figure standing there. But a familiar movement of hands
washing one another told Ras who it was. A cold stillness touched
his heart and did not go away.

June Hastings unlocked the blue suitcase, and the two men
began to paw through the layers of pastel-colored clothes, looking into pockets, peering into the toes of shoes. Before opening
the metal trunk she removed her sunglasses and put them in her
purse. The glance with which she touched Ras was fleeting, but
in the strange light her eyes looked to him like warm gold. Once
before he had known someone with eyes of that color—in Dar es
Salaam.

Several times he had gone there by dhow with his father, sailing
first to Zanzibar and on to what was then Tanganyika. They
would always stay two days—one to sell the copra they had
brought from their plantation, another to visit a man named

Benji, an old friend of his father. The two men would sit together
in the shade of a mango tree, sipping tea, their voices hushed,
their heads bent in serious talk. On the other side of the garden
Ras would play with Benji's youngest son, named after his father.
They drank orange Fanta and stuffed themselves with sweet cakes
and played marbles. Sometimes the girl, who lived in the house
on the other side of the garden wall, would join them. Though
she was the same age as they, rarely could she beat them in a
marble game. Her hair was the color of dark honey, her eyes pale
gold.

Each time they left Benji's house the packet of money his father
had received from the sale of the copra would be smaller than
when he had first received it, but the expression on his father's
face would say that things had gone as he had wished. Ras was
always tempted to ask what business his father had with Benji
that took so much money, but he did not, knowing that when his
father wanted him to know he would tell him. That time came.
"Some day things will not be good on Zemu Island and you and
your mother and your sisters will have to leave. Benji is sending
money for me to a bank in Switzerland. It is in my name and in
yours. Should something ever happen to me, you will know what
to do." Ras remembered how frightened those words had made
him, and how little he had understood their full meaning.

Now he understood, but what good did it do? Those careful
plans his father had made in Dar es Salaam, under the mango tree,
while the sound of marbles clinked in the warm still air, had died
on the beach at Pwani Pwani. . . .

June Hastings turned the key in the lock and lifted the lid of
the metal trunk. The two army men looked up from the blue
suitcase and turned to stare at the contents of the trunk, their
eyes growing round and then narrow. They leaned closer and
then straightened, muttering in Swahili to each other and to the
man in the corner of the room.

Masaka left the shadowed security of the banda wall and moved
to the table. She looked up but made no sign that his presence

was a surprise to her. Ras felt his breath catch as he wondered if she knew who Masaka was.

The lid of the trunk held a collection of tools: files, tweezers, knives, hooks, brushes, a small rake and shovel. In the bottom of the trunk was a roll of netting, a half-dozen liter-sized bottles filled with liquids, and several dozen clear plastic boxes of assorted sizes, separated by layers of cotton wool.

She spoke in a quiet, fluent Swahili that surprised them all. "I have come to Zemu Island to gather specimens of seashells. These are tools I need to find the shells and to clean them." Her hand passed lightly over the contents of the lid and then moved to the items in the lower section. "The large bottles contain cleaning solutions—Clorox, alcohol, vinegar, formaldehyde. These plastic boxes are for the shells after they have been cleaned. Each will be wrapped in a piece of cotton, so it will not be crushed."

She had turned in the course of her explanation so that her glance touched each of them—the two army men, Ras, and Masaka. Ras found it difficult to hide the rush of admiration he felt for her intuition. She might have guessed that Masaka would not understand a lengthy stream of English, but she could not have known how angry he would have become if his ignorance were revealed.

She withdrew a small blue-bound book from the trunk, with a colored photograph of shells on its cover. Ras read the title: *Shells of the East African Coast.* She opened to several pages. Each had some text accompanying the photograph of a shell.

"This book describes shells found along the coast of East Africa. I would like to do the same thing about shells in the waters of Zemu Island."

One of Masaka's large hands reached out for the book. He looked at its cover and turned to look inside. He snapped the book shut and thrust it at her. "You will make a book like this about Zemu Island?"

"I would like to."

"Where did you learn to speak Swahili?"

"In Kenya. I taught English in a school north of Nairobi. My pupils knew their own tribal languages and Swahili. I learned Swahili so that I could teach them English."

Masaka's hands had begun moving one over the other. Ras saw something building in him, but he did not know what it was, or its cause. His concern stirred. When Masaka spoke again, it would not be with an even voice, but with the beginning of some irrational anger. How would the girl react?

"Kenya has declared Swahili its national language! Why do they still teach English?"

Something in Masaka's expression had evidently prepared her for the attack. She only frowned thoughtfully. "English is just one of many subjects taught in Kenyan schools, like arithmetic and history and geography."

Masaka stared at her, and then his face closed over. He motioned to the two men standing mute behind the table. The three of them marched out the door.

Ras stared through the open doorway after them. He was not certain whether to feel relief or worry. It was not like Masaka to give way so easily.

"Can we leave now?" Her voice took him from his thoughts.

"Yes, we can go," he said slowly, unable to free himself of the uneasiness he felt.

"Let's hurry then." She smiled at him, a mischievous smile. "I'm so hungry I could eat a horse!"

Her spirit was contagious. He grinned. "You will insult the Norberts with that kind of talk!" They were both suddenly laughing, and he felt strangely free. He had to remind himself that his position had not changed. He was still a prisoner on Zemu Island. But the gloom of that realization was not as great as it usually was.

They put her suitcase and trunk into the compartment of his car. When they were driving off, he turned to her and asked, "Did you know who he was?"

"Masaka? Not right away. It was so dark at first. After the revolution there were lots of photographs of him in newspapers and magazines, standing on the veranda of the old sultan's palace with the new flag draped over the railing. I was scared stiff when I realized who he was."

"You did not show it."

"I felt it. I've never had a head of state come to the airport and check my luggage before."

"I told you that you were someone special."

"You didn't say *that* special." She leaned back, resting her head against the seat. "Ras, are we going to be seeing a lot of Masaka?"

The road from the airport to the Manga Hotel was narrow. He was behind a donkey cart laden with bananas, driving slowly. It was easy to turn and look at her. She had called him Ras, not Rashid. There were some things about her that were indeed puzzling—the easy comfort he felt, the strange sense of the familiar.

He shrugged. "I cannot speak for Masaka. He is not the most predictable of men."

"Or the most stable. I heard that on the mainland, but I thought it was just gossip, wishful rumor. But it's not. That man is cracking up. I'm not sure it's anything to rejoice about. Zemu Island could be in for a lot of trouble with someone like him ruling."

"That is very dangerous talk."

"And I should know better. You might turn the car around and head straight back to the airport. Please don't. I'd be so disappointed. I've wanted to visit Zemu Island for a long time. I never thought I'd get the chance. It's a long way from Boston."

"Is that where you come from?"

"It's my mother's home. We went there to live after my father died ten years ago. He was a British doctor. We traveled a lot when I was small."

"You had been to Africa then—before the last two years teaching in Kenya?"

"Yes," was all she said.

The last turn brought them into the center of Zemu town, with its narrow Arab alleys that twisted and cut back on each other. To a stranger they were a mysterious labyrinth, but to Ras they were home.

Some of the old pride stirred in him as he stopped the car in front of the hotel and waited for her reaction. The chalk-white walls appeared almost opalescent in the brilliance of the noonday sun. At intervals bougainvillea clung and tumbled in scarlet cascades. The stairway entrance ascended to a wide arch embracing a massive double door carved of ebony. Spikes of polished brass were embedded in the oiled wood and gleamed in the equatorial sunlight.

She was silent beside him, staring, her profile still. After a while she turned. Her eyes were shining. "It's magnificent. I've never seen anything like it. And you were right—it would take an elephant to batter that door down."

He stared at her. "An elephant—I—"

Her soft brown-gold eyes gleamed with mischief. "You don't remember? How absolutely horrid of you!"

How absolutely horrid of you! Where had he heard those words?

Then he heard the clink of glass against glass. He saw the blue marble fly from his hand, hit the white one swirled with red, and split it in two. *How absolutely horrid of you!* she had cried, stamping her foot and running off, disappearing behind the garden wall.

The great double door swung open, splashing reflections of sun onto their faces. An eager young African in a starched white uniform and red velour fez came down the steps and opened the car door on her side. *"Jambo, Memsab, Jambo, Bwana.* Welcome to Manga Hotel."

Winky Norbert was waiting for them at the desk inside. He shook Ras's hand and smiled at the pretty girl with him. His wiry moustache twitched. "Good you didn't get here a while ago. Sheer bedlam with that tour. Couldn't please one of them, no less the lot. If they can't give Zemu more than four hours, I'd rather they stayed away."

"That'll do with the complaining, Winky." Margaret Norbert appeared. "You know very well you loved every minute of it. You haven't been so chipper since the last tour. Twenty-nine lunches are twenty-nine lunches. Makes me feel we're still running a hotel."

She turned to June with a smile that deepened the wrinkles around her mouth and eyes. At fifty-five she was still an attractive woman. "Welcome to the Manga. I don't have to guess who you are. You're June Hastings, our first real guest in a long time."

June smiled. "Thank you. It's as lovely here as I heard it would be. Is there any chance you've given me a room overlooking the courtyard?"

"Take your pick. You can have one next to the Cubans or across from the Russians. The Chinese prefer the hotel down the street."

Winky patted his wife's arm. "Stop twigging the girl, Maggie." Then looking at June, "We've given you a second-floor room that looks right out onto a forest of bougainvillea. I think you'll like it."

The road to Pwani Pwani wound along the edge of coconut plantations and through the ripening groves of clove trees. The warm humid air was heavy with the fragrance of an earlier crop, already harvested and drying in the sun. June had changed into a short blue dress that bared her suntanned arms. She was leaning back against the seat, her hair blowing in the breeze. It was the first time they had been alone since their arrival at the hotel.

"You've had time to remember," she said.

"I'd never forgotten. But it was better to pretend. If I had allowed myself to think, I could not have let you come. This way it has happened without my really knowing."

"It's that bad here, then?"

"Why have you come?"

"Benji sent me."

"Benji? Benji died three years ago."

"I'm talking about Benji the son."

Ras thought of the small boy with the dark eyes with whom he had shot marbles and drunk orange Fanta and gorged himself on sweet cakes—he was a man now. The last time Ras had been to Dar es Salaam, young Benji had been at school in England.

"Where is Benji now?"

"I saw him in Nairobi, but he was leaving for New York."

Nairobi—New York—and he could not even go to Zanzibar.

"Benji sent you. Why?"

"To find out what is happening on Zemu Island. No one on the outside really knows. Only a little has gotten out. I wasn't honest with you when I said I'd not heard of Yukano—I have heard of him. Some people think he is the man who should be ruling Zemu Island instead of Masaka. He would allow the British to return. He would seek American aid, not only Communist."

"What would he do for the Indians? Give them back their lives?" He'd spoken so bitterly that he knew she could make no reply. "Benji has a plan?" he asked softly.

"Not just Benji alone. There are others. But they need someone they can count on in Zemu. Benji wants to know if you will help."

"In what way? To make Yukano head of Zemu Island?"

"You mean he is an African," she said quietly.

He felt the bite of her words, the accusation in them and the challenge. She was no stranger to East African politics. She knew the deep animus that lay between African and Indian. She knew the tumult and bloodshed that had thrust the African into power. For those who had been born to the old way it would never be easy to accept black authority; but to fight it, or pretend that was not the way the tide ran, would be stupid.

"I know the differences between men," he said. "There is little likeness between Masaka and Yukano except for the color of their skin. Zemu will rot under the rule of a man like Masaka. I do not know that it will ever flourish as it once did, but with someone like Yukano there would at least be a chance." He fell silent.

"But how?" he asked after a while. "It would not be enough merely to get rid of Masaka. They would only put someone else like him in his place. And it would be dangerous—more dangerous than you can imagine. Masaka may be stupid, but those behind him are not. I do not think it was his own intelligence that made him suspicious of your visit. He was warned."

She smiled mischievously. "But after today no one will be suspicious."

"What makes you say so?"

"Today we are going shell gathering—and we'll be watched. After they see all the trouble we go to to get a few shells, they will be convinced that shells are the sole reason for my visit."

"Then it is not a pretense?"

"It is, and it isn't. Marine biology is my field. I will write a book about the shells I find on Zemu Island. It will be published, and copies will be sent to the government here. If any doubt over the purpose of my visit still lingers, it will disappear when copies of the book arrive. Yukano went a bit overboard when he talked of Oldavai Gorge—Africans are impressed by such things. They are impressed by books even when they can't read them.

"But Masaka will be reassured—and so will the Cubans and the Russians. Tours from Western nations will begin to come to Zemu Island, and word will spread that Zemu Island is a lovely place. The government will become complacent and think that people have forgotten how Masaka came into power. It will assume there is no one interested enough in the welfare of this small piece of land floating in the Indian Ocean to plan a counter-revolution."

"Those are large words," he said. "The idea is larger still. You are talking about a long time—many months, perhaps years."

"I don't think Benji or the others involved with him have any illusions that it will be easy, that it will not take months of careful planning. They also know they cannot do it without help from someone here on the island—from you. Your position as director of tourism allows you to receive and send letters, a privilege others on Zemu are denied. It is a ready means of communication which cannot be duplicated with anyone else here."

"But every letter I receive or write is censored. They are not as naïve as you think."

She shook her head. "I know. We would use a code."

He listened to her unfold a plan that could not work without him. It was a mad plan that had greater chance of failure than of success—but it offered hope, some hope. Ras realized that until she had come he had had no hope, no hope at all.

They had almost reached the place where he should turn off onto a narrow track that would take them to Pwani Pwani. He had slowed down, looking for it. It would be grown over now—perhaps they would have to leave the car and walk in—it would be difficult with the metal trunk. Ah, there it was—the place marked by a dead tree. The growth was not so thick that he could not drive through part of the way.

"Close your window so you will not get scratched," he said, rolling up his own. Branches strung with thorny vines and moss arched across the once open path. The perfume of ripening guavas had drifted into the car and touched his mind with memory— he had been picking guavas when the first shot came. Other shots followed, the bullets skipping like footsteps across the sand. Like dolls, his mother and the girls had fallen, brilliant piles of crumpled saris on the sand. Then his father, like a dervish, spinning, falling, coughing, dying on the sand. Ras was flattened in the underbrush of vines, the guavas he had picked and put in the front of his shirt squashed and wet and oozing against his chest, warm from the sun, warm like the blood in which his father lay. Pain exploded in his leg. Blackness passed over him, but in his unconsciousness he strained to remember the familiar face among the bearded strangers, the African whose gun had aimed and with lust had killed—Masaka. . . .

His hands were clenched around the steering wheel, whitening his knuckles and making the muscles of his forearms bulge. He stared through the windshield at the beach, at winter glimmering through the suddenly denser tangle of green. He stopped the car, got out, and reached under the seat for the *panga* he kept there. The scent of guavas filled his nostrils as he struck at the vines that choked the path. The broad blade sliced through the ropy lengths as if they were bits of string. Sap oozed and trickled over his hands and arms.

When the path was clear, his arms fell to his sides, the point of the *panga* stuck in the sand beside his foot. His chest heaving, he turned and saw her standing by the car, watching him with her soft golden eyes, questioning, but not asking.

"We always came here to Pwani Pwani—my family. It was our special place. They all died here that first day of the revolution. I was picking guavas. They were walking along the sand. I have not been back, not until today." His dark eyes looked deep into hers. "It is time. I am ready."

She smiled gently and held out her hand. "Let's go, then. There is lots to do."

They each took a handle of the metal trunk and carried it onto the beach, where they placed it in the shade of a palm tree. He left her to open it while he returned for the two buckets she had borrowed from the Norberts.

Along the way he glanced on both sides into the dense tropical growth for a sign of anyone hiding there. They would be watched, but they would never know by whom or by how many. Once before the forest had camouflaged the presence of the enemy.

He started back toward the beach, carrying the buckets. He spied the tree where he had left her and saw the trunk as it had been, unopened. Then he saw her arm raised in the water, waving to him, splashing. He heard her voice and her laughter. He tore off his clothes and went racing into the waves. In a few moments he was shoveling, and she was using the rake.

"Here's a beauty," she cried. "Look at it." She held a brown-and-white spiraled shell in the palm of her hand.

"There must be hundreds of them just like that all over the beach."

"They'd be chipped or cracked. The shells I take back must be perfect." She dropped it into the bucket of formaldehyde solution and reached for a notebook. "Speckled Turret Shell," she said aloud, "otherwise known as *Terebra oculata*."

"What about this one?" he said, extending his hand. She reached for it without looking.

"You don't take me seriously at all!" He could almost see her foot stamp.

"Oh, but I do," he said, tossing the small stone away and giving her a handful of shells he had been saving.

She grinned at him, and then set about recording the names in her notebook.

When the buckets were almost full, she rose. "I want to set some traps in the rocks close to shore. Some shells are nocturnal. It won't take long. Then we can swim until the sun goes down, and come back tomorrow."

He cut squares from the roll of netting that had been in the trunk, and with some thin wire gathered them into makeshift baskets. A small piece of the meat from the Norberts' kitchen served as bait. They laid the traps together, anchoring them with small stones. As they worked their heads were close, almost touching. She spoke softly. "They're watching, I know. But they are stupid—we could be setting mines and they wouldn't know. Someday we will."

She looked up, and her eyes held his for a moment, the expression in them intent and serious. Then in the next instant her head tossed and she was running into the water.

The sun was low in the sky, a fiery orange ball that lit the surface of the transparent pale-green sea with strands of orange and gold. Between the breaking waves the water flowed like the soft folds of an iridescent sari. Ras raced after her and dove into the water, feeling the salt of it sting his eyes, blurring the memory that had begun of a girl he had once loved, a girl who had worn a sari of green threaded with bronze and gold on the last day of her life.

He swam alongside her. "Can you swim to those rocks out there? At the last one there is a deep pool and a cavern. If the light is right, it is a wonderful sight."

Drops of water clinging to her eyelashes sparkled and flew away when she nodded and began an easy stroke beside him.

It was a long time since he'd made the dive, and he wanted to be certain the passage was still clear, certain no rock had dislodged itself. He had warned her to let him lead the way. Her hand was in his as they swam underwater toward an archway of rock leading under a ledge in the rock ceiling.

It was the purple coral he wanted her to see, the sea anemones and the swaying ferns whose undulations were said to have teased love-starved sailors into thinking they were mermaids. It was a perfect time, the sun and tide were just right. There was a small space where they could rise to the surface and rest before they dove again.

"I've never seen purple coral before," she said.

"It is purple only in the water. It turns brown when it is in the air."

He was ready to dive again, anxious to show her more.

"Wait, Ras. The sun will set soon. This is a good place to talk. No one can hear us, no one can see. There are other things you must know—about Yukano and the money that is yours in Switzerland—and the code. It's important that you know the code right away. Should anything happen to me, then you could still get in touch with Benji."

"Nothing will happen to you."

She grinned. "I could drown."

He shook his head. "You swim too well." He smiled to himself, measuring the differences between them. She thought of setting mines in the sea, and he saw saris in the sea. He wanted to show her the mysteries of an underwater grotto he had explored as a child, and she wanted to plan a revolution. "This is not the place. The opening in the rocks above us is like a horn, and our words would be carried across the island."

She looked at him, her eyes doubtful, but he knew she could not take the chance. She needed him. Benji needed him. He would be their tool, as Masaka had been the tool of the Cubans. Was there a difference? Would the people of Zemu Island feel any more loyalty to the man whom counterrevolutionaries would put in the sultan's palace than they did to Masaka? How many people would die?—Africans this time.

Despite his questions, he knew he would do what Benji asked. Not because he wanted revenge, or because success of the counterrevolution would make him free, but because it gave him hope. And without hope no man can live and stay whole.

He took her hand, wishing he could explain what her coming to Zemu Island meant to him. But even if he were able to say it, he was afraid she would think him sentimental and not ready for the task that lay ahead of him.

"We have time for one more dive, and then we must go while there is still light."

They swam toward the shore in the sun's last golden path. In minutes night would fall. They left the water and felt the evening air was cool. She began to run, her wet hair streaming, calling to him, laughing, "Catch me if you can!"

A breeze stirred and furled the water's waves. Dark leaves fluttered, and shadows moved at the forest's edge. Bearded men who looked like trees advanced across the sand. As if in a nightmare he stood immobile.

He heard shots, her one sharp cry, but he looked away so as not to see her body lying crumpled on the sand.

*This haunting little tale treats of that cliché-honored trium-
virate: boss, wife, and secretary. Matters proceed, at the outset,
along fairly traditional lines, for three in romance is one too
many. But then, with delicate touch, a departure transforms the
commonplace into an almost archetypical parable. . . .*

PAULINE C. SMITH

Osborn and Sabrina

He was a handsome and successful businessman while she was a
young and beautiful secretary.

When he called her across the office to take an inconsequential
letter, it was only to watch her walk from her desk to his.

"Miss Varga, would you take a letter, please?" Then he held
his breath as she rose with a fluid motion, gathered up pencils
and notebook, and walked toward him.

She had a way of swaying that was both elegant and provocative.
Seated, her circumspect office skirt molding her curves, she crossed
exquisite limbs with style, and placed the notebook on a perfect
knee with a flair.

Once she had poised her pencil with a "Yes, Mr. Breedlove?"
turning her startling green eyes upon him, all the business termi-
nology with which his brain had long been convoluted fled, leaving only delighted furrows of love and desire.

He usually started the letter with, "I think that's enough for the day, Sabrina. Let's go . . ." his suggestions graduating as their affair progressed, from lunch to a weekend together.

"Yes, Osborn," she always replied, no matter what he suggested.

Not that Sabrina was one to fall, like a ripe tomato, into any pair of outstretched arms. She was selective, discriminate, opportunistic, and besides that, in love. Just as Osborn too was in love, for the very first time. He couldn't remember why it was that he once wanted his wife, nor understand how business could have been an obsessive preoccupation now that he had Sabrina.

He found himself to be a happy man at last, living only for their days of occupational affinity and those too seldom nights of extracurricular intimacy.

"I don't live when I'm away from you," he told her with emotion. "I think only of you, my darling."

"Yes, Mr. Breedlove," she answered if they were in the office, and "Yes, Osborn," alone in some trysting place.

"We are very special, my dear," he said, "like Tristram and Isolde."

"Tris-who and what?" she asked.

"Tristram, my dear, and Isolde. They were famous lovers of medieval romance."

"Just lovers?" she asked suspiciously, "or did they get married?"

"Well," and he tried to remember the legends, "one version has it that Tristram, an Arthurian knight, was forced to flee the country at the time it was discovered that King Mark's wife, who was Isolde the Fair, and he were lovers. Later, Tristram married Isolde of the White Hands and it was through her treachery that both he and his loved Isolde the Fair died."

Sabrina looked puzzled by the complication of Isolde, then she immediately oversimplified the explanation to her own satisfaction.

"So Tristram married Isolde, that's nice," she said. "Osborn," since they happened to be in a motel and all alone, "Osborn, can you fix it so we can get married?"

"Yes, my darling," he promised, holding her close, his heart beating mightily. Osborn never promised her anything he could not fulfill.

Osborn's wife was an attractive woman. She could play a good hand of bridge, follow her partner adequately on a dance floor, drive a car without bashing a fender and always laughed at the right places at her husband's oft-told jokes during company dinners.

If Osborn hadn't found Sabrina, he would have been willing to go on with his wife to the end of his days—thinking he was happy at it too—but there was Sabrina.

"I'll ask her for a divorce," he promised.

The reason he didn't ask immediately was that he was seldom at home anymore, and when he was at home, his wife maintained an aloof and hurt silence so that he completely forgot her to the point that he didn't think about asking the question.

He set Sabrina up in a very nice apartment on the North Shore, he draped her lovely white shoulders in mink and decorated her finger with a pear-shaped diamond.

"Now we're engaged," she announced to him. "Aren't we engaged, Osborn?"

"Yes, Sabrina, we certainly are."

"When will we be married, Osborn?"

He was so busy kissing her that he didn't answer immediately.

"You have to ask your wife for a divorce," said Sabrina. "We can't get married until you get a divorce, Osborn."

That was true. So the next time Osborn went home, Sabrina's words filtered through Osborn's thoughts of Sabrina's body, and he told his wife he would like a divorce.

He was startled by her sudden reaction. She threw her arms wide, turned her eyes ceilingward, screamed, "Never," and to press her point, repeated, at the top of her lungs, "Never, never never . . ." *What did he mean by casting her aside after all the lean times she went through with him* . . . adding a few descriptive phrases, *So some tart could get her claws in him,* and, *probably nothing but a cheap hooker*—words he hardly knew and certainly didn't expect to be a part of his wife's conversation.

He explained it all to Sabrina.

"It looks like we'll have to go on being lovers," he said, "just like Tristram and Isolde."

But she too showed a surprising reaction.

"They got married," she argued as firmly and coldly as ice, "you said so. You said this Tris-whatever and Isolde got married. So what did they do about that king? The king that was married to Isolde?"

Osborn's mind whirled.

"I don't suppose there was any divorce back in those uncivilized times, so what did they do with the king so they could marry?"

Osborn wondered, so caught up with this brand-new version of the legend that he completely forgot the two Isoldes.

"I don't know, Sabrina," he said, perplexed.

"They killed him, Osborn. What else?"

That seemed reasonable. There was always a lot of bloodshed during the medieval period. Osborn drew Sabrina to him, content to let the king die while he got on with living, he and Sabrina.

"So you'll have to kill your wife," said Sabrina.

Osborn, shocked, stepped back and stared at this woman he loved.

She explained. "You see, Osborn, it's the only way we can marry. You do see that, don't you?"

Osborn nodded, preoccupied with the thought that her skin felt like warm ivory.

"So we must plan."

"Yes, I suppose so," he agreed.

From then on, they were very busy planning a murder, when they were not busy with each other. Eventually, it didn't seem to be his wife, thought Osborn, that they planned to do in, but that their elaborate plans were only a pretense, a figment, built around a legend without substance—as was Tristram and Isolde.

Actually, Sabrina did most of the planning, while Osborn watched, in fascinated awe, the flash of her wondrous eyes.

"You could do something to her car," she suggested, "like loosen a wheel or knock out the brakes so she'd crash at the bottom of a hill or go over a cliff."

"But there aren't any hills in town," Osborn reminded her, "and certainly no cliffs. Anyway," he sighed, "I don't know a thing about mechanics. I wouldn't know what to do."

"Oh, for goodness' sake," sighed Sabrina, and allowed him to do what he did know how to do.

"There was a mystery on radio," Sabrina said. "These people were trying to get rid of the wife just like we're trying to do—"

Osborn gave a start of alarmed refutation.

". . . Know what they did?"

Dazed, Osborn shook his head.

"They cut almost through a big chandelier that hung from the middle of the ceiling. Then they fixed it so the wife stood right under it."

Osborn hung onto her words, hypnotized.

"One of them went upstairs, just jiggling the floor a little—stamping, I suppose, hopping around on top of the chandelier, and the other one stayed downstairs to see she didn't move."

"Sabrina!" cried Osborn.

"That chandelier came down with an awful clatter. It was terribly exciting, the clatter and the wife's dying moans and all."

She turned, her arms creeping around Osborn's neck.

"We could do that," she said.

He kissed her. "We don't have a chandelier," he said.

She drew away, disgusted. "You're so—so unequipped for murder. You don't know how to rig a car, you haven't got a chandelier." She sighed deeply at his inadequacy.

Desperately then, he searched for a murder means both within his physical and mental scope.

"If she had a bad heart," he brought out hopefully, "and she had an attack, and was helpless, couldn't move, and called out for her medicine—digitalis, probably—I could keep it from her. Let her die." He shuddered.

"Has she got a bad heart?" asked Sabrina.

"No," said Osborn.

"There. You see?" Sabrina spread her arms in weary indignation. It was a beautiful gesture, one that clogged the breath in Osborn's throat. "You're just a dreamer. I am the realist. I will have to plan this thing from start to finish."

He attempted to kiss her, and while the kiss was not a total failure, still it was not a total success either.

"I think one thing that's wrong with you is that you're so terribly opposed to violence."

"I'm not so sure about that," he said, catching her violently to him.

"Yes," she said, "it's true. And here you call yourself Tris-whatchamacalit, a *knight!*"

His grasp on her loosened as he thought of the knights of old, clanking about in their armor, brandishing whatever it was they brandished, jousting all over the place. And when he came to think of it, Tristram was the most versatile of all the versatile jousting heroes in legendary history, being not only a supreme lover, but the greatest of all dragon slayers, as well. Osborn felt the hot blood of courage pound through his veins. He folded Sabrina in his arms.

"Do not fear, my darling," he said, "it shall be done."

It was about then that the dream started, a recurrently sad, gray dream, night after night, not a hair-raising nightmare but a dream in limbo. A dream of silence of emptiness. Of bars and the shadow of bars of a narrow cot slung against the concrete walls by means of an iron chain. Of a cement floor, gray, all of it gray, a cold gray box. And the silence.

In this dream, Osborn clung to the bars and cried out for help and wakefulness so that he could escape, but no one could hear his cry, for he had no voice. There was no sound at all in the silence.

Osborn became so afraid of his dream that he fought sleep,

but sleep came, and with it came the dream—not always the same every night, but almost, and only imperceptibly different.

Sometimes it was a room, concrete yet, but instead of the cot slung against the wall, a bed against the wall, with brown against the gray . . . and the silence. And loneliness without being alone. In this room, he saw a woman, an older faded woman, who sat in silence beside him on the brown bed in the gray room.

He thought of telling Sabrina about the dream, of confiding his fears that the dream might be a premonition of things yet to come—the gray concrete box a prison cell. If he could only explain it as awful as it was, and that maybe it was a warning not to plan murder.

He thought then of how she would greet his fears, with widespread arms, that expansive gesture, so beautiful yet so contemptuous, the gesture that told him he was no planner, no doer, and without violent action, and he kept his dreams to himself.

Maybe they will stop, he gave himself shallow comfort, with the hopeless certainty that they would not.

"How about poison?" suggested Sabrina brightly. "There's strychnine—no, maybe it's arsenic, that you can give in little bitty doses and finally it's all over."

With his lips against her throat, he explained the hazards of obtaining the stuff and the danger of detection. She was so lovely —so beautiful.

If only the dreams would stop. But they visited him every night, or rather *he* visited *them.* Actually, he walked into them, right into that concrete box of a cell, and then that concrete box of a motel room. He knew now that the dump where he sat in silence with that colorless middle-aged woman was a motel, for he had seen the neon sign in front of the window, first the M, then the O, then the T and E, L—green liquid gas flowing through each letter to finally spell out *Motel,* then fade in the darkness and start all over again.

Like the dreams, the terrifying dreams that weren't actually terrifying, but rather a gray and dismal monotony.

"For heaven's sake," cried Sabrina, "can't you think of *anything,*

Osborn? People get killed all the time. And I bet a lot of them that get killed nobody knows they were even killed, but just think they died by accident. I want to get *married*, Osborn. I can't wait forever."

Her threat by innuendo frightened Osborn more than the dreams. He crushed her to him and babbled off a top-of-the-head plan about a break-in, fake robbery, a shot, and she said that was fine.

But the minute he closed his eyes in sleep, the cuddling and love talk, the warmth and the murmurs were gone, and he was back again in the cell, in a vacuum of quiet, lethargy claiming him, a lethargy of the mind so that he could not think but could only stand there in the stillness listening to nothing, and a lethargy of the body so that his limbs felt leaden and he had to hold himself up by hanging onto the bars.

Then the montage, the slow, hardly noticeable change into the motel room, seated on the brown bed, hands limp between his knees, watching the lazy green gas form the motel letters, sitting next to the drab, middle-aged woman who said nothing.

He would have to tell Sabrina. He could no longer bear the burden of this dream alone. He would have to explain and describe the terrible dream so that she would understand it as a dire prognostication—should they continue to plan and attempt to carry out murder. He would have to tell her.

Without looking at her, he told of the gray cement cell, the bars and shadows the trussed-up cot, the loneliness in which he cried out, without voice and without reply, then of the motel room. He could see the sign now with its traveling green vapor; he could see it, an echo to his dream of the room, the silence, and the middle-aged woman.

"Osborn," cried Sabrina. "Look at me."

But his eyes still followed the echoed green letters.

He talked of the dream, of punishment and regret, and lifted up his hands so he could cover and bury his face, shutting out what was left of the dream that still seemed so real.

"We mustn't do it, Sabrina," he said, his voice muffled against the palms of his hands. "The dream is a warning. We mustn't do murder."

"Osborn, we've already done it."

His hands trembled against his face.

"We did it. Don't you remember? Just like you said—staged a phony break-in and we shot her and left the place a mess like a burglary. . . . Osborn, that was twenty years ago. We're out now, both of us. Osborn, we can get married now. Look at me."

Slowly, he let his hands drop from his face, and slowly he turned to look at the middle-aged woman by his side.

"That wasn't a dream, what you said," Sabrina said. "It was real. It's been real for twenty years. It was the other that was a dream of you and me, young and in love."

A slow shudder shook his body. His groan made only the whisper of a sigh in the gray room.

"If this is waking," he said softly, "and that is sleeping, let me sleep now."

Osborn dropped back upon the brown bed and slept.

The cause of peace—how important, how attractive, how relevant, how vulnerable to perversion of selfish interests. Enter Mr. Gilbert's Behrens and Calder, who have begun to sense the odor of fish in unlikely places. . . .

MICHAEL GILBERT
The Peaceful People

"We call ourselves," said Lord Axminster, "the Peaceful People, and we are gathered here tonight to testify by our presence, our belief in the rightness, the cumulative force, and the inevitable ultimate success of the cause we all have at heart, the great cause of World Peace. It *must* prevail. There will be setbacks. No cause worthy of the name has ever succeeded without encountering, and overcoming, the opposition of bigotry, self-interest, and indifference. These are dragons to be slain, and we will slay them, not grudging the mortification and the wounds, the toil and the discomfort—"

The chair on which he was seated had, Mr. Behrens concluded, been designed by a sadist. Its seat was not only hard, but knobby in all the wrong places. It was tilted at an angle which threw you forward, but it was so short it gave no real support to the thighs.

"—but I will detain you no longer with blasts from my feeble trumpet. The object of our gathering is an exchange of ideas. A cross-fertilization of mind with mind. After we have heard the

report of our international secretary, Reverend Bligh, of the
Unitarian Church of Minnesota, and have considered the financial
statement produced by our hard-working treasurer, Mr. Ferris,
we will be pleased to deal with the many questions which must,
I feel sure, be agitating your minds."

Reverend Bligh plunged straight into business. "Support for
our movement," he said, "continues to be global. In the period
since we last met, messages of encouragement, and donations,
have been received from Anatolia, Algeria, and Andaman Islands,
Bahrain, Bangkok, Barbados—"

The raised edge of the seat dug into the femoral artery, cutting off the blood supply, and causing Mr. Behrens agonizing pins
and needles.

"—Venezuela, Western Germany, Yucatan, and Zanzibar. In the
light of such universal support we should be wrong to consider
ourselves as lonely fighters. We must feel ourselves to be, as it
were, the advance guard of a great invisible army with banners,
marching as to war." Feeling, perhaps, that this was an unhappy
metaphor, he added, "A war for peace," and sat down; whereupon
Mr. Ferris, armed with a bundle of documents, reeled off a quantity of figures. The young man in horn-rimmed spectacles on Mr.
Behren's left woke up and started to make notes. Pins and needles
were succeeded by complete paralysis of the lower leg.

Question time was kicked off with an inquiry from a lady who
had a nephew in Tanzania; it touched on devaluation (dealt with
by Mr. Ferris), the role of the church (a "natural" for Bishop
Bligh), and the iniquities of the government (blocked by Lord
Axminster, whose peerage was political). It did not take them
long to reach Vietnam.

A tall man, with insecure false teeth, managed to ask, "Would
the platform expound to us its proposals with regard to the
unhappy conflict at present decimating the peaceful people of
Vietnam?"

"Certainly," said Lord Axminster. "Our proposal is that the
fighting cease at once."

"On a more concrete plane," said the young man with horn-rimmed spectacles, "how is it proposed that this solution with which we all, of course, agree, should actually be attained?"

"It will be attained automatically, and immediately, when the United States withdraws its armed forces from the country."

When the applause had subsided, Mr. Behrens rose to his feet and said, "Would it be proposed that the South Vietnamese forces should also withdraw from the country?"

"Certainly not," said Lord Axminster. "The Vietnamese of the South would lay down their arms and embrace their brothers from the North in fraternal friendship."

Renewed applause.

When the meeting was finished, Mr. Behrens got out as fast as the state of his legs would allow.

He had spotted a familiar-shaped head of gray hair in the front row. When its owner emerged into the foyer, Mr. Behrens had his back turned and was examining one of the campaign posters. He allowed the gray-headed, red-faced figure to get ahead of him, then followed. A taxi cruised past. The man ignored it and strode on. Evidently he had a car parked nearby somewhere.

Mr. Behrens secured the taxi. He said to the driver, "If I was leaving here by car for the West End, which way would I have to go?"

The driver meditated. He said, "You're bound to go over the railway bridge. Carnelpit. All one way, see."

"Excellent," said Mr. Behrens. "Get to the railway bridge and stop there."

"Want me to follow someone?"

"That's the idea."

"Police?"

"Special constable."

"You look a bit old for a policeman."

"They're so short of men these days," said Mr. Behrens sadly. "They have to call up anyone they can get hold of."

It was an interesting chase. The gray-haired man was a bad-tempered driver and took a lot of chances with traffic lights and other motorists, but the taxi driver stuck to him with the ease of an expert angler playing a freshwater fish. They finished up, fifty yards apart, outside a house in Eaton Terrace. Mr. Behrens noted the number and signaled the taxi driver to keep going. Once they were around the corner he redirected him to the Dons-in-London Club. He had a long report to write.

Two hundred miles to the north, in the industrial outskirts of a Midland town, a different sort of meeting was taking place. A couple of hundred men, mostly in overalls or old working clothes, were crowded into the small open space in front of the main gates of the Amalgamated Motor Traction Company's factory. Since it was the lunch hour, many of them were eating sandwiches, out of small dispatch cases, but all were listening to the speaker.

"Punchy" Lewis had a jerky but forceful delivery. He had learned the value of short simple sentences, and his timing was expert. Lord Axminster could have learned a lot from him.

"And who gains from this lovely arrangement? Who actually gains from it? I'll tell you one thing. *We* don't. And if *we* don't, who does? You don't need to be a genius at mathematics to work that out. Who gains?"

"*They* do," shouted the crowd.

Mr. Lewis smiled down on his listeners. "You heard what they call it! They call it a new deal. That's not what I call it. I call it a crooked deal. A deal with a stacked deck. And shall I tell you who's champion at stacking cards?" Pause for effect. "The bloody Yanks, that's who."

There was a roar from the crowd.

Mr. Calder, who was standing inconspicuously in the rear, found it difficult to tell whether the applause was a tribute to the speaker's timing, or whether there was genuine warmth in it.

"That's what I said. The bloody Yanks." Lewis turned his head toward the building behind him and shouted, "And I hope you heard *that* in the board room." Swinging around on the meeting and lowering his voice to a conversational level, he added, "What we've had plenty of since these bloody Yanks took over Amalgamated Motors is trouble. A big handout of trouble. Now they want us to crawl in and lick their boots and say thank you for a lovely new deal. If *you* want to do that, *I* don't."

Mr. Calder became aware of movement behind him. The workers who wanted to get back, because the lunch break was over, were forming up in some sort of order at the rear of the crowd, which blocked the way. Lewis saw them too.

"I notice some of our mates," he said, "hanging around the back there, waiting to crawl in. That's why we're holding our meeting right here. Because if they want to crawl in they'll have to crawl past us, and we can just see them do it."

There were police there too, Mr. Calder noticed, in plain clothes as well as in uniform. Leading them was a superintendent, with the beefy red face and light blue eyes of a fighter. He pushed his way through the crowd and made straight for Lewis.

He said, "Stand back. Clear the way there. If these men want to get in, you've got no right to stop them."

Over the growing crowd noises Lewis could be heard shouting. "We've got our rights under the law! We're picketing this gate. Peaceful picketing."

The superintendent said, "Take that man."

And then pandemonium broke loose.

Mr. Calder had every intention of keeping out of trouble. He started to back away. As he did so, someone tripped him from behind. He put his hands out to save himself and received a violent blow to the middle of the back. Until that moment he had assumed that the hustling was accidental. Now he knew better. Instead of trying to turn, he let himself go, falling across the trampling legs. Two men tripped over him, and he pulled a third man's legs from under him, squirmed onto his hands and knees, and crawled to temporary safety behind the human barricade he had created.

As he scrambled to his feet he could hear the police whistles shrilling for reinforcements. A crash proclaimed that the plat-form had gone down. Mr. Calder waited no longer. He ran toward the side road, where he had left his car.

When he got there, he saw there was going to be more trouble. A truck was now parked across the nose of his car, and two men were sitting in it, watching him.

He said, "Would you mind moving that truck? I want to get out."

The men looked at each other, then climbed slowly out, one on each side of the cab. They were big men. One of them said, "What's the hurry, mate? You running away or something?" The other laughed and said, "Looks as if someone's been roughing him up already."

"That's right. And if he doesn't mind his manners he may be in for more."

Mr. Calder said, "I'm getting tired of this." He opened the door of his car. Rasselas came out and looked at the men, lifting his lip a little as he did so. Mr. Calder indicated the man on the right, and the dog moved toward him, his yellow eyes alight. The man stepped back quickly. As he did so, Mr. Calder hit the second man.

It was not a friendly blow. It was a left-handed short-arm jab, aimed low enough to have got him disqualified in any prizefight-ing ring. As the man started to double up, Mr. Calder slashed him across the neck with the full swing of his right arm, hand held rigid. The man went down and stayed down. Mr. Calder then transferred his attention to the other man, who was stand-ing quite still, his back against the truck, watching Rasselas.

"You can either move the truck," said Mr. Calder, nursing his right hand, which had suffered the impact, "or have your wind-pipe opened up."

"You would appear to have been in the wars," observed Mr. Fortescue. "That's a remarkably perfect example of a black eye that you have. How did you acquire it?"

Mr. Calder said, "I was trodden on. By a plainclothes police-man, actually."

"I trust you weren't attempting to assault him."

"I wasn't attempting to do anything except keep out of trouble. I was tripped from behind, hit as I went down, and trampled on."

"Accidents will happen."

"There was nothing accidental about it. I was on the edge of the crowd, minding my own business. But someone had spotted me. There were two more of the heavy brigade waiting for me by my car. Luckily I had Rasselas with me, and that evened things up."

"I see. And what was your impression of the meeting?"

"Manufactured, for public consumption. A very skilled piece of stage management by people who knew their job backwards. A couple of hundred genuine strikers, at least twenty professional agitators, and an equal number of reporters, who'd been tipped off beforehand that something was going to happen and were ready with cameras and notebooks to record it for posterity."

"It may not prove," said Mr. Fortescue, "that having reporters there was really such a good idea. The police impounded all the photographs they'd taken. I have copies here. Is there anyone you recognize?"

Mr. Calder looked at the photographs. Some of them seemed to have been taken from a window overlooking the scene and showed the whole crowd. Others were close-ups, taken by reporters in the melee itself. There was a fine shot of the platform going down and Punchy Lewis jumping clear.

"Is that Superintendent Vellacott on the ground?"

"It is indeed. He was very roughly handled and is now in the infirmary. He's still on the danger list."

Mr. Calder had carried one of the photographs over to the window to examine it. He said, "There are one or two faces here I seem to recognize."

"Indeed, yes. Govan, Patrick, Hall—"

"An all-star cast. What are they doing with them?"

"They're being held. The chief constable would like to charge them. He's very upset about his superintendent. I've tried to persuade him that it would be unwise. They'll make a public show out of the trial. If they're convicted, they're martyrs, and if they're acquitted, they're heroes."

Mr. Calder was still intent on the photographs. "That's me," he said. "You can just see my foot sticking out." He picked up another one. "What beats me is, who puts the money up for a show like this? Twenty top-class agitators at twenty-five pounds apiece. And they wouldn't get Punchy to come from South Wales for less than a hundred quid."

"Part, at least, of their funds come from a liberal and philanthropic body known as the Peaceful People. You may have seen their manifestos in the papers."

"I have indeed. I thought they were a harmless and woolly-minded lot of intellectual pinks."

"Behrens has attended six of their public meetings in the last two months. He found them excessively boring."

"*My* meeting wasn't boring!"

"Last night he thought he recognized Sir James Docherty in the audience. He followed him home to check up. It was Sir James."

"Odd place to find our current shadow foreign secretary."

"Sir James is an odd man," said Mr. Fortescue.

He said the same thing to the home secretary that afternoon.

Mr. Fortescue had served six home secretaries, and the incumbent was the one he admired most—a thick Yorkshireman, sagging a little now, but still showing the muscle and guts that had brought him up from a boyhood in the pits to his present job.

He said, "If things go wrong for us at the next election, Fortescue, he'll be one of *your* new bosses. I wish you luck with him. He was here this morning, complaining about some customs officer who had dared to open his bag when he was coming back from one of his trips to Paris. He asked me to discipline him. I refused, of course. Don't let's talk about Sir James. I want to hear about the riot."

"Calder was in the crowd. He confirms what we'd suspected. It was a put-up job. Aimed at the American management of Amalgamated Motors."

"Motive?"

"Anti-Americanism is the easiest platform for any rabble-rouser today."

"The easiest *and* the most dangerous. An open split between ourselves and the Americans would benefit the Russians enormously. And the Chinese still more. Who were behind this show? Do we know?"

"It was paid for, if not actually run, by the Action Committee of the Peaceful People. The main body is respectable, aboveboard, and full of public figures. It holds meetings, writes to the papers, and collects funds, which it hands over to its Action Committee, without much idea, I would suspect, of how the funds are going to be used."

"The tail wagging the dog, eh. They'd want more than casual money to finance the sort of national pressure they're keeping up."

"Yes," said Mr. Fortescue. "I fancy they're getting regular subsidies."

"Where from?"

"I'd very much like to find out. But it's not going to be easy. Some organizations are easy to penetrate. But not this particular committee. It's too closely interrelated. The members all know each other personally. They've worked together for years. If we tried to slip anyone in, it would simply be asking for trouble. The sort of trouble Calder ran into at the meeting."

He told the home secretary about it. The Yorkshireman said, "Ay, they're a rough crowd. What do you suggest?"

"We shall have to tackle it from the outside. Slower, but more certain. The first thing is to trace the money. It comes from somewhere abroad. Regularly, and in largish amounts. The Bank of

England is confident that it's not done by credit transfer. This
money actually comes in—that is, it's brought in physically. If we
knew how, it would be a start. Either the money would lead us
to the man, or the man to the money. When we've got proof, we'll
let the Peaceful People know exactly how they're being used.
They won't like it. And they'll stop financing their Action Committee. Without money they can't function."

The home secretary had listened to this exposition in silence—
a silence which continued after Mr. Fortescue had finished. At last
he said, "I don't have to tell you that things are moving very fast
in international politics at the moment. Personally, I'm not un-
hopeful. The outcome might be very good. On the other hand, it
might be very bad. And the smallest thing could tip the balance.
So don't take too long."

The offices of William Watson (Paris) Limited, Importers and
Exporters, are in a small street running south from the Quai des
Augustins. The head of the firm is a Mr. Mackenzie, but should
you ask to see him you will invariably find that he is absent, on
temporary sick leave. You will be invited to return in a week's
time.

If you know the form, you refuse to be put off and inquire instead for his deputy, Mr. Rathbone. Mr. Behrens evidently knew
the form. He was shown into an outer office and passed, after
scrutiny by a severe gray-haired lady, into the inner sanctum,
where a surprisingly youthful Mr. Rathbone was trying his hand
at a French crossword puzzle.

When the preliminaries had been concluded, he said, "Your
last signal stirred things up a bit, I can tell you. Do you mind ex-
plaining what's happening?"

Mr. Behrens said, "It's a long story. Four men were pulled in
after a strike meeting in the Midlands. A Welshman named
Lewis and three others. They had some trouble with them."

"Was that when the superintendent got kicked?"

"That's right. Well, they found money on all of them. New

notes, in sequence. And it was hot money—part of the proceeds of two bank jobs pulled by the Barrow gang last year. But—and this is the odd part—we knew for certain, because we'd had a reliable tip, that the loot had left the country. It was taken across the channel on the night of the robbery and was out of the country before the news of the robbery broke. It was cached somewhere here, in Paris, until the heat cooled off. Then it was offered, discreetly, for sale. At a heavy discount, of course. Three months ago the Chinese bought the lot."

"So that's why you asked us to keep an eye on their trade commission."

"That's right. We thought it might give us a lead."

"Well, we've got something for you. Whether it's a lead or not I don't know. You'll have to tell me."

Mr. Rathbone went across to a cabinet labeled "Export Samples," unlocked it, and extracted a folder.

"The only thing we've noticed in the least bit odd is that one of their chauffeurs has been paying regular visits, after dark, to a small place called the Hôtel Continental. It's a moderate-sized dump in the Place Languedoc. Not too expensive, much used by businessmen from England, civil servants coming to conferences, government delegates, and people of that type. The sort of place where they serve bacon and eggs for breakfast without being asked."

"And what does the chauffeur do when he gets there?"

"He disappears into the kitchen. What happens after that we haven't been able to find out."

"Possibly he has a girl friend in the kitchen staff."

"Maybe. When he's not being a chauffeur he's a colonel in the Chinese Army—so I think it's unlikely."

"Even colonels have human feelings," said Mr. Behrens. "But I agree there might be something in it. Could you get a list of all the guests—particularly the English guests—who have stayed at the Continental during the past six months?"

Mr. Rathbone extracted a list from the folder and said, "Your

wishes have been anticipated, sir. It goes back to the beginning
of the year."

Mr. Behrens studied the list. Two names on it, which occurred
no less than four times, appeared to interest him.

The prison interview room was quiet and rather cold. Punchy
Lewis, in custody, looked a smaller, less magnetic figure than
Punchy Lewis on a platform. His thin white face was set in ob-
stinate lines. He said, "It's bloody nothing to do with you where
I got the money from. It's not a crime in this country to own
money, or have they passed some law I haven't heard about?"

"If you don't realize the spot you're in," said Mr. Calder, "it's
a waste of time talking to you." He got up and made for the door.
A policeman was sitting outside, his head just visible through
the glass spyhole.

"No one's persuaded me I'm in a spot," said Lewis. "I didn't
do anything. If the police charge in while I'm speaking, and get
roughed up, they can't blame me. I didn't incite anyone. Every
word I said's on record. I've got nothing to be afraid of."

Mr. Calder perched on the corner of the table, like a man who
is in two minds whether to go or stay. He sat there for a long
minute while Lewis shifted uneasily in his chair. Then he
said, "I don't like you. I don't like the people you work for. And
if I didn't want something out of you personally, I wouldn't lift
a finger to help you. But that's the position. You've got one piece
of information I want. It's the only thing you've got for sale.
And I'll buy it."

"Talk straight."

"You think you're going to be charged with incitement, or assault, or something like that. You're not. The charge is receiving
stolen goods. And you'll get five or seven for it."

"The money, you mean? Talk sense, man. I didn't know it was
stolen."

"That's not what the police are going to say. Do you know
where that money came from? It was lifted from a bank—by the
Barrow gang last year."

"And just how are they going to show I knew that?"

"Be your age. They've already got two witnesses lined up who saw Charlie Barrow handing it to you in a Soho club."

"It's a lie."

"All right," said Mr. Calder calmly. "It's a lie. But it's what they're going to say, all the same. They don't like having their chaps kicked in the head. They're funny that way."

"The bloody sods," said Lewis. He thought for a moment, then added, "They'd do it, too."

Mr. Calder got up. He said, "I haven't got a lot of time to waste. Do we deal or not?"

"What's the proposition?"

"I want to know where that money came from. Who gave it to you. When and where and how. Details that I can check up. You give me that, and the charge of receiving goes out of the window."

Sir James Docherty said to his wife, "I'm afraid I'm off on my travels. It's Paris again."

"Oh, dear," said Lady Docherty. "So soon?"

"Needs must, when public duty calls. Is there any more coffee in that pot?"

"I can squeeze out another cup. Who is it this time?"

"I've got semiofficial talks with De Bessières at the Quai d'Orsay. There are occasions"—Sir James dropped two lumps of sugar into his coffee—"when the French government finds it easier to make unofficial suggestions to a member of the opposition than to the government. Then they can disclaim them if things don't work out."

"I'm sure they like talking to you because they know that you'll be foreign minister, as soon as the electorate comes to its senses."

"Maybe," said Sir James. "I'll be taking Robin with me."

A faint shadow crossed Lady Docherty's face. "Do you think you ought to?" she said. "He's been away such a lot. Four times to France, and those trips to the Midlands—"

"My dear," said Sir James, "you're talking as though they were

holiday jaunts. He's not wasting his time, you know. He's studying political science. And what better way to study political
science than to see politics in action. When he comes to France
with me he meets important people—people who matter. He can
see the wheels of international politics turning. When he goes
to the Midlands it's to study these industrial strikes at first
hand."

"Those terrible strikes. Why do they do it?"

"You mustn't assume," said Sir James, scooping the sugar out
of the bottom of the cup with his spoon, "that the faults are all on
one side. Management can be quite as bloody-minded as the workers. More so, sometimes."

In the next forty-eight hours a lot of apparently disconnected
activities took place. Mr. Calder spent the time working as a
porter in Covent Garden helping to load the trucks of an old
friend of his in the fruit trade. His spare time was divided between betting shops and public houses, neither in short supply
in that neighborhood. The money he made in the former he
spent in the latter.

Mr. Behrens, who had reserved a room at the Hôtel Continental in the Place Languedoc, spent his time making friends with
the hotel staff.

Young Robin Docherty had a prickly interview with his class
tutor at the London School of Economics. The tutor said that if
Robin spent all of his time running errands for his father in the
Midlands and trotting across to Paris with him in the intervals,
he was most unlikely to complete the scholastic side of his
studies satisfactorily.

The home secretary answered two questions and three supple-
mentaries about the strikes and disturbances which were para-
lyzing the motor industry. And Mr. Fortescue attended to the
customers at the Westminster branch of the London and Home
Counties Bank, granting one overdraft and refusing two.

Mr. Calder came to see Mr. Fortescue on the third day.

He said, "What Lewis told us has checked. I still don't know how the money gets into this country from France, but as soon as it does get here it's taken to a betting shop in Covent Garden. The Action Committee meets in the back room of a pub just down the road. It's on their instructions that the cash payments are handed out from the bookmakers. That's as much as I've been able to learn. I can't get any closer to these people. Some of them know me."

Mr. Fortescue considered the matter, rotating a silver pencil slowly over in his hand as he did so. Then he said, "If you've evidence that stolen money is passing through this betting shop, there should be no difficulty about getting permission to listen in to their telephone."

"You ought to get some useful tips on the races," said Mr. Calder.

Mr. Fortescue did not smile. His eyes were on his pencil. "Some sort of arrangements must be made for the reception of the money."

"That probably takes place after the shop's shut. There's a back entrance."

"No doubt. What I mean is, they must know when to expect the money and who's going to bring it. If we could find that out, we could put our finger on the courier. Then we might be able to backtrack to the person who brings it across the channel. We shall have to do it very carefully."

"You will indeed," said Mr. Calder. "These boys have got eyes in the back of their heads."

It was exactly a week later when Mr. Fortescue called on the home secretary and made his report.

"When you gave us permission to listen in to that betting shop, we started to make some real progress. It was the calls after hours that interested us. They were very guarded and came through different intermediaries, but we were able to trace them to their original sources."

"To the carrier of the money?"

"To his house."

"Excellent. Who is the man?"

"The owner of the house," said Mr. Fortescue with a completely impassive face, "is Sir James Docherty."

For a moment this failed to register. Then the home secretary swung around, his face going red. "If that's a joke—" he said.

"It's not a joke. It's a fact. The point of origin of these messages is Sir James's house in Eaton Terrace. Sir James also happens to be a member—a founding member—of the Peaceful People. Taken alone, I agree, neither of these facts is conclusive."

"Taken together, they're still inconclusive. You told me that the Peaceful People were backing their Action Committee with money. The messages might have been about that."

"They might have been," said Mr. Fortescue, "but they weren't. They had nothing to do with the official business of the society at all. And here are two other facts. One of my men has been making inquiries in Paris. He has established that there is a regular courier service between the Chinese Trade Commission and the Hôtel Continental. *Which happens to be Sir James's regular pied-à-terre in Paris.* Add to that the fact that Sir James's visits are usually arranged at official level. And that this enables him to bring in his valise, which is said to carry official papers, under diplomatic exemption."

The home secretary said, "Do you really believe, Fortescue, that a man in Sir James's position would lend himself to smuggling currency—a criminal maneuver?"

"Whether or not I believed it," said Mr. Fortescue, "would depend in the last analysis on my estimate of his character."

The home secretary turned this reply over in his mind for a few moments. Then he grunted and said, "He's a loud-mouthed brute, I agree. And I loathe his politics. But that doesn't make him a crook."

"I am told that he is something of a domestic tyrant. I would not assert that he beats his wife, but she certainly goes in considerable awe of him. His only son, Robin, has been forced to study political science and is dragged around at his father's chariot wheels, no doubt destined to be turned into a junior model."

"And that's our next foreign secretary. A fascist with a taste for gunboat diplomacy. What do you want to do? Tap *his* outgoing calls?"

"Yes. And have his mail opened. And have him watched day and night, in England and in France. If he's our man, he'll slip up, sooner or later, and we've got to be there to catch him when he falls."

"*If* he's our man," said the home secretary. "And if he isn't, by any chance, and if he finds out what we're doing—there'll be an explosion which will rock Whitehall from end to end."

"So I should imagine."

"The first head that will roll will be mine. But make no mistake about it, Fortescue. The second will be yours."

The young customs officer at Heathrow Airport produced a printed form and said, "You know the regulations, sir?"

"Since I have traveled backwards and forwards to Paris some twelve times this year," said Sir James Docherty, "I think you may assume that I have a nodding acquaintance with the regulations."

"And have you made any purchases while you were abroad?"

"None whatever."

"Or acquired any currency?"

Sir James looked up sharply and said, "I don't *acquire* currency when I travel. I spend it."

"I see, sir. Then would you mind opening this valise?"

"I would mind very much."

"I'm afraid you must, sir."

"Perhaps you would be good enough to examine the seal on the lock. I take it you are capable of recognizing an embassy seal?"

"Yes, sir."

"And perhaps you would also read this note from our ambassador, requesting you to confer the customary exemption from

search on this bag, which, I might add, contains important diplomatic documents."

The customs officer glanced at the letter, then handed it to
the thickset man in a raincoat who was standing beside the counter. This man said, "I'm afraid, sir, that I have an order here,
signed by the home secretary, overriding the ambassador's re-
quest."

"And who the hell are you?"

"My name's Calder."

"Then let me tell you, Mr. Calder—"

"I think we ought to finish this in private."

Sir James started to say that he was damned if he would,
realized that he was shouting and that people were starting to
look at him, and resumed his public-relations manner.

"If you wish to continue this farce," he said in a choked voice,
"by all means let us do it in private."

"But it wasn't a farce," said Mr. Calder. "There were three
thousand pounds, in fivers, stowed away flat, at the bottom of his
valise."

"What explanation did he give?"

"He was past rational explanation. He screamed a bit and
stamped and foamed at the mouth. Literally, I thought he was
having some sort of fit."

"But no explanation?"

"I gathered, in the end, that he said someone must have been
tampering with his baggage. Frame-up. Police state. Gestapo.
That sort of line."

"I see," said Mr. Fortescue. He said it so flatly that it made Mr.
Calder look up.

"Is something wrong, sir?"

"I gather," said Fortescue, "that Sir James has managed to persuade our masters that we have made a very grave mistake."

"But good God! I *saw* the notes. We all did. How does he suggest they got there?"

"He suggests," said Mr. Fortescue sadly, "that Behrens put them there. I am seeing the home secretary in an hour's time. I rather fear that we may be in for trouble."

"Incredible though it may seem," said the home secretary, "it really does appear that the one person who couldn't have put the money there was Sir James himself—unless he bribed half the ambassador's private staff."

"What exactly happened?"

"Our ambassador had a highly confidential document—a memorandum in the general's own hand—and Sir James offered to act as courier. The head of chancery put the document in Sir James's valise—which was almost empty, as it happens—saw the valise sealed, and handed it to the ambassador's secretary, who took it back to the hotel and himself saw it locked up in Sir James's bedroom. The secretary didn't leave the hotel. He stayed there, lunched with young Robin, and the two of them escorted the valise to the airport."

"And what was Sir James doing all this time?"

"Sir James was having lunch with our ambassador, the French minister of the interior, and the wife of the French minister of the interior."

"How, precisely, is it suggested that the notes got into the valise?"

"There's no mystery about that. Microscopic examination of the seal—what was left of it—shows that it had been removed, whole, with a hot knife and refixed with adhesive. Probably during lunch hour."

"And it's suggested that Behrens did that?"

"He was at the hotel."

"So were two hundred other people."

"You don't think, Fortescue, that he might—just conceivably—have thought he was being helpful."

Mr. Fortescue said, "I have known Behrens for thirty years.

Impossible." After a pause he added, "What is Sir James going to do?"

"He's been to the Prime Minister. He wants the people responsible discovered and dealt with."

Mr. Fortescue smiled a wintry smile. He said, "I do not often find myself in agreement with Sir James, but that sentiment is one with which I heartily concur. I shall need to make an immediate telephone call to Paris."

"I'm afraid you won't catch Behrens. He's on his way back."

"Excellent," said Mr. Fortescue. He seemed to have recovered his good humor. "Excellent. We may need him. The person I wished to speak to was the ambassador's private secretary. Perhaps your office could arrange it for me? Oh, and the manager of the Hôtel Continental. Then we must have Behrens intercepted at the airport and brought straight around to Sir James's house—to meet me there."

"You're going to see Sir James?"

"I have really no alternative," said Mr. Fortescue genially. "In his present mood, he would certainly not come to see us, would he?"

Sir James was at ease in front of his drawing-room fire, the bottom button of his waistcoat undone, a glass of port in one hand, an admiring audience of two, consisting of wife and son, hanging on every word.

"And it might have come off," he said, "if I hadn't been wide-awake and, I admit it, had a bit of luck. I could have been in a very awkward spot."

"And now it's them who are on the spot," said Robin with a grin.

"In the old days," said Lady Docherty, "they'd have had their heads cut off."

"Even if they don't lose their heads, I think we can be sure that the people concerned will lose their jobs. I'm seeing the Prime Minister again tomorrow. I wonder who *that* can be?"

"I'll go," said Robin. "The girl's out. What do I do if it's a reporter?"

"Invite him in. The wider the publicity this deplorable matter receives, the better for"—he was going to say "my chances at the next election," but changed it to—"the country."

Robin came back, followed by two men. "I don't think it *is* the press," he said. "It's a Mr. Fortescue and a Mr. Behrens."

"I see," said Sir James coldly. "Well, I've nothing much to say to you that can't be said, in due course, in front of a tribunal of inquiry, but if you've come to apologize, I'm quite willing to listen. No, stay where you are, my dear. And you too, Robin. The more witnesses we have, the better."

"I agree," said Mr. Behrens.

"Kind of you."

"It would be appropriate if your son were to remain, since most of what I have to say concerns him." Mr. Fortescue swung around on the boy, ignoring Sir James, "I've just spoken to the ambassador's private secretary in Paris. He tells me that you were away from the luncheon table for nearly half an hour. Making a long-distance call, you said. Why did you lie about it?"

"Don't answer him," said Sir James. But the boy appeared to have forgotten about his father. He said, in his pleasant, level voice, "What makes you think it was a lie, sir?"

"I know it was a lie because I've talked to the hotel manager. He tells me that no long-distance call in or out was recorded during that period. On the other hand, Behrens here saw you leave the dining room. He followed you up to the bedroom, saw you go in, and heard you lock the door."

"And who do you suppose," fumed Sir James, "is going to believe your agent provocateur?"

"Well, Robin," Mr. Fortescue went on, "if you *weren't* telephoning, what were you doing?"

Sir James jumped up and forced himself between them. "I'll deal with this," he said. "If you think you can shift the blame onto my son on manufactured evidence—"

"Don't you think he might be allowed to speak for himself?"

"No, I don't."

"He'll have to, sooner or later."

"Unless you can produce something better than the word of your own spy, he's not going to have to answer at all."

"Oh, there's plenty of evidence," said Mr. Fortescue mildly. "Robin's been a member of the Action Committee of your society for two years—that's right, isn't it, Robin? I would surmise that during all that time he's been using *your* diplomatically protected luggage to bring back funds for the committee from France."

"Lies," said Sir James in a strangled voice.

"He has also taken a personal part in a number of demonstrations. He was up in the Midlands last week—"

"Collecting information for me."

"No doubt. He also put in some time kicking a police superintendent. Have you the photographs, Behrens?"

Sir James glared at the photograph. "A fake!"

Robin said, "Oh, stop bluffing, Dad. Of course it isn't faked. How could it be?"

There was a moment of complete silence, broken by Lady Docherty, who said, "Robin," faintly.

"Keep out of this, Mother."

Sir James recovered his voice. He said. "Your mother has every right—"

"Neither of you," said Robin, silencing his parent with surprising ease, "has any rights in the matter at all. I'm twenty-one. And I know what I'm doing. You talk about violence and ruthlessness, Dad. But that's all you ever do—you and your Peaceful People. Talk, talk. I don't believe"—a faint smile illuminated his young face—"that you've ever actually hit anyone in your life. Really hit them, meaning to hurt. Have you?" Sir James was past speech. "Well, I have, and I'm going to go on doing it, because if you truly believe in something, that's the only way you're going to make it happen—in your own lifetime, anyway. By breaking the law and hurting people and smashing things. And young people all over the world have seen it. They know what to do. Don't talk. Kick out."

Mr. Fortescue said, "I take it that includes kicking people when they're on the ground."

"Of course," said Robin. "It's much easier to kick them when they're lying down than when they're standing up. Why not?"

"I left that to Sir James to answer," said Mr. Fortescue, sometime later, to the home secretary. "He's a politician and used to answering awkward questions."

If we needed to be reminded that the crime story and the super-
natural are not without common ground, we have the present tale,
which otherwise seems to escape classification. Many loose ends,
much unexplained—anathema in the detective story—but how
powerful and disturbing the cumulative effect is here.

J. F. PEIRCE
The Total Portrait

Some days stand out in our lives more than others. For me such a day was a Friday in May of 1952. The mail that day brought only one thing of interest—an envelope addressed to me in care of my publisher. Inside were a round-trip plane ticket to Santa Fe and an address. Nothing more.

I was at loose ends at the moment, ready for a vacation, for something different. But even if I'd been in the midst of something big, I would have gone. My curiosity would have made me. I called the airline, checked the afternoon flight, then started to pack.

William Randolph Hearst had died at the end of April, and I had cranked out a biography of that multifaceted man in less than two weeks. At the time I was caught up in a racket that might be called "instant journalism." I had got into it six years before when one of the paperback publishers had hired me to write a book on Van Meegeren, the artist who had counterfeited Vermeer's paintings during the war. The publisher had given me just two weeks to knock out fifty thousand words.

Remember the multitude of books that came out after Eichmann was captured, after Eisenhower died, after the Kennedys and Martin Luther King were assassinated? There were a dozen on the newsstands about each of them within a matter of weeks. That's instant journalism.

In most cases you've never heard of the authors. And for good reason. Nobody in his right mind would write such a book. It's killing to body and mind, and most of all, to spirit. Some are "committee" jobs, the work of a dozen writers published under a single pseudonym. But most are a paste-and-scissors patchwork of clippings from articles and other books. The editor who hired me told me how to go about it.

I hired a couple of college students to comb the libraries for newspaper and magazine articles about Van Meegeren, then read and regurgitated them, half-digested, into a Dictaphone for a secretary to type up. I didn't even correct the galleys. The editor did that himself.

After it was over and I'd had a chance to catch my breath, I asked the editor, "Why me?"

"Because of the book you wrote on Vermeer," he answered.

Because of a book published five years before, a book that had sold exactly 167 copies, fifty-nine of which I'd bought at a remainder price to give to relatives and friends. Actually it was a rewrite and expansion of my college thesis that a publisher, now no longer in business, had mistakenly seen fit to print.

At any rate, searching for a writer, the editor had looked up books and articles on Vermeer, seen my name on a number of them (I'd written articles on Vermeer for art magazines, too), and obtained my address from one of the magazines. It was as simple as that.

My book, *Van Meegeren, Counterfeiter or Collaborator?*, came out in record time, before I'd even had a chance to spend my ad-

vance—which, as it turned out, was the only payment I received
for it. After that I made it a practice to write all such books for
a flat fee, paid in advance.

The address I'd been given was that of a house hidden in the
foothills some distance from Santa Fe. At first glance it looked
like any other adobe dwelling, but up close it turned out to be a
dun-colored concrete building that resembled a small fort. Its
massive oak door was decorated with wrought iron, but the
metal seemed more for reenforcement than ornamentation.

As I was about to knock, the door was opened by a little man
with quick, precise movements. I started to introduce myself, but
before I could say anything, he said, "Come in, Mr. Reynolds,"
and my mouth was still open as I entered. Obviously he was expecting me, but he had no way of knowing exactly when I would
arrive. For that matter, I could have cashed in the ticket and
pocketed the money.

He gestured to a chair and said, "Coffee—black," and then
disappeared through an archway before I could answer.

I glanced about. What little furniture there was seemed lost
in the room. I was reminded of the home of a friend who had
built too big a house, then couldn't afford to furnish it. Though
there was no north window, it was obviously an artist's studio.
The light for painting was artificial, spotlights and the like. A
small painting was clamped in an easel at the far side of the room,
near a huge stone fireplace.

I crossed to examine the painting, expecting it to be a work
in progress, but was surprised to discover that it was of the man
who had admitted me, my host, showing him some five or six
years younger.

Though I'd never seen the painting before, it was irritatingly
familiar. Then recognition came with a sudden shock. The painting had the same style and composition as a Vermeer, the same
palette and patina, the same brush strokes. It was the work of an
artist who could have forged a Vermeer painting. I wondered

if he would have tried it if Van Meegeren had not anticipated him and been caught.

"From your expression," my host said beside me, "I can tell that you've added two plus two and come up with five."

I hadn't heard him return.

I looked at him more closely. He was wearing a T-shirt with horizontal blue and white stripes, blue denim trousers, and navy-colored canvas slippers. His face, his hands, his clothes, were flecked all over with paint, reminding me slightly of the pointillist style.

I judged him to be five-two (I towered over him) and to weigh at most one-twenty. He had curly black hair, and eyes of an unbelievable cornflower blue that looked as though some artist had painted them.

His face was unlined, as if he never used it or as if it were a mask that he hid behind to keep from revealing his emotions. His complexion beneath the flecks of pigment was a pasty white. I took him to be one of the night people. He looked thirty-five, but I know now that he was my own age—forty.

He handed me a cup of coffee, and I thanked him.

"I'm Sloan Frazier," he said, his voice as expressionless as his face.

I recognized the name. In fact, I'd seen examples of his work. He painted portraits of society women and their children for substantial fees. In his own way he was the same kind of artistic hack I was.

"As you can see," he said, nodding toward the self-portrait, "I'm out of step with my time. I paint with skill and precision at a time when shapeless daubs suggest more to mindless men than beauty or reality."

His speech sounded memorized. I'm not sure now what he went on to say, but there was no question in my mind that he'd taught himself to paint like Vermeer, only to be foiled by Van Meegeren's arrest and exposure, a victim not so much of the time as of timing.

"What do you want of me?" I asked when he seemed unable to come to the point.

For answer he said, "Let me show you," and crossing the room, he drew back a curtain of beige monk's cloth that covered one entire wall.

I had assumed that the curtain shut out the light from a tier of windows overlooking the valley below, but instead it concealed a miniature art gallery: seven paintings of uniform size and shape, all masks. And when he turned on the overhead lights, I realized with a shock of surprise that they were all of *me*. Seven portraits of me at different ages, from childhood to old age.

These paintings were not "Vermeers," but sophisticated, multi-colored "Rorschach tests" in which the viewer saw not only what was on the surface of the canvas but also what was hidden in the convolutions of the subconscious mind. The colors had been laid on heavily with a palette knife, and the hard light on the built-up layers of paint cast subtle shadows, giving the masks a three-dimensional effect that added to their air of mystery, to what one saw or thought he saw.

I was standing before a mask of me during my years in the army, shortly after my wife's death. I could recall no other painting exactly like it, yet it was similar to several made at the time— or rather, like a pastiche of all of them combined.

Frazier gestured toward three connected lines, like a V with a flat bottom, painted on the floor in front of each picture, then said, "Each line is at the right distance from the paintings to give the best view."

I was standing on the center line, the flat bottom of the V.

"Move to the diagonal line on the left," Frazier commanded.

I did as directed, and a second mask came into focus, and I was shocked to see myself as a beast of prey, cruelty and evil underlying every feature.

"That's me?" I said.

Instead of answering, Frazier gestured to the diagonal line to my right I moved, and as my toes touched the line, a third mask of myself at that age came into focus. This mask gave me the look of a poet, a version of myself I found easier to rationalize.

I stepped forward, to the picture, and discovered that it was not one painting but three. Ribs of some rigid material had been attached to the surface of the canvas, and both sides of the ribs were painted, so that looking at the picture head-on I saw one mask—the ribs disappearing from view—and looking at it from the right or left I saw another mask, painted on the sides of the ribs. From the middle line the ribs seemed to merge, to form a solid plane. And though each of the three masks was different from the other two, all three were clearly related.

"You're wondering what it means," Frazier said.

"Yes, though I suppose each portrait represents me at a given age and that all seven represent my entire life. Shakespeare's seven ages of man."

"Right. But there's more to them than that. The mask seen from the left of each portrait represents your physical or animal nature at that age—which of the seven deadly sins possessed you or will possess you and to what degree. The mask seen from the right represents your aesthetic or spiritual nature. The two together shape the center portrait—you as others see you, as you perhaps see yourself, your good and evil qualities blended in the role you play."

As Frazier talked, I sipped my coffee and studied each of the paintings in turn, comparing them with what I knew, or thought I knew, about myself at the period depicted. I could feel Frazier's gaze on me as he watched my reactions, saw the shocks of recognition that jolted me as I discovered things that I had not known about myself, but that I now knew to be true from the insights which the paintings gave me.

The center portrait of me as a schoolboy was the Buddha-like mask I'd presented to the world at that time. The same painting seen from the left was Gluttony incarnate—I had been extremely fat as a boy; whereas the one seen from the right showed a thin, intense, owlish youth, old before his time.

Frazier put my thoughts into words. "Who was it who said, 'Inside every fat man is a thin man screaming to get out'?"

I shrugged and moved along the line. The center mask of the fifth portrait resembled me to a marked degree; still, it wasn't me. It had a leonine cast foreign to my countenance.

"It doesn't look like me," I protested.

"It will. It will," Frazier answered.

Gertrude Stein had said as much about the portrait Picasso had painted of her, and he had replied in kind. And in time she had grown to look like her portrait. Could this happen to me, I wondered.

The center painting of the final portrait showed me as an old man looking into space, into nothingness. No, not nothingness. Into hell. I shivered.

"I—*it* looks almost insane," I said.

"Almost?" Frazier said mockingly.

I remembered an episode from the autobiography of Arnold Genthe, the photographer who took the famous photographs of the San Francisco earthquake: He wrote of seeing the philosopher Nietzsche in old age, sitting in a room staring into space, obviously insane, and described him as looking like an eagle who had flown too near the sun.

Though I swear I did not speak aloud, Frazier summed up what I'd been thinking: "Like Icarus, who flew too near the sun—and fell," he said.

I turned and stared at him a moment dumbly, but his expression told me nothing, and I returned to my study of the paintings. Teilhard de Chardin said, "Give a man a mask, and he will tell you all about himself." Give him many masks which he can hide behind, I thought, and he will reveal his whole world.

"What gave you the idea for all this?" I asked.

"Many things," Frazier answered. "The original suggestion came from a visit I made to a palace in Sicily. The nobleman who built it was a hunchback, the butt of much cruel humor. To revenge himself he had his garden decorated with statues of those who had taunted and ridiculed him, each statue in some way deformed to reveal the human weaknesses, the secret vices, the hidden humps, of the person represented."

How many hidden humps did Frazier have, I wondered.

"My reading added other things," he continued. *"As You Like It* suggested the seven ages of man; *Dr. Faustus,* the seven deadly sins; *The Picture of Dorian Gray* and *Dr. Jekyll and Mr. Hyde,* the double nature of man, the difference between appearance and reality."

"But how did you get to know me?" I demanded. "From reading about me? From my work? How were you able to portray me at so many ages? From photographs that show what I am or was, from pictures of my family that show what I might become? And how did you get such photographs?"

Frazier smiled, but with his eyes only.

"Would you believe me if I said it was ESP?" he asked.

"No."

"Too bad. Because that's the answer."

"It would be easier to believe you're in league with the devil."

He cocked his head to one side as if considering the possibility.

"That, too," he said matter-of-factly.

Everything about him made me angry, though I tried not to show it. Of course, what really angered me was that this stranger knew more about me than I knew about myself, that he had revealed things to me I had hidden from myself.

At last, unable to control myself any longer, I all but shouted, "Either you're a con man or a blackmailer! I don't know which."

"Not a great artist?" he said, pretending to be hurt.

"What do you want of me?" I demanded. "Why did you choose me for your victim?"

"Because I want you to write up what I'm doing—painting a portrait of the total man, from birth to death. One that reflects what he was, what he is, what he will become. A series of revelations."

"So that he can change if he doesn't like what he sees?"

I hadn't liked much of what I'd seen in my portraits.

Frazier shrugged. "I don't believe one can change," he said.

"You're a fatalist?"

"No. I just don't believe one can change his basic character. Not to any significant degree. I think that once you establish what you are, you can't change what you'll become."

"I see."

"Do you?" he said contemptuously.

My anger flared again. I raised my arm to strike out at him, then remembered what I'd seen in one of the paintings, and the movement metamorphosed into a gesture toward the painting. "You give me the look of a murderer," I said. "I don't consider myself capable of committing murder."

Frazier glanced at the portrait of me as a soldier.

"Oh, I've killed," I said, "but that was war—impersonal. I had no choice. It was kill or be killed. I regret it now. But at the time I didn't think about it much—it had to be done."

"But you didn't try to avoid doing it. You weren't a conscientious objector."

"No," I confessed. "In fact, I enlisted. If I hadn't, I might never have been taken." Not wanting to think about it, I changed the subject. "What you really want of me," I said, "is an advertisement—to sell your paintings."

"Not one. Several."

Again he smiled with his eyes only, and something told me to stay out of it; but it was too good a story. I finished my coffee and set the cup on the stone mantelpiece.

"Say I do," I said, "what's in it for me?"

"You've already decided."

It was true. I couldn't deny it.

"How much do you want for these?" I asked, making a sweeping gesture to take in all the paintings.

"Three thousand each," he answered without hesitation, "or twenty thousand for all seven."

I sucked in my breath involuntarily.

"Or I'll make you a complete set of color photographs for two hundred and you can use them to illustrate your articles."

I started to shake my head—but instead, I nodded. . . .

The articles were duly written and illustrated with selected views from the twenty-one photographs. And the articles sold without difficulty to expensive, limited-circulation magazines subscribed to by the very rich—men in big business, international society, and government who could afford portraits that sold for a minimum of twenty thousand dollars.

Six months passed before the first of the articles was published. By then I was in the Culion leper settlement in the Philippines undergoing treatment for leprosy, which I had apparently contracted in the South Pacific during the war. I was in Japan doing a series on Oriental art when I took ill. Actually the symptoms had appeared in me two years earlier, but my physician, being unfamiliar with the disease, had treated me for tuberculosis, which it resembles. The symptoms had been mild, and neither of us had taken them seriously.

But in Japan I had an acute attack, and the doctor the hotel recommended recognized the symptoms immediately and made arrangements for me to go at once to Culion.

During my first few years there I failed to respond to treatment. My condition got worse, and I became weaker and weaker from recurrent inflammation of the kidneys. Then, slowly, I began to recover, and after years of treatment with the highly toxic drug dapsone, I was finally pronounced cured and permitted to return home.

This is not the place for a detailed account of either leprosy or its treatment; therefore, I will merely catalog its effects on me. Discolored patches appeared on my skin. My eyebrows fell out. My nose and ears became thickened and enlarged, my nails hard and clawed. My breathing and speech were impaired, and I experienced a loss of sensation and muscular power. Fortunately, on my recovery, I regained most of my natural resistance.

During my eleven years at Culion I devoted my time to study

and writing. Among other things I wrote a book, *Mask of the Lion*, in which I discussed leprosy and described my own leonine appearance. The money I received from this writing, along with a small inheritance from my parents enabled me to be self-supporting.

On my return to the United States early in February 1964 I picked up the mail that had been held for me by my publisher, including copies of the magazines that had printed my writings. Thumbing through these magazines, I came across one of the articles I'd done on Frazier. Over the years I had forgotten all about him. Now memory came flooding back, for the picture that illustrated the article could have served as the dust-jacket illustration for my book *Mask of the Lion*. I shivered. I had grown to look like Frazier's painting.

I remembered standing in front of the original in Frazier's studio and saying, "It doesn't look like me," and Frazier's matter-of-fact reply: "It will. It will." And again I shivered.

What had happened to Frazier, I wondered. I had been cut off from the world, true, but if his paintings had made any sort of splash, surely the waves would have reached me.

I crossed to the telephone, but calls to editors and collectors brought me no information. Most of them remembered reading my articles on Frazier, but none recalled hearing anything further about him. I even tried getting Frazier's telephone number, but if he had a phone, the number was unlisted.

The next day I searched the *Art Index* for reference to him. Except for my own articles, I found none.

The one result of my inquiries was a brief syndicated story in the newspapers about my return home.

Two weeks later I received an envelope, postmarked New York City, that contained a news clipping and the illustration from my article on Frazier. Nothing more.

The clipping, which was some years old, was an obituary of the internationally famed architect Ernst Stern. At one time I had planned doing an article on Stern and had collected everything I could find about him, looking for a lead that might suggest a different approach to the man and his work. But I found none—at least, none that I cared to use. An article in one of the news magazines gave the impression that though the old man was married—to a woman many years his junior—and the father of two lovely young daughters that—

Nothing had been spelled out, so obviously nothing could be proved, but there were references to "his handsome male secretary" and to his surrounding himself with "attractive young men." None of the other articles contained similar references. They concentrated on the old man's outstanding work.

After reading the obituary, a brief description of Stern's death by his own hand—he had put the barrel of a shotgun in his mouth and pulled the trigger—I turned to the illustration of me. Across its face someone had scrawled *Murderer!*

I was more puzzled than shocked. What did it mean, I wondered. Then it hit me. All the articles on Stern had referred to his narcissism. His office was decorated, not with illustrations of his works—as one would expect—but with paintings, photographs, and sculptures of himself. Obviously he would have been interested in having Frazier do his portrait and would have been able to afford it.

I rented a car at the airport and drove out to Frazier's studio. Again it reminded me of a fortress. And this time I recognized why. It had no windows. Once more the door was opened before I could knock, and again I had the feeling that Frazier was expecting me.

The studio room we entered was now elegantly furnished, and a fire crackled in the huge stone fireplace. Frazier gestured to a chair, and I sat down.

"I see you have grown to look like my painting," he remarked.

It was a statement of fact. I would have thought there'd be an air of smugness about him, but there wasn't. He seemed more subdued, almost afraid.

I handed him the envelope I'd received in the mail, and he glanced at the clipping, then at the illustration. He looked up, his face devoid of expression.

"So your game *was* blackmail," I said.

He didn't deny it, and I continued, "Stern was a homosexual. You guessed it, then painted his secret for all to see."

"No," Frazier said. "Not his secret—his secrets. His masks revealed many secrets that he had concealed, not from himself, as you concealed yours, but from his family, his friends, his associates—from the world. His animal and spiritual masks looked nothing like him at any age."

"Then why didn't he just deny them?"

"I don't know. Their very ugliness seemed to fascinate him."

"Perhaps he wanted to view them in secret, remind himself of what he was. Like Dorian Gray."

"No. Once he'd paid me the sixty thousand that I asked for them, he burned them on the spot—in that fireplace. He committed suicide the next day."

I stared into the fire and saw the old man as he watched his secret life go up in flames. No matter what his crimes, I thought, he hardly deserved that.

"No," I said. "He didn't commit suicide. You murdered him."

It was a moment before Frazier answered. When he did, I could barely hear his voice above the fire's crackle.

"Yes," he confessed. "I murdered him—with *your* help."

The words froze me. I felt completely numb. Then the numbness burned away, and I knew I had been used. But what bothered me was that I had known I was being used, had let myself be used. Rage flared up in me—as much at myself as at Frazier. I sprang to my feet, the beast in me suddenly gone mad, and struck out at him, and struck and struck. . . .

I've always been suspicious of people who claimed they blacked out before committing some horrible crime. Perhaps afterward, I thought, but not before. Now I'm not sure. Certainly there was a moment when the beast within possessed me, directed my actions. The next thing I knew, I was standing over Frazier's bloody, mangled body. I checked to see if anything could be done for him, but he was beyond human assistance.

My first reaction was to notify the police, but before I did, I searched for any paintings that Frazier might have hidden, so that I could destroy them. But except for some concealed behind the monk's-cloth curtain, I found none. And after viewing those, I decided not to turn myself in, hoping that in time my writing would serve some larger purpose and atone for my act.

The paintings that made me decide were of Frazier himself. I'll not describe all of them, only the fifth of his self-portraits, the center mask of which had deep scratches across one check as if from the claws of a lion. Frazier's face now bore similar scratches.

The fifth mask seen from the left was largely in red and black, with touches of blue and yellow. It seemed on fire, the flames suggesting horns, giving a satanic cast to the features. The mask seen from the right was faceless—a mere skull-like outline with gaping holes where the eyes, nose, and mouth had been. Tears of zinc white dripped from the eyeless sockets. The features of this mask had collected in a shriveled heap at the bottom of the painting where the tears had washed them.

There were only the five paintings—no sixth or seventh.

I had the strange feeling that Frazier himself had sent me Stern's obituary, that he had scrawled *Murderer!* across the face of the illustration, knowing that they would bring me here. The postmark on the envelope meant nothing—all sorts of people advertised that they would remail letters from New York for a small fee.

But why had Frazier done it? Why had he brought me here, knowing I would kill him? *Why?* So that he could be punished? Were the masks really the result of ESP, or of research and intuition? Is there such a thing as fate—or do we control our own destinies?

At times I seem to glimpse an answer. Life must retain its mystery if it is to have a meaning. To know what is coming and to be unable to change it is untenable. Not knowing makes life an adventure from day to day. We must fly ever upward toward the sun, till its brightness blinds us and its fire melts the wax of our wings and we plunge earthward to our death.

But more and more, like Baudelaire as he lay dying in that all-white room in Belgium, I feel the wind from the wings of madness. . . .

To a glorious melange of absurdities and eccentricities, add an author's keen ability to tie things together with thread we hadn't realized was there and you have the likes of the following, featuring—as Ellery Queen put it in introducing the story originally —"the most unusual weapon in the history of fictional (and factual) crime. . . ."

R. BRETNOR
A Matter of Equine Ballistics

If Alastair Drummond of Skrye had not escaped from the tower in 1654 and taken service in Muscovy under the Czar Alexei Mihailovitch to fight the Polonian and the Turk, more than three centuries later his descendant, Alastair Alexandrovitch Timuroff, would probably not have been a dealer in antique arms. Nor would he have been in the north of England trying to buy the great Lessingham Collection when the curious case of the horse Hinchpeth came to public notice. Nor would he ever have been, among his many brief careers, an officer in the cavalry of the Argentine Republic. In short, given all these *ifs*, the violent and tragic death of Sir Cedric Substance would have remained unsolved—or, even worse, might have been "solved" erroneously.

Timuroff was the guest of Major Mark Drummond-Mowbrey, M.C., chief constable of Hallamshire and a distant relation.

Like the Russian Fanshawes, the Timuroffs had always maintained their British connections, sending their eldest sons at least
to be educated at Edinburgh or Oxford, and sometimes bringing
brides back to Russia, until the revolution tumbled everything
down. The chief constable had, indeed, known Timuroff since
boyhood. Besides, he had been a close friend of old Lessingham's,
and he collected Scottish flintlock pistols, in which the Lessingham Collection was particularly strong. He was being very helpful to Timuroff.

They were having breakfast on the loggia when the news
reached them. It was a splendid midsummer day: you could look
down on the valley from the village of Upper Tiptilton at one
end to Lower Tiptilton at the other, with the squat town of
Frognall just showing its dull factory roofs in the middle-dis-
tance, and the absurd parapet of Parmenter's Folly rearing up
out of the trees halfway to Lower Tiptilton. Timuroff and his
host had been arguing, in a friendly way, about horses, Timuroff
maintaining that all horses were incredibly and incorrigibly stupid, and Drummond-Mowbrey asserting with fervor that they were
the best friends a cavalryman like himself ever had.

"In fact, Tim," he suggested, "after lunch let's ride down to
the battle together. I'd imagine my boots and breeches still fit
you—"

"The *battle?*" Timuroff interrupted.

"Didn't I tell you? The reenactment of the Battle of Woads—
Wars of the Roses, I think. They're going to lay siege to the
folly, storm it, and burn the place down. It's been condemned
anyhow, to make way for something dull and socialistic. Pilfer and
Crombie and Substance and their crowd have their siege engines
down there all ready to go. They brought them in yesterday, behind tractors, with half the Tiptilton youth dressed up in
medieval costumes. It's for sweet charity's sake, naturally—the
tourists are expected to leave behind hundreds of pounds."

Timuroff is a hard compact man—so much so that he usually
looks a bit smaller than his five-foot-eleven. His forehead has a

touch of the Tartar about it, which seems strange over eyes and a jaw straight from the Hebrides. The scar on his left cheek—the result, as he puts it quite truthfully, of a car accident in Montevideo—runs from the trim corner of his graying moustache to his cheekbone. He groaned, but his groan, as always, sounded implausible.

"Must we go?" he complained. "All collectors are crazy, but these let's-go-back-to-the-past, let's-build-siege-engines people are the maddest of all. Why would anyone want to spend twice the price of a Rolls-Royce on an enormous catapult or ballista?"

"They're useful," replied the chief constable. "You can bundle up enemy ambassadors and send them back over the walls with your compliments."

"Well, if you'll promise me *that* as part of the program, I'll even ride one of your nags," Timuroff said.

"You can take that lovely tall mare that Mary's been riding." Drummond-Mowbrey was obviously pleased. "You can prance up and down watching the carnage, like Napoleon in one of those David paintings—" He broke off. A car had just screamed its brakes at the front of the house. "Now, who can *that* be?"

Car doors banged; voices were heard; and presently a mountainous man in a black suit and bowler hat came around the corner of the house.

"Oh, my God," muttered Drummond-Mowbrey.

"Who is he?" asked Timuroff.

"He's Police Superintendent Hesiod Plumley. He is a bird of ill omen. Whenever anything really dreadful happens, he rushes to tell me in person; then he accuses me falsely of meddling too much in procedural matters. And he always declaims as if he were reading Blair's *The Grave* at a funeral. Well—" He rose; the bird of ill omen was now within earshot. "Good morning, Plumley. Is anything wrong?"

The superintendent advanced in an ominous silence. Six feet away, he came to a halt, his dewlaps quivering. *"Wrong, sir?"* he boomed dismally. "You may well ask what is wrong. Murder's been done, sir. If I may say so, murder most foul! The first murder we've had hereabouts"—he opened his notebook—"since July the twelfth, nineteen-thirty-seven."

"An interesting datum," said the chief constable, "but who has been murdered?"

"Sir Cedric Substance, sir."

"How? Who did it? Out with it, Plumley!" Drummond-Mowbrey was visibly shocked by the news.

"How? Well, I suppose one might say he was shot, sir. In a manner of speaking, that is."

"How the devil can one be shot in a manner of speaking?"

"Ah, sir! You see, he wasn't shot ordinarily. He was shot with a *horse*."

The chief constable sat down, speechless; and Timuroff stepped into the breach. "I've heard of people being shot *on* a horse," he observed. "I've heard of people being shot *from* a horse. I even knew one poor fellow who was shot *by* a horse; it kicked over a gun at the stables. But, Mr. Plumley, how does one shoot a man *with* a horse?"

Mr. Plumley regarded him with disfavor. "The late Sir Cedric Substance"—he consulted his notebook again—"was shot to death with a horse named Hinchpeth, the property of Mr. Randolph Pilfer of Tiptilton Manor, Lower Tiptilton, near Frognall, et cetera."

"Good God, of *course!*" Timuroff exclaimed. "Hugh, has Pilfer or one of his lunatic friends built a trebuchet lately?"

The superintendent ignored him. "The horse Hinchpeth," he intoned, "was propelled through the air from and by an obsolete engine of war, also the property of the aforesaid Mr. Randolph Pilfer, at the hands of a person or persons unknown."

"*Trebuchet?*" said the chief constable. "Is that the kind with about a thirty-foot arm and a few tons of stones in a bucket to make it take off? If that's it, then Pilfer did build one. He was pleased as Punch. Went around bragging how he'd scored off Substance, who had only a catapult."

"The horse Hinchpeth," Mr. Plumley went on, "was impelled

through the air for a distance of thirty-eight yards, over the moat, and struck the deceased at the foot of the tower known as Parmenter's Folly, where he was walking or standing."

"Rather good shooting," remarked Timuroff.

"Death, I am happy to say, was instantaneous. The very considerable mass of the horse Hinchpeth fractured the skull of the victim. The report of the autopsy surgeon will doubtless reveal other grave injuries. If I may say so, sir"—Mr. Plumley nodded with vast satisfaction—"murder is an unhappy business."

The chief constable sighed. "It is indeed, Plumley. Substance was no friend of mine, but he's always been part of the landscape. I feel sorry for Cecily—she was fond of the pompous old ass." He shook his head sadly. "Well, I suppose an investigation is called for. We'll drive down to the folly and join you there."

The superintendent began to turn red. "That will not be necessary, *Major,*" he declared. "I have already investigated the affair. The poor broken body"—his voice fell funereally—"has been taken away. The next of kin have been notified. *If* I may say so, sir, these matters are far, far better left to the professional police, whose training and background qualify them to make an accurate assessment."

Drummond-Mowbrey betrayed irritation. "Plumley, are you an expert on horses?"

The superintendent made it clear that he was not.

"*I* am, Plumley. So is Mr. Timuroff here. You will have two former cavalrymen to assist you. Our training and background qualify us especially to solve all problems concerning them."

"Besides," Timuroff added, "I, Alastair Alexandrovitch Timuroff, am the world's foremost authority on the ballistics of the horse. My knowledge will be of inestimable value to you."

The superintendent opened his notebook. He asked Timuroff to spell his name. "Well," he said, "that's as may be, but I regret to inform you, gentlemen, that we of the police already know the identity of the murderer, and that as soon as a warrant is issued, I shall take him into custody."

"Who the deuce is it?" demanded the major.

"Mr. Randolph Pilfer," said Plumley. "If I may say so, sir, the jaws of justice are about to close on him."

Whatever comment Drummond-Mowbrey might have made was cut off by a housemaid, who informed them that Miss Cecily Substance had phoned, in tears, to ask whether he was driving down to the folly, and whether she could ride with him. He said yes, of course.

As they got into the car, Timuroff tried to cheer him. "You know, Mark," he declared, "I'm beginning to be interested in this murder of yours. In San Francisco I'll dine out for a month on the horse Hinchpeth and your man Plumley. And I'll probably really become the greatest authority on equine ballistics. I'll write papers for the Arms and Armor Society. You know, *The Horse's Flight from Engine to Target* and *How Properly To Truss the Dead Horse for Firing.* That sort of thing. Of course, it may turn out not to have been a murder after all."

"What do you mean?"

"Perhaps," said Timuroff, "it was an accident. Maybe they just didn't know the thing was loaded."

"Tim, shut up. I didn't like Substance, but I do like his niece. Besides, Randolph's a friend of mine, even if he is crazy. I just wish there was more I could do, but I really don't like to interfere with Plumley's handling of things."

"I'm sorry, Mark." Timuroff was sincerely contrite. "But the whole business does seem a little far out, doesn't it? Who on earth would name a horse Hinchpeth?"

"He was named after a butler," replied Drummond-Mowbrey, "of whom the family was particularly fond. The man died, I believe, and they named the horse after him. It was a lumpy fat thing as old as the hills, and a great pet of the children's. Used to follow them everywhere hoping for sugar."

"Hinchpeth seems an odd name even for a butler."

"Oh, *his* name really was Inchpeth. He was a bit loose with his aitches, you see."

"I see," murmured Timuroff.

"Funny things, names. If it weren't for names, probably there'd have been no ill will between Randolph and poor Substance. Of course, it was all on Substance's side. Randolph just tried to laugh off the whole thing—at least, in the beginning. It was only later that he got really irritated. You see, Cecily and Ronnie Pilfer—he's Randolph's son—have been wanting to get married for three years now, but Substance was dead set against it. You know his firm, Worth and Substance?"

Timuroff, long a reader of *Country Life,* had indeed seen the name. However, he had merely ticked it off as a specimen of the curious nomenclature of British estate agents, which includes such well-known samples as Giddy & Giddy, Sanctuary & Son, and Ralph Pay, Lord, & Ransom.

"Well, Substance got the notion that Ronnie was really trying to weasel his way into the firm, which would then, in due course, become Worth, Substance & Pilfer, or even worse, Pilfer, Worth & Substance—which I admit might not have inspired confidence in the customers. Of course, there wasn't the least danger of it. Ronnie's much too decent, and besides, he's a naval architect on the way up. But it kept Substance awake nights. Finally he went to Randolph and suggested in all seriousness, that he change the name from Pilfer to Paillefer, which would have the added advantage of sounding aristocratically Norman. Randolph was pretty rude to him, I'm afraid, in an earthy Anglo-Saxon sort of way."

"And then came the trebuchet?"

"Not right away. But Substance kept pushing the silly Paillefer idea, and making unpleasant remarks, and finally Randolph had the huge thing put together. Substance was awfully annoyed; he used to wander around muttering and mumbling about it until even Cecily began to think he was slipping a cog. Well, I thought I'd just fill you in on the background, but let's say no more about it right now—she'll be waiting for us there at the gatehouse." He pointed at a chimneyed roof directly ahead.

Cecily Substance stepped out into the road as he put on the

brakes. She wore a tweed jacket and jodhpurs, but Timuroff could see that she had forgotten all about riding. She said a few words to a gnarled old man walking with her, then came on alone. Timuroff opened the door, got out, and gave her the front seat, a gesture she acknowledged abstractedly. She was a very tall, very dark blond with a delightful complexion, beautifully feminine but somehow not truly beautiful. Nor were her tearstains responsible; the imperfection was more subtle. It was only after they had exchanged a few words that Timuroff detected what was wrong. Miss Substance's nose, and not only her nose but her personality, reminded him gently but inescapably of the great Duke of Wellington.

They got under way again, Drummond-Mowbrey clucking avuncular advice, Timuroff putting in that well-bred minimum required of any concerned and courteous stranger, and Cecily Substance assuring both of them that, thank you, she was now going to be perfectly all right. It had been a great shock, of course, especially when that wretched policeman Plumley—she dabbed her eyes—asked all those silly questions about secret enemies. But s-somehow it—well, she'd not been surprised, because Uncle Cedric had been terribly angry when he stalked out after supper. When he hadn't returned by morning, she just *knew* something terrible had happened—

Timuroff and the major exchanged glances.

"B-but it was such a dreadful thing to d-do!" she sobbed indignantly. "I can't imagine how anyone could do that to a horse. Why, *everybody* loved Hinchpeth. Only Uncle Cedric thought he was a nuisance; he used to swear like anything when Hinchpeth followed him, you know, for sugar. I hope the poor beast was a-already dead when—when—"

"I'm sure he was, Cecily dear." The major reached across and patted her. "Otherwise they couldn't very well have, well, *loaded* him."

Timuroff, considering the unusual moral values revealed in this conversation, said nothing.

"At least," declared Miss Substance in a firmer voice, "we won't have to wait very long. That Plumley promised me he'd have the wicked criminal fettered—those were his very words—by noon today." She noticed the unhappy look on the major's face. "You don't think he'll fail us, do you? If he doesn't catch him, it'll be simply terrible!"

Drummond-Mowbrey groaned audibly. "My God, Cissie, didn't he tell you whom he's planning to arrest? He's getting out a warrant for Randolph!"

Miss Substance sat bolt upright. The hint of Wellington was suddenly stronger than before. "He's stark, raving mad!" she cried out. "He's addled. He—he's a kook! It's unthinkable—why, Hinchie was one of the family! Besides, if Randolph's arrested, it'll just spoil *everything!*"

"Not between you and Ronnie, surely?"

"Of course not! I mean *today*. We'll have to cancel the whole thing—the battle, and knocking down the folly. We'll have to give back all their money, and if we try again later on, then nobody will come, no matter how much we advertise. Look there! Just look at that!"

The twisting road had finally made up its mind and was meandering along the military crest that overlooked Parmenter's Folly and the battlefield of Woads. Now the cupped green slopes around the moat were clearly visible. So were the combatants-to-be, a scattering of the upper-middle classes dressed as knights and noblemen, and any number of the yokelry got up as men-at-arms, churls, and varlets.

In their midst crouched the grim engines of approaching war: three great catapults, two ballistae, and, conspicuous among them not only because of its vast size but because it obviously had been fired, Mr. Randolph Pilfer's trebuchet, its mighty arm straight up in the air. Around the edges, gathering thick and fast, were the first-comers of the crowd, with their wives, in-laws, dogs, and noisy children, in numbers far beyond all expectation.

"Cecily," exclaimed Drummond-Mowbrey, "surely you aren't

expecting a public entertainment—not after what's happened!"

Miss Substance looked him in the eye; then she looked Timuroff in the eye for good measure. "The show," she said decisively, "must go on. It is what Uncle Cedric would have wished. His death was tragic." She sobbed again momentarily. "It was certainly a bit premature. But wasn't it just the sort of death he would have chosen? Better than lingering in a nursing home, I'd say. Besides, it's the first time something like this has happened in the family—at least, since the Crusades. And anyway, it's really what brought half these people here—they heard it on the wireless this morning."

The inconsistencies of the female mind, like those of certain French military firearms, had always fascinated Timuroff. Shuddering slightly at the thought of what Miss Substance might be like when she eventually became a dowager, he asked why the arrest of Mr. Pilfer would cause the cancellation of festivities.

"Because," replied Cecily Substance, *"he's* the MC, the Commander-in-Chief, the Grand Panjandrum. Right now, so far as all these people are concerned, Uncle Cedric's death is just a mystery; it makes things more dramatic, don't you see? But if they put the nippers on old Randolph, then it becomes Murder, and everything will be impossible." She turned back to Drummond-Mowbrey. "You're the chief constable—you'll have to make him stop, that awful Plumley man, I mean."

The chief constable's face was flushed. "My dear child, I don't like him either, but he's a conscientious policeman trying to do his duty. The course of justice—"

"Pooh!" said Miss Substance. "Well, if you're afraid of him, then I suppose we'll simply have to *find* whoever really did it. Probably it was someone like those Puggett brothers, somebody really stupid. It shouldn't be too difficult to find the culprit. You'll have at least two hours to do it in."

The major groaned again. "The Puggett brothers," he told Timuroff, "are deaf-mutes. They are illiterate. They can perform simple tasks when patiently instructed with graphic gestures, but it would be almost impossible to interrogate them."

"Uncle Cedric used to hire them to work his catapult," Miss Substance said. "I wonder if he himself wasn't planning to shoot somebody else with Hinchpeth, and they misunderstood?"

The car was now picking its way through toward the area of the engines, which the police, much in evidence, had cordoned off. More and more of the folk they passed were girded for the fray, armed and costumed so diversely that any uninformed observer might reasonably have supposed the Battle of Woads to have lasted at least from that of Hastings to Culloden Moor. One of Plumley's minions passed them through, and they halted finally on the meadow behind the line of engines, where gay pavilions with bright fluttering pennants had been set up in preparation for the tournament which would precede the battle.

Beside the drawbridge, close under the wall and with two legs in the air, lay a dead horse. They spied it simultaneously as they left the car, but only Cecily Substance commented on the sad sight. "You know," she said, "since poor Hinchpeth's already copped it, is there any reason why we can't use him over again? Over the walls, you know. He'd be quite a dramatic climax, wouldn't he?"

Luckily, Drummond-Mowbrey did not hear this suggestion. He had been summoned to the aid of two elderly ladies from the R.S.P.C.A., concerned about the possible fate of four live percherons due to be ridden in the tourney.

In front of the pavilions had been placed a platform heraldically adorned. On it were benches fanning out from a splendid elevated throne, and on the throne, broad and apple-cheeked, sat Mr. Randolph Pilfer. He wore a furred robe of some magnificence, which Timuroff correctly guessed to have been designed for the role of Boris Godunov, and on his head reposed a kingly crown. Pages bearing such symbols of his sovereignty as sword and scepter stood at either hand, and he himself, in the midst of his busy entourage, was trying valiantly to cope with all the cares of state, summoning and dismissing, deciding weighty issues, reproving the unworthy. He was perspiring freely, for the presence of

Superintendent Hesiod Plumley in the immediate background was contributing nothing to the brave panoply of medieval war.

The superintendent stood with two grim companions, and his expression, though still quite suitable for churchyard wear, was now indubitably that of one who, hungrily awaiting the arrival of a warrant, is certain that his hunger will soon be satisfied.

"If it flaps its big black wings, watch out!" announced Cecily Substance in a penetrating voice. "That means it's going to flip over and peck poor Hinchie's eyes out."

"Good morning, miss." Stiffly, Plumley ignored her remarks. "I am happy to report that the ends of justice have been properly served. We have gathered much new evidence—incontrovertible evidence, if I may say so, miss."

"They've probably already been pecked out." Miss Substance cocked her head appraisingly. "The creature looks revoltingly well fed."

Plumley regarded her reproachfully. "We of the police," he told her, "are used to obloquy. If I may say so, miss, sticks and stones may break my bones, but aspersions—even unpleasant ornithological aspersions—can do me no real injury." He favored them with an appalling grin. "Nor can they undermine the evidence we have. We have a note, found in the victim's pocket, asking him to meet Mr. Pilfer by the engines at eleven o'clock—and we have two eyewitnesses.

"Last night, at a few minutes past eleven, the Puggett brothers, Sam and Ludlow, aged twenty-nine and thirty-four respectively, of Tilton Undertree, saw the suspect, Mr. Randoph Pilfer, work the trigger mechanism of his traybooshay, causing it to fire, thereby bringing about the dreadful death of Sir Cedric Substance, whom they had previously observed crossing the drawbridge which, I regret to say, he was fated never to cross again."

"Poppycock!" said Sir Cedric's next of kin. "Pure, shameless, driveling idiocy. And we're going to prove it."

She had made no effort to modulate her tones; and now a

young man, who had detached himself from the group around the throne, quickened his pace and came to her. He was of middle height, with what would ordinarily have been an open cheerful countenance; his scarlet surcoat, over chain mail, sported three golden griffins, and he carried a two-handed sword. He clanked ominously as he walked, glared even more ominously at Superintendent Plumley, and seemed completely lost in the glories of the past.

After chivalrous platitudes had been exchanged, Miss Substance introduced him as Ronald Pilfer, and Timuroff gained his immediate favor by complimenting him learnedly upon his arms. But he was not to be distracted long. Suddenly he gripped his sword, bared his teeth, and demanded loudly, "Fair maiden, has yonder knave, yon ill-bred varlet, dared to molest you? Only tell me, and I shall split him to the chine! Or perhaps even a little further."

Superintendent Plumley puffed, spread his wattles, and reminded him that British law forbade cleaving to or beyond the chine, and all other forms of violence to all persons civil or military—except, of course, occasionally in the performance of their duties. "Indeed, if I may say so, gentlemen, it even forbids—though perhaps not explicitly—shooting people to death with horses. As we shall see. Oh, yes *indeed*—as we shall soon see! And may I also add that—as I'm sure our chief constable here will testify—we of the police are no molesters of young ladies! Our characters are constantly subjected to the severest scrutiny."

"What a strange interpretation!" remarked the unrelenting Miss Substance. "We of the police must have a horribly dirty mind."

"*Cecily!*" The chief constable had rejoined them just in time to overhear the last of this exchange. He was properly horrified. "Cecily, that was an *outrageous* thing to say! Plumley, I'm sure Miss Substance will apolo—"

He was too late. The superintendent, turning with a wounded-walrus roar, was bellowing orders at his underlings, sending them off to thwart thieves, pounce on pickpockets, and (with special emphasis) manacle molesters.

Finally the chief constable indicated that they might as well resume their march. "Well," he said unhappily, "there go our chances of any cooperation from that quarter. Cecily, don't you realize what a pickle poor Randolph's already in?"

Ronnie Pilfer retorted hotly that Plumley was a base-born clod who was plotting to commit *lese-majeste* by seizing the person of the king. Drummond-Mowbrey argued that, while it was hard to take Superintendent Plumley seriously because the man was such a bloody mountebank, his powers were very real and very, very serious.

Timuroff, who was beginning to suspect what made the superintendent tick, asked if anyone would mind if he wandered off and rejoined them in the royal presence in ten or fifteen minutes? Then he dropped quietly back and made his way to where Mr. Plumley stood wrapped in gloom, anger, and high purpose. Coming up behind him, Timuroff sighed heavily by way of introduction.

Plumley turned. "What do *you* want?" he growled suspiciously.

"Want?" replied Timuroff, all innocence. "Why, I want nothing, except perhaps to understand the ways of man. What I have heard today distresses me. You, Superintendent Plumley, are a policeman. You may not understand. But we who've seen the world across the footlights of a stage, who've worn the sock and buskin—ah!" He sighed even more deeply than before. "We know only too well that 'All the world's a stage, and all the men and women merely players.' We watch them as they strut and fret, all unaware that the final curtain, Death, awaits us all."

Plumley's jaw dropped. "You think I do not understand?" he cried. "Only too well indeed, if I may say so, sir! Oh, that's the pity of it." Abruptly, suspicion raised its head again. "Do you mean to tell me that you have played *professionally?*"

"I played Mercutio from Belfast to Bologna," lied Timuroff. "I have been Sir Lucius O'Trigger in Los Angeles, Faust in Ottawa, and Othello in more towns than I can name. Yes, and for one too brief season I was Tamburlaine, because Tamerlane, or Timur, is supposed to have been my ancestor; Sir Tancred would allow no one else to play the part. I was triumphant! The stage was my career; since boyhood I had dreamed of nothing else. But it was not to be. Vile critics brought me down. I fled into the army of a foreign land."

Timuroff was proud of his two speeches, which he had tried to make us Plumleyesque as possible; and now he witnessed their complete success. The superintendent had at long last found a kindred soul; it was his turn to sigh, abysmally.

"I too have had the same experience, Mr. Time-you're-off. I have aspired. I have been cast down. 'Of comfort no man speak: Let's talk of graves, of worms and epitaphs; Make dust our paper and with rainy eyes/Write sorrow on the bosom of the earth.'

"I was to the theater born. My fond father, unhappily no more, headed a repertory company, Plumley's Players. As a babe in arms I made my first appearance in such productions as *The Scarlet Letter*. As a mere child I was Moth and Mustardseed, for often we presented scenes from *A Midsummer Night's Dream*, Father having been universally proclaimed the greatest Bottom of them all. Nor shall I soon forget the vast applause which greeted my success as Peter Pan at Brighton. Oh, how I wish the great Sir Tancred Solomon had seen *me* then!" His voice broke. "B-but no! 'Twas not to be. Poor Father died. I was apprenticed to an undertaker, I know not why. My talent, all unknown, shriveled, died."

"Oh, surely not!" Timuroff patted him on the back consolingly. "Surely, Superintendent, you have been able to employ your skills and your theatrical perceptions as well in your profession as I in mine?"

Plumley's gloom did not lift, but it did seem to thin a little around the edges. He admitted that his dramatic background had given him a distinct advantage, sometimes earning him the plaudits both of his superiors and the press. He lowered himself to a convenient hummock—

" 'For God's sake, let us sit upon the ground/And tell sad stories of the death of kings—' "

Obediently, Timuroff sat upon the ground beside him.

" 'How some have been deposed; some slain in war; Some haunted by the ghosts they have deposed; Some poisoned by their wives; some sleeping killed—' "

"Some shot to death with horses," thought Timuroff.

" '*All murdered!*' " intoned the superintendent. "And, if I may say so, sir, that king we're looking at"—he gestured at Randolph Pilfer on his throne—"will also meet his fate, his just and dismal fate. Had Hesiod Plumley never trod the boards, he might have gotten off scot-free. Had I not mastered the arts of wordless pantomime, the terrible truth could not have been extracted from the dull minds of those two hulking boors, both deaf and dumb since birth. Not only did they witness the firing of the traybooshay, but earlier they observed Mr. Pilfer leading the horse Hinchpeth by a rope."

"Incredible!" exclaimed Timuroff. "You got all this with gestures?"

"With gestures *and* expressions, if I may say so, sir. For instance, when I conveyed the picture of that awesome instrument hurling death at poor Sir Cedric, my features had to mirror its intent even while my body limned the functioning of its mechanism. Then, in return, I had to be alert to each emotion that displayed itself upon their brutish faces. You, Mr. Time-you're-off, as an accomplished thespian, might have been able to do much the same—had you, of course, had my years of rigorous training and experience in the police."

Timuroff protested modestly that he did not deserve this compliment. Then, having obtained the information he was after, he listened politely to a few more minutes of theatrical reminiscence, declared that his confidence in British justice had been restored, and broke off the conversation with genuine regret.

All was not calm around the throne when Timuroff returned to pay his delayed *devoirs*. Miss Substance, looking more than ever

like the eve of Waterloo, made a remark under her breath about
people who gave aid and comfort to the enemy; and Drummond-
Mowbrey, as nervous as the rest, introduced him first to his
Majesty, then for a second time to Ronnie Pilfer, then to a lean
Dame Marigold, who was excited because she could find no one
fitted to command the brave defenders of the folly and deliver a
final speech of defiance from its doomed battlements, and finally to
a Mr. Robertson, the local veterinarian.

Miss Substance resumed her interrupted exhortation angrily.
"What's the matter with the lot of you?" she demanded. "At any
moment our vulture's going to swoop down, and all you do is
moan and run around in circles. Why aren't *we* out trying to get
new evidence?"

"My dear Cecily," protested Drummond-Mowbrey, "I'm sure
we're all aware of what's at stake. But, just as Plumley says, we're
not professional policemen, and time's running out, and—well, I
admit I don't know which way to turn."

"My God, can't any of you think of *anything* to do?"

There was a despairing silence, punctuated by throat clearings
and the shuffling of feet. Timuroff waited till he was certain that
there would be no more positive reaction. Then he said politely,
"I have thought of several things to do."

Miss Substance sneered, but king and court set up an instant
clamor, snatching at the unknown straw held out to them.

Timuroff held up a hand for silence. "First," he said, "we may
well need more time. Therefore let's start by having the crown
prince change costumes with the king. In a pinch, Ronnie will be
able to run faster than his father." He smiled. "Isn't it lucky for
the criminal classes that the British police aren't allowed to carry
guns?"

Agreement was immediate and virtually unanimous. Only
Drummond-Mowbrey protested weakly that, after all, he was
chief constable, and wouldn't they be, well, obstructing justice?

"Then," Timuroff went on, "we'll need a Polaroid. And a notepad of some sort. And I should like a photo of Sir Cedric. You see,
I'm going to finish questioning the Puggetts. I'm not sure that

Superintendent Plumley got all the information they possess."

The camera was almost immediately forthcoming, and Timuroff quickly took recognizable pictures of Randolph Pilfer, of the defunct Hinchpeth, and of the trebuchet. Cecily Substance —though she expressed serious doubts about his sanity—produced a likeness of her uncle from her purse. Timuroff was now ready. "Hugh," he suggested, "why don't you stay up here so that Plumley won't realize what we're doing? Miss Substance, I'd like to have you come with me. You know the country people hereabouts, and I do not."

Prince Ronald held his peace. Miss Substance, declaring that she would go with anyone if it would help to save the day, attached herself to Timuroff. King Randolph said, "Mr. Timuroff, if you can stop this ludicrous arrest, I—all of us—shall be forever in your debt."

"All I'll require," said Timuroff, "is gleaners' privileges."

"What?"

"A fine medieval custom, your Majesty. We dealers in old arms descend upon a battlefield and gather all the weapons of the slain. And of the badly wounded too, of course—though that can sometimes get a little stickier."

He bowed. Miss Substance curtsied. Escorted by a page, they took their leave.

The Puggett brothers were not hard to find. The page discovered them behind a catapult, drinking bottled beer; and Timuroff's conclusion, at first glance, was that they were not as stupid as everyone believed. They were big, clumsy men, rawboned, with huge hands, feet, and ears. But the expression in their little eyes was one of cunning—low cunning possibly, but cunning nonetheless—and their deaf-and-dumbness had not prevented them from being *au courant* with the winds of fashion.

Their clothing and adornments—from filthy moccasins and skin-tight sackcloth trousers past gaudy plastic vegetables on strings to floppy hats and Farmer Giles beards—were mod, as mod was being interpreted by a musical ensemble called the Living

Twitch. Timuroff decided that he had done wisely to fill his
pockets with shillings and half-crowns; he very obviously began
to transfer a few of them from one hand to the other.

The Puggetts' first reaction was unfavorable. Ludlow drove an
elbow into Sam's brisket and pointed angrily. Sam made a rude
gesture indicating, at the least, that they preferred to remain
alone. Then both recognized Miss Substance and, simultaneously,
the legal tender Timuroff was juggling. At once, cunning and a
coarse *bonhommie* replaced cunning and hostility on their faces.
Ludlow drove his elbow into Sam again and pointed at the beer,
and Sam hospitably offered two bottles, one of which Timuroff
graciously accepted.

After that the interview proceeded at the rate, roughly, of one
coin per question. Timuroff learned almost immediately that the
Puggetts were not quite illiterate, for they could read and write
the numerals and their own names. He found out, too, that they
disliked Superintendent Plumley, who had paid them not a
penny. And he discovered that Ludlow, especially, had a primitive
talent with the pencil, snatching it at the first opportunity and
producing a series of sketches which made everything he had
witnessed the night before completely clear.

There were, of course, minor hitches. Ludlow insisted on stimulating Sam's memory with his elbow, and Sam occasionally replied in kind. However, a proffered coin always prevented actual
fratricide. Finally, when nothing more was to be learned, Ludlow
offered beer again, which this time Timuroff refused politely, and
Miss Substance responded with a pound note, which was accepted
instantly. They parted on the best of terms.

Timuroff was pleased. Not only had he succeeded in his purpose, but he had converted Sir Cedric's heiress into a friend and
ally.

""Well!" she declared, eyes flashing. "*That* settles Mr. Plumley's hash! I can hardly wait to see his beak drop open when we
tell him. He'll probably regurgitate"—she shuddered slightly—
"you know, hair, bones, all that sort of thing, the way owls do."

"A fascinating prospect," said Timuroff. "But hadn't we best wait? He hasn't any chance of getting a conviction, but *he* still doesn't know it—and in his present mood we can't convince him in time to stop him making the arrest—not without good hard evidence to back us up. So let's not even tell his Majesty the king; let's just say things are looking up, and that we're hopeful."

"I daresay you're right, but you deserve *some* credit. The way you got through to those Puggetts was simply wonderful."

"It was just that I knew more about my audience than Mr. Plumley did, Cecily—and that I'm not half as stagestruck."

Then, while they walked the remaining distance to the royal seat, Timuroff discussed more pleasant matters, praising Ronald Pilfer's great two-handed sword, and asking casually whether it was an old family heirloom with which its owner couldn't bear to part.

The group about the king was still milling uncertainly, disconcerted by the change in his identity; and Timuroff took advantage of this to march up demanding instant action, the utmost haste, and no questions asked. He was ably and penetratingly seconded by Cecily Substance, who quelled the faltering hesitations of the chief constable.

"Mark," Timuroff said, "if you and I and Mr. Pilfer here, and of course Mr. Robertson, start right away, perhaps we can check out Hinchpeth's remains and the folly too before Plumley descends on us. We'll leave the impostor"—he smiled at Ronnie Pilfer—"to delude the Plumleyan eye. Cecily can stay with him to speed him on his way when the great hour arrives. Now, let's get cracking."

The chief constable bade farewell to Dame Marigold, who was still frantically trying to recruit a guardian of the keep; the true king issued a few last-minute orders; Mr. Robertson began to hum "The Flowers of the Forest" dolefully; and, as inconspicuously as possible, they strolled toward the drawbridge.

"Mr. Pilfer," asked Timuroff, as they pushed through the thickening crowd, "you were observed last night firing off your trebuchet. This is part of Superintendent Plumley's web of evidence. Did you fire it?"

"Just before I went home I did. Some fool had left the arm drawn back and ready. Even though there was nothing in it, I didn't want it to go off and hurt anyone."

"Is it easy to draw back?"

Mr. Pilfer blushed. "Easier than they used to be. I have a geared-down engine in it. Otherwise it'd be too much work, and churls and varlets come pretty high these days."

"By the way, how do you load it?"

"We use a fork-lift when we're practice-shooting, but today we'll have the soldiery push stones up ramps."

"Are you aware that you were also seen leading the horse Hinchpeth toward the trebuchet?"

"Must've been those miserable Puggetts, though how they got the message through, I can't imagine. I found the beast tied to a wagon back of the pavilions. I supposed some kid had ridden him down bareback—they do that sort of thing. It was much too late by then to take him home again, so I moved him down by the trebuchet, where there's grass, and I had a rope there long enough to let him graze. I suppose that crazy Plumley thinks I slaughtered him and hoisted him up into the basket?"

"I'm afraid so," replied Timuroff. He refrained from mentioning that, to those who did not build ancient siege engines, the idea of those who did shooting each other with dead horses might not seem at all far-fetched. "The superintendent believes that he has established motive, opportunity, and means—the three classic requirements. Besides, he has enough contributory evidence to justify arresting you—unless we can demolish the evidence, of course. There's that note you wrote to the deceased, for instance."

"My God, that was day before yesterday. I asked Substance to meet me at eleven in the *morning*—yesterday morning."

They had by then crossed the moat and were surveying Hinchpeth, whom a man-at-arms was guarding from a ring of open-mouthed small boys. Robertson, the vet, was the first to comment. "If I hadna been told he was a horse," he stated solemnly, "I believe I would have taken the creature for a hinny, which, as you weel know, is a mule the other way around, but wor-r-rthless."

"I see your point," said Timuroff, "but doesn't that neck betray a touch of dinosaur somewhere in his ancestry? I can think of nothing else that might account for it."

Mr. Pilfer, aggrievedly, pointed out that, while Hinchpeth might indeed have been a compendium of the worst points of horses, he had possessed a spirit of rare gentleness and beauty. "And believe me," he added ferociously, "whoever killed him is going to pay for it!"

In death Hinchpeth was an unlovely sight. He was a very fat horse, with very thin, very uneven extremities. His scruffy coat was of a mottled mud color. His lips had curled back from long yellow teeth which betrayed immense old age, and his stiffened limbs, all badly damaged, pointed in a variety of directions. While Mr. Robertson and Drummond-Mowbrey knelt to examine him more closely, Timuroff devoted his attention to the surrounding territory. After a few minutes he turned back to them. "Mr. Robertson," he asked, "can you say whether Hinchpeth was alive or dead when he hit the ground?"

The veterinarian replied judiciously that it was a little difficult to say positively without an autopsy, but that confidentially and just between themselves, aye, the horse had been alive. "Or at least," he added, "as alive as it probably has been during the past twelve years. But, och! what's the difference? The injuries would have killed two teams of perfectly sound horses."

"Yes," said Timuroff, "and considering the nature of these injuries and the animal's long flight through the air, isn't it strange that he appears to have landed, squashed Sir Cedric, and remained pretty much *in situ?* Look—" He pointed to the shrubbery between Hinchpeth and, scarcely fifteen feet away, the folly's wall. "He doesn't seem to have richocheted at all."

"I never thought about that," said Drummond-Mowbrey, "but

is the trebuchet a high-angle-of-fire weapon? Could he have fallen practically straight down?"

"Hardly. Anything fired from a trebuchet is lobbed. The angle's fairly high, but not much higher than a horse taking a tall fence steeplechasing—and look how far they can roll after a fast fall. I told you I was the world's foremost authority on the ballistics of the hor—"

He stopped abruptly. A tumult of shouts, police whistles, piercing screams, and running feet had burst out in the crowd.

"What's that?" cried Mr. Pilfer.

"Quick!" snapped Timuroff. "Let's get inside the folly. Plumley's trying to serve his warrant. Mr. Robertson, if Superintendent Plumley comes this way, please delay him as long as possible. We've only minutes to find whatever we're looking for."

"Ah, weel," Mr. Robertson replied, "if I canna see where you are going, certainly I canna tell the man where you have gone." And as Timuroff hustled the other two away, he turned back to his examination. In the crowd the royal raiment appeared and disappeared as young Pilfer sought to outdistance his pursuers.

"What the devil do you expect to find in here?" protested the chief constable a little irritably as they passed through the sally port.

"Who knows?" said Timuroff. "The good investigator must try everything."

The front aspect of Parmenter's Folly made it appear a great, square, lowering keep. Once inside, however, one saw that it was indeed only one and a quarter sides of such an edifice, the quarter, off at one end, crumbling into deliberately contrived ruin, the rest achieving a similar effect through long neglect.

"Not much stone in it," commented Drummond-Mowbrey. "Just enough for looks. Most of it's lath and plaster.'

"Can we get up to those two turrets over the sally port?" asked Timuroff.

"We can," Pilfer answered. "We've kept the place locked up, but I have keys even though Substance owned it—more evidence,

I suppose Plumley'd say." He fished in the scarlet surcoat's ana-
chronistic pocket. "Here they are, two to the downstairs doors
leading to the ramps and two more to the turret chambers—His
and Hers, we used to call them. On moonlit nights Parmenter's
wife—her name was Guinevere or Isabeau or something like that
—would come out through that long embrasure in her turret, right
over where poor Hinchpeth's now lying, and stand on a little iron
balcony they had there. She always wore a filmy Burne-Jones sort
of nightie, with her long hair streaming down over her shoulders.
Then he'd sing to her from a gondola on the moat, twanging his
lute. As she was awfully overweight, and as he always sang lilting
love songs in Middle Scots, the effect must've been quite memorable."

As he talked, Mr. Pilfer unlocked one of the doors, admitting
them to a dark and cobwebbed corridor. "After she died, when
he'd become pretty well crippled by arthritis, he pulled the stairs
clean out and had these ramps put in, so that a couple of stout
village lads could push his wheelchair up into her bower—not out
of sentiment, you understand, but so he could sit in the embrasure
and take pot-shots at this and that with his old Genoese cross-
bow. He was a vile shot and never hit a thing, which was lucky,
because a couple of times toward the end he tried to wing one of
the local peasants. He was a bit of a nut, really."

"Did he build siege engines?" Timuroff asked mildly.

"Not a bit of it," replied Mr. Pilfer. "He was just one of those
silly mid-Victorian romantics—no scientific spirit whatsoever."

They made their way up a long ramp and down another corridor, and, with the king beginning to puff slightly, repeated
the process two more times. Finally they stood before the portal
of the bower. Mr. Pilfer again produced his keys. The door
creaked open. And—

"There," cried Timuroff triumphantly, "is our evidence!
Randolph Pilfer was not the murderer of Sir Cedric Substance!"

"I'll be damned!" exclaimed Drummond-Mowbrey.

"Wh-why—why, this is incredible!" Randolph Pilfer gasped.
"Perhaps now we'll find out who really killed him."

"There's no time for that now," said Timuroff. "I'll take a look around, then Mark and I can show poor Plumley the error of his ways. You'd best wait here; the sight of you at this point would just infuriate him."

Quickly he examined the floor of the empty room, with its souvenirs of spiders, bats, owls, and rodents. From it he picked up a few shreds of scarlet paper. "I'll take these along to help persuade him," he announced. "But we'll leave the real evidence right here; it'll be more impressive. Come on, Mark, let's go."

From the drawbridge they saw that the pretender had been taken into custody. Three of Plumley's men had dragged him back to the royal platform to prevent his rescue by a threatening crowd of ardent royalists. Superintendent Plumley, majestic in his wrath, was lecturing all and sundry on the impropriety and peril of defying British law.

"Mark," said Timuroff, coming to a halt, "I wonder if you'd mind my handling this? I think I may be able to bring him around without blood being spilt."

"You're handling things quite nicely, it seems to me." Drummond-Mowbrey smiled wryly. "If you were a British subject, I'd resign and recommend you for my job."

Timuroff took his notepad from his pocket:

> Dear Friend and Fellow Player [he wrote],
> I send this message in great haste and secretly, for the wrong people must not know of it.
> Shocking new evidence has been discovered which changes the whole case, and I strongly urge you—indeed, for the sake of your talent and career, I beg you!—to do nothing before I have a chance to tell you of it. At the moment, after much persuasion on my part, the Chief Constable is, I think, amenable. Come to the trebuchet immediately.
> Faithfully,
> Alastair Timuroff

"That ought to do it," he remarked, folding the document and whistling to a lad of eight or ten. "Here's a shilling for you, son. Take this note to that big man over there, the angry, purple one. It won't matter who sees you, but act as if you're trying not to be seen. Catch on?"

The boy dashed off, yelping excitedly. They saw him vanish in the crowd, reappear on the platform, then sneak his way very obviously to Plumley's side; they observed the superintendent read the paper, hesitate, crumple it into his pocket, and then, with a word or two to his subordinates, depart.

As they took off for the rendezvous, Dame Marigold, more agitated than ever, buttonholed the chief constable, demanding that a true guardian of the keep be found for her immediately.

"Madame," interjected Timuroff firmly, "I can assure you that Major Drummond-Mowbrey and I shall soon have just the right man for your purpose."

They met a troubled Plumley by the trebuchet. "You were wise to heed my warning, superintendent. No, do not say a word!" Timuroff held a conspiratorial finger to his lips. "Come with us! We wish to show you everything."

He led the way across the drawbridge once again. He spent several minutes pointing out the technicalities of Hinchpeth's impact and injuries. Then he led Plumley through the sally port and up into the tower.

When they descended shortly afterward, in the company of the erstwhile accused, it was obvious that the superintendent, if not a broken man, was at least bent badly out of shape. His face was pallid. His jowls had lost their buoyancy. He walked as though he carried the weight of a dead horse on his shoulders. But for all that, he did not shirk his duty. Heavily, followed by Timuroff, the chief constable, and the restored king, he mounted to the platform. So tragically did he hold his hand up to command attention that instantly all were still.

"A terrible error has been made," he announced sepulchrally, "an error for which we of the police apologize and which we infinitely regret. New evidence has, if I may say so, come to light. It has not yet revealed precisely how the late Sir Cedric Substance met his death, nor at whose hands, but it has shown beyond doubt—" Here Plumley choked and, for a moment, had rather heavy going. "It has shown beyond any doubt whatsoever that Mr. Randolph Pilfer is completely innocent. All charges against him have been dropped."

"Long live the king!" shouted nobles, knights, and commoners. "God save good King Randolph!"

Miss Substance, having embraced the crown prince (who was promising everyone high wassail in the Great Hall come sundown), shouted out, "Long live Mr. Timuroff!" But no one else took up the cry.

"I'm glad somebody appreciates me," Timuroff said to the chief constable. "I'm sure Plumley doesn't, or he'd be telling them the truth, the whole truth, and nothing but. He knows how the late Sir Cedric Substance met his death as well as you and I know."

"Probably he's waiting until the show is over. Anyhow, here he comes, poor devil. Looks a bit flattened out, doesn't he?"

"Well, we'll soon fix that." Timuroff moved off to intercept the superintendent. "The curtain has not fallen for our hero. . . . Dame Marigold!" he called. "Dame Marigold? Ah, there you are. Here's someone you simply have to meet—"

The day went off famously, and many of its happenings, much embellished, were woven into the tapestries of local folklore and local history. Wearing Miss Substance's favor, Sir Ronald acquitted himself honorably in the tourney, prevailing over a number of opponents until he was unhorsed abruptly by a grizzled knight who happened to be a retired rough-riding sergeant major of the Blues. Before the jousts there had been minor combats between the common folk, who cheerfully bruised each other with wooden swords, quarterstaves, and dummy battleaxes. There had been shooting at the popinjay and at the mark. There had even been a lovely fist fight between the Puggett brothers, who had set to over their last bottle. The crowd was in a fine medieval mood.

During the lull before the battle and the siege, the gnarled

old man who had been with Miss Substance at the gatehouse appeared leading three horses, one of hers and two of Drummond-
Mowbrey's—apparently someone had been in touch with him by
nonmedieval telephone. Close on his heels came a boy carrying
two pairs of the chief constable's boots and breeches, into one set
of which Timuroff was reluctantly persuaded. There was nothing
for it but to watch the battle from a convenient grassy knoll,
where the lovely tall mare snorted, danced, pranced, and cara-
colled, and drew everyone's attention, as Timuroff, bowing to
social pressure, put her through her paces.

The attackers, of course, were triumphant; the defenders beat a
disorderly retreat across the drawbridge; the wounded screamed
and writhed realistically enough to satisfy every schoolboy in the
audience; and Miss Substance, her nostrils flaring, surveyed the
field as though, with Boney's armies hastening back to France,
she were regarding the Torres Vedras Lines.

Then it was announced that the last desperate assault upon
the keep would soon begin, and, as trumpets blared, a defiant,
solitary figure appeared in Mrs. Parmenter's embrasure. Superintendent Plumley wore a leather jerkin, a cuirassier's breastplate,
a Cromwellian lobster-tail helmet, and great jackboots. Held in
his right hand was a huge halberd; and while the awe-struck
crowd momentarily held its breath, he launched into the first
mighty stanzas of "Horatius at the Bridge." It was a magnificent
performance, which earned him a highly favorable review from
the dramatic critic of a Dublin paper who happened to be drinking his way through rural England; and when he asked who would
stand at his right hand and keep the bridge with him, it was all his
constables could do to restrain the volunteers.

However, Plumley was not able to turn the course of recon-
structed history. At the critical moment someone—Timuroff suspected Cecily Substance, who had ridden down to inspect the
troops manning the engines—caused the trebuchet to fire prematurely, and the horse Hinchpeth was sent sailing through the
air to crash against the turret, rebound, break off a tree branch,

and strike again almost at the moat's edge. Actually, *vis-a-vis* the superintendent, Hinchpeth hit about twenty feet low at eight o'clock. But he hit effectively.

The horse's flight was taken for a signal, and instantly catapults and ballistae discharged their fearsome stones and giant shafts. Horatius, who had been about to plunge into the Tiber, disappeared. The crowd went wild. And the besiegers, massed around their battering ram, surged forward uncontrollably. Fortunately, perhaps, the Greek Fire, which was supposed to have been catapulted into the folly a little later on, fell short into the moat and fizzled out; and the fire brigade were able to do the incendiary bit more safely and tidily with gasoline.

It was a great day for almost everyone, including Timuroff. Old Mrs. Lessingham had admired his horsemanship, and the purchase of the Lessingham Collection was practically assured. Ronnie Pilfer, prodded by Cecily into gratitude for his father's timely rescue, had remembered that his sword, by no means an heirloom, had been purchased by a cousin at a country auction in 1947, and had presented it to the rescuer. Even the tall mare had shown herself to be so responsive and amiable an animal that Timuroff privately apologized to her for his general estimate of equine intelligence.

After Ronnie had been persuaded that Cecily's bereavement was not a time really suited to high wassail, they drove back together to a quiet dinner, Timuroff and Drummond-Mowbrey in the front seat, the two Pilfers flanking Miss Substance in the rear. As soon as they were clear of the dispersing visitors, Cecily's fiancé leaned forward. "Mr. Timuroff," he asked, "who on earth *did* kill Uncle Cedric?"

"Nobody killed him," Miss Substance said. "He—" She dried a solitary tear. "He committed suicide."

"He *what?*" exclaimed both the Pilfers simultaneously.

"It's really very simple," said Timuroff. "I think there's no doubt whatever that Sir Cedric's mind had come unhinged, and that in his distorted world Mr. Randolph Pilfer was the enemy.

What gave him the idea of engineering his own death and blaming it on you, we'll never know, but having you convicted by your own horse and your own trebuchet must have seemed a specially sweet revenge."

The Pilfers and Miss Substance murmured pityingly.

"At any rate, he counted on your motive, your instrument, your opportunity, and the fact that there'd be witnesses to testify to this and that, all in an atmosphere sufficiently—shall we say, eccentric?—to make an otherwise improbable occurrence believable. Yesterday evening he must have led Hinchpeth down to the battlefield himself. He had equipped himself with several lumps of sugar, and with two enormous firecrackers with long fuses. I imagine he also had a flashlight."

"He always had a little pocket torch—to keep the goblins off, he used to say," put in Miss Substance.

"He probably went back and forth several times getting things ready, and it must've been on one of those occasions that the Puggetts saw him. He found Hinchpeth again where Mr. Pilfer had tied him, and led him over to the folly. Tugging at the halter, and using sugar when that didn't work, he got him all the way to the top story and into my lady's bower. He lit his fuses—I daresay he'd timed it all carefully earlier in the day—quickly locked the door, and hurried down again. The firecrackers went off—*BANG! BANG!*—and Hinchpeth, terrorized, leaped through the only exit. And that was that. Actually, it was a rather clever plan. If no one but the superintendent had been involved, it might have succeeded."

"I still don't understand how you managed to convince Plumley so decisively," said Ronnie Pilfer. "Surely it wasn't just the paper from those—what did you call them?—firecrackers."

"Oh, no. That would have been too easy to explain away. The evidence we showed him was much more conclusive. When your father saw it, up there in the turret room, he was too upset to realize its true significance. But it proved conclusively that Hinchpeth had been there and that he'd leaped from the embrasure, and Plumley saw at once that that meant suicide.

"Sir Cedric made two errors. The first was in not foreseeing that some horsy people might get in on the investigation. That was bad enough, but the second was disastrous." Timuroff smiled. "Knowing little or nothing about horses, he neglected to watch *both* ends of Hinchpeth instead of just the one he was leading."

When I was first involved in the process of selecting Mystery Writers of America Edgar winners in 1968, we chose Warner Law's short story "The Man Who Fooled the World." At the awards banquet early in 1969 Mr. Law expressed mild surprise that we had considered his story a mystery, but this understandably did not lead him to decline his bust of Mr. Poe. Since that effort, a delightful tale of iniquity in the world of art and celebrities, Mr. Law has all too seldom gone to the criminous well, so it is an unusually great pleasure to present this cheerful caper. . . .

WARNER LAW
The Harry Hastings Method

Susie Plimson says I should keep on practicing my writing. She's been my teacher at Hollywood High Adult Education in the professional writing course and says I am still having trouble with my syntaxes and my tenses, and very kindly gave me private lessons at her place, and she is dark-haired and very pretty and about my age (which is twenty-five) and, in addition, she has great big boobs.

Susie says if I really want to be a professional writer, I should write about what I really know about—if it is interesting—and while I did do a hitch in the navy some time back, I was on a destroyer tender and never heard a shot fired except in practice, which I don't think is a highly interesting matter to describe.

But one thing I know a lot about is working the houses in the Hollywood hills. The people who live up there are not particularly stinking rich, but then, I've never been interested in valuable paintings or diamond necklaces, anyway, because what do you do with them?

But there are usually portable radios and TV sets and auto tape decks and now and then there is some cash lying around, or a fur, or a few pieces of fairly good jewelry, or maybe a new leather jacket—all things easy to dispose of.

This is an area of winding streets and a lot of trees and bushes, and the houses are mostly set back from the street and are some distance from their neighbors, and so it is an easy vicinity to work. There's no bus service up there at all, so everybody needs a car or two, and if there is no auto in the carport, you can be pretty sure that no one is home.

There are rural-type mailboxes on the street, and people are always stuffng them with business cards and circulars, like ads for house cleaning and landscaping and such, so I had a lot of cards printed for various things, like for a house-painting firm, and some for the "Bulldog Burglar Protection Agency," which say we will install all kinds of silent burglar alarms, and bells will ring in our office and we will have radio cars there in a few minutes. I also have some Pest Control and House Repair cards. None of these firms exists, of course, but neither do the phone numbers on my cards.

But while I drive slowly around the hills in my little VW bus and put my cards in the boxes, I can get a pretty good idea of who is home and who isn't, and who is gone all day, and so forth.

By the way, my truck is lettered with: H. STUSSMAN INC. GENERAL HOUSE REPAIRS on one side and FERGUSON PEST CONTROL. EVERYBODY LOVES US BUT YOUR PESTS! on the other side. I make these up myself. My theory is that nobody can ever see both sides of my truck at the same time, which will really confuse witnesses, if there are any. Of course I change the truck signs every week, and every month I paint the truck a different color.

When I decide that a certain house is ripe for hitting, I go and ring the doorbell. If I am wrong and someone is home—this is seldom—I ask them if their house happens to be swarming with disease-infested rats. Since there are no rats at all in these hills, they always say no and I leave.

If nobody answers the doorbell, it is, of course, another matter. Most of these houses have locks that could be opened by blindfolded monkeys. Not one of them has any kind of burglar alarm. There are watchdogs in some houses, but these I avoid, because you never know a friendly dog from a vicious one until you've been chewed up. And, of course, I would not hurt any dog if you paid me.

What I am getting to is about one particular house up there. It's a fairly new one-story modern style, up a driveway, but you can see the carport from the street below. In casing the place for some time, I figured that a man probably lived there alone. There was only one car, a great big new Mercedes, and this man drove off every weekday morning at nine. I saw him a few times and he was a nice-looking gentleman of about forty-five. He was always gone all day, so I guessed he had an office job.

So one day, I drove my truck up the driveway and got out and saw a sign: BEWARE OF THE DOG—and, at the same time, this little pooch comes out of a dog door and up to me, and he is a black bundle of hair and the wiggliest, happiest little puppy you ever saw. I picked him up and let him lick my face and saw that he had a tag on his collar that read: CUDDLES, MY OWNER IS HARRY HASTINGS. There was also a phone number.

I rang the doorbell, but nobody came. The front-door lock was so stupid that I opened it with a plastic card.

Inside—well, you have never seen such a sloppy-kept house. Not dirty—just sloppy. There was five days' worth of dishes in the sink. I found out later that this Harry Hastings has a maid who comes and cleans once a week, but meantime, this character just throws his dirty shirts and socks on the floor. What a slob.

I turned out to be right about his living alone. There was only one single bed in use—which, of course, was not made, and I doubt if he makes it from one year to the next. There was no sign of any female presence, which I don't wonder, the way this Hastings lives.

One of his rooms is an office, and this was *really* a mess. Papers all over the desk and also all over the floor. This room stank of old cigarette butts, of which smell I am very conscious since I gave up smoking.

From what I found on his desk, I learned that this Harry Hastings is a TV writer. He writes kind of spooky stuff, like this Rodney Serling. I took one of his scripts, to study. From his income-tax returns, which were lying around for all the world to see, I saw he made nearly $23,000 gross the year before.

But most of the furniture in the house is pretty grubby, and the drapes need replacing, which made me wonder what this character spent all his money on, besides the Mercedes. He had a new electric typewriter and a great big color-TV set, which would take four men to move, and a hi-fi, but no art objects or decent silver or gold cufflinks or things like that.

It wasn't till I went through his clothes closet that I found out that most of his bread went into his wardrobe. There was about $5,000 worth of new apparel in there, most of it hand-tailored and from places like where Sinatra and Dean Martin get their outfits. Very mod and up-to-date. I tried on a couple of jackets, and it turns out that this Hastings and me are exactly the same size! I mean *exactly*. These clothes looked like they had been tailored for me alone, after six fittings. Only his shoes didn't fit me, sad to say.

I was very pleased, indeed, I can tell you, as I have always had trouble getting fitted off the rack. Also, I like to dress in the latest fashion when I take Susie to nice places.

So I took the entire wardrobe, including shirts and ties. I decided to take the typewriter, which I needed for my writing-class homework. The machine I had kept skipping.

But I wanted to try out the typewriter before I took it, and also, I thought I would leave a note for this Hastings, so he wouldn't think I was some kind of crude thug. So I typed:

Dear Mr. Hastings:
   I am typing this to see if your typewriter works O.K. I see that it does. I am not taking it to sell it, but I need it because I am trying to become a professional writer like you, which I

know because I saw your scripts on your desk, and I am taking one to help me with my work, for studying.

I wish to make you a compliment anent your fine wardrobe of clothes. As it happened, they are like they have been made for me only. I am not taking them to sell them but because I need some good clothes to wear. Your shoes do not fit me, so I am leaving them.

I am also not taking your hi-fi, because there is a terrible screech in the treble. I like your dog, and I will give him a biskit.

A Friend

Well, some three months or so now passed, because there was no sense in hitting Hastings' house again until he had time to get a new bunch of clothes together.

But when I thought the time was ripe, I drove by there again and saw a little VW in the carport, and also, there was a big blond woman shaking rugs.

I drove up and asked her if her house was swarming with disease-infested rats, and she said she didn't think so but that she was only the once-a-week cleaning lady. She sounded Scandinavian. I took note that this was a Wednesday.

I went back the next Monday. No car in the carport. But on the way to the house, there was a new sign, hand-lettered on a board, and it read: BEWARE! VICIOUS WATCHDOG ON DUTY! THIS DOG HAS BEEN TRAINED TO GO FOR THE TESTICLES! YOU HAVE BEEN WARNED! PROCEED NO FARTHER!

Well, this gives me pause, as you can well imagine. But then I remember that this Hastings is a writer with an ingenious and inventive mind, and I do not believe this sign for one moment. Cuddles is my friend. So I start for the house, and suddenly, this enormous Alsatian jumps through the dog door and runs straight at me, growling and snarling, and then he leaps and knocks me down, and sure enough, starts chewing around my crotch. But then out comes Cuddles, and I am sure there is a dog language, for he woofed at this monster dog as if in reproach, as if to say,

"Knock it off. This is a friend. Leave him alone." So pretty soon, both dogs are licking me.

But when I get to the front door, I find that this Hastings has installed a new, burglar-proof lock. I walk around the house and find that there are new locks on both the kitchen door and the laundry-room door. They must have set Hastings back about seventy-five bucks.

There are also a lot of sliding-glass doors around the house, but I don't like to break plate glass, because I know how expensive it is to replace. But I finally locate a little louvered window by the laundry-room door, and I find that by breaking only one louver and cutting the screen, I can reach through and around and open the door.

Inside, I find that the house is just as messy as before. This guy will *die* a slob.

But when I get to his bedroom, here is this note, Scotch-taped to his closet door. It is dusty and looks like it has been there for months. It says:

Dear Burglar:
Just in *case* you are the same young man who was in here a few months ago, I think I must tell you that you have a long way to go before you will be a professional writer.
"Anent" is archaic and should be avoided. A "wardrobe of clothes" is redundant. It is "biscuit," not "biskit." Use your dictionary!
I know you are a young man, because both my cleaning woman and a nineteen-year-old neighbor have seen you and your truck. If you have gotten this far into my house, you cannot be stupid. Have you ever thought of devoting your talents to something a little higher than burgling people such as me?
Harry Hastings

Inside his closet are two fabulous new suits, plus a really great red-and-blue-plaid cashmere sports coat. I take these and am about to leave when I remember there is something I want to tell Hastings.

In his office, there is a new electric typewriter, on which I type:

> Dear Mr. Hastings:
>   Thank you for your help. In return, I want to tell you that
> I read the script of yours I took and I think it is pretty good,
> except that I don't believe that the man should go back to his
> wife. I mean, after she tried to poison him three times. This is
> just my opinion, of course.
>   I do not have a dictionary, so I am taking yours. Thank you.
>   A Friend

I, of course, do not take this new typewriter, partly because I
already have one and also because I figure he will need it to make
money with so he can replace his wardrobe again.

Four months go by before I figure it is time to hit the house
again. By this time, my clothes are getting kind of tired, and also
the styles have changed, some.

This time, when I drive up to the house one afternoon, there is
a new hand-lettered sign: THIS HOUSE IS PROTECTED BY THE BULL-
DOG BURGLAR PROTECTION AGENCY! THERE ARE SILENT ALARMS
EVERYWHERE! IF THEY ARE TRIPPED, RADIO CARS WILL CONVERGE AT
ONCE! PROCEED NO FARTHER! YOU HAVE BEEN WARNED!

Come *on,* now! I and I alone am the *nonexistent* Bulldog Burglar Protection Agency! I'd put my card in his mailbox! This is
really one cheapskate smart-ass bastard, this Harry Hastings.

When I get near the house, the dogs come out, and I give them
a little loving, and then I see a note on the front door:

> Dear Jack:
>   Welcome! Hope you had a nice trip. The key is hidden
> where it always has been. I didn't have to go to work today.
> I've run down the hill to get some Scotch and some steaks. Be
> back in a few minutes. The gals are coming at six.
>   Harry

Well, this gives me pause. I finally decide that this is not the
right day to hit the house. This could, of course, be another of
Hastings' tricks, but I can't be sure. So I leave.

But a few days later, I come back and this same goddamn note

to Jack is still on the door, only now it is all yellowed. You would
think that this lame-brain would at least write a new note every
day, welcoming Bert or Sam or Harriet or Hazel or whoever. The
truth is that this Hastings is so damn smart, when you think about
it, that he is actually stupid.

The broken louver and the screen have by now been replaced,
but when I break the glass and cut the screen and reach around to
open the laundry door, I find that this bastard has installed chains
and bolts on the inside.

Well, as any idiot knows, you can't bolt all your doors from the
inside when you go out, so one door has to be openable, and I
figure it has to be the front door; but the only way I can get in
is to break a big frosted-plate-glass window to the left of it and
reach through and open the door. As I said, I'm not happy to
break plate glass, but this Hastings has left me no choice, so I
knock out a hole just big enough for me to reach through and
open the door and go in.

This time, there is *another* note on his closet door:

> Dear Burglar:
> Are you incapable of pity? By now, you must be the best-
> dressed burglar in Hollywood. But how many clothes can you
> *wear?* You might like to know that my burglary insurance has
> been canceled. My new watchdog cost me one hundred dollars
> and I have spent a small fortune on new locks and bolts and
> chains. Now I fear you are going to start smashing my plate-
> glass windows, which can cost as much as ninety dollars to
> replace. There is only one new suit in this closet. All my other
> clothes I keep now either in my car or at my office. Take the
> suit, if you must, but never return, for, by God, you will be
> sorry, indeed, if you do. I have a terrible revenge in mind.
>   Harry Hastings
> P.S. You still have time to reform yourself.
> P.P.S. I don't like his going back to his poisoning wife, either.
> But the network insisted on a "Happy Ending."
>   H. H.

Well, I am not about to fall for all this noise about pity. Any
man who has a dog trained to go for my testicles and who uses my

own Bulldog Agency against me is not, in my mind, deserving of too much sympathy.

So I take the suit, which is a just beautiful Edwardian eight-button, in gray sharkskin.

Now, quite a few months pass and I begin to feel a little sorry for this character, and I decide to let him alone, forever.

But then, one day, when I am out working, some bastard breaks into my own pad, which is three rooms over a private garage in Hollywood. This son of a bitch takes every stitch of clothing I own.

By this time, I am heavily dating Susie Plimson, and she likes good dressers. So, while I am not too happy about it, I decide I have to pay Hastings another visit.

No dogs come out this time when I walk to the front door. But on it is a typed note, which says:

> HELGA! DO NOT OPEN THIS DOOR! Since you were here last week, I bought a PUMA, for burglar protection. This is a huge cat, a cougar or a mountain lion, about four feet long, not including the tail. The man I bought it from told me it was fairly tame, but it is NOT! It has tried to attack both dogs, who are O.K. and are locked in the guest room. I myself have just gone down to my doctor's to have stitches taken in my face and neck and arms. This ferocious puma is wandering loose inside the house. The S.P.C.A. people are coming soon to capture it and take it away. I tried to call you and tell you not to come today, but you had already left. Whatever you do, if the S.P.C.A. has not come before you, DO NOT UNDER ANY CIRCUMSTANCES OPEN THIS DOOR!!

Well, naturally, this gave me considerable pause. Helga was obviously the blond cleaning woman. But this was a Tuesday, and she came on Wednesdays. Or she used to. But she could have changed her days.

I stroll around the outside of the house. But all of the curtains and drapes are drawn, and I can't see in. As I pass the guest-room windows, the two dogs bark inside. So this much of the note on the door is true.

So I wander back to the front door, and I think and I ponder. Is there really a puma in there, or is this just another of Hastings' big fat dirty lies?

After all, it is one hell of a lot of trouble to buy and keep a puma just to protect a few clothes. And it is also expensive, and this Hastings I know by now is a cheapskate. It costs him not one thin dime to put this stupid note to Helga on his front door and, God knows, it would terrify most anybody who wanted to walk in.

Susie told us in class that in every story, there is like a moment of decision. I figured this was mine.

After about five minutes of solid thought, I finally make my decision. There *is* no puma in there. It's just that this smart-ass bastard wants me to think that there is a puma in there.

So I decide to enter the house, by breaking another hole in the now-replaced frosted-plate-glass window to the left of the front door. So I break out a small portion of this glass.

And I peer through this little hole I've made, and I see nothing. No puma. I listen. I don't hear any snarling cat or anything. No puma. Just the same, there *could* be a puma in there and it could be crouching silently just inside the door, waiting to pounce and bite my hand off when I put it in. Very carefully, I put some fingers in and wiggle them. No puma. And so I put my arm in and reach and turn the doorknob from the inside and open the door a crack. No snarl from a puma—whatever pumas snarl like. I open the door a little wider and I call, "Here, pussy-pussy! Here, puma-puma! *Nice* puma!" No response.

I creep in very cautiously, looking around, ready to jump back and out and slam the door on this beast, if necessary. But there is no puma.

And then I realize that my decision was, of course, right, and there is no goddamn puma in this goddamn house. But still, I am sweating like a pig and breathing heavily, and I suddenly figure out what Susie means when she talks about "the power of the written word." With just a piece of writing, this bastard Hastings transferred an idea from his crazy imagination into my mind, and I was willing to believe it.

So I walk down the hall to his bedroom door, which is shut, and there is *another* typed note on it:

> Dear Burglar:
> O.K. So there is no puma. Did you really think I'd let a huge cat mess up my nice neat house?
> However, I am now going to give you a *serious warning*. DO NOT OPEN THIS DOOR! One of the engineers at our studio has invented a highly sophisticated security device and I've borrowed one of his models. It's hidden in the bedroom and it works by means of ultrasonic waves. They are soundless and they have a fantastically destructive and permanent effect on brain tissue. It takes less than a minute of exposure. You will not notice any brain-numbing effects at once, but in a few days, your memory will start to go, and then your reasoning powers, and so, for your *own* sake, DO NOT ENTER THIS ROOM!
> Harry Hastings

Well, I really had to hand it to this loony character. No wonder he made a lot of money as a writer. I, of course, do not believe *one word* of this, *at all;* therefore, I go into the bedroom and hurry to see if there is any hidden electronic device, but, of course, there is not. Naturally.

Then I see another note, on the closet door, and it says:

> Dear Burglar:
> I don't suppose I should have expected you to believe that one, with your limited imagination and your one-track mind. By the way, where do you *go* in all my clothes? You must be quite a swinger.
> There are only a few new things in the closet. But before you take them, I suggest you sniff them. You will notice a kind of cologne smell, but this is only to disguise another odor. I have a pal who was in chemical warfare, and he has given me a liquid that can be sprayed inside clothing. No amount of dry cleaning can ever entirely remove it. When the clothes are worn, the heat of the body converts this substance into a heavy gas that attacks the skin and produces the most frightful and agonizingly painful blisters, from the ankles to the neck. Never forget that you have been *warned.*
> Harry Hastings

Well, I don't believe this for one moment, and so I open the closet door. All there is is one pair of slacks and a sports coat. But this coat looks like the very same *plaid cashmere* I took before and the son of a bitch stole from *me!* But then I realize this could not be so, but it was just that Hastings liked this coat so much he went out and bought another just like it.

Anyway, I find myself sniffing these. They smell of cologne, all right, but nothing else, and I know, of course, that this kind of gas stuff does not exist at all except in Hastings' wild imagination, which I am coming to admire by now.

As I drive back to my pad, I start to laugh when I think of all the stupid and fantastic things that Hastings has tried to put into my mind today by the power of suggestion, and I realize that he almost succeeded. *Almost,* but not quite.

When I get home and climb the outside stairs to my front door, there are three envelopes taped to it, one above another. There are no names on them, but they are numbered, 1, 2, 3. I do not know what in hell all this could be about, but I open 1 and I read:

Dear Burglar:
The plaid cashmere coat you have over your arm right now is *not* a replacement for the one you stole. It is the *same identical coat. Think* about this before you open envelope 2.
Harry Hastings

Well, of *course* I think about this as I stand there with my mouth sort of hanging open. All of a sudden, it *hits* me! *Harry Hastings* was the son of a bitch who stole all his clothes back! But how did he know where I *live?* How could he know I was going to hit his house *today?* My hands are all fumbles as I open 2. Inside it says:

Dear Burglar:
To answer your questions: On your *third* visit to my house, my young neighbor saw you and followed you home in his car, and so found out just where you live. Later, in my own good

time, I easily entered this place with a bent paper clip and re-
trieved my own clothes. Today, my neighbor called me at my
office and said you were inside my house again. Later, I phoned
him and he said you had come out, with my coat. So I've had
time to come here and write and leave these notes. I also have
had time to do something else, which you will read about in 3.

Harry Hastings

I open this third envelope very fast indeed, because I figure that
if Hastings knows all this, the fuzz will be along any minute. In it,
I read:

Dear Burglar:
    I got the puma idea from a friend out in the valley who has
one in a large cage in his yard. Long ago, I asked him if I
might borrow this huge cat for a day sometime, and he said yes
and that he didn't like burglars, either. He has a large carrying
cage for the puma. I called him this morning the moment I
heard you were inside my house, and he drove the puma right
over *here,* and we released the huge cat inside your place. She
is now in there, wandering around loose. I have done this partly
because I am vengeful and vindictive by nature and partly because I've made my living for years as a verisimilitudinous
(look it up later) writer, and I deeply resent anyone I cannot
fool. The puma that is now inside is my childish way of getting even. This is no *trick* this time! If you have any brains at
all, DO NOT OPEN THIS DOOR! Just get out of town before the
police arrive, which will be in about half an hour. Good-bye.
                                                Harry Hastings
    P.S. The puma's nome is Carrie—as if that would help you any.

Well, I read in a story once where somebody was called a
"quivering mass of indecisive jelly," and that is what I was right
then. I simply did not know *what* to think or believe. If this was
any door but mine, I could walk away. But all my *cash* was hidden inside, and I *had* to get it before I could leave town.

So I stand there and I sweat and I think and I think and after a
long time, it comes to me that *this* time, this bastard Hastings is
finally telling the *truth.* Besides, I can hear little noises from

inside. There *is* a puma in there! I know it! But I have to get *in* there, just the same!

I finally figure that if I open the door fast and step back, Carrie might just scoot past me and away. But maybe she will attack me. But then I figure if I wrap the sports coat around one arm and the slacks around the other, maybe I can fend off Carrie long enough to grab a chair and then force her into my bathroom, the way lion tamers do, and then slam the door on her, and then grab my cash and run out of there, and the police can worry about her when they come.

So this is what I decide to do, only it is some time before I can get up the nerve to unlock the door and push it open. I unlock the door and I stand there. But finally, I think, "Oh, hell, you *got* to do it, sooner or later," and so I push my door open and stand back.

No puma jumps at me. Nothing happens at all. But then I look around the corner of my door and *Harry Hastings* is sitting inside. Not with a gun or anything. He is sitting very calmly behind the old card table I use as a desk, with a cigarette in his mouth and a pencil in his hand, and I see one of my stories in front of him.

I walk in and just stand there with my face on and cannot think of any clever remark to make, when he says: "Tell me one thing. *Did* you or did you *not* really believe there was a puma in here?"

If I remember right—I was pretty shook up then—I nodded and I said, "Yes, sir. Yes. I really did."

Then he smiled a big smile and said, "Well, thank heavens for *that*. I was beginning to think I was losing my grip. I feel a little better now. Sit down. I want to talk to you. By the way, your syntax is terrible and your grammar is worse. I've been making some corrections while waiting for you. However, that's not what I want to talk to you about. Sit down. Stop trembling, will you, and sit down!"

I sat.

As I write now, I am the co-owner and manager of the Puma Burglar Protection Agency. Harry Hastings is my silent partner and he put up two thousand dollars for financing. Susie helps me with my accounts. I have 130 clients now, at five dollars a month each. The reason it's so cheap is that we use the Harry Hastings Method. That is, we don't bother with burglar alarms or things like that. I just patrol around and keep putting up and changing signs and notices and notes on front doors. Already, the burglary rate in my area has been cut by two-thirds.

This very morning, I got a little letter from Harry Hastings with two new ideas for front-door notes. One is: CLARA! I HAVE ALREADY CALLED THE POLICE AND THEY WILL BE HERE IN MINUTES! DO NOT CALL THEM AGAIN! GEORGE IS LOCKED IN THE BATHROOM AND CAN'T GET OUT, SO WE WILL BE SAFE TILL THEY GET HERE!

The second one is: NOTICE! BECAUSE OF A FRIGHTFULLY CON-TAGIOUS DISEASE, THIS HOUSE HAS BEEN EVACUATED AND QUARAN-TINED. IT MUST ABSOLUTELY NOT BE ENTERED UNTIL IT HAS BEEN FUMIGATED!

Harry Hastings says that I should be sure to warn the house-holder to remove this notice before any large parties.

Welcome to the bailiwick of the classic con, the tradition-en-shrouded swindle—but with a bit of a deadly twist. . . .

MORRIS HERSHMAN
Willing Victim

Carl Peck said easily, "This is for you," giving his waiter the last bill in his wallet.

Peck coughed politely a couple of minutes after that functionary was gone. The man at the next table in this restaurant, a hard-looking fellow in the mid-fifties, glanced up from a copy of *Inventor's News*.

He was dressed as expensively as Peck, but his clothes weren't nearly as loud, Peck noticed.

"I seem to have spent my last five dollars just now." Peck smiled. "Could you lend me enough to pay my bill?"

"I beg your pardon?"

"If you lend me ten and walk to my cottage with me, I'll give you ten dollars back." He shrugged in the silence that followed. "I can give you twenty, if you'd rather. The amount makes no real difference to me."

He wasn't surprised to see quick interest lighting the older man's face. Rich people, as Carl Peck had found out during ten years or so of making deals with them, will do almost anything at all for a few extra dollars.

"Well, I heard the waiter call you by name, so you're obviously registered.as a guest," the older man said, brushing a hand at the dust motes that gleamed and whirled in the sun's rays across the length of his table. The hard face didn't change as he nodded. "I'll be glad to accommodate you, sir. Your interest rates are excellent."

Peck began walking a step or two ahead of the older man down the tree-shaded path to his rented cottage close to the year-round luxury hotel; but the older man caught up and kept to Peck's pace without making any complaint.

"I was a little startled when you said that thing about interest rates just before," Carl Peck told him in a thoughtful tone of voice. "I hadn't remembered about interest rates in years."

"Apparently not," the older man agreed, rolling his copy of *Inventor's News* into a horn and swatting a fly with it. "If you were an inventor, though, you'd have to—"

"But I am," Peck said quickly, grateful because the point had been brought up by the hard-faced older man. Then he did his best to look confused. "That is, I—well, I did invent something once, but frankly, I'd rather not talk about it."

"Suit yourself. I can be closemouthed, too."

"Money," Peck said lazily, as if being closemouthed about a certain subject was exactly what he wanted, "doesn't have to worry anybody who's really farsighted."

"All the same, you're the one who was embarrassed at table," the older man said crisply. "I have some respect for money, thank heavens, and that sort of thing doesn't happen to me."

"I don't have any respect for it," Peck said, more and more grateful that the talk was going like he wanted it to. "Manufacturing it is a mechanical process that needs plates and inks and paper. If there was a way to erase the inking on a one-dollar bill and then produce a ten or a twenty or a fifty with it, we'd all be rich. It's a matter of inks, when you come right down to it. Your wealth is ruled by the ink on your bills."

"Money would become worthless if everybody had access to a

mechanical process like that." Thoughtfully the older man added. "The process would be useful in the hands of one or two people, but those people would be rich. Not like you or me, I mean, but really rich."

Carl Peck managed to keep from smiling. Never in a long career had he run across a single wealthy man who admitted directly or otherwise to being in excellent shape financially. Every one of them thought of himself as being reasonably well off or comfortably fixed, but not rich. Never rich. And it was amazing, when you come to think of it, how often a wealthy man could positively drool at the notion of earning some more money.

"People with any such invention," the older man said realistically, "would have to keep quiet about it."

"Maybe so." Peck nodded. "But they'd be less than human if they could resist the temptation to brag about it occasionally."

"Then they'd better be less than human or face ruin."

"I don't think an occasional brag will—oh, here we are. My little shack."

It was one of the most expensive cottage accommodations that the hotel offered. The older man, who was staying in a smaller room that was part of the huge building they had come from, looked at Carl Peck as if he had never before come across such a spendthrift.

"How much money did I promise you?" Carl Peck asked negligently. "Twenty dollars, wasn't it?"

"Fifty," the older man said promptly.

"All right. I'll have to ask you to wait outside while I get the money. I'll try not to take very long."

Peck slipped into the cottage before the older man could start to protest. He locked the door noisily, then closed and locked every window before shuttering it.

From one of the locked drawers he pulled out a thick roll of bills and a heating pad. He plugged the cord from the heating pad into an electrical outlet, then took a fifty dollar bill from the roll of bills and held it against the pad. While it was simmering gently, Peck reached down for a bottle of green ink. He allowed a drop of it to reach his left forefinger and smudged part of the fifty-dollar bill with it.

It would take another minute for the bill to warm up sufficiently, he judged, and in that time he glanced at the locked drawer which held what he sometimes thought of, with a chuckle, as the infernal machine. Many a time he had "demonstrated" it by putting a bill into the top of it and seemingly taking out the same bill without a mark on it, then putting it into the upper half of the machine and apparently cranking it out as a ten- or twenty- or fifty-dollar bill.

Carl Peck was never surprised that so many suckers believed such a crude confidence game. With wonders on every side nowadays, suckers had become more gullible than ever. And the rich ones were more gullible than any others in this technological civilization that had turned into a con man's paradise.

At this very minute there was a sucker, a genuine fourteen-carat pigeon, waiting for him in front of his door.

Quickly now, Peck disconnected the heating pad and put it away. When he opened the door a few inches and stood firmly against it as if to block any view inside, he saw that the older man, the pigeon, was standing less than six inches away.

Carl Peck offered the bill and said, "Here you are, Mr.—uh, I don't even know your name, come to think of it."

"Henry Sebastian," the older man said, wincing as he touched the heated bill and looking wide-eyed at the smudge of green ink. He gaped at Peck.

"My name is Carl Peck," Peck said, taking a step backwards. "P-e-c-k. I'll see you around, I'm sure. Mr. Sebastian."

Sure enough, the pigeon phoned him next morning.

"You've found a money-making process, and not even a bank can tell the difference," Mr. Sebastian started, almost incoherent with excitement. "I'll buy it for—well, it makes no sense to offer cash, but perhaps you'd be interested in negotiable securities, Mr. Peck. Does anybody else know about this?"

"Nobody does, but I'm not sure I want to sell," Peck said very slowly.

"But you admit I'm right, you admit it. I'm coming over to see you right now, and I promise it'll be well worth while."

But this visit didn't turn out to be worth Carl Peck's while. Not at all.

Carl Peck, in fact, never knew what hit him when he opened the door to Mr. Sebastian, he never regained consciousness.

Mr. Henry Sebastian stepped away from the body, pocketing a certain tool which he had invented years ago and which wouldn't be detected as having caused anything but heart failure. That tool was the first of the two workable inventions he had ever made, and he disliked using it for this.

He forced two bureau drawers open, and then the curious-looking black box was in sight. With the special implement he was carrying, Mr. Sebastian, of all people, promptly destroyed the money-producing machine.

When he was finished he glanced at Peck's body and said, "Damn fool for talking so much." He sighed. "Tell the truth to one person, and it'll be told to others, inevitably—and in time nobody will be safe. No one. No one at all." Mr. Sebastian shrugged his shoulders.

His morning's work had played hob with the expensive suit he was wearing, Mr. Sebastian noticed regretfully. It was a shame, but if necessary he could always go back to his city residence for a while and crank out enough money for another suit.

How best to describe this story? An eerie chorus from the night song of our race? A paean to the price of progress? No matter—it's only the husk of a junkie feeding his habit off in a dirty corner well away from the sensibilities of us gentler folk. . . .

DONALD OLSON
The Blue Tambourine

In the shabbiest precinct of a city so long tainted by economic blight that he is even denied the companionship of his own image in the grime-crusted windows of its vacant buildings, Willie de Garde stoops to snatch a starving cat from a dark doorway, pops it into the sack he carries for this purpose, and then hurries on, for the night air is sharp, winter close at hand. A cold fog shortens the streets and makes pretty but useless golden roses of the street lights.

The young man cradles his furry prize tightly against his chest, as if to revive it by contact with his own strong young heart, and his steps quicken as he approaches an old brick building whose facade still bears faint traces of a gaudy elegance. It is a theater called the Oriental Garden, the only theater in town which has made no concessions to the changing habits of its patrons, and consequently has lost all but a special few. It has not modernized its marquee, nor improved its lighting, nor installed retractable seats or refreshment stands, and it continues to show movies consistently lacking in appeal to the general public.

The almost total darkness does not confuse Willie, who knows his way around and can find his usual seat with no other guide than a few spots of orange light where mandarin-colored bulbs glow eerily beneath plaster bas-reliefs of Chinese maidens wearing kimonos that are now chipped and paintless. Overhead, a similarly despoiled jet-black dragon with only one red bulb of an eye holds in its teeth a huge black-and-crimson Chinese lantern.

Those who still patronize the Oriental Garden seek something other than entertainment: a place to sleep, a place to hide, a place to hope for one of those exceedingly rare occasions when some black-sheep cousin of Eros might lead to a nearby seat a figure whose needs, communicated by signals as universally understood by the initiated as the Morse code is by the fraternity of wireless operators, might correspond to one's own.

Occasionally one might see, it's true, a white-skinned leg extended at a grotesque angle, and a spiderlike hand creeping and crawling from ankle to thigh, but it is more often to the solitary passions that the Oriental Garden caters. It is a popular refuge, for instance, of lonely drunks who stumble into the orchestra to sleep off a binge after offering rumbling, gratuitous criticisms of whatever story is unfolding above them on the tarnished silver screen.

Like these others, Willie de Garde comes to the Oriental Garden for a purpose, and no sooner is he seated than his eyes peer through the gloom as anxiously as a seaman's through coastal fog, until, perhaps from nearby, perhaps from the other side of the theater, he hears the jingle of the blue tambourine, a sound which violates the silence no more harshly than a discreet cough, and which is repeated at intervals until he has found his way to Mrs. Rainfyre's side.

Without the sound of the blue tambourine she might never be located, for she dresses always in black from head to foot, in garments as out of fashion as her face, a face rather like those that peer out of pre-Renaissance paintings, a Margaritone or a Cavallini, a somber, slant-eyed face as ravaged by time as the plaster faces of the Chinese maidens on the frieze above their heads.

"Buona sera, Poet," she greets him as he slips into the seat beside her. "What have you brought me?"

"A choice ingredient for your witch's brew. Another cat."

As usual, she ignores this little dig, just as she drops no hint of what she does with the creatures he brings to her. Nor does he ever ask. It's none of his business.

As he drags the unprotesting cat out of his sack, Mrs. Rainfyre settles her black umbrella against the farther seat and deftly plunges the animal deep into her own black leather shopping bag.

"Quick!" he whispers, for having fulfilled his part of the bargain, he is eager for the customary payment; his eyes begin to water and his lips to burn as she rummages in yet another bag as if for some trifle requiring much fishing about to locate.

"Ecce!" she murmurs as a figure looms dimly beside them in the aisle, groping blindly along the dark, narrow row of empty seats.

"He can't see! Hurry."

"Ah, *pronto, pronto,"* she hisses, mimicking his urgency as her yellow fingers fasten upon the glimmering hypodermic, while the other hand grips his already bared arm, pumping up the vein and finally puncturing it with a deft thrust of the needle.

As she puts away her instrument, she engages in familiar small talk, to which he scarcely listens. "How goes the poem? Soon finished?"

His body droops limply against the seat. "Soon . . ."

"Ah? But not *too* soon, one hopes."

He is so little aware of her now that he misses the faint note of alarm in her voice. "You have other—customers," he murmurs.

She strokes his thigh with an impersonal touch, cold and sexless. "You are my favorite, *care."*

As soon as she departs, carrying her bags, her umbrella, and her blue tambourine, he too drifts out into a foggy drizzle in which the golden roses on their iron stems appear to expand and throb above him, and as he passes through squalid alleys, his mind in a state of swiftly laddering exaltation, a cascade of brilliant images floods his brain so that he fears it will explode before he reaches his own room and can transfer them onto paper. He moves very quickly now.

This creative mood is sustained for an unusually long period, and he is not aware of its passing until one garish dusk as he stands at the window of his room and watches the sun, like a mad arsonist lighting fires in the windows of buildings across the street, while the sky above this conflagration grows purple with news of an approaching storm.

Being above all else a poet, Willie de Garde seeks no logical explanation for the way in which Mrs. Rainfyre manages to be in the Oriental Garden whenever he has something—a cat, a puppy, a rat, a bird—to exchange for her ministrations; he is happy to grant to her occult powers of divination, in spite of having seen her on the street one day, all in black and carrying her usual luggage, stooping to crush a wad of bills into the grubby hand of a dwarf, who thereupon whispered something in her ear which sent her scurrying off in another direction. Apparently, Mrs. Rainfyre paid a whole brigade of street creatures to keep her informed of the desires and movements of her clientele.

When next he creeps into his seat at the Oriental Garden, Willie is shaking with something besides the craving of his burning nerves, for this time he harbors the secret of betrayal, the giddying knowledge that this will be the last time the odious harpy stabs him full of dreams, for the poem is almost finished and he will spend a vagabond winter in the South. He speeds merrily toward the jingle of the blue tambourine.

"*Buona sera*, Poet."

Her perfume is as offensive and rank as the stench of brimstone in the halls of heaven. "Hurry!" he pleads. "I need it!"

She doesn't move. "Ah, Poet, we all have special needs tonight."

"Shoot me! Shoot me!"

"Slowly, Poet. Tonight you must pay for my merchandise."

He jabs at the bag in which she has deposited the gray squirrel he brought her. "I've paid, beldame!"

She jiggles a note of laughter out of the blue tambourine. "These pets you bring me—you think *they* pay for what you get?"

"Give it to me!"

"Will you pay?"

"I'll steal a lion from the zoo in broad daylight! But give—"

"Look. Empty." She opens the black bag, and he plunges his hand deep inside, drawing it out damp and trembling.

"I must have it! Now!"

"So you will, *care*, so you will. We're going to leave this place together and go where you will be given what you crave—in return for a small service," she whispers.

They leave the theater, and she leads him through a twist of streets and alleys to a tenement in an even more desolate part of town. In a filthy vestibule a dozen rusty mailboxes hang empty and unlabeled on the leprous wall. A bulb glimmers at the top of a long flight of steps.

A flight above this ill-lit landing they stop outside a door upon whose frosted pane has originally been painted in black letters the words:

RAINFYRE

PHOTOGRAPHER

However, the second word has been unskillfully scratched out, and underneath has been inscribed the word ESCHATOLOGIST. Mrs. Rainfyre pauses to let him read this before taking a key from her pocket and letting him in.

In a room as dismal as the Oriental Garden, a man sits quietly reading at a cluttered table. He looks as if he had been glued together out of miscellaneous pieces of chalk and string, for there is a curious incompatibility about his features; nothing seems to match. His glasses are so thick they give the illusion that his eyes are actually inside the lenses instead of behind them, rather like monstrous green buttons laminated in plastic spheres. The top of his head is covered by a cap made from a woman's silk stocking; the lobes of his ears sprout grizzled white whiskers. Willie scarcely notices any of this, so fascinated is he by the man's right arm, which ends in a flipper instead of a hand, an elongated tapering paddle of tissue and skin. The left hand is normal, although extraordinarily tiny and delicate, like a girl's.

"My husband," gravely announces Mrs. Rainfyre.

His voice is a passionate squeak. "Honored, dear boy. I know you well, already, I feel." A nod toward his wife. "Forgive my not offering my hand, but, as you see . . ." And he deliberately waves the grotesque flipper in Willie's face, at the same time laughing with a sound like breaking glass. "A congenital inconvenience, most distressing at such a time."

"A crucial time," adds Mrs. Rainfyre darkly.

Willie feels faint. "I need—" he starts to say, and Mrs. Rainfyre, leaving her husband to help the youth to a chair, hurries into another room, returning with a hypodermic wrapped in gauze. She no longer has the blue tambourine. Willie tenses his arm, but she merely lays the instrument on the table.

"Yes," purrs Rainfyre. "You need your—medicine. Of course. The inconstant muse must be enticed, mustn't she? I can't tell you how thrilled Mrs. Rainfyre and I have been to have been permitted to play the role, so to speak, of patrons of the arts in the life of so gifted a young man."

In the silence following this remark there comes from behind an inner door the distinct sound of the blue tambourine. Rainfyre smiles at his wife. She consults a clock on the wall. "You had best tell him what you must, and quickly. It grows late."

Rainfyre gets up and circles the table, thumping its surface with that obscene flap of flesh, while with his good hand he removes his glasses and massages his eyes.

"Mrs. Rainfyre is right, Mr. de Garde, and though I deplore the necessity of offering so abbreviated an explanation of what we're going to do, I have no wish to conceal from you the reason for which we require your service. At this very moment I am engaged in the most important experiment of my career, an experiment that will crown years of prodigious labor and research. Research, I might add, financed solely by the commercial enterprise of Mrs. Rainfyre, and the demand for that commodity which she has been abundantly able to supply."

Again, from behind the door, comes the jingle of the blue tambourine, and Rainfyre smiles and says, "Once we pass through that door, there can be no turning back. I tell you now, young friend, you are here under no duress, nor will you be coerced into taking part in the experiment for which we require your assistance—provided you leave at once and never come near this place again. But hear me! Mrs. Rainfyre will make no further visits to a certain tawdry cinema where you have so liberally availed yourself of her services. You will never see Mrs. Rainfyre again. You must employ some new device to woo your muse, or find some other agency. Which will not be easy, for this service of Mrs. Rainfyre's is seldom extended on such generous terms. Am I not right?"

Willie's head droops forward onto his folded arms, his body racked by the savage pangs of his addiction. The poem . . . the poem . . . so near completion . . . if only . . . if only . . .

"Many poets have paid a higher price than you shall be made to pay," whispers Rainfyre, as if reading his mind. "You are the reincarnation of Poe. The shade of Baudelaire. The ghost of Verlaine. An artist to your soul. Your work is your life, as is mine. Upon fulfilling your part of this little business you will be given what you and your muse crave, and as a bonus—hear this—the very instrument of your pleasure in an exquisite velvet-lined case, and with a sufficient amount of that commodity of Mrs. Rainfyre's as will make you a king of dreams, and your muse a slave."

To Willie de Garde, writhing in misery, it sounds like the promise of heaven. He nods his agreement.

Rainfyre vanishes on his tiny feet into another room of the flat, and Willie raises his head and stares at the glittering receptacle of his anodyne, which Mrs. Rainfyre, sensing his intention, snatches quickly out of his reach. Then she removes a locket from inside the collar of her dress and hands it to him. Through the mist that stings his eyes he sees the picture of a young girl of not more than nine or ten, with luminous dark eyes and massive ringlets.

"Our daughter, Poet. She died less than a month after her father took that picture. A drunken motorist ran her down in the street, crushed her little dancing legs. When they carried her to us in the house where we lived, she was—"

"Still alive!" Rainfyre comes back into the room, wheeling before him on a squeaky-castored tripod a bulky crepe-covered object. "She lay for hours, broken, helpless, dying so very slowly. Near midnight she raised her little hand and weakly beckoned me. I looked into those eyes which had been rigid as stones with pain and saw such radiance she might have become an angel before death. Her eyes seemed to light the room, and she said in a strong, clear voice: 'Papa, papa, make them hurry. It's so pretty!' "

Behind his glasses Rainfyre's eyes expand like soap bubbles, seem sure to burst. "*It's so pretty!* Her precise words, Mr. de Garde. A moment later she was dead."

Raindrops tap against the black-curtained windows like the fingers of beggar children pleading to be let in. No one moves.

Rainfyre removes the shroud from the object and reveals an enormous camera of apparently antique vintage but fitted with innumerable shiny devices as terrifying as those that menace the waiting patient trapped in the dentist's chair.

Taking from his pocket three small pieces of stiff white paper, he lays them before the poet, who examines them gingerly, trembling. He sees nothing but overexposed snapshots, dull on one side, glossy on the other, with vague bluish streaks on the glossy side.

"These, Mr. de Garde, are photographs of the last optical image in the brain of a dying guinea pig, one of the expendable creatures you so kindly procured for us. They're of no interest. I erred in the calculation of perceivable light-ray intensity."

Again, behind the door, the jingle of the blue tambourine. There is a look of mild urgency in the smile that crosses Mrs. Rainfyre's face; her husband continues speaking, however, with no sign of haste.

"This, you observe, is a camera, with many sophisticated refinements. For several years I was a professional photographer. Now, as you may have read on the door, I am an eschatologist, an explorer of those ethereal regions my colleagues have heretofore ignored, although essentially it involves the same problems of timing and lighting. To oversimplify further, my boy, there is an instant between life and death when one is neither wholly out of this life nor entirely within the other. After the death of my beloved child, and with nothing but her deathbed cry to inspire me, I devoted myself to the exploration of that mystical borderland, and finally—yes, with this very camera!—devised a means of recording in black and white a picture of that afterworld whose radiant beauty illuminated my dying angel's face. With the brains of the animals you have procured for us I have mastered the enormous technical problems, and now—*now,* Mr. de Garde . . ."

Willie de Garde scarcely listens to this madness, so acutely painful are the symptoms of his body's deprivation. "Please! Give me . . . give me . . ."

"Yes, yes, soon, my boy. Very soon. Now, come, observe."

Rainfyre takes the poet's arm and leads him to the door, pushes it quietly open. In the middle of a smaller room, a young girl sits on a straight-backed chair in a soft pool of light. She has long red hair and skin almost as white as the simple dress she wears. In her hands she holds the blue tambourine, and she smiles with infinite sweetness as she gently taps it with her fingertips. She is totally blind, and sits stiffly, as if posed.

Though there was no perceptible sound as the door opened, she turns toward them. "Mr. Rainfyre?"

"Are you fatigued, child?"

"Oh, no. I've been listening to the rain and answering it with the blue tambourine. As long as I do that, the rain won't turn to snow."

"Are you warm enough?"

"Yes."

"It won't be long," he promises. "We're nearly ready to take the picture."

Rainfyre motions Willie back into the other room and shuts the door behind them.

"You have glimpsed the rarest of treasures, Mr. de Garde— *total innocence.* A privilege, even for a poet. Our search for such perfect, pristine innocence makes a tale in itself, but we haven't time to entertain you with it now. Suffice to say it was most exhaustive and ended where it began—in this very building. She lives alone in a hole of a room on the floor above us, where she sits in the dark crocheting fancywork in exquisite designs, which she tries to sell by hawking them from door to door. If anyone deserves heaven, that child does."

The sight of the girl and the knowledge of what this madman plans to do with her momentarily distracts Willie from his own misery. He starts to protest, but Rainfyre hushes him with a threatening movement of the unformed hand.

"Don't distress yourself, my boy. The animals you brought to us died painlessly, and so will she." His magnified eyes roll upward in reluctant submissiveness to fate. "One would prefer to employ the brain of some hideous sinner, quite naturally. Alas, this is precluded by certain insurmountable technical problems. If you will pardon me for once again oversimplifying, and not to sound too flippant, one would need a most sophisticated flash device to take photographs of hell. So we had to skip that idea. And we needed, you must see, someone of unimpeachable purity in order to take pictures of heaven."

By now Mrs. Rainfyre is becoming quite agitated. She starts plucking at her husband's sleeve and casting urgent glances at the clock, but he goes on just as imperturbably. "Don't ask me to explain how the actual process works—a matter of electrical impulses flowing between the child's brain and the internal mechanism of this specially adapted camera. She thinks it's merely another picture. I've used her as a model for conventional photos on several occasions in order to dispel any qualms she might feel. She is patient and indefatigable. A saint. Her passing will be swift and humane, and at the last quick pulse of life the marvelously sensitive eye of this camera will register the visual image that flashes instantaneously across the optical nerves of her brain on the very threshold of the infinite."

Willie listens to all this with mounting nausea, while out of the corner of his eye he never loses sight of that fascinating steel instrument in Mrs. Rainfyre's hand. Loathing and revulsion serve only to quicken the burning appetite that has drawn him to this lunatic's room. He fights to keep alert.

"You are wondering precisely what you shall have to do?" says Rainfyre. "As you can see, I'm somewhat handicapped by this." He waves the flipper. "And I'm also afflicted with a coronary weakness that forbids undue exertion. Nor is my wife strong in anything but spirit. We must therefore rely on you, my young friend, to dispose of the—er—remains. You must carry the girl's body in a laundry bag down all these stairs to the alley. No one will see you, and once you've got to the river . . . You understand."

As he speaks, the photographer has been deftly, with his one good hand, rolling up Willie de Garde's sleeve, while Mrs. Rainfyre circles the table, the needle poised and ready.

"When you've completed your little errand, you might wish to come back here, and Mrs. Rainfyre will make you a lovely cup of tea. Yes. We might have a little celebration, just the three of us, and you could read us your poem. Wouldn't that be nice?"

Now he is opening the door into the inner room, and Willie sees the girl in white playing happily with the blue tambourine, and then Rainfyre begins wheeling his terrible machine toward the door, pushing it along with the help of his tapering, fishlike flipper.

Willie's eyes are on the glittering shaft of the needle, but just as Mrs. Rainfyre extends it toward his naked arm he cries out and tears away from her grasp. Without realizing he is doing so, he snatches up the three photographs from the table as he lunges toward the door. Mrs. Rainfyre shrieks. An unlikely roar comes from the puny photographer.

Down, down, down the rickety steps he flies, crashing from wall to wall, bursting through the door and into the deserted street.

Breathless, he runs like a wild man through dark canyons of vacant buildings, big white crystals of snow settling upon his eyes and cheeks and lips like icy moths, and no matter how far and fast he runs, he still hears in his head the mad jingling of the blue tambourine.

Near the end of the street a gust of wind tears the small white photographs out of his hand. He claws at the air to retrieve them, and thinks he has, but when he reaches the river and opens his fist he holds nothing but a handful of snowflakes.

The Yearbook of the Detective Story

Abbreviations: EQMM—Ellery Queen's Mystery Magazine
AHMM—Alfred Hitchcock's Mystery Magazine
MSMM—Mike Shayne Mystery Magazine

BIBLIOGRAPHY: 1971

I. Collections

1. Aiken, Joan: *The Green Flash and Other Tales of Horror, Suspense and Fantasy*. New York: Holt, Rinehart and Winston. Fourteen short stories of mixed themes; no detection.
2. Chandler, Raymond: *The Midnight Raymond Chandler*, with introduction by Joan Kahn. Boston: Houghton Mifflin Co. Two novels, four short stories, and Chandler's essay "The Simple Art of Murder."
3. Christie, Agatha: *The Golden Ball and Other Stories*. New York: Dodd Mead & Co. Fifteen stories, most of them hitherto uncollected in book form in this country.
4. du Maurier, Daphne: *Don't Look Now*. New York: Doubleday & Co. Five stories of romantic suspense.
5. Eden, Dorothy: *Yellow Is for Fear*. New York: Ace Books. Five stories of romantic suspense.
6. Gallico, Paul: *The Zoo Gang*. New York: Coward, McCann, & Geoghegan, Inc. Four entertaining tales about an aging quintet from the French Resistance and their enterprising approach to anticrime on the Côte d'Azur.
7. Gardner, Erle Stanley: *The Case of the Crimson Kiss*. New York: William Morrow & Co. A 1948 Perry Mason novelette and four short stories from the pulps, 1921–1939, none about Mason and none previously printed in book form.
8. Gardner, Erle Stanley: *The Case of the Crying Swallow*. New York:

William Morrow & Co. A Mason novelette from 1947 and three pulp short stories (1931–1949) about lesser-known series characters.

9. Goulart, Ron: *Ghost Breaker*. New York: Ace Books. Nine stories about psychic detective Max Kearny.

10. Goulart, Ron: *What's Become of Screwloose? and Other Stories*. New York: Charles Scribner's Sons. Ten stories of science fiction, half of them also criminous.

11. Hoch, Edward D.: *The Judges of Hades*, with introduction by Hans Stefan Santesson. North Hollywood, California: Leisure Books. Five stories of supernatural mystery and detection, about Simon Ark.

12. Hoch, Edward D.: *The Spy and the Thief*, edited and with introductions by Ellery Queen. New York: Davis Publications. Seven short stories, each about master spy Rand and master thief Nick Velvet, all from *EQMM*, 1965–1970.

13. McAuliffe, Frank: *For Murder I Charge More*. New York: Ballantine Books. Four more mad commissions of intrigue and skulduggery for Augustus Mandrell.

14. Morrison, Arthur: *Martin Hewitt, Investigator*. Philadelphia: Oswald Train. Reprinting of a collection of seven detective stories first published in 1894 and out of print for more than half a century.

15. Ritchie, Jack: *A New Leaf and Other Stories*, with introduction by Donald E. Westlake. New York: Dell Publishing Co. Eighteen criminous short stories, sixteen of them from *AHMM*.

16. Sayers, Dorothy L.: *Lord Peter*, compiled and with an introduction by James Sandoe. New York: Harper & Row. All twenty short stories about sleuth Lord Peter Wimsey, plus an essay by Carolyn Heilbrun and a Wimsey parody by E. C. Bentley.

17. Woolrich, Cornell: *Nightwebs*, edited and with a long introduction by Francis M. Nevins, Jr. New York: Harper & Row. Sixteen stories, largely from Woolrich's pulp writing, plus an exhaustive checklist of his work.

II. Anthologies

1. Greene, Hugh, editor: *More Rivals of Sherlock Holmes: Cosmopolitan Crimes*. New York: Pantheon. Detective stories from the period between 1891 and World War I.

2. Hitchcock, Alfred, editor: *Alfred Htichcock Presents: I Am*

Curious (*Bloody*). New York: Dell Publishing Co. Thirteen stories from *AHMM* 1960–1969.

3. Hitchcock, Alfred, editor: *Down by the Old Bloodstream.* New York: Dell Publishing Co. Fourteen stories from *AHMM* 1960–1969.

4. Hitchcock, Alfred, editor: *Stories To Stay Awake By.* New York: Random House.

5. Hubin, Allen J., editor: *Best Detective Stories of the Year—1971: 25th Annual Collection.* New York: E. P. Dutton & Co. Fifteen of the best criminous short stories published for the first time in the U.S. in 1970.

6. Hubin, Allen J., editor: *Best of the Best Detective Stories: 25th Anniversary Volume.* New York: E. P. Dutton & Co. Twenty-four stories, one from each of the regular anthologies in the first quarter-century of *Best Detective Stories of the Year.*

7. Masur, Harold Q., editor: *Murder Most Foul.* New York: Walker & Co. Fifteen stories in the 1971 annual from the Mystery Writers of America.

8. Playboy Magazine: *The Peeping Tom Patrol.* Chicago: HMM Publishing Co. Eleven stories of crime and suspense from *Playboy.*

9. Queen, Ellery, editor: *Ellery Queen's Anthology: Spring–Summer 1971.* New York: Davis Publications. Sixteen stories in the semiannual softcover anthology from *EQMM.*

10. Queen, Ellery, editor: *Ellery Queen's Anthology: Fall–Winter 1971.* New York: Davis Publications. Fifteen stories in the semiannual softcover anthology from *EQMM.*

11. Queen, Ellery, editor: *Ellery Queen's Headliners.* New York and Cleveland: World Publishing Co. Twenty stories from the 1970 issues of *EQMM;* the twenty-sixth anthology in the hardcover series.

12. Queen, Ellery, editor: *The Golden 13.* New York and Cleveland: World Publishing Co. The first prize winners from the thirteen *EQMM* international short-story contests, 1945–1956, 1961.

III. Critique and Reference

1. Barzun, Jacques, and Wendell Hertig Taylor: *A Catalogue of Crime.* New York: Harper & Row. A listing, highly personalized, fascinating and provocative in its extensive annotation, of more than three thousand volumes variously enjoyed by the co-authors in some fifty years of diligent reading.

2. Bruccoli, Matthew J.: *Kenneth Millar/Ross Macdonald: A Checklist,* with introduction by Kenneth Millar. Detroit: Gale Research Co. Here listed are *all* of Millar's works up to the date of publication—books, short stories, articles, sketches, reviews, interviews, and verse.

3. Donaldson, Norman: *In Search of Dr. Thorndyke.* Bowling Green, Ohio: Bowling Green University Popular Press. A definitive work on R. Austin Freeman and his remarkable detective creation.

4. Hall, Trevor H.: *The Late Mr. Sherlock Holmes.* New York: St. Martin's Press. Seven essays on the Great Detective.

5. Kaye, Marvin: *The Histrionic Holmes: An Analysis and Dissertation on the Impersonatory Genius of Sherlock Holmes.* Culver City, California: Luther Norris. An affectionate examination of Holmes the actor.

6. La Cour, Tage, and Harald Mogensen: *The Murder Book.* New York: Herder and Herder. A magnificent pictorial history of the genre.

7. Nevins, Francis M., Jr., editor: *The Mystery Writer's Art.* Bowling Green, Ohio: Bowling Green University Popular Press. An excellent collection of twenty-one wide-ranging essays.

8. Quayle, Eric: *The Collector's Book of Books.* New York: Clarkson N. Potter. A knowledgeable illustrated account of the joys of book collecting, with a short chapter on detective fiction.

9. Randall, David A.: *The Ian Fleming Collection of 19th–20th Century Source Material Concerning Western Civilization Together with the Originals of the James Bond—007 Tales.* Lilly Library Publication Number XII. Indiana University. Contains descriptions of typescripts and author's copies of the Bond stories, with some annotation, as well as relevant illustrations.

10. Tuska, Jon: *Philo Vance: The Life and Times of S. S. Van Dine.* Bowling Green, Ohio: Bowling Green University Popular Press. An informative collection of essays and checklists by Tuska and others, particularly concentrating on Van Dine as filmed.

AWARDS

Crime Writers Association (London)

Gold Dagger Award—James McClure, *The Steam Pig* (London: Gollancz; New York: Harper & Row)

Silver Dagger Award—P. D. James, *Shroud for a Nightingale* (London: Faber & Faber; New York: Charles Scribner's Sons)

Mystery Writers of America

novel—Frederick Forsyth, *The Day of the Jackal* (Viking Press)

American first novel—A. H. V. Carr, *Finding Maubee* (G. P. Putnam's Sons)

short story—Robert L. Fish, "Moonlight Gardener" (*Argosy*, December)

NECROLOGY

(the assistance of George Wuyek in collecting the data recorded here is gratefully acknowledged)

1. Nigel Balchin (1908–1971). Not generally regarded as a mystery writer, but a number of his novels closely approach the genre.

2. A. H. Z. Carr (1902–1971). Author of many works of nonfiction, but also of a number of mystery short stories and, in the year of his death, of his first detective novel, *Finding Maubee*.

3. Anthony Berkeley Cox (1893–1970). As Anthony Berkeley and Francis Iles, produced some of the best detective fiction coming out of Britain during his active writing period (1926–1939).

4. August Derleth (1909–1971). Prolific in an astonishing variety of literary forms, and noted in our field for his Judge Peck novels and, more widely, for his abundant Holmes pastiches about detective Solar Pons.

5. H. F. Heard (1899–1971). Author of several well-received detective novels, such as *A Taste for Honey* (1941), over which looms the dim and shadowy figure of the Great Detective.

6. Helen Hull (1888?–1971). Wrote two mystery novels, the first—*A Tapping on the Wall*—winning the Dodd Mead prize competition for college faculty members in 1960.

7. Inez Haynes Irwin (1873–1970). During 1935–1946, author of several novels about police detective Patrick O'Brien.

8. Wolfe Kaufman (1905–1970). Wrote a single mystery novel, *I Hate Blondes* (1946).

9. Manfred B. Lee (1905–1971). Co-author with Frederic Dannay of the incomparable Ellery Queen stories and novels.

10. Leonard H. Nason (1895–1970). Author of the espionage novel *Contact Mercury* (1946).

11. Raymond Postgate (1896–1971). In addition to a number of volumes of nonfiction, wrote three crime novels, of which *Verdict of Twelve* (1940) should particularly be noted.

12. Clayton A. Rawson (1906–1971). Amateur magician, author of the detective stories about the Great Merlini and managing editor of *EQMM* 1963–1970.

13. James Reach (1909?–1970). Author of three mystery novels during 1949–1954.

14. Gilbert V. Seldes (1893–1970). As Foster Johns, wrote two mystery novels, *The Victory Murders* (1927) and *The Square Emerald* (1928).

15. Viola Brothers Shore (1890–1970). Author of two mystery novels, *The Beauty Mask Murder* (1930) and *Murder on the Glass Floor* (1932).

16. Samuel Spewack (1899–1971). Wrote two mystery novels, *The Skyscraper Murder* (1928) and *Murder in a Gilded Cage* (1929).

17. Wilbur Daniel Steele (1886–1970). Noted American short-story writer, among whose output are numbered some excellent criminous tales.

18. Philip Wylie (1902–1971). Celebrated and prolific iconoclast, who also produced some ten mystery novels, several in collaboration with Edwin Balmer.

HONOR ROLL

(Starred stories are those included in this volume)

Poul Anderson, "The Queen of Air and Darkness," *Magazine of Fantasy and Science Fiction*, April.

George Antonich, "Trouble in Xanadu," *MSMM*, June.

William Arden, "Clay Pigeon," *Argosy*, March.

William Bankier, "The Road Without a Name," *EQMM*, November.

Phyllis Bentley, "Miss Phipps Exercises Her Metier," *EQMM*, February.

* Robert Bloch, "The Play's the Thing," *AHMM*, May.

Ray Bradbury, "My Perfect Murder," *Playboy*, August.

Gary Brandner, "The Eraser," *MSMM*, April.

———, "Nobody's Perfect," *AHMM*, June.

Jon Breen, "The Dewey Damsel System," *Wilson Library Bulletin*, April.

*R. Bretnor, "A Matter of Equine Ballistics," *EQMM*, September.

William Brittain, "Falling Object," *EQMM*, February.

———, "Mr. Strang Finds an Angle," *EQMM*, June.

———, "Mr. Strang Lifts a Glass," *EQMM*, May.

James Cairns, "The Benefactors," *Cavalier*, April.

Michael J. Carroll, "Man and Boy," *EQMM*, April.

George C. Chesbro, "The Drop," *MSMM*, October.

———, "The Shadow in the Mirror," *AHMM*, March.

Robert Colby, "Shadows on the Road," *AHMM*, November.

*Michael Crichton, "The Most Powerful Tailor in the World," *Playboy*, September.

Avram Davidson, "Summon the Watch!," *EQMM*, October.

Miriam Allen deFord, "The Ubiquitous Heir," *AHMM*, March.

Don DeLillo, "In the Men's Room of the Sixteenth Century," *Esquire*, December.

Mary Louise Downer, "After the Lights Are Out," *EQMM*, October.

Robert Edward Eckels, "To Catch a Spy," *EQMM*, September.

*———, "Vicious Circle," *EQMM*, June.

———, "The Waldemeer Triptych," *EQMM*, July.

Charlotte Edwards, "Unknown Woman," *AHMM*, September.

Stanley Ellin, "The Payoff," *EQMM*, November.

Richard M. Ellis, "Shoplifter's Christmas," *AHMM*, January.

Robert L. Fish, "Moonlight Gardener," *Argosy*, December.

G. E. Fox, "Nightmare!" *Adventure*, February.

Anthony Gilbert, "When Suns Collide," *EQMM*, April.

Michael Gilbert, "Accessories After the Fact," *EQMM*, December.

*———, "The Peaceful People," *EQMM*, March.

C. B. Gilford, "Fatal Charm," *AHMM*, March.

———, "Murder in Mind," *AHMM*, June.

Kathryn Gottlieb, "The Gun," *EQMM*, January.

Ron Goulart, "Monte Cristo Complex," in *What's Become of Screwloose? and Other Stories*, Scribner's.

———, "Orczy Must Go!," *AHMM*, September.

———, "Passage to Murdstone," *Magazine of Fantasy and Science Fiction*, October.

Len Gray, "Adventures of Herbie and Big Sal," *EQMM*, June.

*Morris Hershman, "Willing Victim," *MSMM*, March.

Edward D. Hoch, "Blood Money," *MSMM*, September.

———, "Dead on the Pavement," *AHMM*, July.

———, "Die-Hard," *MSMM*, February.

*———, "End of the Day," *EQMM*, February.

———, "The League of Arthur," *Argosy*, September.

———, "The Leopold Locked Room," *EQMM*, October.

———, "A Little More Rope," *AHMM*, March.

———, "The Sound of Screaming," *MSMM*, November.

———, "The Spy Who Knew Too Much," *EQMM*, August.

———, "The Theft of the Dinosaur's Tail," *EQMM*, March.

———, "The Theft of the Satin Jury," *EQMM*, June.

Clark Howard, "The Juror," *MSMM*, August.

———, "The Keeper," *AHMM*, October.

Michael Innes, "Comedy of Discomfiture," *EQMM*, September.

Jerry Jacobson, "The Abraxas Affair," *MSMM*, April.

William Jeffrey, "A Case for Quiet," *AHMM*, August.

Leo P. Kelley, "Sweet Tranquility," *AHMM*, June.

Gerald Kersh, "Gambling Fever," *EQMM*, January.

George Grover Kipp, "Downright Murderous," *AHMM*, December.

*R. A. Lafferty, "Enfants Terribles," *EQMM*, June.

Allen Lang, "The Case of the KO'd Computer," *AHMM*, September.

*Warner Law, "The Harry Hastings Method," *Playboy*, April.

———, "Payoff on Double Zero," *Playboy*, October.

Richard O. Lewis, "Black Disaster," *AHMM*, February.

———, "Showdown," *EQMM*, February.

John Lutz, "Games for Adults," *AHMM*, December.

———, "The Real Shape of the Coast," *EQMM*, June.

Dana Lyon, "The Bitter Years," *EQMM*, September.

John D. MacDonald, "He Was Always a Nice Boy," *EQMM*, March.

Anthony Marsh, "The Candidate," *AHMM*, April.

Alberto N. Martin, "Angel of Death," *AHMM*, January.

Berkeley Mather, "Treasure Trove," *EQMM*, July.

*Richard Matheson, "Duel," *Playboy*, April.

Florence V. Mayberry, "The Beauty in That House," *EQMM*, May.

Frank McAuliffe, "The German Tourist Commission," in *For Murder I Charge More*, Ballantine.

Patricia McGerr, "This One's a Beauty," *EQMM*, November.

McGarry Morley, "Testimony of a Witness," *EQMM*, March.

Helen Nielsen, "The Perfect Servant," *EQMM*, November.

John O'Brien, "Ludwig Soaring Down," *EQMM*, July.

M. G. Ogan, "The Night Is for Dying," *MSMM*, May.

*Donald Olson, "The Blue Tambourine," *AHMM*, February.

Dennis O'Neil, "Report on a Broken Bridge," *EQMM*, December.

A. F. Oreshnik, "The Expert," *MSMM*, June.

Josh Pachter, "Sam Buried Caesar," *EQMM*, August.

Gary Paulsen, "The Kidnapping Kit," *MSMM*, October.

David Peele, "The Cataloging on the Wall," *Wilson Library Bulletin*. April.

J. F. Peirce, "The Hot Tamales Murder Case," *EQMM*, December.

*———, "The Total Portrait," *EQMM*, April.

Hugh Pentecost, "Jericho and the Dead Clue," *EQMM*, December.

John Pierce, "Exercise Number One," *EQMM*, September.

———, "The Pig Sticker," *EQMM*, January.

———, "The Ropewalker," *EQMM*, October.

James Powell, "The Gobineau Necklace," *EQMM*, March.

———, "Three Men in a Tub," *EQMM*, September.

Bill Pronzini, "The Man Who Collected 'The Shadow,'" *Magazine of Fantasy and Science Fiction*, June.

Ellery Queen, "The Odd Man," *Playboy*, June.

Carl Henry Rathjen, "Ear Witness," *AHMM*, April.

Newton Rhodes, "The Hero," *MSMM*, July.

* Joan Richter, "The Prisoner of Zemu Island," *EQMM*, October.

Jack Ritchie, "The Griggsby Papers," *MSMM*, October.

*———, "Take Another Look," *AHMM*, August.

———, "The Violet Business," *AHMM*, September.

Richard M. Rose, "The Hard Cure," *MSMM*, September.

Carole Rosenthal, "A Specialist in Still Lifes," *EQMM*, February.

Jaime Sandaval, "Judge and Jury," *AHMM*, September.

Richard A. Selzer, "A Single Minute of Fear," *EQMM*, January.

Frank Sisk, "A Convention of Wooden Indians," *AHMM*, July.

———, "Roundhouse," *AHMM*, October.

———, "Slay the Wicked," *AHMM*, May.

Pauline C. Smith, "My Daughter Is Dead," *AHMM*, November.

*———, "Osborn and Sabrina," *MSMM*, August.

———, "That Monday Night," *AHMM*, August.

R. L. Stevens, "The Physician and the Opium Fiend," *EQMM*, July.

Dante Stirpe, "Bad Spot," *EQMM*, June.

Jeff Sweet, "Nightmare in New York," *EQMM*, August.

Julian Symons, "Experiment in Personality," *EQMM*, July.

Lawrence Treat, "Crime at Red Spit," *EQMM*, April.

———, "Jackpot," *EQMM*, May.

———, "R as in Rookie," *EQMM*, October.

Calvin Trillin, "Safely Deposited," *Playboy*, December.

Jeffrey M. Wallmann, "Now You See Her," *MSMM*, March.

———, "The Pattern of Murder," *MSMM*, November.

Dori White, "Flight from Fear," *Good Housekeeping*, February.

*Alan K. Young, "Ponsonby and the Classic Cipher," *EQMM*, December.

ABOUT THE EDITOR

Allen J. Hubin is editor-publisher of *The Armchair Detective,* a periodical devoted to news about books and writers of detective fact and fiction. He lives with his family in White Bear, Minnesota.